Fairy Tales

Fairy Tales

Robin

FURPLANET

Fairy Tales

Production copyright FurPlanet Productions © 2025

Copyright © Robin 2025

Cover Artwork and illustrations © Slate 2025

Published by FurPlanet Productions
Dallas, Texas
www.FurPlanet.com

eBook ISBN 978-1-61450-669-0
Paperback ISBN 978-1-61450-668-3

First Edition Trade Paperback 2025

This book is dedicated to Duo and Tempo, without whose never-ending enthusiasm and encouragement it would not exist. Also, an extra special thank you to Kiri, who is surely enjoying her wings.

CHAPTER ONE

The first of autumn's fallen leaves crunched under heavy work boots as Tamara made her way down the dark forest path. A cool wind stirred the stray hairs escaping from her messy bun, bringing the sounds of the night to the coyote's swiveling ears. Along with the rising wind moaning through the trees came the bright chirping of crickets. Hooting owls. A few late tree frogs. The rustle of small creatures in the undergrowth. Somewhere not too far distant, the barely discernible presence of wild deer.

Reassured, she hitched her backpack higher and continued on toward the bridge.

Small pockets of moonlight began to peter through the tree branches. The faint shoosh of rushing water joined the other night sounds as the narrow path opened out onto a wider trail that merged into abandoned railroad tracks. Only a few yards out loomed the angular structure of a trestle bridge, left to rust on its own time.

Preoccupied with studying the swirling water beneath the bridge, she almost missed the other girl. Almost. Tamara caught sight of her at the last moment and stopped in her tracks, ears shooting stiff and tail bristling in surprise.

The cat was dressed all in white, wearing a long, flowing summer dress woefully out of season. She stood at the edge of the bridge, one hand delicately resting on one of the support struts of the lattice that arched overhead. In her other arm, she held a bouquet of white lilies. The strong wind lifted her long ginger hair as she gazed soulfully up at the full moon and eddying clouds, illuminated almost ethereally by its glow.

Three thoughts crossed Tamara's mind in quick succession.

That is the most beautiful girl I've ever seen.

She's going to jump off that bridge.

She's going to fall right through that ward and let the damn fairies out.

The coyote shrugged slowly out of her backpack and lowered it carefully to the gravel of the old railway track, the glass bottles inside tinkling gently. She stepped forward, hands out non-threateningly, and cleared her throat. "Uh, excuse me, miss?"

Obviously caught off guard, the girl on the bridge sucked in a sharp gasp. She clutched the flowers to her chest, wobbling alarmingly on strappy silver heels as she spun to face Tamara. "Oh!"

"Listen, I know this may seem like a good idea right now, but you probably won't even die if you jump off this bridge—just get really wet, cold, and hurt." Well, she might actually drown given the depth and current at this part of the river, but there was no sense in egging her on.

"What?" The cat blinked at her in puzzlement—she had enormous green eyes—and suddenly began to laugh. "Oooh! Oh no, dear, I'm afraid you're mistaken! I'm not up here to jump."

Tamara let her arms drop, ears tilting in confusion as much at the thick British accent as the statement it delivered. "You're not?"

"Of course not!"

"Then what the flip are you doing up there?"

"Trying to get the best shot, of course." It was said matter-of-factly, as if it were the most obvious thing in the world.

"Shot? What are you—?" Then she saw it. Off at an angle, unobtrusive in the shadows of a looming strut, a small tripod topped with a camera.

The cat carried on obliviously. "I had to wait all month for the moon to get full again, and when it rained this morning I was so disappointed, but then it cleared up and turned into the most perfect night, don't you think?"

"Wait." Tamara held out a hand to stop her, trying desperately to deny what she'd just heard. "Are you telling me you climbed out on a rusty old bridge over the deepest part of this river in the middle of the night to take a *selfie?*"

"Not a selfie," the other girl corrected, tail tip twitching. "A glamour shot. My name's Madeline, by the way. What's yours?"

Tamara rubbed at her forehead, that finicky spot next to her right brow piercing that throbbed when a headache was imminent. "Oh, for the love of—!" She took a deep breath in. Let it out slowly. "Just. Just get down from there before you really do fall, you—you *photographer.*"

Madeline gave a small, dainty huff, straightening her dress. "There's no call to say it like an insult."

She turned toward the camera, flowers slipping in her arms. The wind blew, moaning down the tunnel of trees that lined the river gully. It whipped her hair, carried several of the lilies airborne, and wrapped the hem of her dress around her ankles. She wobbled.

Sometimes Tamara hated it when she was right. She lunged forward as the other girl let out a squeak of alarm and began to windmill, then tripped over her heels on the rotting wood of the deck and pitched sideways into the thin air above the river.

It all seemed to happen in slow motion. The cat fell with an expression of bewildered dismay, copper hair and white dress flowing in the moonlight, scattered lilies suspended in the air around her.

Then Tamara was on her stomach, the front of her baggy blue flannel filling with splinters, a delicate wrist gripped tight in one white-knuckled hand. "Hang on, I got you!"

Madeline flailed, frazzled tail tracing panicked arches through the air as her free hand clawed willy-nilly for something, anything, to grasp onto. "Ah, help me! Don't let me fall!"

"That's exactly what I'm trying to do and it would help me immensely if you'd stop smacking around and grab my hand!" Tamara growled, teeth clenched with exertion and adrenaline.

To her surprise, the order was followed. The cat gulped a deep, shaky breath and stilled herself, then groped upward purposely to grab the coyote's helping hand. The tip of her lashing tail passed through the barely visible, moonlight-glitter surface of the magical ward hovering flat between river and bridge.

Tamara knew the instant it happened. She felt the rush of energy race up through their joined arms, standing every hair on her body on end. The rune circle seemed to ignite with golden light, casting the wavering shadows of coyote and cat along the side of the trestle.

Madeline gasped sharply, craning her neck to glance down below her own swinging feet. "What—?"

The ward failed.

With a buzz like a thousand angry wasps, a swarm of pixies erupted into existence. They poured up out of the ward, swirling and zigzagging around the two on the bridge as they made their ascent, each trailing a bright tail of light like a shower of embers billowed out of a bonfire.

The buzzing very nearly drowned out Tamara's howl of rage and frustration. The cat in her hold hung limp, staring wildly about her with open-mouthed awe.

With a heave Tamara forced herself from her stomach to her

knees, hauling Madeline's surprisingly light form with her. Once the other girl was pulled safely onto the bridge, shoved rather unceremoniously away from the edge, the coyote sprinted for the dark lump of her backpack on the gravel path.

The pixies were a lost cause—something that would have to be dealt with later. Whatever might be behind them was not.

She raced back, one hand already fumbling inside her pack for the box of chalk that had, naturally, fallen to the very bottom. She ran past Madeline, barely noticing the cat sitting stunned, surrounded by a small cluster of pixies that twirled and fluttered around her.

Chalk finally in hand, Tamara dropped her pack and frantically began to scratch out a new rune ward on the mostly rust-free side of a girder. Symbols for binding, rebuttal, endurance, and not a few strongly worded curses were woven together as fast as her hand could draw them. The final mark complete, she dropped the chalk, grabbed at the air above the new ward, and pulled.

Energy thrummed from the rushing water beneath her, the wind above her, and the growing forest around her. The symbols began to glow. Slowly, the whole circle lifted gently off the metal surface. As soon as it was free, Tamara hurled it over the edge. Unaffected by the wind, it landed unerringly over the breach and stuck. There was a final rippling flash as it took hold. Then, nothing.

The pixies felt, just as the coyote did, the proverbial door slam. As the rift between worlds closed, the swarm rose and, with a flurry of deeply unpleasant squeaks and shrieks, scattered into the night like a flight of bottle rockets.

Powerless to stop so many of them at once, Tamara could only watch glumly as the small lights disappeared as quickly as they had come. Shoulders slumped, ears drooping, she looked back down at the tightly closed, now-invisible opening to the fae realm for a long, long moment.

A rhythmic buzz behind her, less like a wasp than a hummingbird, snapped her back to her side of reality. She turned, hackles raised, then paused.

Madeline was still sitting on the bridge, the white folds of the dress pooling around her and no doubt attracting an impressive share of splinters. Less than an arm's length from her a lone pixie hovered, its golden glow illuminating her perfect features.

Fae and cat regarded one another with equal curiosity. It cocked its head, blunt muzzle wrinkling, long pointed ears that only passingly resembled any earthly species' twitching.

Slowly she leaned forward, balancing with one palm on the

ground as she tentatively reached up to touch the glittery little vermin.

The whole thing looked like a Renaissance painting, and Tamara was once more struck by the other girl's nearly ethereal beauty even as she shook off the distraction—*focus!*—and took a careful step forward.

Naturally, the board she stepped on creaked sharply.

The pixie jerked to attention, shot her one evil glance, and disappeared into the darkness upriver like a tiny comet, leaving only a shower of quickly fading sparks.

In the vacuum of buzz-less quiet left behind, the river burbled. Tree branches rustled in the wind. Far away, a train whistle blew mournfully.

Fists clenched, Tamara rounded on the cat. "*You!* Do you have *any* idea what you've done? There are at least a hundred of those little monsters on the loose because of you! It'll take me weeks to catch them all! I—"

Madeline, still on her knees, stared up at her dumbly. Her lip began to tremble. Huge, moonlit green eyes filled with tears.

The coyote balked. "What? No, stop that. Why are you crying? You're not hurt." Her ears flagged warily. "Are you?"

The ginger shook her head negatively, delicate hands coming up to cover her eyes as the tears spilled over with a sniffle and a soft sob.

Tamara's anger deflated almost as quickly as it had built. Here was this air-headed little thing who had nearly fallen off a bridge (even if it had been her own stupid fault), been pushed around (even if it had been necessary at the time), and then obviously been terrified by something she couldn't explain. And who was probably freezing cold, on top of it all.

With a sigh, Tamara shrugged out of her flannel. Her dusty brown fur stood up a bit as the cool wind went right through the thin black t-shirt she wore underneath. She sank down beside the other girl and draped the flannel around bare, shaking shoulders. "Here. Look, I'm... I'm sorry I yelled at you. It wasn't really your fault. I mean, it *was* your fault, but it was an accident. I can fix it—"

The cat pitched forward, burying her damp face in Tamara's collarbone with another muffled sob. Sharp claws pricked unintentionally as hands clenched in the front of her shirt.

"Oh, jeez. It's okay, don't cry." Awkwardly, Tamara pulled her into what she hoped was a comforting hug. The smell of lavender and the brush of soft fur overtook her senses. With one hand she gently smoothed mussed copper hair, mentally berating herself for noticing such tactile details. "It's okay. It's over now. That must have been pretty scary for you, huh?"

Madeline pulled back slightly to look up at her, tears making tracks through the short fluff of her cheeks. Her whiskers wobbled as she tried valiantly to make words. "F... fff..."

Feeling oddly protective, Tamara soothingly petted the fuzzy little triangles of her ears. "Shh, shhh. It's okay. You don't have to—"

"Fairies are *real!*" the cat wailed, flinging her arms around the coyote's neck and squeezing alarmingly as she bawled. "I've never been so *happy!*"

Tamara let her arms fall limply. "You have got to be kidding me."

It took several minutes to separate herself from Madeline, who hung around her neck like a wool scarf with the worst case of static cling imaginable, but at last, Tamara managed. The cat sat back and began the arduous process of collecting herself as the coyote found her backpack once more.

"Oh dear, I'm sure I look a fright," the ginger tittered shakily. She had produced a compact mirror from somewhere (Tamara rather suspected the front of her dress) and was looking into it with great concentration as she wiped her eyes and straightened her hair.

Tamara frowned sourly, setting out a row of tiny glass bottles and a velvet bag of crystals and stones. "You look better after falling off a bridge than most people look walking out of a salon. I wouldn't worry."

The comment sailed right over the other girl's head. She closed the mirror with a snap and focused on what Tamara was doing, tail tip twitching with interest. "What's that you're doing? Are those magic potions?" She gasped with what sounded suspiciously like delight, hands flying up to her mouth. "Oh my goodness, are you a witch?"

"Yes," Tamara answered flatly, "I'm a witch." She held a bottle up to the moonlight, examined it critically, and dropped a small green stone into it. "It's a secret."

"Oh, I won't tell anyone. I won't tell a soul!" She was practically vibrating with excitement, clutching the borrowed flannel tighter around her shoulders. "This is incredible—I can't believe this is actually happening!"

"I just bet you can't." Carefully, the coyote transferred the water to a second bottle, leaving the stones at the bottom of the first, and passed her hand in front of it three times. "Here. Drink this." She thrust the full bottle at the cat.

"What is it? What does it do?" Despite the questions, the bottle was accepted instantly.

"It's spring water imbued with the light of the full moon and a swirl of citrine. And, y'know, some witchy magic. Nothing big. It'll help you calm down, sleep deeply, and have pleasant dreams." And also remember nothing of this unfortunate meeting come sunup. If there was one thing she could be confident in, it was her skill at memory charms. "Go on, drinky drinky."

The whole draught was gracefully sipped without further bidding.

"It's late," Tamara pointed out as she was handed back the empty bottle. "You should head home. You didn't walk here, did you?" Surely not. Town was more than a few miles away.

Madeline shook her head and gestured back along the path, the opposite way Tamara had come. "Oh no, I drove. My car is just around the bend there, where the old road stops." Her whiskers suddenly stood out like straight pins. "But—but how could I possibly go home with a cloud of fairies on the loose?"

"Pixies," Tamara corrected, ears angling back in distaste. "They're pixies. And now that they're stuck here, they're probably hunkering down in the forest for the night and thinking up ways to be horrible. You should get home and get some rest."

"But you're going to find them?" the cat pressed.

"In the morning," Tamara said firmly, trying hard not to think about what a pain in the tail that would be, not to mention how long it would take. Far beyond tomorrow morning, she was sure. "But anyway, I'm leaving. You can do what you want, but I'd recommend you leave too."

Madeline's ears drooped rather sadly. "I suppose you're right."

Packing up her equipment, the coyote rocked back onto her feet and offered the other girl her hand.

Taking it, Madeline rose much more gracefully. And held on. "Will I see you again?" she asked, hand squeezing Tamara's almost beseechingly.

"Well... it's a small town. I'm sure you will."

The cat brightened visibly, all sunshine and smiles once more. "Oh, good! I'm so glad. My name's Madeline, remember? Madeline Babcock. But you can call me Maddie—that's cuter, don't you think? Don't forget!"

"I won't forget." As if she could. Somehow, after what had happened during the last half hour, the thought of casting a memory charm on herself was almost appealing.

Tamara dutifully waited while the camera and tripod were

collected and lovingly tucked into a canvas carrying bag. For good measure, she walked the other girl to the opposite end of the bridge and pointed her firmly toward where her car must have been waiting just out of sight. "Go straight home, okay?"

The anti-anxiety properties of the draught should be kicking in sooner than later. The authorities would probably assume that she'd fallen asleep behind the wheel if they found her car in a ditch the next morning and the cat snoozing on the floorboard, but it would be bad if she collided with something beforehand. Like a tree. Or a pedestrian.

"I will, I promise." Madeline paused to unwrap the borrowed flannel from her shoulders. "Thank you for lending me this. And for saving me. And for—"

"Don't mention it. Really." Tamara shrugged back into her shirt, firmly ignoring that it now smelled of lavender. "Well, see you around, Maddie."

Somehow managing to walk perfectly in her ridiculous high heels, the cat shouldered her photography bag and started down the path, the moon lighting her way. Before reaching the trees, she paused and looked back. "Oh, wait, Miss Witch. You never told me your name."

There was no point in refusing if she was bound to forget anyway. "It's Tamara."

"Tamara." It sounded almost musical on the other girl's tongue. "That's lovely! I'll see you soon then, Tamara. Can't wait!" With a smile and a wave, she disappeared around the bend and was lost to sight.

The coyote watched the path for a while in silence until a car engine started up and a glimmer of headlights shone through the trees. With a quiet sigh, she turned and began the long walk home.

It was past midnight when Tamara reached home. The moon was high in the sky, but under the spreading boughs of a monstrous oak tree, the small cabin lay, as always, in perpetual shadow.

The front door swung open as she reached it, allowing her to stumble tiredly inside. As she dropped her backpack in the entryway and bent to unlace her boots, it closed behind her without a sound. Small, flickering balls of light began to form along the creases where the ceiling met the wall. When she stepped up into the living area, one detached and floated down to bob along at her side. A board creaked underfoot as she passed the archway into the kitchen, answered by a groggy, grumpy croak from the darkness.

"Go back to sleep," she growled, digging up her sleeve for a bra strap. "I'll tell you about it in the morning."

There was a soft rustling, then silence.

Articles of clothing fanned out behind the coyote like a snail trail as she oozed toward her bedroom. By the time she flopped into bed, she was down to underwear and the t-shirt. Without raising her face from the pillow, she snapped her fingers, and the ball of light bobbled back the way it had come, disappearing into the shadows of the hallway.

After a long moment, Tamara rolled onto her back.

"Tonight could have gone better," she informed the ceiling rafters.

No reply was forthcoming. Not that she had expected one. The oak tree was almost always silent at night.

On the corner of the old wooden bed, leaning heavily against the headboard, sat a small stuffed bear long past what even a generous observer would call "shabby." It had no eyes and was floppy from long years and many embraces compacting the stuffing, but Tamara pulled it into her arms with the ease of familiarity and curled around it. The scent of chamomile tea and the memories of a soothing lullaby immediately relaxed her.

Tomorrow.

Tomorrow was another day that she would start afresh. The task ahead was daunting, but surely nothing the local witch, born and raised, couldn't handle.

A big job starts just the same as a small one; one step at a time. Somewhat comforted by the thought, she squirmed gracefully under the blankets and buried her face in the pillow once more. *Hope that crazy cat got home alright.*

Pending natural selection hadn't run its course by then, the feline photographer would wake in the morning as Tamara was preparing to hunt pixie, the events on the bridge faded in her mind to nothing but a hazy dream.

On the edge between sleep and wakefulness, the coyote's last conscious thought was a fleeting regret that, if she ever did see Madeline again, the other girl wouldn't spare her a second glance.

CHAPTER TWO

The next morning was Saturday. As witches did not get days off, Tamara was up with the sun. Filled with determination, resolve, and toast, she strode purposefully around the kitchen.

From the back of a worn wooden chair, an enormous crow watched impassively as she filled her backpack with paraphernalia. Her bag of crystals; the box of chalk; a ball of twine; a water bottle; a collapsible butterfly net that glimmered faintly in the light; and a plastic insect collecting box, likewise glimmering with translucent runes of containment.

"We need to get these things under control as soon as possible," said coyote to bird, pulling a glass jar of old-fashioned iron nails out of the pantry. "We'll keep searching until sunset."

The crow uttered an incredulous croak.

"Yes 'we,' you overgrown feather duster. Don't be lazy." Tamara dropped two nails into the reservoir of a brightly colored plastic water pistol. "You'd just be flying around town with your buddies all day anyway. Keep an eye out for pixies and let me know where, if you find any." She filled the squirt gun at the kitchen tap, plugged it, and stuck it into her belt with a smile of grim satisfaction.

With a petulant caw and a ruffle of feathers, the crow hopped across the table and onto the sill of the open window.

"I know pixies destroy nests. If they come near yours, eat them."

Seeming to realize that it had lost the argument, the corvid departed with a great flapping of wings. A lone pinfeather settled gently to the tabletop.

Swinging her backpack onto her shoulders, the coyote followed.

Main Street was hopping when Tamara rolled into town, her beat-up blue truck joining the flow of Saturday morning traffic.

The farmers market was in full swing near the fairgrounds, a blur of pumpkin orange and chrysanthemum yellow. The air was laden with the sweet smell of the first ripe apples. A nearby playground teemed with squealing children. The patio of the local coffee shop overflowed with patrons as the mild wind of the last days of summer lazily spun the colorful umbrellas overhead and tinkled the wind chimes under the eaves.

It was there the coyote felt the first disturbance. Swiftly changing lanes, she whipped into the parking lot of the Java Flow and watched intently from the last open parking space, keeping both her physical and magical eyes trained on the patio.

Her patience was rewarded. A small, sparkly form zipped out from under a rainbow-colored umbrella, shot through the wind chimes with a loud clatter, and disappeared through the side door on the heels of a harried-looking rabbit hefting a crate full of single-serve deli salads.

Tamara scowled. She hopped out of the truck, checking herself over with quick pats. Wallet: check. Wristbands stitched with the runes of her best memory spell: check. Hem of flannel covering the squirt gun: double-check.

The aroma of strong coffee and the overly enthusiastic wailing of pop music over the speakers assaulted her senses as she stepped inside. Like the patio, every seat in the place was full of patrons, pastries, and idle chatter. Tamara scanned the room quickly, faces and forms blurring to unimportance as she searched for telltale sparkle. None was forthcoming, but the pixie was still there—she could sense it, an annoying itch at the back of her neck that raised her hackles against fae magic.

It can't hide forever. There's too much temptation to screw something up in here. The little monster would blow its cover. All she had to do was wait it out.

The line was long but moved quickly, and soon she was face to face with the same barista she had seen outside.

"Hi, what can I make for you today?" the rabbit greeted with a pleasant smile that belied the controlled chaos around her.

"Do you have any recommendations?" asked Tamara, who

couldn't remember the last time she'd been to a coffee shop and had no idea what to sip on as she loitered.

"The special today is half off a scone with the purchase of our new matcha latte, any size. The matcha is one hundred percent organic!" The promotional button pinned to the strap of her apron said 'Whisky Business' and depicted a small bowl and bamboo tea whisk.

"I'll have that, then."

"What size would you like the latte and what flavor of scone can I get for you?"

"Just a small is fine. Blueberry, if you have it."

"Sure thing!"

The rabbit was punching in the order when a tall aluminum canister fell off a shelf behind her and hit the cabinet below with a bang. A rain of chocolate sprinkles showered both her and the workstation.

Despite a startled bounce and a squeak of alarm, the barista bunny recovered quickly and took in the situation at a glance. "Oh, shoot! That shelf is installed crooked, I swear. Josh, can you—?"

As a border collie with a broom and dustpan bustled over, Tamara shot a sharp glance at the empty space where the container had been, noting a faint trace of quickly fading glitter.

Turning back to the register, the rabbit focused on Tamara again. She smiled brightly. "Hi, what can I make for you today?"

The coyote sighed. So there were a couple of minor drawbacks to spells that made people mentally delete all memory of you after breaking a conversation. "I'll have the special. Small matcha latte, blueberry scone."

"Sure thing!" The rabbit reached out to key in the order, then paused. "Huh. That's weird." She squinted at the register, where the order was already entered and awaiting payment. "Uh, that'll be seven ninety-five, please."

Tamara handed her a ten. Dropping her change in the tip jar, she moved to the sideboard to wait for her drink, dark eyes still scanning the café. All she needed was for her prey to get distracted enough to get careless and move out into the line of fire.

"—looked right at me, then it flew off up the river like a little Roman candle!"

Tamara went stock still. Her ears swiveled cautiously backward, honing in on a very familiar British lilt.

"So you almost fell off a bridge, got rescued by a witch, and then saw a swarm of fairies?" A new voice, laced with amusement. "That's a good one, Maddie. Are you going to write that story up for your blog?"

As casually as she could, the coyote aimed a glance over her shoulder.

"It's not a story, it really happened," Madeline exclaimed indignantly, leaning across a small table and into the personal bubble of the chubby gray tabby cat sitting with her. "Ellie, you have to believe me! This is serious."

The barista's voice suddenly chimed in. "Excuse me, miss? Were you waiting for something?"

Tamara jerked back to the counter. "Matcha. Scone."

"Oh, of course!" Shaking her head, the rabbit passed her a cup and a paper pastry bag. "Sorry, I completely spaced who we made that for. I must be totally out of it today."

The coyote gave a distracted nod of thanks, attention already focused back on the table in the corner where the gray tabby was trying to placate the ginger.

"Okay, okay, I'm sorry. Whatever happened last night, I get that it's really important to you," the new cat was saying, nervously finger-combing her brown ponytail. "But what do you want me to do?"

"Not insinuate that I'm making up stories, for one." Despite her narrowed green eyes, backward-angled ears, and twitching tail tip, Madeline was just as lovely sitting in an overstuffed armchair in a coffee shop as she had been bathed in moonlight the night before. Today, she was wearing a slightly more practical pair of white ankle boots, a long pleated skirt, and a pale purple blouse. A purple headband was affixed on one side with a tiny pink heart nestled in front of her ears.

"Not insinuate you're making up stories, and...?"

"Well, obviously I need you to help me find her so I can help her."

"So, what, we go door to door and ask everyone in town if they know any coyotes about our age who just happen to be witches hunting for fairies?" the gray cat asked, expression carefully neutral.

Tamara slowly turned until she completely faced the other girls, barely feeling the uncomfortable heat of the cardboard cup she held against her palm.

The blasted cat remembered. Remembered the pixies. Remembered *her*.

The blasted cat in question gestured rather wildly with her own cup, the string of a teabag fluttering haphazardly from it. "Yes, if we have to!"

"Maddie," her friend began gently, "are you sure—"

The teacup descended audibly against the tabletop. "I've never been so sure of anything in my life." She leaned forward once more, this time with a look of entreaty. Her manicured claws dug into the scuffed wood at the table's edge. "Ellie, please. Please. I've spent all this time—all these years—questioning myself, why I'm so odd, thinking maybe I made it all up after all. But last night, I..."

Madeline paused. Her brows furrowed. Then, as if sensing Tamara's gaze, slowly looked over at her.

Their eyes met.

"Miss Witch!" the cat shrieked, leaping to her feet with a look of utter glee that wouldn't have been amiss on the face of someone being presented with a million-dollar check from Publishers Clearing House.

All the hair on Tamara's body rose to the occasion as every eye in the place landed on them. She slunk quickly toward the table. "Uh, new Dungeons and Dragons game," she laughed weakly to a gaggle of middle-aged moms who stared blatantly as she passed. "My friend's just—real excited. Yeah."

Madeline was babbling by the time Tamara reached her. "Oh my gosh, Miss Witch—Tamara—I knew I'd see you again! And so soon! Were you looking for me, too? Have you found any fair—"

Tamara thumped the latte and scone onto the table, grabbed her by the arm, and clapped a hand firmly over her mouth. "You are very loud," she growled, dropping into the armchair and pulling the cat down with her. It was a tight squeeze, but they both fit, just barely.

The gray cat, startled, had pulled her legs up into the chair and curled her striped tail around her knees. The black tip of it flicked rapidly in agitation as she stared at the coyote, clearly at a loss for words.

Tamara passed her free hand through the air as if pulling an invisible curtain across the little corner. Instantly, all the café-goers who hadn't already lost interest in the sudden commotion looked away and went back to their own business as if nothing had happened at all.

"Are you through?" she asked pointedly, frowning at the other occupant of the chair.

Behind the hand covering everything but her whiskers and pink nose, Madeline nodded quickly. "Sorry," she squeaked as she was released. "I was excited."

"Apparently."

The gray cat eyed them both, one finger flicking back and forth between them. "Sooo. You two know each other?"

"We've met. Recently." Having never dealt with a situation

quite like this before, Tamara erred on the side of civility and offered her hand. "Name's Tamara."

"Eleanor. Eleanor Elena Elizabeth Golding. But you can call me Ellie." As they shook, the tabby seemed to relax a bit, uncurling from her defensive posture in the chair. "Okay. So. I'm assuming you're the coyote Maddie's in a frenzy about, so please be honest with me." She pointed at Madeline, who was still staring at Tamara and practically vibrating with excitement. "Did she really almost fall off a bridge last night?"

Tamara, who had been braced for questions about witchcraft, pixies, or magic in general, couldn't help but huff a laugh. "I wish I didn't have to say yes, but…yes."

"Maddie!" Ellie hissed, tail fluffing in a reproach. "A selfie is not worth dying over!"

"It was a glamour shot!"

A loud rumbling, sputtering sound brought the discussion to an abrupt halt as all three girls paused to look. Across the café, the latte maker was having issues.

"Laurel," the border collie yelped frantically, arms and apron covered in goop as he tried to shield his face. "Something's wrong with the milk steamer!"

"Turn it off, turn it off!" the rabbit directed, covering her own head with a serving tray as globs flew. "Is that—oh my god, it's… butter? The steamer's turning the milk into butter!"

Tamara grit her teeth at the high-pitched, squeaking laughter that was almost, but not quite, drowned out by the chaos behind the counter.

Ellie stole a sip from the bottle of artesian cola at her elbow that didn't manage to hide her grin. "Wow, that machine is hella broken. Glad I never drink coffee." She took her eyes off the scene, caught sight of Tamara, and almost dropped her cola. "Whoa, who are you?"

"You know who she is," Madeline frowned. "You were just introduced. Don't be rude."

Before Tamara could comment, the pixie broke cover. It zipped out from behind the malfunctioning steamer, still laughing, and took refuge on the blade of a slowly spinning ceiling fan.

Madeline squeezed Tamara's arm tightly. "Oh my gosh, oh my gosh, did you see?" she squealed delightedly, sparkling green eyes fixed on the fan.

"See what?" Warily, Ellie looked away from the coyote to scan the ceiling.

"How could you not have seen that?" the ginger demanded.

"More importantly, how *did* you see that?" Tamara asked, feeling less in control of things than she had in a long, long time. Seeing the fae on a lonely old bridge in the moonlight and seeing them on a bright, sunny morning in a crowded café were two very different matters.

Ellie looked down again and frizzed, her follicles getting quite the morning workout. "Oh my god, who are you?"

"Oh, for crying out loud!" Tamara pulled off her wristbands and crammed them into her pocket. "I don't have time for this. Tamara Ridgemount. Coyote. Bridge."

"Oh. Oh, well, looks like Maddie found you after all." Looking both confused and slightly relieved, the tabby relaxed once more. "I'm—"

"Ellie. Maddie's friend. Nice to meet you." Calculatingly, she watched the lazy rotation of the fan. The pixie was riding it, giggling gleefully on every pass. There was no way she could get in a clear shot from below.

Madeline too watched, smiling widely. "How adorable! It's having such fun."

"What are you two looking at?" Ellie too looked, tail swishing in confusion. After a moment of hard staring, she squinted. "Wait. Is there a bird on the fan?"

"What do you mean, a bird?" Madeline looked personally offended. "That is clearly a—"

23

"Oh wow, is it seriously that late?" Ellie had caught sight of the wall clock past the fan. "Sorry, I have to get going."

Tamara gave an internal cheer. Not that there was anything wrong with the other girl, per se, but the situation was already too complicated. The fewer distractions, and the fewer witnesses, the better.

"You're leaving? Now? But..." the ginger cat pointed beseechingly at the fan.

"I told you earlier that I had work this morning. I'll text you when I get off." Chugging the last few mouthfuls of her soda, Ellie grabbed the messenger bag hanging off the backrest of her chair. "It was nice meeting you, Tam. If you know Maddie, I'm sure we'll see each other again. Bye!" Then she was gone, dropping her soda bottle in the recycling bin on her way out the door.

Confronted with a vacant seat, Tamara noticed suddenly that she was still sandwiched into one chair with Madeline. Though it was surprisingly not unpleasant to be squeezed against her soft, fragrant form, the coyote stood. Delicate claws immediately latched onto the back of her flannel.

"You're not leaving too, are you?" came the almost pleading mew.

"I'm moving to the other chair."

"Oh." Madeline dropped her hands and eyes quickly to her lap, the insides of her ears flushing pink. "Thank you. For not leaving."

"I'm not going anywhere without that pixie, so you don't have anything to worry about." Tamara sank into the recently vacated chair, which conveniently provided an even better vantage point.

The little nuisance in question seemed to be getting bored with the fan. It had stretched out on its chosen blade, making it even less of a prime target, and was watching the floor below.

Madeline watched it watching the room, the look of wonder returning to her face. "So it really is a fair—uh, pixie."

"Unfortunately." Tamara fingered the squirt gun at her side.

"Why can't anyone else see it? Ellie called it a bird!"

"I shouldn't tell you," the coyote said bluntly. "Anyone who can't use magic has no business learning anything about the fae, for their own safety."

The feline achieved almost total deflation; face falling, shoulders slumping, ears drooping.

Tamara sighed, already regretting the decision she'd made. "But I'm going to tell you anyway. I don't know how or why, but you can see the fae. And you remembered me. I've never met anyone who wasn't even fazed by my memory charms."

"Really?" The return of that hopeful smile was like the sun coming out from behind a cloud.

"Yeah, really. So ask questions, I guess. I'll try to explain it so you can understand."

"Then..." The cat got no further, trailing off as she met the witch's eye.

After several moments of nothing, Tamara knocked on the tabletop. "What? Do I have something on my face?"

Madeline gave herself a little shake. "Sorry. I didn't notice in the dark last night, but you have black eyes."

It probably shouldn't have been surprising that a girl who could see pixies could see through such a basic glamour, but it was still unsettling to have the steadfast cosmetic disguise she'd used since Kindergarten torpedoed so casually.

"It's... it's a witch thing." Her eyes, like those of her mother and her grandmother before her, were black as moonless midnight. "People used to say it's because of our black, godless souls." Pierced brows danced as she grinned wickedly, hoping for a rise from the prim cat.

"They're beautiful."

It was so completely the opposite of what she had been

expecting—weird, creepy, freaky—that she reared back in surprise, tail bristling stiffly. "Oh. Well. Thanks, I guess." Thrown off-kilter, she fumbled her untouched scone out of the nearly forgotten pastry bag and took a large bite. "Uh, what were we talking about?"

"You were going to tell me why no one else can see the pixie," Madeline supplied eagerly.

"Right, right." Refocused, Tamara took a swig of her latte, now lukewarm. "The simple answer is that people see what they want to see. Their eyes might see a pixie, or a unicorn, or whatever, but their brain says 'no, that doesn't exist' and blows it off. Or turns it into something else that's more acceptable. Like your friend. She saw us looking at something, so something clearly had to be there—but pixies 'aren't real,' so in her mind, it became a bird. Simple, really."

"But it can still happen? People can see magical things sometimes?"

"Sometimes," the coyote allowed. "It's easier if you're already lost, or afraid, or alone in an unfamiliar place. Your brain lets its guard down on what's normal or not. And little kids can see a lot of things that adults can't because they haven't closed their minds to the possibilities of the universe yet."

"I see," the cat breathed, whiskers standing stiff. "So that's why…" She looked skyward again, where the pixie had abandoned the fan blade and was industriously tangling the pull cords together.

Tamara followed her line of sight and growled in satisfaction. "Finally." She drew her squirt gun.

Alarmed, Madeline reached across the table to grab her arm. "Wait, what are you doing? Don't hurt it!"

"I have to slow it down somehow," Tamara argued, swatting away the interfering hands. "I'm not going to kill it—just knock it down." Then she could grab it, stash it in the carrier, and finally be out of there.

Unfortunately, the pixie seemed to sense that something was amiss. It dodged the second she pulled the trigger and the shot of iron water hit the pull cord knobs dead on, making the chains sway. The pixie spiraled wildly and darted out the door behind a pair of college students, flashing a rude gesture as it did.

"Damn it!" Tamara leaped from her chair and ran out with a jangle of the bells over the door, Madeline shouldering her purse as she followed hot on the witch's heels.

More shots were fired on the sidewalk outside the café, but the quarry was just too nimble. Easily flying out of range, it looked back over its shoulder long enough to blow a smug raspberry at the angry coyote. Thus distracted, it flew straight into traffic.

There was an audible smack as it hit the windshield of a minivan. It rolled up the glass, over the top of the passing vehicle, and spiraled down to flop on the centerline like a stunned sparrow.

Madeline covered her mouth in horror.

Staring at its motionless form, Tamara let the squirt gun arm fall limply to her side. "Well, I guess that's one less pixie to worry about."

The cat broke from her side and ran into the street.

"Oh my god, you idiot, stop!" Tamara screeched, but the other girl had already dodged a pothole and a frantically beeping moped and was kneeling on the asphalt, scooping the crumpled form of the pixie into her hands.

A jeep was cruising toward her and showed no signs of slowing.

Tamara moved before her brain could catch up. Her legs carried her off the sidewalk as her hands flew into the motions of spell casting. Skidding in between Madeline and the oncoming vehicle, she threw her arms up and braced.

The jeep ground to a halt with a jolt and a shudder, its grille less than a foot from her outstretched hands. Through the windshield, two nearly identical teenaged foxes stared back at her in shock.

"Watch where you're going, you little punks!" she barked.

Crouched on the pavement behind her, pixie cradled protectively to her chest, Madeline gave a wordless squeak of awe.

"That's two you owe me, Powderpuff," the coyote growled, shaking the numbness out of her arms.

The young male fox behind the wheel leaned out the window. He was wearing an anime t-shirt and looked slightly shaken. "Hey, are you alright?"

At almost the same instant, a vixen so similar she could only be his sibling popped out the passenger window, ears back and teeth bared. "Get out of the road, you morons!"

Narrowly resisting the urge to flip the bird to a brat who looked like she was still in high school, Tamara grabbed Madeline by the elbow and pulled her to her feet. "We're fine," she told the male fox curtly. "Pay more attention next time."

"R-right."

Back on the sidewalk, she watched the jeep roll away with a line of honking cars behind it. The boy was still watching them in the rearview mirror, while the girl stared suspiciously out the window until they were swallowed up in the traffic down the block.

Turning to the cat whose elbow she still held, Tamara gave her a shake. "Would you please try to keep in mind that I'm not Luke Skywalker? Stopping a ton of metal moving thirty miles an hour is actually really hard, you know."

In reply, a double handful of damaged pixie was thrust at her. It was leaking what looked eerily like glitter glue onto the other girl's outstretched palms.

Tamara leaned away with a grimace. "Eww."

"We have to help it," Madeline blurted urgently. "I think it's dying!"

The coyote gently pushed the insistent hands and their slightly squishy burden away. "I think that's a pretty accurate assessment, but what do you want me to do about it?"

"Something. Anything. You're a witch. You know magic! Save it, please!"

Tamara looked up from the distasteful mess she was honestly surprised the other girl was still touching. "Look, I don't... aaaand you're crying again."

Green eyes were indeed suspiciously damp. Her whiskers trembled, lower lip quivering noticeably.

Tamara sighed and rubbed her eyes with the heels of her hands. Though it was barely midmorning, she suddenly felt very tired. "Do you really care about that thing that much? They're magical vermin. There are millions of them on the other side."

"Well, yes," Madeline sniffed, as if the answer was obvious. "It doesn't matter how many more of them there are; this one right here is hurt and it needs our help. We can't just leave it to die in the street. P-poor little thing, it probably didn't even know that c-cars are dangerous." The tears spilled over, dripping down her cheeks to dot the fabric of her blouse.

After a long moment, Tamara turned and walked toward her truck, beckoning over her shoulder for the cat to follow.

"Does—does that mean you'll help?" she called anxiously, trotting quickly to catch up.

"Minor fae stop glowing if their life energy expires," the coyote explained tersely, pulling her backpack out of the truck. "After they're dead, they turn to dust. Pixies are obnoxious in every conceivable way, so that one will probably turn into a pile of glitter that won't ever come out of the upholstery." Unzipping the backpack, she dumped its contents into the truck bed and held it out. "Put it in here where it's dark. If it doesn't glow, there's nothing I can do. If it does, then... I'll try."

Madeline quickly, but gently, lowered her hands into the

darker interior of the empty bag. "It's... it's glowing! I think? Darn it, it's so bright I can't tell."

Without thinking, Tamara stepped closer to her side, pressing their shoulders together to make a deeper shadow. She lifted the bag, Madeline adjusted her arms, and they both peered intently inside, so close to one another that the tips of their ears touched.

From the bottom of the backpack, a small, feeble light flickered.

"Okay, get in." Mind made up, Tamara was instantly in motion. "That was super weak. We probably don't have a lot of time."

"Right!" With no hesitation, Madeline scampered to the passenger side and struggled in somewhat awkwardly, given the height of the cab, the length of her skirt, her encumbering purse, and the half-dead pixie she was trying not to jostle.

Tamara already had the engine running by the time the cat managed to gingerly pull the passenger door shut. Rather than watching her struggle to buckle an old and cantankerous seatbelt one-handed, she leaned across the cab and did it for her after the second fumble.

Madeline squeaked in surprise as she was firmly strapped in.

"No time. Let's rock n' roll."

They sped out of town faster than was strictly legal, but once a plan was in place, Tamara was nothing if not determined to see it through. She considered and mentally discarded spell after potion after incantation, while the girl beside her crooned soft reassurances and entreaties to the last creature on earth Tamara ever thought she would be dedicated to preserving.

If there's one thing you can count on, it's the thing you didn't count on.

Grumbling under her breath, she stepped harder on the accelerator.

CHAPTER THREE

Gravel flew as the old truck blazed up the long wooded drive and skidded to a stop in front of the cabin. Almost before the engine died, Tamara was out of the cab and leaning into the bed as she stuffed her scattered supplies back into the backpack.

Madeline slipped from the passenger seat. Craning her neck, she gazed up wonderingly at the towering oak tree that seemed to cradle the old structure as protectively as she still held the injured pixie. "This is where you live?"

"Home sweet home," the coyote grunted, absently surprised that the bothersome fae hadn't poofed into nonexistence en route and turned the interior of her truck into a rolling disco.

"I've driven down this road before on shoots and seen your little lane! Who would have thought we were so close all that time."

Ears back, Tamara captured the water bottle that had rolled into a rusted crevice and dropped back to the ground. "Doesn't surprise me. The drive's supposed to be unnoticeable to anyone not wearing a postal uniform, but I kind of doubt there's much of anything you can't see. Come on."

"Witches get mail the old-fashioned way?" The cat trotted quickly behind as Tamara jogged up to the front door. "For some reason, I thought there might be more owls involved."

"My grandmother really liked mail-order catalogs," Tamara dismissed. "Those get heavy fast." The door sprang open as she approached, beckoning Madeline to follow. "This way, quick. If you want to keep that thing alive, we don't have a lot of time."

The pointed reminder of the life and reduction-to-glitter-pile urgency of the situation seemed to work, as her feline visitor followed her straight inside with minimal gawking. Pausing only to snag a thick, leather-bound tome from the overflowing bookcase in the den, Tamara headed for the kitchen.

"So, I've given this a lot of thought, and there's only one option I can come up with." A broad sweep of her arm and the thick wooden surface of the kitchen table was cleared and ready. "Pixies aren't of this world, so any healing charms or potions I could try on it wouldn't be very effective, let alone yank it back from death's doorstep. We have to attach it to an energy source."

"You mean like an outlet?" Madeline asked, ears and whiskers stiff in concentration as she glanced quickly around the room.

Unprepared, Tamara couldn't help a bark of laughter at the mental image. "No, not like—I mean life energy. Pixies are made up mostly of concentrated magical energy, so that's what they live on. But it is a pretty tiny fae, so binding it to something non-magical from this world should work anyway."

"Oh, good. Let's do it!"

"Okay, but hear me out." Tamara thumbed nervously through the book until she found the page she was looking for and laid it open on the table. "There are some things in this cosmos that a witch just isn't willing to do, and donating life juice to a pixie is one of them. They make me itch."

"Then... then use mine instead," Madeline volunteered instantly, shooting another fretful look into her cupped hands before holding their burden imploringly toward the other girl.

"You understand what that means, right? I'd be binding this thing to you magically. Your body would have to take the strain of supporting another being. It would siphon off your very life force like a sparkly little parasite."

"Yes, that's fine."

"You're sure? They exist to cause havoc. It'll ruin your house. Destroy everything you love."

"Yes, I'm sure!"

"You won't ever be able to get rid of it. It'll follow you everywhere. Probably even to the bathroom, they're obnoxious little—"

"Just do it before the poor thing dies, for goodness sake!" Madeline shouted, tail a ginger bottlebrush lashing in agitation.

Despite herself, Tamara quailed a bit in the face of the cat's sudden ire. "Whoa, whoa, okay! Yes. Doing it right now; here we go."

Hastily digging some chalk out of a drawer, she carefully began to copy the rune circle in the book onto the wood of the table. Madeline watched, pacing fretfully behind her, and within a few minutes, the detailed markings were completed.

"Okay, that looks right," Tamara mumbled, letting the chalk roll away. "What's next?" She bent over the book once more, running a finger quickly across the aged ink. "It says 'first subdue ye yon fae unto even the very brink of its demise'—I guess the car already did that part, never mind."

"Just what kind of spell is this, exactly?" Madeline asked nervously, holding the pixie a bit closer.

"Well, normally it's for binding a powerful faery to a witch to increase the witch's magic. The fae don't really take too well to being enslaved, so it's kind of a given that you need to beat them in mortal combat first."

"And you've done this spell before?"

"Not exactly, but I'm almost totally sure it'll work. The binding command is fairly basic, all things considered, and like I said, that is a pretty small fae." Tail wagging in concentration, the coyote tapped the center of the rune circle. "Okay, lay it down here. And then go wash your hands, eww."

The pixie was carefully lowered into position. Its head lolled. One wing, dragonfly-delicate, bent at an odd angle. It looked, by all accounts, lifeless, but the lack of visible dust around its tiny form afforded a glimmer of hope.

Madeline hovered, obviously hesitant to be parted from it for even a moment.

"The sink's right there," Tamara directed pointedly. "Try not to get any soap in the jar with the tadpoles; they're the last ones I'll find this year."

"Oh, of course."

As the cat hurriedly scrubbed, Tamara retrieved a battered first aid kit from a storage cupboard. From that, she dumped a packet of alcohol swabs and a hypodermic needle wrapped in paper. "Ready to do this?"

"Yes!" Madeline reached for the hand towel on the rack, hesitated at some dubious staining, and wiped her hands on her skirt instead as she quickly returned to the table. "What should I do?"

"The spell calls for blood from the person it's being bound to. Just a few drops should work, I think." She passed the swab and needle over. "Can you prick yourself, or do you want me to—?"

"Is that it? No trouble at all." With no hesitation, the ginger accepted the needle and jabbed her index finger without so much as a wince. "Where does the blood go?"

Tamara blinked. "Um, anywhere in the middle of the circle. Do you sew?"

"I dabble," Madeline admitted lightly as a red smear was applied next to the pixie. "Sometimes the only way to get exactly the costume you're dreaming of is to do it yourself, you know? Getting pricked is a necessary hazard."

The coyote nodded seriously. "Like getting kicked by unicorns."

Before Madeline could do more than open her mouth to squeak in delight, she was motioned to the one chair at the table that didn't have an article of laundry draped on it.

"Okay, sit down. You're going to feel faint very soon. Last chance to back out now."

Very primly but very firmly, Madeline settled into the appointed chair. Her claw tips sinking into the armrests were the only hint at her wavering nerves. "Please, let's do it quickly before anything happens."

Tamara scanned the book once more. Confident that they were as ready as was possible, she glanced up, black eyes meeting deep green. "On three, then."

Carefully polished nails sank deeper into the scuffed wood as the cat gulped quietly. "On three."

"One." Tamara raised her hands over the rune circle. Her fingers and palms began to warm, testing out the tension of unfamiliar signs. "Two." A hush descended over the cabin as energy began to gather. The old oak's leaves ceased to rustle, birds falling silent among its branches. "*Three.*"

The witch let go.

The rune circle blazed up like blue fire. For a moment it eclipsed all other light, then sank down into deep shadow that seemed to plunge the whole kitchen into darkness. The oak tree groaned in disapproval as the buildup of energy released with a palpable crack, plunging over the still form of the pixie before leaping out to engulf the one whose blood had been given.

Madeline had no time to scream.

Heart hammering, hackles bristling, Tamara stood statue-still as reality twinged, warped, and snapped back into focus around her. The vacuum of energy she had created evened out, filled itself in, and returned to what it once had been—with the small exception of a gossamer-thin, faintly shimmering, rapidly fading strand of light between the markedly less damaged fae and the cat curled tightly in the chair.

"I did it!" Tamara howled, ears and tail popping up gleefully as she punched the air in triumph. "Yes! Maddie, I think it worked!"

Very slowly, Madeline unwound from her defensive ball. She blinked owlishly, back and forth between Tamara, the pixie, and her own hands. "It did? I... we..." Haltingly, she stood, wobbly as a new fawn, and reached across the table to where the rune circle was already disappearing into nothingness.

There was something almost artful about the way her legs gave out, Tamara noticed with detached attention to detail.

Madeline fell like a fairytale princess, as Sleeping Beauty surely did after pricking her finger on the spinning wheel: eyes fluttering shut, delicate features going lax, arm gracefully outstretched. There was a thump as she landed facedown on the table. Barely an inch from her reaching fingertips, the fully mended pixie stretched, yawned unconcernedly, and, with the faintest poof of chalk dust, curled into a sleeping ball with its tufted tail over its face.

The coyote leaned over the table, peering down with some concern. "Maddie? Hey, Maddie? Madeline?"

Gravity slowly pulled the unconscious girl's upper body from table to floor, where she flopped like an overcooked noodle.

Well. This could be problematic.

For the second time in as many days, Tamara found herself supporting that light, willowy form as she gathered Madeline off the laminate. Hefting the cat into a bridal hold, she transported her impromptu houseguest to the sofa in the den.

A cursory check of vitals proved that she had, indeed, merely fainted and not expired. Her pulse was steady, if a bit slow. Her breath remained deep and even. The tiniest, most delicate of snores ascended.

Tamara heaved a quiet sigh of relief. Sure it was *possible* to cover up a case of accidental magical demise, but it was also something she really didn't want to deal with at the moment. Or ever.

There was a strict 'no shoes on the furniture' policy, so Tamara helpfully unbuckled and removed Madeline's little white ankle boots, placing them neatly together beside the sofa. At that point, it seemed the hospitable thing to also tuck a soft throw pillow beneath her head. The den was cool—too cool?— so an afghan was gathered from an old cedar chest in the corner and tucked lightly over the sleeping feline.

Only then did she remember the pixie and return to the kitchen to collect it.

Her crow was perched on the tabletop, feathers fluffed irately as it hopped menacingly toward the snoozing fae.

"No! No no no, stop that!" The witch pounced, seizing her familiar with both hands and holding him at arm's length as he flapped and cawed crossly. "Yeah, I said you could eat them, but not *that* one. Because I just winged the hardest magic I've ever done in my life to keep it alive, that's why!"

With a mighty flap and an air of great disgust, the crow struggled from her grasp and flew back out the window.

Unaware of its second near miss with oblivion, the pixie slept soundly.

Tamara scowled down at it. "I hate you, just so you know."

A soft whimper from the den brought her back to the task at hand. When she peeked around the corner, the cat on the sofa was twitching restlessly in her sleep, ears flat and unhappy against her headband. One hand had escaped the folds of the afghan and groped across the blanket sluggishly, unconsciously seeking.

Tamara turned back to the kitchen with a sigh. "Okay, you little… creature. Time to go start making nice with your new mistress."

She pinched the pixie gingerly by the scruff and lifted it off the table. Almost immediately she put it down again, her hand tingling and itching unpleasantly. Rubbing the back of the offended appendage, she frowned. So direct contact was out. She made a mental note to add gloves into her pixie-hunting arsenal.

A short dig through the gadget drawer failed to turn up the pasta tongs. Now that she thought about it, those were probably still out in the garden shed and very possibly contaminated with belladonna. A pair of disposable chopsticks did just as well.

Limp as yesterday's spring roll, the sleeping pixie was carefully hoisted, transferred into a salad bowl, and carried into the den. After a moment of deliberation, Tamara tipped it out directly on Madeline's chest.

The cat's hand came up at once to curl over it, pressing it close to her heart with a tiny, contented sigh.

Tamara rubbed awkwardly at the back of her neck, feeling oddly out of place in her own home. What should she do now? It wasn't yet noon. Madeline would be feeling the effects of the binding spell for hours, and the coyote was loathe to leave her side until she was back on her feet. Not because she was *concerned* or anything, of course; it was just that leaving a stranger and a fae, harmless as they seemed, alone in her house would be sheer madness.

But she also couldn't just stand there watching the other girl sleep, either.

I should be exhausted too after casting a spell like that, she thought suddenly. *Why aren't I?*

Once, many years ago, she had attempted a spell that should have been beyond her ability and succeeded. She had then missed two days of school, unable to stay awake for more than a few minutes at a time as her body fought to rebuild the stores of magical energy she had blown through. Now she felt tired, sure, but it was the normal kind of tired that casting any large spell would make her and was undercut by a buzz of accomplished adrenaline.

I guess I haven't really tried to do any new spells for a while. Not any proper ones, at least. Maybe I've just been getting stronger and haven't realized it?

Deep in contemplation, Tamara's unfocused gaze slowly zeroed in on something. It was the bra she had discarded late the night before. It lay directly in the middle of the carpet. Ears low in embarrassment, she scooped it up. Just her luck that the first house guest she'd had in years would not only be the feline model of Barbie but also burst in when she hadn't picked up after herself in a week. Or was it two?

Well, guess I know what I'm doing today.

She snuck a last look at the sofa, from which a soft purr had begun to thrum. For a moment the sound struck her as abnormally dissonant, until she realized that one sound was actually two. Both cat and pixie were purring, in almost perfect sync.

Shaking her head slowly, the witch rolled up her sleeves.

Madeline slept until late afternoon.

Ironically, she came awake just as Tamara was collapsing into an armchair nearby, finally good and tired from the hours of chores she had done.

"Oh, you're up."

With a whimper of pain, the cat tried to lever herself upright. "Nnnh, my head..." Then she gasped, eyes popping open, hand flying up to touch the pixie just beginning to stir on her bosom. Seeming weak with relief at its presence, she flopped back onto the pillow. "Oh, thank goodness! I was afraid it was all just a dream."

"You mean like I was hoping you'd believe this morning?" Tamara sighed, pushing herself up out of the chair. "Take it easy. Sit up slowly."

"What time is it?"

"Past four."

"So late." One hand to her forehead, the other over the pixie, Madeline glanced around the room with a wince. "May I have my purse, please?"

Having moved it off the kitchen counter an hour ago while cleaning, Tamara went straight to the coat rack to collect the bag. Of course Madeline had someone at home that she would want to call, after disappearing all day without warning. "Here. I'll get you some water."

When she returned a few minutes later with the glass, Madeline was upright on the couch, the groggy pixie draped over her shoulder. She was closely inspecting her face with a purple hand mirror.

"You've got to be kidding me."

"I look a mess," the cat fretted, poking at the area under her eyes. "Do I seem haggard?" She made a rather manic face that forced her slightly drooping whiskers to attention.

"You look like starlight and dewdrops," Tamara deadpanned. "Drink this."

Sheepishly, Madeline tucked the mirror back into her purse and accepted the cup. "Sorry. Of course, what really matters is that the pixie is… alright…" She peered suspiciously into the glass. "What is this?"

"Water."

"Why is it brown?"

"There're powdered herbs in it. For your headache."

"Erm. Thank you, but perhaps I could have an aspirin instead?"

Tamara's ears went back. "Did you just ask a forest witch to support big pharma by buying overpriced, non-organic painkillers?"

"Heavens no." Madeline held her nose and drank, tail curling into a disgruntled question mark.

The pixie, apparently amused by her grimace upon finishing, snickered drowsily.

"That's what I thought." Tamara took the glass back. "Come on, bring your sparkly little scourge. I'll take you home."

The ride back to town—more specifically, back to the Java Flow where Madeline's car had been parked all day—was weirdly peaceful.

The pixie remained calm and docile, content to be held in Madeline's arms and watch out the window as forest and field rolled past. From time to time, it looked up, gazing into her face with bright, curious eyes.

"Hello, little love," she cooed softly, her emerald eyes misty even as her smile never wavered. One thumb gently stroked its cheek fluff.

Tamara glanced over, nose wrinkling at the display. "You seriously like that thing that much?"

"More than I think I'll ever find words to say. Seeing them all last night, holding him now, meeting you, and finally knowing magic is real... I'm so happy it feels like my heart might burst."

For the first time, Tamara felt the worming sense that maybe she should start asking some questions of this odd girl who could see the fae, was immune to memory charms, and could accept the existence of an entirely different angle of reality so readily. But witches, as a rule, had a thing about minding their own business.

"You sure that's not just a magical parasite draining energy out of your vital organs?"

"Yes, I'm sure!"

When they reached the coffee shop, business had slowed enough with the approach of dinnertime that there were only a few cars in the parking lot. Tamara guessed instantly which one belonged to Madeline. Sure enough, she was directed to park next to the yellow Volkswagen Bug.

"Isn't she cute? Her name is Daisy."

"That doesn't surprise me at all. It really doesn't." Despite herself, the coyote smiled. "It suits you."

One hand on the door handle, Madeline smiled back. "Well, I suppose I ought to be getting home. Thank you again for saving him." The pixie was head downward in her purse, only its tufted tail visible over the edge as it pillaged. "Thank you for everything."

"You might not be thanking me after spending the night with that thing. Might be a good idea to stop and buy a birdcage on the way home."

"I'm sure that won't be necessary," the ginger demurred primly.

After a moment of inner conflict, Tamara held out a hand. "Give me your phone."

The cat's ears popped up questioningly.

As far as irresponsible acts went, binding a fae to a non-magical being and then letting them both wander off into the sunset had to be near the top of the list. "I'm giving you my number. Just in case."

A phone in a pastel pink, cupcake-patterned case was extended almost reverently. Madeline watched in awe as Tamara punched the number into her contacts. "I can't believe it! To think, witches have cell phones."

The coyote's jaw dropped, tail bristling in consternation. "Wha—of course I have a phone! This isn't the Dark Ages."

Apparently, her offended expression was humorous, as Madeline tried and failed to cover a fit of giggles and twitching whiskers with a polite hand. "Sorry."

Tamara plopped the phone back into her hand. "That's it. Take your sparkle-vermin and get out before I change my mind and hex both of you."

Still giggling, Madeline slipped out of the truck. "See you later, Miss Witch."

"Seriously, get a birdcage." Tamara leaned out the driver's window as the cat unlocked the little yellow Bug. "And eat soon or you're going to crash. Pretend like you have low blood sugar now or something."

"I wiiill," came the singsong tone of one who was definitely not taking a situation seriously enough. "Bye-bye!"

It was harder than Tamara wanted to admit to put the truck in gear and pull away. She cast one last look into the rearview mirror as the cat climbed into her car, carefully holding the purse containing her newly acquired companion to her chest.

Realistically, she had done all she could in the short time available to make sure the ditzy girl knew what she was getting into. Madeline had insisted on making her pixie-infested bed and now she was just going to have to sleep in it. With a firm nod to herself, Tamara pulled out of the parking lot and headed for home.

She was halfway back when her phone buzzed from her pocket.

Well, that didn't take long.

At the next stop sign, a four-way at the center of converging fields of yellowing soybeans with not another vehicle in sight, she checked the message. The number registered as unknown, but the text could only be from one person.

//Isn't he the most adorable thing you've ever seen?!?!?!//

It was accompanied by a photo of the pixie sitting in the cup holder of the Volkswagen, hugging a French fry that looked like a two-by-four in its twiggy arms.

Tamara's muzzle convulsed as at least four separate emotions fought for dominance. Then, like the stages of denial playing on fast forward, resigned bemusement won out.

Sometimes all you can do is wait and see.

CHAPTER FOUR

It was just past breakfast the next morning when the next text came through.

Tamara had decided, somewhat belatedly, that an immediate full-scale pixie capture would be ill-advised without some kind of holding facility ready to receive them. Knee-deep in lumber, chicken wire, and bits of scrap iron, she dropped the wire cutters to tug out her phone as it chimed.

//Sorry to bother you, but might you have time to meet up this morning? It's URGENT//

The request was only surprising in that it hadn't happened sooner. //Meet in the park @ 10// she typed back, already striding toward her truck. //By the pond.//

She kind of wanted to say 'I told you so' in person.

Madeline was waiting when she arrived.

The cat was sitting on a park bench half surrounded by willow trees at one end of the park's small pond. Hands folded in her lap, she gazed pensively at the wavering shapes of gold-fish gliding languidly past beneath the water.

Tamara stopped at the edge of the trees and watched her.

Today the cat wore a simple pair of blue jeans, purple sneakers, and a light green jacket. At odds with the most casual outfit the coyote had seen her wear to date, her long hair fell over her shoulder in an intricate braid that shone in the dappled sunlight through the willow branches. Chicory flowers had been woven into it, blue petals peeking through loops of gleaming copper.

Tamara wanted to take a picture. Instead, she stepped forward. "Yo."

Madeline glanced up at her approach, then giggled. "Good morning!"

"Morning. What's funny?"

"Oh, nothing." She twirled the tip of her braid self-consciously. "Just had a funny thought. *'The Witch in the Willows.'*"

"Would probably be more interesting than the original." Tamara dropped down on the bench beside her. "Where's your sparkly shadow?" She could feel traces of the pixie's magic, but it was hard to pin down an exact location beyond that it was likely somewhere within the boundaries of the park.

"He's close. He wanted to explore, but I asked him to stay nearby."

"Right." The witch nodded, getting right to business. "So, I figure I'll just use the highest level severance spell I can find. The binding was supposed to be permanent—at least until you use up all the fae's magic and it withers away to dust—but since you're not using any magic from it, this is probably a special case."

The cat eyed her with some concern. "What on earth are you talking about?"

"Getting you out of the binding spell, obviously. Don't

worry. Now that it's healed up, it won't die if I undo the spell. Probably."

Ears back, frowning deeply, Madeline scooted slowly away.

Tamara watched the retreat, baffled. "You... weren't going to ask me to undo the spell?"

"Of course not! Ravel is going to stay with me forever!" The ginger's tail poofed in offense, swishing back and forth between two of the wooden bench slats.

New law of nature: this girl is never going to do anything *the way I expect her to.*

The witch closed her eyes for a long moment. When she opened them, her expression and tone had returned to a carefully schooled neutral. "I take it last night went well, then?"

Madeline brightened, irritation falling away almost instantly. "Oh yes, it was wonderful! He was so curious that he explored my room top to bottom. He had a bath with me and slept on my pillow. It was lovely."

"And he—*it*—didn't break anything? Didn't mess anything up at all?"

"Well, he did break one vase. But it wasn't on purpose! I think he wanted the marbles at the bottom. It was no bother. He just needs some toys of his own so he won't be so keen to go after things he shouldn't."

Wrists on her knees, Tamara shook her head slowly. The wind blew pleasantly, ruffling her ponytail and twirling a curtain of yellow-tinged willow branches around them. "Well, that's great for you. So what did you want to talk to me for? Sounds like you've got everything under control."

"Oh no, this is very important." Madeline pulled a tablet from her bag and swiped in. She tapped for a moment before handing the device to Tamara. "Please take a look and tell me: do you notice anything odd about these photos?"

In the first shot, the pixie's rear half protruded from a dresser drawer. In the next, it was wearing a lace handkerchief like a cape. In another, it slept peacefully on a pillow, its internal glow the only source of visible light in a darkened bedroom.

"Odd in ways other than the fact that you took—" Tamara skipped quickly down the screen, "—over two hundred pictures of a pixie in less than twenty-four hours? Not really. Did you use the wrong filter?"

"No. Just like I thought. There's nothing wrong with my photos; she just can't see him."

The coyote handed the tablet back. "You tried to show it off, huh? I told you that most people can't see the fae."

Madeline nodded glumly as she locked the device and tucked it away.

Tamara slouched on the bench, searching for a delicate way to phrase her next words. Not that she would normally hold anything back, but her short association with Madeline had done nothing to convince her that the cat was anything less than a decent girl. Kind and tender-hearted. Spacey but sweet. Someone whose feelings Tamara found that she didn't want to hurt.

"Look. I get that you're excited about all this. And I guess it's normal to want to tell people about the things you're excited about. But you might not want to go around telling people that you have a pet fairy. It sounds kind of…"

"Crazy. I know."

Tamara looked up at the quiet admission. "Not that I'm calling you crazy," she assured quickly, "because you're not. You're just a cat with a pixie issue."

Madeline giggled softly. "Right." Ears drooping, hands in her lap, she studied her twiddling thumbs. "And I understand what you're saying. Believe me, I do. I only really wanted to show him to Ellie. She's my very best friend, you know."

"The tabby you were with at the coffee place, right?"

The ginger nodded before an irritated pout flashed across

her face. "All she saw when I sent her the photos were blurry shots of my room. She asked if my camera lens was smudged. Smudged! *My* lenses, smudged? The nerve."

Tamara bit her lip to keep from grinning. "Sounds rough." She thought for a moment. "Did you tell her what the pictures were of before you sent them?"

"No. I said something like 'oh my gosh, you won't believe this!' Which she didn't."

"Okay. Remember how I told you that people's brains can't just wrap around things they don't think should exist?"

"Yes."

"Send her another picture, but say something like 'look at this neat fairy doll I bought' or 'I'm trying out Photoshop.' Give her something to work with that doesn't challenge her perception of reality. She might be able to see it then. Then you get to share your pixie and she doesn't question your mental state."

Madeline's mouth dropped open at the simplicity of the suggestion. "That's absolutely brilliant! I'll try it."

With a satisfied nod at the cat's satisfaction, Tamara stood. "Good."

"Oh, are you going already?" Madeline asked, apparently disappointed.

"I should. Got a project going that won't build itself. But good luck with your friend." She took one step and fell flat across the path in front of the bench with a startled yelp, raising a cloud of dust. "Oww! What the—?"

Her ankles had been tied together, so gently she hadn't even noticed, with a length of tightly braided willow branches.

A squeaky laugh flittered from the tree.

Madeline covered her eyes in mortification. "Ravel, nooo!"

"And this," Tamara snarled as she inelegantly flopped and struggled her way into a seated position, "is why I hate pixies."

"I'm sorry—I'm so sorry," Madeline babbled. She scrambled

off the bench and dropped to her knees to help untangle the witch. "I had no idea he was doing that!"

Their hands bumped, fingers getting in one another's way as they each tugged at the branches. After the third collision, Tamara shooed her away with a huff. "I didn't think you did."

The pixie swooped down to land on the backboard of the bench. Still giggling, it chirped at Madeline and then pointed gleefully to Tamara.

"Yes, I see what you did, and it was very naughty!"

Its head tilted in confusion, long ears swiveling. It squeaked questioningly.

"This lady saved your life," the cat scolded, arms folded crossly. Her agitated tail drew patterns in the dust behind her. "You need to be nice to her. Falling down like that could have hurt her, do you understand?"

"Somehow I don't think it grasps the concept," Tamara grumbled. She ripped the last of the willow branches off her left boot and inspected the braided strands. "That thing wove these together like this?"

Madeline nodded eagerly. "Oh yes. He's very good at tying and untying things—aren't you, Ravel? Mummy's going to buy you some ribbons to braid so you won't knot up her cords and chargers again, yes she is."

Tamara snorted, tossing the handful of willow away. "Ravel the sparkle-vermin. Well, I guess if you had to name it, at least it's something fitting."

The cat smiled bashfully in response.

"Are you sure you only want one scoop?"

"Uh, yeah. One scoop is fine." Tamara awkwardly accepted the ice cream cone being thrust upon her. "Thanks, but you didn't have to buy me anything."

"Nonsense! You've helped me so much, treating you is the least I can do." Digging into her purse, Madeline traded a bill for a cone topped with three towering multicolored scoops.

Ravel watched curiously from the hood of her jacket, unnoticed by the raccoon dishing up the ice cream.

Tamara wasn't sure how her morning had come to this. One minute she was walking back toward the small parking lot, the chatty cat trailing almost hopefully at her side, and the next she was being pulled excitedly along in the wake of the ice cream truck's cheerful tune as it rolled slowly toward the playground.

They chose a picnic table between the swing set and the edge of the wooded acreage that ringed the town's park with a half-moon crescent of trees. Behind them, a small brook babbled beneath a wooden bridge where it flowed along the border of the tree line. Before them, a pack of children chased each other, screeching at ear-piercing decibels, around the playground equipment.

Flattening her ears as the small bat hanging upside down from the jungle gym let out a terrific shriek, Tamara took a lick of strawberry. "This is pretty good."

"Mm-hmm!" Madeline attacked her own treat with gusto. "I love ice cream. Want to try some of mine?" She thrust the melting cone out invitingly. A rivulet of pink and blue cotton candy trickled down into chocolate territory, which in turn oozed lower to muddy up lemon crème.

The coyote politely declined.

"So, what's the project you're working on? Does it have to do with the rest of the pixies?"

Tamara crunched sourly into the top side of her cone. "My whole life now has to do with the rest of the pixies. Basically, I'm building a giant bird cage to keep them in when I catch them."

"You're not going to hurt them, are you?" Madeline asked, clearly worriedly.

Another burst of merriment rose from the playground. Ravel buzzed his way out of her hood and fluttered away to investigate.

Ears back, Tamara watched him go with a frown. "Of course not. I just have to have a way to keep the ones I catch in one place until I get all of them. Then I open a way to the fae realm, shove them all back in, and close it as fast as I can. It's not like opening the front door—you only want to do it once."

"Would it really be so bad? To let them stay in our world?" Madeline asked timidly. "Surely they're too small to really do any harm."

The witch gave her a flat, black stare that was only somewhat hampered by the strawberry ice cream on her lip. "Seriously? Causing trouble is the only thing they know how to do. The only reason there hasn't been more mayhem than a possessed latte machine is because they've only been in this reality a day and a half."

Looking sad, the cat lapped thoughtfully at her melting cone. Her eyes followed Ravel as he flittered from merry-go-round to slide to swings, curiously following one child after another, and paused to hover in fascination above the sandbox where a tiny otter was digging with a brightly colored plastic pail and scoop.

"I know they're small, but they can do a lot of damage," Tamara implored, increasingly desperate to get the point across. "Believe me, I have firsthand experience with that. A bunch of them got loose earlier this spring."

"Really?" Madeline's ears perked in interest.

"Only ten or twelve, but that was more than enough. Nothing like what I'm dealing with now."

"What happened?"

"A lot of frustration and inconvenience happened is what, but the summarized version is that a little old muskrat went to the ER when a pixie knocked a potted cactus off a second-floor balcony and I had to cast the biggest memory spell of my life to make eighteen witnesses forget they saw a floating pickup truck."

Madeline stared.

"One crawled in the gas tank of a diesel at the Pit Crew gas station and barbeque," Tamara elaborated, ears flicking irritably at the memory.

"Did it... did it die?"

"Uh, yeah. It definitely died. And apparently, pixie death glitter does weird things to engines." The coyote crammed the last bite of ice cream cone into her mouth. "I still can't figure out if they're super smart or super stupid."

Deep in serious philosophical conversation, the two barely noticed as the little otter was collected from the sandbox. Still waving his shovel and pail, he squeaked happily from his father's arms as they approached the ice cream truck.

Ravel darted after them.

"I wonder if maybe they don't have many natural enemies in the fairy world," Madeline mused, still looking queasy. "They don't seem to be very aware of dangers, for such little creatures."

"Yeah, could be." Tamara wiped her slightly sticky hands on the hips of her jeans. "But that's just one more reason I need to catch them and get them back where they belong, right? They don't get hurt, we don't get hurt, everybody wins."

Madeline daintily wiped her mouth with a paper napkin. "I suppose so..."

At the ice cream truck, the tiny otter was proving more interested in the glittery distraction than the promise of a frozen treat.

"Bur. Bur!" Pail in one hand, he pointed insistently at the circling pixie with the plastic shovel.

The adult otter laughed, bouncing the squirming pup in one

arm as he took a cup of ice cream from the raccoon vendor. "You see a bird, buddy? Good job. What color is it?"

"Bur!"

Madeline reached across the picnic table and tapped the witch's arm excitedly. "Tamara, look! That baby can see Ravel. Isn't that precious?"

Tamara snorted in amusement, tail giving a preoccupied wag. "Yeah, cute." Then she squinted suspiciously. "What's it doing?"

The pixie dove, zipping rapidly back and forth between the father's legs.

With a gasp, Madeline surged to her feet, banging her knee in the struggle to extract herself from the picnic table's wooden embrace. "Ravel, no—!"

The coyote was faster. Whipping her legs out from under the table, she sprinted toward the ice cream truck. Behind her, the cat nearly tripped, the toe of her sneaker catching on the edge of the bench board, but regained her footing and dashed after Tamara.

They were barely halfway across the grassy, open space when the otter turned away from the truck's counter and staggered over his tangled shoelaces. He fell as only someone with the body shape of an upright noodle could: like a tree, straight down. His torso rotated like a corkscrew. When he hit the ground shoulder first, he was the only one to do so—his pup, held tightly to his chest, never touched the grass.

The cup of ice cream came down on the little otter's head with an audible splat.

The plastic pail came down on top of the pixie.

The little one, silent surprise quickly replaced with upset, began to wail.

Tamara skidded to a stop as the pail began to rise off the ground, buzzing faintly from beneath. She grabbed it as it floated past her knees. Luckily, both the father otter and the ice cream vendor, who had rushed out of her truck to help, were too busy soothing the crying pup to notice.

Madeline jogged up beside her a moment later, distress stamped across every fair feature.

Flipping the pail right side up, the coyote dumped the pixie out into the other girl's hands. It squeaked indignantly as her grip tightened around it.

"Take that thing and go wait over there," Tamara whispered harshly, pointing toward the stand of willow trees.

Madeline nodded rapidly, the points of her tiny fangs digging guiltily into her lower lip. She cast one last glance at the chaos by the ice cream truck and walked quickly away with Ravel held firmly to her chest.

Pail in hand, Tamara tried to school her expression away from anger and back to pure concern as she approached. "Excuse me, are you okay?"

The otter father looked up at Tamara in surprise as the grandmotherly raccoon helpfully lifted his sniffling pup out of his arms. "Oh, yeah. We're fine, thanks. Just tripped up a bit." He shot a vexed look and a webbed hand at his inexplicably knotted shoelaces. "I have no idea how these got so tangled up…"

"I think your kid dropped this," the witch declared somewhat louder than necessary as she held out the pail.

With the hand not picking at his laces, the otter accepted it. "Hey, thank you. He's all about putting stuff into things right now. Look buddy, she found your bucket."

The pup seemed to be over his fright. Eyes crossed, he licked repeatedly at his nose as trickles of melting ice cream dripped onto the tip of it.

The ice cream lady laughed, booping his sticky nose. "There we go, all better. Now let's see if we can get you a little cleaner."

He squeaked delightedly as she produced a string of napkins out of her sleeve.

Satisfied that the situation was under control, Tamara

departed with a quick wave. She could only hope that Madeline hadn't cut and run with the cause of the trouble.

Luckily, the cat's voice reached her as she neared the path at the edge of the pond, drifting closer as willow strands parted under her hands.

Madeline stood with her back to the water, secluded from the rest of the park by a curtain of wind-blown branches. Her ears lay almost flat against her hair. The tip of her tail twitched grimly among the thistles and crabgrass.

Ravel cowered on her cupped palms. His ears low, long tail curled defensively around himself, he chirped up at his mistress in confusion and dismay.

"What did I just tell you not half an hour ago? Tripping people is *bad*. It *hurts*. We do *not* hurt people!"

Ravel flinched at the hard edge of her tone.

Even Tamara, out of sight among the leaves, had to admit that there was something to be reckoned with in the ginger's current bearing. Like an angry Kindergarten teacher, maybe.

"Do you remember how it felt when you got hit by that car? That hurt you. It hurt you so badly that you almost went 'poof!' and died. When someone is hurt enough—when someone dies —they go away and they don't come back. Ever."

She dropped her hands. The pixie took flight, so quickly that he barely dipped from the spot where he'd so recently been supported.

Madeline opened her purse with a snap of the magnetic clasp. "I want you to go in here and think about what you did. I'll tell you when it's time to come out."

Looking as wretched as a fae could look, he shot one last soulful glance at the cat and zipped into the bag trailing faint sparks.

Tamara stepped out of the cover of the trees. "I have to say, that's the first time I've ever seen a fae get put in time-out."

Madeline seemed to deflate as she approached. Her tail

stopped its restless twitching and drooped limply, picking up a cocklebur without her notice. "Do you think he'll still like me now?"

Her bottle-green eyes brimmed with tears, but she had not, as yet, begun to cry. Knowing what she knew of the other girl's tendencies, Tamara was unreasonably proud.

"That thing is bound to you with the strongest ties in our earthly realm. You're its morning sun and its evening star." She patted the cat's slumping shoulder awkwardly. "It still likes you."

Madeline sniffled.

"Seriously though, you did good. That was your first Command. You gave it strongly and for a good reason, and your fae obeyed without a struggle of wills." Never mind that it was just a pixie—for a non-magical being, Tamara decided the other girl deserved the kudos. "Most witches have a hard time getting that result."

A tiny, stuttered sigh. "I just hope he learned his lesson. I hate having to scold."

"Welcome to life as a pixie mom." The witch's tiny smirk melted almost as quickly as it formed. "But do you understand what I mean now? These things cause problems and misery wherever they go. I have to send them back to the fae realm. You get that, right?"

Madeline wiped at her cheek and looked up, sparkling green gaze meeting deep, infinite black. "No."

Tamara's mouth dropped open so far and fast that it made a noise. "What?"

"I said, no. I don't agree with you." With one last sniff, the cat drew herself up. "I don't deny that they cause trouble. That's obvious and I can see it now. But I don't agree with you that they're nothing but evil little creatures that harm people for fun. I think they're… they're just new. Brand new. And they don't know any better, yet."

Tamara, who wasn't sure what she could say to that, said nothing.

Madeline straightened and managed a smile. "Well, 'stiff upper lip' and all that! We should start finding the rest of the pixies as soon as possible."

The coyote shook herself, ponytail flipping. "Uh, we?"

"Yes, of course. You and I and Ravel. I'm sure he can help us somehow, once I explain—"

Tamara turned on the heel of her work boot and began to walk away. "Forget it. You can help me most by keeping your pixie out of trouble and staying out of my way."

"But—but wait!" The cat scampered after her, catching her by the arm imploringly. "You said on the bridge that there are more than a hundred of them. You can't capture that many on your own. It would take forever."

"I've always been on my own. I can handle it."

"No woman is an island!"

"Unless they're a witch. Let go."

Before Tamara could even spare a thought to consider what a spectacle they were making, the clinging cat being towed along behind her like a fluffy ginger pull toy, there was a commotion from the direction of the woods.

A windblown tumult of chestnut hair topped with black-tipped triangular ears popped up from the creek bed. A young vixen scrambled up the embankment through the elderberry and bindweed.

On her heels came a second fox, annoyance and trepidation written all over his face as the other charged heedlessly ahead.

They were the jeep-driving teenagers from the day before.

Tamara bristled instinctively before reason prevailed. There was nothing to worry about, she reminded herself firmly. She recognized them, but there was no way they would remember her.

The vixen headed right for the two by the willows, springing lightly through the grass on bare, muddy feet. A few steps behind, her brother, pants rolled up to his knees, carried two pairs of sneakers slung over his shoulder by the laces.

"Hey, hi there!" She raised a similarly muddy hand in greeting as she neared. The sleeves of her red sweater were pristine. "Remember us? We totally didn't run over you yesterday, even though you were standing in the street like idiots—"

"Kari!" the boy hissed, ears back and one wary eye on the coyote.

For a moment, Tamara felt like she was having an out-of-body experience.

Twice. Twice in a week, her memory alteration skills had failed her. But why? Yesterday, everyone else had forgotten her immediately thanks to her charmed wristbands. The barista, the patrons at the café, Madeline's friend—

Ellie. *Now* she remembered. She had taken off her wristbands to talk to the other cat, stuffed them in her pocket, and never put them back on. She hadn't even been equipped with her first-line defense when the fox brats had almost hit them, and who wouldn't remember an incident like that without magical intervention?

Madeline, still hanging on the witch's arm, perked in recognition. "Oh! Yes, of course we remember you. Hello."

Tamara frowned sourly, mostly at herself. *Get it together, Ridgemount. You're getting distracted. You can't afford distractions.*

She made a mental note to dig that pair of pants out of the laundry basket later. Washing machines could do a number on hand-stitched spells.

The vixen smiled charmingly, displaying a number of perfectly white teeth. "Sooo, you two look well. Like, really well. Very healthy and un-smashed." She laced the tips of her grubby fingers and flipped her tail beatifically. "Like two upstanding ladies who wouldn't even think about calling the cops on us."

"We would never," Madeline hastened to assure. She kept a

firm grip on Tamara's elbow, as if the coyote would sprint away if she relaxed her attention for a moment. "No harm done."

The girl let out a sigh of relief. "Oh, okay. Just making sure. You didn't really look like someone who would get a couple of kits' driver's licenses revoked when we just got them."

"I was driving, not you," the boy muttered, eyes still on Tamara. He, like his sister, had striking gray eyes, like frost being born at the edge of a November lake.

Trying not to look like she was doing so, Tamara looked the pair up and down. Seeing them up close, the familial relationship was more than obvious—to the point that if she didn't know that nature intended it to be impossible, she would swear the two were identical twins. Their hair, the same shade of chestnut, spiked up into a cowlick in exactly the same place between their ears, though the vixen's was pulled up in a high half-tail and her brother's into a shorter one at the back of his neck. Their facial structures were the same, though his were less delicate. And their silver-gray eyes gazed back in perfect tandem, almost eerie in their sameness.

A cold chill, unbidden, crawled down the witch's spine.

"What are you staring at?" the vixen demanded abruptly, ears back and tail swishing.

Tamara blinked herself back to the present.

"Just some dirty kits," she drawled coolly. Though she had to admit, albeit privately, they had done a great job keeping everything but their hands and feet clean. When she went into the water for smooth stones and potion ingredients, all bets were off on how filthy she would become. "Aren't you two a little old to be playing in the creek?"

"Aren't you old enough to mind your own business?" the girl shot back.

Her brother cleared his throat loudly and delivered a warning elbow to her ribs. "We were just messing around. Catching crawdads."

Tamara nodded shortly. "Fun. I used to do that as a pup."

"Really? So did I!" At her side, Madeline fluffed at the apparently fond memory. "Right after my family came over from England."

It was the first time Tamara had heard the cat talk about anything from her past. Before she could do more than wonder idly how long ago that had been, the vixen squeezed back into the conversation.

"Yeah, yeah, that's fascinating. But now that we've all made nice—what was that sparkly thing that went in your purse a minute ago?"

As that charming, toothy smile turned expectantly on Madeline, Tamara tucked one hand behind her back and began to weave signs.

"Er. Um." Clearly spooked, the ginger let go of Tamara's arm to wrap both of her own protectively around her bag. Her tail hairs rose, poofing the already voluminous appendage to a frankly ridiculous girth. "Nothing. There's nothing in my purse."

The vixen frowned, fists on her hips and clearly unimpressed. "Yeah, and that's why you're hugging it like it's full of diamonds."

"I'm sure I don't know what you're talking about."

"You were picking something sparkly up off the road yesterday, too. Come on, I won't mess with it, just let me see." She took a determined step forward.

Madeline took a defensive step back.

Tamara raised her hand. The building energy of the spell released with a rippling ping. "Something sparkly, huh? Was it a hummingbird? They're gathering to go south this time of year."

The young vixen stopped in her tracks, rusty red ears swiveling slowly like satellites that had lost a signal. "Humming...? Um. I don't think so... I think?"

Madeline watched the exchange from where she had taken

refuge slightly behind the coyote, still carefully hugging the pixie within her purse.

"Then maybe it was a dragonfly," Tamara offered, waving a hand vaguely at the pond. "There are all kinds of them with all the water around here. Kind of quick and shimmering. Did you see one out of the corner of your eye?"

"No, I—maybe?" the white tip of a bushy red tail flipped in confusion. "Maybe it was. I... can't really remember, now."

"Hey, that's okay," the witch soothed with a smile, gentle and understanding. "It happens to everyone sometimes."

"Yeah." The vixen nodded to herself, reassured. "What were we talking about?"

Her mirror image suddenly appeared between the two. "We should talk about going home, if you're done bothering these people we don't know. We need to work on our science project."

The vixen blinked rapidly as her brother's arm went around her back. She shook herself, as if waking from a daydream. "Huh?"

"Science. Project."

"Oh. Right. Sure." She allowed herself to be shepherded in the direction of the parking lot, ears still swiveling dazedly.

"Be careful on your way home. Don't do drugs. Stay in school. Eat your veggies." Tamara waved casually after them. For a moment she thought she saw the boy's hackles rise, his arm tighten noticeably around his sister, but just as quickly she was sure she had imagined it.

As soon as they were out of earshot, Madeline released the death grip on her purse. A relieved squeak issued from within. "That was absolutely brilliant!" she gushed. "How did you do that? It was magic, wasn't it?"

"Persuasion spell." Tamara kept watching until the foxes climbed into their jeep and the purr of the engine began. "That girl is way too sharp."

"She saw Ravel."

"I don't think she actually saw him as he really is, but she saw *something*. That's a lot more than most people would. But if you can get someone to start doubting their own perception, suggest a concrete explanation for them to latch onto—most of the time that's even more effective than messing with their memory."

"That's amazing," the cat breathed, watching the jeep as it turned out of the parking lot. When she turned back, Tamara was walking away. "Hey, wait! Where are you going?"

"Home, to work on my pixie cage. Prison. Aviary. Whatever. Before anything else happens."

"I'll come with you." Feline footsteps pattered through the grass as Madeline's purple sneakers hurried to catch up.

"No dice. I'm not coming back to town today."

"Then I'll drive myself and follow you there. I still want to help you."

Tamara turned a frustrated eye on her persistent follower. "Do you even know how to use power tools?"

"I'm very good at measuring and holding." The cat's white whiskers stuck out stubbornly.

The witch heaved a deep sigh. "Fine. Do what you want. But you have to keep that pixie under control and I'm not responsible for any accidents."

Madeline brightened instantly. "Deal!"

They left the park in a procession of two.

Tamara did her best to ignore the fact that her very practical old truck was being closely tailed by a little yellow Volkswagen as she set her sights on open fields and the forest beyond. That proved something of a challenge, as every stop sign brought a wave of bouncy pop music from behind.

A glance in her rearview confirmed that the pixie had been redeemed from time-out and was happily swinging from the strand of sparkly charms hanging below the cat's mirror. A thin vapor of glitter gusted from the open window.

If the other girl was so set on offering her assistance, there was no use wasting the energy trying to get her to change her mind. The witch would simply have to stand back, keep watch, and let nature take its course in convincing the silly cat that she was in over her head.

Sometimes the only way to learn a lesson is the hard way.

CHAPTER FIVE

"Okay, not bad. But we have to do better."

Tamara studied the pixiary with a critical eye. Inside, four pixies amused themselves with varying degrees of contentment among a scattering of branches, piping, and thrift shop toddler toys. The newest addition, having just been introduced to its new accommodations, glowered ungratefully from a perch near the ceiling.

To the witch's surprise, the ginger cat had proven helpful in the construction of the cage. They had begun working in earnest early in the afternoon two days ago, and by the evening of that same day, the structure had been complete. It stood nearly as large as the garden shed it abutted, wooden beams supporting chicken wire woven through with all the scrap iron they could find. The sheet of tin that served as a roof had been salvaged from the ramshackle chicken coop of an abandoned farmhouse several miles down the road.

A veritable mural of wards and charms finished it off. The wards, mostly for containment, were interlocked with charms for illusion and sheltering—an illusion to be sure that any trespassers, however unlikely, would only believe that Tamara owned a coop full of cranky pigeons, and sheltering per Madeline's insistence that, well, the nights *were* getting a bit chilly, and what if it rained?

Madeline, standing nearby, gave the captive fae an anxious look. "Four in two days is fairly good, though, isn't it? Five in three, if you count Ravel."

Oblivious to the plight of his fellows, the pixie in question was happily occupied dive-bombing the tiny fishpond in the corner of the yard with acorns.

"That still leaves ninety-five on the loose, give or take a handful." Tamara chewed thoughtfully on a claw tip. "Where did you find this one?"

"The glass wholesale shop on Main. You know, Frank's Glass & More? They have a bunch of mirrors set out on the sidewalk near their window display. I was walking back to work with my lunch and that little one flew right into a mirror."

The coyote snorted in amusement. "So that's why it looks hungover. And why you brought it over in a takeout container."

"I'm just glad he didn't try to get away once I had him. It would have been terrible if he had gotten loose in the shop while I was working." Looking tired at the mere thought, the ginger settled into one of the rare sunbeams to penetrate the oak tree's branches, slanting across an old garden bench near the base of the trunk.

"I'd say you have no idea, but you saw what happened at the coffee place. Where do you work, anyway?"

"Photo Finish. I help in the shop a few days a week, and the owner lets me stay in the little flat upstairs for free."

Tamara knew of the camera shop, as most of the town's residents knew about the little stores that lined Main Street. It always had a charming display of antique cameras in the window, along with, weirdly, an extensive collection of the tiny artificial birdies that had presumably once been used to coax people into not looking cross-eyed for their portraits.

"Pretty sweet deal."

"Oh, it's quite fun. Most of the business nowadays is repair and resale of older camera models, so I mainly help with the online auction postings and electronic recordkeeping. But I do try to give customers pointers when they come in, and keep things nice and tidy on the sales floor."

The witch wondered vaguely if maybe she needed to buy an old camera. Strictly for aesthetic purposes.

"The owner keeps odd hours, so I always have time for photo shoots. And my photography blog, of course."

Finally deciding that the imprisoned pixies weren't plotting a sudden escape, Tamara joined the other girl on the bench. The late afternoon sun was warm, but the cool breeze was a constant reminder that autumn wasn't far away.

"You really like taking pictures, don't you?"

"Well, it is my oldest hobby. I like to think I've gotten rather good at it by now." She gave Tamara a sidelong glance. "Do you have a hobby of some sort?"

The question took the coyote off guard. She blinked. "I'm a witch."

Madeline's laughter was so bright it didn't sound even a little bit condescending. "That isn't a hobby—that's a thing that you are! What's something that you like to do for fun?" Then, as if struck by a sudden thought, she sobered. "Assuming that you were born a witch, of course, and you didn't decide to work to become one."

"I was. All witches are born. Real ones, I mean. Non-magical beings can practice witchcraft and get some results if they genuinely believe that they will, but real magic is like breathing water. Unless you're born with the ability, it's not something you can learn."

The cat nodded, tracing aimless shapes in the dirt with the toe of her shoe. "That makes sense, I suppose. If just anyone could learn to do magic, the whole world would know about it by now."

"Right." A dry oak leaf drifted down, was caught by the breeze, and moored itself in Tamara's already messy bun. "But something I do for fun, huh…" Frowning in concentration, she plucked out the leaf and put her hair back up. "I guess I like to fish. And I kind of collect more crystals than I really need for my spellcraft."

"Really? I love to fish! Though I've only been the once. And I accidentally hooked my Uncle Trevor through the ear. And they never took me back after that."

The coyote valiantly fought a smile. "Can't imagine why."

Ravel had finally lost interest in tormenting the goldfish. He fluttered over, did a lazy barrel roll over their heads, and came to rest on Madeline's shoulder. She reached up to stroke him fondly with a polish-tipped finger.

A dark shadow plunged from the tree with a hair-raising cry.

Madeline screamed like a kettle boiling over. She bolted from the bench, waving her arms madly around her head to ward off the terror that had descended upon them. Ravel shot in the other direction with a flash of sparkles and an only slightly higher-pitched shriek.

Tamara laughed so hard she nearly slid out of her seat.

"You," she informed the intruder breathlessly, "are an asshole."

Highly pleased with himself, her crow familiar strutted back and forth along the now empty span of bench beside her.

Madeline, breathing hard, peeked out from behind the shed where she had taken cover. Her tail, when it swished into view, was so large in circumference that Tamara doubted that she could get both her hands around it without compressing the fluff. "What—what on *earth*—?"

The harder the coyote tried to stop giggling, the less it

worked. "Hey, it's okay," she called, beckoning the cat with a laughter-weakened hand. "He won't hurt you. He's just a jerk."

Madeline looked less than convinced but warily scooted back into the open.

Tamara offered the bird her wrist. He deigned to step onto it, and she raised him to chest level. "This is Raven."

The ginger blinked. "But that's a crow."

"No, I mean his name is Raven." Tamara ran a hand down his back, smoothing ruffled plumage. A pinfeather drifted loose. "Gran was a big Edgar Allen Poe fan."

"He's tame?" Madeline drifted closer, curiosity replacing the nervousness in her eyes.

"He's my familiar."

"What does a familiar do? Help you with spells?"

"Sometimes. He brings me things he finds, lends me extra energy for my magic, keeps an eye on things in my territory from the air. Eats my chips. Y'know, familiar stuff." She extended her arm. "Want to hold him?"

Cat and bird sized one another up. "Will he let me?"

"If he doesn't want to, he'll just fly away."

Slowly Madeline aligned her forearm with Tamara's. The crow considered. One foot stepped daintily over, followed by the second, and he was perched fully on the ginger's wrist.

Glassy black eyes peered at her. An inky head cocked in concentration. "*Pretty.*"

Madeline's whiskers went stiff with surprise. "He talks!"

"He says a few words. Non-crow language words, I mean." Tamara couldn't help but smile at the display. Who knew that her familiar made such a good wingman?

Not that she was trying to impress the other girl, or anything.

"*Pretty.*" With a soft croak, the corvid sidled sideways up the cat's arm.

Madeline's free hand went to her cheek as she tittered. "My

goodness, what a charming fellow. So clever! I think you're very pretty too, Raven."

The crow reached her shoulder. Then it leaned down, matter-of-factly, to peck at the pendant of the necklace she was wearing. "*Pretty.*"

Tamara facepalmed.

"…Oh. I see." The insides of the cat's ears pinked. Regally, she inclined her head and looked away. "Flattery will get you nowhere."

The witch held out her arm. The crow stepped back with a last, longing glance at the necklace. Ravel zipped down from the foliage of a nearby maple tree and took refuge under Madeline's hair, squeaking what could only be insults at the intruding creature that had dared to perch upon his mistress.

"Did you actually want something, or did you just come by to be a featherhead?" Tamara asked grumpily, transferring the bird back to the garden bench.

A flurry of caws and croaks erupted as the crow went into a flapping, high-stepping dance.

The coyote's ears and tail popped to attention. "Really? That many? Are you sure? That's perfect!"

Madeline watched the exchange in utter befuddlement. "What's he saying?"

"He says a bunch of pixies are camped out in the beehives in that big orchard just north of here! Probably close to twenty of them. They're hard to count when they zip around."

"You understood all that?" the cat asked wonderingly. "Well, never mind, I suppose a witch would have to be able to understand her own familiar. More importantly, why would pixies want to take over a beehive?"

"Easy shelter, maybe. Or they have a sweet tooth. Or the buzzing caught their attention. Or all of the above." Tamara surged to her feet, fist clenched in resolve. "But whatever. The point is, this is our chance to bag a bunch of them at once without having to hunt all over the county." She glanced upwards, noting the growing slant of the light through the tree-tops. "It's too late in the day now, but tomorrow we can mount an assault."

"I can get off work by two," Madeline supplied eagerly. "Will that be soon enough? Please wait for me!"

"That should be fine. Just get here as soon as you can." The witch looked the cat up and down, from silk blouse to velveteen flats. "And try to wear something... practical."

"That's not exactly the kind of practical I had in mind."

"Oh?" Madeline blinked innocently down at her spotlessly tidy designer overalls and cherry-patterned sneakers. Braided pigtails fell over the faintly striped ginger fur exposed by her lacy shoulderless top. "But we're going to an orchard."

"To hunt rogue fae, not do a photo shoot for Southern Living." Studiously averting her gaze from shapely feline shoulders, Tamara gathered the last of her gear off the front porch step.

The cat trotted along at her side, Ravel peeking from the breast pocket of her overalls. "So, what's our plan?"

"When you want to calm down a swarm of bees, you make them drowsy with smoke." A backpack leaf blower was lowered into the truck bed next to a large metal feed bucket and a coil of rubber hose. "Charm the kindling and it just might work on pixies."

"Will the farmers be keen on us meddling with their hives?"

Tamara tugged at the lapels of her khaki uniform shirt. "It's in the best interest of everyone involved to cooperate with the Forest Service, ma'am."

"You've thought of everything!" Madeline marveled as they climbed into the truck cab. On her third try, she managed to tame the finicky seatbelt, tucking the strap behind her back so as not to squash the pixie at her chest. "You could go anywhere in these parts, impersonating a forestry worker."

The coyote snorted in mock offense. "Impersonating? Excuse you, I'm on the payroll. On-call specialist, Invasive Species Program." She patted the patch sewn onto one sleeve. "I get called in about once a week. Ask me about emerald ash borers. Giant hogweed. Pygmy unicorns."

Madeline looked startled. "You have a job? Other than being a witch? I had no idea."

"Yeah, well. The world's a lot smaller than it used to be. The days when witches could just hide away from it all are long gone." The truck pulled out onto the main road with a grumble of protest and a cloud of dust, setting course for the afflicted orchard.

Somewhere high above, a lone crow tracked their progress through the dull, muted green of the dying summer.

Face to the sun, braids swaying in the wind from the open window, the cat breathed a deep, happy sigh. "What perfect work for a forest witch to do, though. It's like it was made for you."

"Pretty much. Everything I do in uniform is something I'd be doing anyway, so why not get paid for it? Getting the degree was kind of a pain, though."

"But why go to school for something that's in your very nature? Surely you could have used magic to fudge the records."

A pothole appeared from nowhere. The bump popped Ravel halfway out of his pocket with a squeak of surprise.

The witch frowned.

Because the easy way was rarely the right way.

Because she couldn't sit alone in an empty house anymore.

Because it was what her grandmother would have wanted.

"Because going to public school and college taught me how to blend in with the magically deficient. And keep up with the advances of modern technology. And occasionally talk to something other than a bird, plant, or reptile."

Madeline's green eyes widened hugely.

"FYI, snakes are horrible at conversation. Don't even try."

The cat's delighted laughter struck her as much more pleasant than she thought it strictly should have.

"I knew it! I knew it all along. Didn't I tell you yesterday—didn't I tell you, Barb?—those are no ordinary wasps in my beehives!"

From the veranda of a stately old farmhouse, a graying groundhog chattered with righteous fury.

His wife rolled her eyes, wiping rubber gloves on the apron tied around her rather pronounced middle. By the stains left behind, she had recently been in the kitchen—either murdering someone or canning beets. "Calm down, Gus. Now, what did you say we're dealing with, honey?"

Tamara squared up authoritatively. "Asian giant hornets. Just a few can wipe out an entire colony of honeybees in a single afternoon. Snap their heads right off."

"Over my dead body!" Gus raged. "Those bees pollinate my livelihood! They make the best honey in the tri-county area!"

"Are they dangerous?" Barb asked, glancing nervously in the direction of the hives. "The grandbabies are coming to spend the day with us tomorrow."

"Extremely dangerous. Two inches long. Fast fliers. Sting repeatedly. The venom causes flesh degeneration, kidney failure, anaphylaxis. I can keep going."

The farmer squinted grimly, rolling up the sleeves of his jacket. "I'll get the kerosene."

"Heavens, Gramps, you'll do no such thing!" His wife seized him firmly by the arm. "You'll leave this to the professionals, is what you'll do. A sting from those monsters would flare your kidney stones up in a heartbeat."

"Sir, if you'll lend us some of your beekeeping gear, I'm very confident we can get this outbreak under control."

His stubby, bushy tail flicked uneasily. "Dealt with these things before, have ya?"

The coyote nodded, projecting an air of calm certainty. "I have. Some specially treated wood smoke and we'll get your hives cleared out in no time. Most of your bees are probably hiding out nearby—odds are they'll swarm back before sundown."

"I sure hope you're right." The groundhog looked over her shoulder. "What about that one? She gonna be alright?"

Madeline waved excitedly from the truck.

Tamara scratched the back of her neck with a little cough. "She's from—uh. The entomology department. To collect a specimen sample. Yeah."

It was probably a good thing her inherent pessimism kept her from assuming that having a tagalong on the job would be easy.

A few minutes later, properly suited, they made their way across the orchard toward the beehives. A gentle wind ruffled the leaves of the fruit trees, sending ripening apples swaying on their branches. Rows of cherry and newly harvested dwarf pears seemed to bask in the mellow sun, relieved that their season of toil had ended.

Leaf blower on her back, smoke pot in hand, the witch led the way.

Braids peeking out the bottom of her borrowed mesh beekeeping hood, Madeline followed dutifully with a butterfly net and a pillowcase. Ravel, who had been ordered into silence for the duration of the mission, watched with interest from the designated pixie pocket.

With every step, the buzzing itch of fae magic grew stronger. So did buzzing of a different sort.

"There are the bees." Tamara pointed to several balls of very irritated insects clinging to branches near the middle of a nearby tree. "I figured they wouldn't go far. They know it's way too late in the year to swarm off and get another hive put together before the cold comes."

"I hope the pixies didn't ruin their honeycombs," the cat fretted.

"Me, too. The sooner we get them out of there the better. Ready to do this?"

Gripping the handle of the butterfly net, Madeline nodded determinedly.

Tamara turned her back to the farmhouse as she knelt to cast her spells. Better to err on the side of caution when the groundhogs were undoubtedly watching from the safety of their home. In a moment, abnormally thick and voluminous purple billows were pouring from the metal smoker pot.

"Ooh, pretty."

"Just be ready with that net, okay? I made this stuff extra strong so it'll affect fae, but they might still be able to make a break for it. And don't walk into it yourself, for the love of all that's holy."

"Right."

As stealthily as she could while strapped to a leaf blower, the coyote crept toward the hive box where the concentration of magic hung the strongest. Behind her, Madeline raised the net in one hand, ready to strike, and took hold of the blower's pull cord with the other.

"Rev me!" Tamara barked as they came in range.

The ginger yanked the pull cord. The leaf blower thrummed to life. A thick blanket of smoke was instantly propelled into the bottom of the hive. A cacophony of buzzes and panicked squeaks erupted.

"You're sure this won't hurt them?" Madeline asked nervously.

"Absolutely positi—"

The top blew off the beehive as the pixies made their escape. Tamara yelped and Madeline screamed in surprise as the cluster ascended—only to make it less than three feet into the air before they began to dip and spiral wildly in the swirling cloud of smoke.

"It's working," Tamara yelled, angling the air stream of the blower to add to the disorientation. "Get 'em, Maddie!"

Still screaming, the cat began to run, swinging the net wildly while trying to avoid the smoke. In the confusion, Ravel slipped from her pocket. In a moment he was looping and swooping in corkscrews with the less domesticated rabble, squeaking with glee.

Ears back, the witch laughed maniacally, wielding her blower without mercy. "Begone from these lands, glittery pestilence!"

"I think you might be enjoying this a bit too much," Madeline wailed, scooping up three pixies as they tumbled past head over tail.

"So are they!"

It was true. More and more pixies joined the chaos as those who had been hiding in the other hives got wind of what was happening. Rather than attempting to flee, they did exactly the opposite, diving into the miasma of their own accord. Two crashed drunkenly into one another and fell directly into the cat's net, giggling crazily.

Within minutes, it was over. The most resilient pixies tumbled to the ground like fallen leaves, overcome by dizziness and exhaustion. Abandoning the now useless net, Madeline hurried about with the pillowcase, collecting them by hand like Easter eggs from among the grass.

Tamara circled the perimeter, helpfully blowing them into

tiny piles where they lay, twitching and sparkling erratically. "That actually went a lot easier than I thought."

Peering into the pillowcase, Madeline started. "Oh, dear." Unerringly finding her own bonded pixie among the fallen masses, she delicately plucked him out by the scruff. "Are you alright, love?"

Ravel chirped in agreement, eyes still rolling woozily.

"Well, I'm certainly glad you had fun. Succumbing to peer pressure, indulging in substances, contributing to the general havoc—"

Tamara bit her lip viciously. It wasn't enough to stem the eruption of giggles. She turned quickly away, choking off the blower and covering her laughter with a coughing fit. "Oh, wow. There's sure a lot of—ha!—ragweed out here in these open fields, huh?"

Covered in beekeeping mesh, pillowcase of buzzed pixies in hand, the ginger tried to look cross. Her quivering whiskers belied her mirth for a few seconds until she broke down laughing helplessly. "You got a bunch of innocent little pixies intoxicated! That's terrible."

"I'm a very wicked witch. What do you want from me?"

"You're wicked, and I'm the queen of England."

When the hilarity had calmed, the two gathered their supplies. Madeline sorted gently through the makeshift bag, counting their catch. Tamara settled back into herself and then reached out into the world around her.

At some unspoken signal, the closest cluster of displaced honeybees began to return to their hive.

"What are you doing?"

"Giving them my blessing. Letting them know it's safe to come back home."

Madeline watched the thrumming procession with a look of wonder. "You know... none of these pixies are sticky. I don't think they were after the honey at all."

The witch carefully lifted the lid off one of the still-empty hive boxes with some surprise. "You're right. The combs are fine. That's a relief." She gently replaced the square and stepped back as the first of its residents landed. "So what were they here for?"

Madeline fondly patted the little warm lump in her overall pocket. "Maybe they were just looking for a place to call home."

———

"Twenty-three. Plus four in the cage, plus yours. That's almost a third of them!" Polishing an apple on the front of her uniform, Tamara crunched into it with triumphant gusto.

They had pulled up at the cabin as the shadows of late afternoon began to lengthen. Madeline carefully held the bag of pixies. The bed of the truck bore a bushel basket of apples and pears, an assortment of cherry jam and pear preserves, a crock of apple butter, and two large mason jars of canned beets; a treasure trove of gifts from the grateful farmer and his wife.

Madeline peered into the pixiary with some concern. "They look a bit ill."

"They're just coming down. They'll be fine by morning." Licking some juice off the back of her hand, the coyote considered the wide, glassy eyes of the newly caught pixies as they lay draped around the interior of the enclosure. "Think they've got the munchies? We could give them some chips."

"What I think we should do," Madeline proclaimed loudly, ignoring the witch's not-so-muffled snickering, "is try to find more of them all in a bunch like that. It makes much more sense than chasing them down one by one, don't you think?"

"Yeah." Smile fading, Tamara tossed the apple core into the brambles where the forest met the edge of her yard. "That's the hard part, though. Raven finding the ones in the orchard was pure luck. I only pick up on their magic if they're closer than half a mile or so, and there's a lot of area to cover."

"Could we lure them in somehow?"

"I wish. I tried laying traps in the spring. They feel me the way I feel them. They're too smart to fly into a witch's Holding."

"Well then, why don't we do it at my flat? There's a little balcony outside my bedroom. We could set up some bits and baubles that would attract them, and Ravel being with me might help them know there's nothing to fear."

Tamara considered. She couldn't see any real reason why the other girl's idea wouldn't work. "If you're really okay with it, then sure. Let's give it a shot."

"Wonderful! I'll get started first thing in the morning. What do you think would make a pixie come to a window instead of flying into it? Ellie works at the art and hobby shop; I'm sure she'll give us a discount—"

Tamara froze. Her ears and tail popped straight up.

Madeline noticed her pause. "What's the matter?"

After only a moment's consideration, the witch made up her mind. "Do you know how to climb trees?"

"Well, yes, of course." The cat looked bewildered. "But what does that have to do with anything?"

Tamara beckoned her urgently. "Follow me, quick. And bring your camera."

At the mention of photos, Madeline sprang into action. The purses she carried were always large, Tamara had realized over the past few days, because there was always a camera inside them. In a moment, she had collected it and hurried to the oak tree at a jog as the coyote hoisted herself onto the lowest of the massive branches.

"What's up there?" she asked excitedly, looping the carrying strap around her neck and swinging herself gracefully up beside Tamara. Leave it to a cat to be right at home in a tree.

"Come up and see."

Hand and footholds were worn smooth in the bark, etched by the passage of long years' use. The coyote climbed quick and steady, Madeline easily keeping pace just beneath her as they ventured higher. In half a minute the roof of the cabin below was entirely hidden by layers of leaves and browning acorns.

When they broke through the canopy, the surge of light was almost blinding after the comparative gloom of the forest below. The sun sank slowly in the west. Before them, the tops of the trees stretched for miles, a carpet of golden green that fairly glowed in the evening light.

Straddling a branch wider than her torso, Madeline shielded her eyes with one hand and gaped. "It's absolutely beautiful! I've never seen golden hour from this angle before."

Tamara stood balanced behind her, scanning the skies. As the quiet click of a camera shutter joined the birdsong and soft rustle of leaves, she reached down to pat the other girl's shoulder. "Take a look over there."

Squinting against the setting sun, Madeline lowered her camera and looked to the north. "Oh!"

Above the treetops, a tide of life was rolling toward them on a thousand jeweled wings.

The monarchs came by the hundreds, riding the breeze like all the leaves of autumn had gotten impatient and made their entrance unannounced. As if drawn by an unseen beacon, they soared toward the oak tree.

"Butterflies," the cat gasped. "I've never seen so many butterflies! Is this—?"

Tamara nodded. "The migration. They go every year around this time, but I never know when until it happens." She leaned against the solid trunk behind her, the wind gently combing through her hair and tail. "I don't think they do, either. One day they just suddenly realize that summer's leaving them behind, and they go."

The fastest flutterers were nearing the tips of the branches.

The thrum of their wingbeats, their heartbeats, the stirring of the air currents disturbed by their motions; she could feel it all when she focused in, like tiny, welcome sparks against her skin. The witch closed her eyes, reaching out with her own being.

When the fields lie bare and the snow is deep, we remember you, living motes of amber and obsidian. When the sun grows warm and the south winds blow, remember us, and reach out your wings to us once more.

Her eyes opened slowly, to tiny, tickling feet against the edge of her ear. Everything around them was covered in butterflies. They buffeted into the branches, squabbling over the best leaves for their evening perches. A dozen or so had settled on Madeline.

"Hey. Aren't you going to take some pictures?"

The cat's tail ceased its entranced sway with a start. She glanced up at the coyote with an almost sheepish grin. "You know, they're so beautiful that I completely forgot."

Very slowly and carefully, so as not to disturb her passengers, she raised the camera. The soft clicking resumed as the sun began to dip below the tree line, turning the western clouds as orange as the creatures around them.

"Want me to get a shot of you?"

Madeline was adjusting settings before the question fully formed. "Please! Please and thank you!"

Tamara took the camera carefully, looping the strap tightly around her wrist as she climbed to a better position. "Yeah, well. I've seen what happens when you try to take selfies from high places. Hey, put the tongue away or I won't take any, brat."

Giggling, Madeline cupped her hands around a monarch and smiled happily. The last rays of the sinking sun caught the copper in her hair, the fire in the wings around her.

Tamara swallowed, suddenly dry-mouthed, and snapped the most beautiful photo she'd ever taken.

They climbed down as the last rays of the sun disappeared over the horizon, bathing the woods in purple twilight. The resting butterflies hung like ornaments from the branches overhead.

"Come back tomorrow morning if you want," Tamara offered as the cat tucked the camera back into her purse, making ready to leave. "Hitting up the hobby shop wouldn't be a bad idea. They probably have a ton of stuff we could turn into pixie bait."

"I'll be here!" Madeline checked her pockets for her keys and her pixie. "Well then, have a lovely night. And... thank you." She fiddled almost bashfully with her key ring. "Thank you so much for showing me the butterflies. That was incredible. Some photographers wait their whole lives for an opportunity like that."

Tamara shrugged uncomfortably. "You don't have to thank me. I needed to go up and wish them well on their migration anyway."

"But you didn't have to let me come with you. Or remember that I'd want to take photos. You're a very sweet person."

"Right," the coyote scoffed with a roll of eyes darker than the shadows in the undergrowth.

"You are! You're incredibly sweet, and I'm so glad we've become friends."

Before Tamara knew quite what was happening, the cat's arms were around her, squeezing her into a determined hug. She made a highly inelegant yippy noise as all her fur abruptly stood on end. But hugs demanded counter-hugs, didn't they? After a moment of frantic internal screeching, one arm rose woodenly and delivered an awkward series of pats to the ginger's back. "...me too."

Ravel squawked indignantly from between them.

"Oh, so sorry, love," Madeline shooshed, pulling quickly

away to peer down into the pocket of her overalls. "Did I squish you? Never mind, we're going home." Hitching her purse higher on her shoulder, she flashed that hundred-watt smile at Tamara once more. "See you tomorrow!"

"Yeah. See you." The witch waved limply as the cat climbed into her little car and drove off down the drive with a parting beep.

Tamara stood lost in thought long after the tail lights had disappeared. Slowly she reached up, pinching her cheeks until her ears fell flat and her eyes began to water. "Oww."

A questioning caw heralded Raven, who swooped down to land on her shoulder a moment later.

"It's nothing. You sleeping inside tonight?"

"*Pretty,*" the crow croaked coyly, rotating his head to look at her upside down.

Tamara scowled. "Don't even go there."

"*Pretty!*"

"Yeah, pretty. Pretty hopeless." The screen door at the back of the cabin banged behind her as she sulked indoors, crow feet gripping tightly to the cloth of her uniform top. "And pretty stupid, getting sidetracked when pretty things are the last thing I need to be thinking about right now."

With a disgusted sound, Raven launched off her shoulder and flapped the short distance from the mud room into the kitchen, to the top of the refrigerator.

"I guarantee you, she's straight," the witch called after him, kneeling to unlace her boots. "Probably the prettiest, straightest girl in this whole town. It's useless to even think about it."

The crow presented his silky black back to her pointedly.

"Feather duster," she muttered.

Though it was barely fully dark, Tamara decided to get ready for bed. She ran a hot bath in the old claw-foot tub and settled in for a relaxing soak. The handful of dried herbs she added from the jar by the rug sent up a soothing aroma—and reminded her of enchanting green eyes.

Toweling and blowing her coarse fur dry made her mind drift to soft ginger stripes and bare, creamy collarbones.

Falling into soft blankets reminded her of warm arms wrapped around her for the first time since she couldn't recall when.

"We are totally different!" she howled exasperatedly into her pillow, fists and feet thumping the small mattress stubbornly. "It would never work!"

In the darkness outside, the oak tree rustled in the wind. The cabin settled with a comforting creak.

Doubting yourself kills more opportunities than failure ever has a chance to.

The silence ticked on for several minutes. Near the ceiling, a small cluster of witch-lights bobbed an unhurried circuit of the rafters. In the kitchen, Raven cawed sleepily to himself.

Face down in the pillow, Tamara heaved a slightly smothered sigh. "…fine. I'll think about it."

CHAPTER SIX

Morning brought two visitors. Only one of them was expected or welcome.

Cheerful knocking joined the chorus of birdsong outside.

"Door's open," Tamara yelled somewhat distractedly from the kitchen. She hadn't been aware that knocking could convey cheerfulness, and yet.

Madeline sallied in, a spring in her step and a cardboard box in her hands. "Good morning! My, it's a gorgeous day, isn't it? There's even a little nip in the air! Autumn's such a lovely time of year. I can't believe it's almost... here?" She paused in the arch between the den and kitchen, blinking at the sight before her. "Do you often entertain birds at breakfast?"

The witch placed a small dish of crushed corn flakes on the table. A gray mourning dove bobbed its way across the tabletop, cooing happily. Raven hovered nearby over a bowl of blueberries, swallowing them down like they were going out of season. Like most crows, he had a fondness for nibbles and kept close tabs on his favorite produce.

"Only the featherhead I live with. This one just showed up."

The cat placed her box, from which the sugary aroma of

pastries arose, on the counter. "It looks very comfortable here. Is it a familiar, too?"

"She's *a* familiar. Not *my* familiar." Tamara threw a handful of corn flakes into her mouth, crunching moodily. "She brought me a summons."

Green eyes widened hugely as Madeline accepted the small piece of paper. "Like a summons to jury duty? Do you have to appear in witch court? Is witch court even a thing?"

"That's kind of what it feels like when the coven gets together. But no."

Madeline glanced at the message. "Your aunt wants you to come by for a visit? How nice!"

"Auntie is an honorific. But she is kind of a friend of the family. Are these donuts? I'm eating a donut."

"Please, help yourself. That's why I brought them." Madeline scanned the note once more. "She has impeccable penmanship. And good taste in stationery." There were tiny roses along the borders. Its writer had used pink ink.

Tamara absently lifted the lid of the pastry box, glanced in at the donuts, and let out a yell to match the sudden shriek of the pixie inside. "Oh, yuck! Now they're contaminated!"

Ravel zipped away, trailing sparkles and sprinkles across the countertop.

Madeline slapped the summons down and gave chase. "Stop, you—you're covered in frosting!"

Tamara shut the box and left the room.

———

"I'm so sorry about that. He hid in my purse when we went into the bakery and I thought that's where he stayed." Ears down, hands folded, the cat looked much more contrite than the pixie in her lap. "I suppose I should have known so much silence was suspicious."

"S'fine." Tamara took a large bite out of a slice of peanut butter toast with one hand and flipped the truck's turn signal with the other. One knee helped steady the worn steering wheel.

Leaving the forest behind, they were swiftly getting into the heart of the fields and farmland that made up so much of the surrounding landscape.

"It's not fine. He behaves so beautifully when we're at home, and I think I was stern enough to make him understand there'll be no nonsense inside stores, but all bets seem to be off any other time."

The witch stuffed the last toast corner into her mouth. "So he's like a kid who turns into a brat when mom's full attention isn't focused on him anymore."

"I suppose that's one way of putting it." The cat smiled ruefully, stroking the pixie's back with her thumb. "Mostly it feels quite nice to be somebody's mum, though."

Ravel's long, pointed ears shot up. "Mum?"

Crumbs sprayed across the dashboard as Tamara choked on her toast. "Sweet Earth Mother," she coughed, thumping herself on the chest with the hand that wasn't keeping the truck on the road. "It—it spoke?"

Madeline scooped Ravel into her hands, raising him excitedly to face level. "Yes, yes, that's right! I am your mum! Say it again, Rav? Please?"

"But—but they can't speak! It was probably just copying the sound you made or something, right?"

Trapped in the cat's cupped palms, he pointed to her with a decisive squeak. "Mum."

Madeline all but squealed with delight, bringing the pixie up to her cheek for a vigorous nuzzle. "Oh my goodness, you are so clever. Such a clever boy! Such a little love you are."

"Mum," he purred happily, hugging her nose.

Shocked to her core, Tamara could barely take her eyes off

the spectacle in the seat next to her long enough to keep them from careening into the corn. "Auntie Peg's not going to believe this."

Eugenia Peg lived in exactly the kind of place one might expect to find a hearth witch. The small cottage sat at the end of a long dirt lane, flanked by gardens of all types—rock gardens, wildflower beds, and vegetable patches that seemed to go on for acres before finally blending into the natural landscape of the uncultivated fields that surrounded them. Tall lilac bushes stood in rotund glory on either side of the house.

Tamara shut the truck door with a bang. "Welcome to Meadowcrest."

"It's lovely." Madeline slid down from the passenger seat, brushing imaginary dust from her skirt. She looked nervously up the cobblestone path to the front door. "Perhaps I should have asked this before now, but is it really alright that I came along? Your summons didn't say anything about bringing a plus one. And I'm not even magic."

"Eh, it'll be fine. Peg's actually pretty social, for a witch. Worst thing she could do would be try to cast a memory spell on you, and we know how well that works."

The cat snickered, whiskers and spirits lifting. "I suppose you're right." She opened her purse. "Ravel, you're going to wait in here until I tell you that it's alright for you to come out. And if I do say you can come out, you will be a good boy and not disturb anything that belongs to this nice lady. Understand?"

With an agreeable-sounding chirp, the pixie folded his wings and executed a graceful swan dive into the bag. The tuft of his gold-glittered tail vanished with a wiggle.

Tamara carefully shouldered her backpack and led the way up the walk. Before her hand could come near enough to knock, the door popped open. A short, stout hedgehog stood before them.

"Tammy, sweetheart!" She wasted no time gathering the coyote into the kind of firm, obligatory hug dispensed by maternal figures in the later stages of life. The tips of her round ears came up just past Tamara's chin. "It's so good to see you. It's been too long."

Tamara winced. "Hi, Auntie Peg." She returned the hug gingerly, with careful pats to the older witch's spiny back. "It's only been a few months. Midsummer, remember?"

"Like I said, too long." Her quills perked and lowered cheekily. "Come on in, don't be shy—well, who's this now?" Her pointed nose crinkled in confusion.

Madeline waved sheepishly from behind Tamara. "Hi."

The coyote stepped aside. "Uh. Auntie, this is my friend, Madeline."

"Oh, please, just call me Peg." The hedgehog bustled forward to enthusiastically shake one of Madeline's hands in both of her own. "A pleasure to meet you, sweetie." She looked up into the ginger's face with an air of great intensity. A subtle shiver rustled through her spines. "A real pleasure."

Looking highly relieved, Madeline beamed happily. "Oh no, the pleasure's all mine! And please, call me Maddie."

Peg patted the cat's hand warmly. "What a pretty name. It's so nice to meet one of Tammy's friends. She never talks about 'em, so I was beginning to think she didn't have any."

Tamara's ears went back. "Rude."

"But I can certainly see," Peg continued with a conspiratorial wink, "why she brought you here with her."

The coyote's ears popped up again just as quickly, their delicate insides igniting in a sudden flush. "You—you can?"

"Of course I can. At my age, I've been around the block a few times." She leaned closer to Madeline with a whisper. "This isn't your first run-in with the fae folk, is it, honey?"

Madeline gawked. "How ever did you know that?"

Tamara started. "Wait, what?"

Peg paid her no mind, suddenly shepherding Madeline through the entryway. "But anyhow, let's not stand here at the door letting the flies inside. Come in, girls, come in. We have a lot to talk about."

The hedgehog's kitchen was warm and fragrant with the scents of freshly brewed tea, homemade cookies, and the perfume of the late-season flowers outside. Bouquets of them stood in vases, bottles, and bowls on every flat surface. Bunches of drying herbs hung upside down from the ceiling and walls. Sunbeams spilled in through large windows over the sink.

Madeline purred contentedly from a bench at the table, hands cradling a china teacup. "Mmm, it's so cozy. I feel like I could lay my head down and take a nap right here."

"That's what happens when you wander into the domain of a hearth witch," Peg cackled, brandishing a plate of cookies at Tamara.

"Did you really go to the trouble of summoning me just to feed me?" Tamara huffed. She took a cookie. Then one for the other hand, as an afterthought. Peg's baking was second to none.

"Well, of course not. But what's a get-together without a little small talk?" The hedgehog's spines quivered in consternation. "Visiting first, shop talk after." She brightened. "Did you happen to catch the monarchs heading off yesterday evening?"

"We did, actually."

"Oh my goodness, it was brilliant," Madeline gushed, perking up over her chamomile. "It was the most beautiful thing I've ever seen! Well," she amended thoughtfully, "except maybe all of the pixies that night on the bridge, but it hardly seems fair to compare the poor butterflies to otherworldly beauty like that."

"Well, so much for small talk," Peg chuckled. "Alright. Let's talk about the pixies. Why don't you show me your little friend, honey?" She cast a pointed glance at Madeline's purse.

"You can feel their magic like Tamara can?" the ginger asked, pulling the bag across the tabletop.

"Yes, indeed. Fae magic is on an entirely different plane than mortal magic. A witch would have to be dead or darn close not to sense it. Especially when it walks right up to her door and comes in for tea."

The purse was pulled open with little fanfare. Cautiously, the pixie peeked over the edge.

"It's alright, love," Madeline coaxed. "You can come out if you behave yourself. Auntie Peg wants to say hello."

Ravel rose from hiding much more warily than usual. Hovering above the open purse, he sized the hedgehog up. When she did nothing but blink back passively from across the table, he fluttered up and flattened himself possessively across the top of Madeline's head.

"Ravel, what are you doing?" she laughed, ears angling ticklishly. "You're so silly."

Peg made an appreciative sound. "I have to say, Tammy, that's a heck of a job you did on the binding spell. That's your first one?"

The coyote nodded, brushing cookie crumbs from her chin. "Yeah."

"Don't know that I'd want to tackle it, myself. That's very deep spellcasting." The older witch chuckled to herself. "But you already know that. No matter how hard I try, I always end up talking to you like a pup. Guess you'll always be a little nipper to me."

Tamara looked away with a snort, ears down and flushed.

"Can we talk about the problem at hand, please? I assume you called me here to discuss the infestation in town."

"It had crossed my mind, yes. How did they all get here? I've never felt a swarm this big in all my life."

Madeline suddenly became very interested in a speck at the bottom of her teacup.

"There was a tear starting above the river. Near the trestle bridge down the north fork from Riverglen. I patched it with a ward. Went back a week later to check on it and the ward failed while I was there."

The hedgehog bristled in surprise. "Your ward broke down? You do better work than that." She squinted suspiciously. "What happened?"

Madeline coughed and squirmed delicately. "Um. I did."

Tamara sighed, pinching her forehead near the little silver ring. "It was an accident. She was on the bridge taking pictures and she almost fell right through it."

"My tail touched it," Madeline offered meekly. "Just the very end bit. I'm sorry."

"Aaaaahhh." Peg settled back into her chair. "Now I understand. Of course a ward holding back the fae realm fell for someone like you."

"What do you—?" Tamara started.

"Well, what's done is done. How many do you think got out?"

The coyote frowned. There was a trail here somewhere she was trying to follow and no one was being helpful. "Uh. Close to a hundred, give or take a dozen. We already caught almost thirty."

"That's a good start. But hurry, if you can. Have you seen what they're getting up to in town?"

"We were there for two of the… incidents. And they ran the bees out of their hives at Sugar Tree Orchard."

Peg nodded in annoyance, drumming her fingernails on the

tabletop. "I was in the drive-through at the Royal Burger yesterday and one got into the speaker system. You know how well those work on the best days. Just while I was sitting there, the driver in front of me and the young fellow taking the orders got into a fistfight through the drive-through window."

Madeline's cheeks puffed out as she fought not to laugh, whiskers quivering mightily.

"But at least no one's gotten hurt yet, that I know of. That's the important thing. Besides a few of the pixies, anyway."

The cat's merriment died abruptly. "What do you mean?"

"I mean, they're reckless. Or just oblivious." The old witch rose from the table and placed her teacup in the sink. "I saw one of the little things ride a branch directly into a wood chipper last week."

Madeline clapped a hand over her mouth in horror. Ravel bobbled on her head like a strange accessory before taking flight to seek a steadier perch.

Tamara rubbed frantically at her brow piercing. "Oh my god..."

"Yes, over by the library. It was quite a sight. Those poor gardeners couldn't figure out why all the sawdust kept coming out sparkles." Pulling open a cabinet drawer, Peg rustled around inside. "This one here flew into the bug zapper on my back deck. I had to sweep it up off the top of the patio table." She held up a zip-top sandwich bag. It appeared to be full of craft glitter.

Knowing exactly which way the wind was blowing, Tamara hurriedly leaned forward and laid a hand on Madeline's shoulder. "Hey. You gonna cry?"

"Mmm... mmmm—!" Green eyes were already brimming as the ginger fought the oncoming flood.

"Listen. It's okay. I know it makes you sad. But it happened fast, right? They didn't even know what hit them. And that's why we're catching the other ones as fast as we can, right? So this doesn't happen to any more of them."

Lower lip still aquiver, Madeline nodded dutifully with a little sniff.

The hedgehog looked on in wonder. "Bit of a tender heart, aren't you? Well, that's not a bad thing." Setting the sandwich bag mercifully aside, she reached for the kettle. "Cheer up, honey. Have some more tea. Isn't it nice that Tammy's helping you collect them? Most witches would take the easy way out."

"And what way is that?" Madeline asked rather sharply.

Behind her, Tamara made frantic 'X' motions with her hands that went entirely unheeded.

"Pixies are such a nuisance that most just opt to destroy them on the spot. Or catch them just to juice them later. That glitter they leave behind is almost completely made of concentrated magic energy. That's really useful when you're a serious spell-caster or potion-maker—"

"But you simply *can't*," Madeline wailed, spinning in her seat to grab frantically at the hem of Tamara's flannel. "They're intelligent! Tamara, you have to tell her. Tell her!"

Wondering for at least the hundredth time how she had ever gotten into this mess, the coyote patted the other girl soothingly about the head and shoulders. "Chill, okay? There's not going to be any juicing." With Madeline hanging around her middle, she cast a look back at their hostess. "She's... she's right, though, Peg. They're smart. They can learn."

Arms crossed, the older witch watched them like a daytime TV drama. She looked like she didn't know whether or not to laugh. "So can parrots, honey. So can octopi, I've heard."

"No, not like this. They're not just intelligent; they're self-aware. Or they can learn to be."

"What makes you think so?"

Tamara glanced around the kitchen. She whistled. "Hey, sparkle-vermin. Ravel."

There was a rustle across the room. The pixie's head popped

out of a vase full of coneflowers on the china cabinet. He looked at the party at the table with a quizzical squeak.

Tamara pointed to Madeline, who had finally loosened her death grip. "What is Maddie?"

His eyes brightened. "Mum!"

Peg stood a bit straighter as the pixie flew back into the cat's arms.

"Rav, look." Collecting herself somewhat, Madeline pointed to the bouquet of roses on the table. "Pick me some petals, please. I want more than five but less than eight."

There was an immediate flurry of floral destruction. When the leaves and stems stopped falling, Madeline was proudly presented with seven red petals. They looked like oven mitts in the pixie's small hands.

"Thank you. Clever boy! Now watch." She dropped the petals into her teacup and hid the cup behind her back. "Alright. Now, do I still have the petals?"

He nodded gleefully, zipping behind her to dig into the cup. "Ye!"

"What do you think?" Tamara asked the hedgehog. "We're not reading too much into this, right?"

Fingers steepled, Peg placed them to her lips. "I think," she said slowly, beady black eyes glued to the pixie, "if this isn't just parrot smarts, you're opening up a whole new can of worms, Tammy. We've always known the big ones—the real faeries—are sentient beings. But I don't know any witch who'd tell you that pixies are anything but feral fae pests."

"I know." Tamara nodded seriously. "And I'm not denying the 'pest' part. But they're mentally on par with our familiars, at the very least. We can't get rid of them like they're mindless. They need to go back to the fae realm. If they survive in this world long enough to be caught, anyway."

Madeline looked up at her like she'd hung the moon, face radiating gratitude.

Peg shuffled solemnly closer.

Tamara yelped in shock as her cheek was grabbed and given a sound, jiggling pinch.

"You're exactly like your grandmother," Peg cackled happily. "Never content to leave things alone. Always have to fan the fire. Leave it to you to stir up a moral conflict over pixie extermination, of all things."

"Will you leggo of my fasch?" the coyote slurred, ears back and tail bristled. "It hurtsch."

The sudden sound of an engine in the driveway interrupted them. Both witches paused.

"Who'sch tha'?" Tamara asked with some difficulty.

Peg finally released her cheek with a frown. "I'm not sure. I'm not expecting any other company today." Her eyes narrowed in the direction of the front door as she concentrated. A moment later, though, her expression smoothed. "Oh, never mind. I know who it is. Should have known."

Within seconds, without a knock or a chime, the door opened. Frantic footsteps padded down the hall. An old red squirrel rushed into the kitchen. Without acknowledging anyone in the room, she made a beeline for the refrigerator and began to pillage.

"Something I can help you with, Myma, dear?" Peg asked loudly.

"Don't mind me," the intruder chattered, her front end hidden somewhere among the lettuces. "Just borrowing some new moon water. The batch I had was in a pitcher and I used it to make lemonade."

Madeline watched, aghast. Whether she was more offended by the blatant disregard for proper etiquette or the fact that the newcomer was wearing pink and green paisley yoga pants with yellow Crocs, Tamara couldn't say.

The squirrel withdrew with a labeled plastic jug that might once have held a gallon of milk. Leaving the refrigerator door wide open, she turned away and caught sight of the platter on the counter. "Ooh, cookies."

"Myma," the hedgehog said sharply, rapping her knuckles on the table.

"Hmmph?" She looked over, one cookie already inside her cheek pouch and a second in the process of passing her lips. The jug sat forgotten by the platter.

"Would you care to greet my other guests?" Peg asked pointedly as she got to her feet and closed the refrigerator. She gestured at the coyote and cat. "I'm sure you remember Tamara."

Tamara, who highly doubted that, nodded as politely as she could manage. "Hi, Auntie Gorse."

The squirrel looked her over. One eye pointed ever so slightly off to the left. Her bushy tail, which had a kink in the middle, flicked. Suddenly her head cocked alarmingly to one side. "Aren't you Tabitha's girl?"

"I'm her granddaughter."

"Eh. Close enough, I suppose." Her head remained tilted. A third cookie vanished. "How is she these days?" A snowfall of crumbs dusted the floor.

Peg clapped a despairing hand to her brow. "Myma, Tabitha has been gone for many years. Remember? We went to pay our respects."

"Oh. Right." Her head jerked back into position with a full-body twitch. "Sorry, child. Time tends to blur when you reach a certain age."

"I'm twenty-four," Tamara grumbled.

"Got yourself a daughter yet?"

The coyote's ears went back. Her hackles rose. "No, I do not."

The squirrel reached for cookie number four. "Better get a move on, then, while you're still young and pretty." She looked Tamara up and down, from her flyaway ponytail to the torn-out knees of her blue jeans. "Might want to see a stylist, though. Not everyone's born with it."

Tamara set her teeth together tightly and didn't say a word.

Madeline stood abruptly, thrusting out a hand. "Hello! Do allow me to introduce myself. I'm Madeline. I'm Tamara's friend."

It was as if Myma noticed her presence for the first time. She zeroed in, ignoring the proffered hand in favor of leaning close to stare at Madeline intently with deep, black eyes. The ginger took an uncertain step back. Her legs hit the bench and she sat back down with a sudden bump.

The squirrel's head cocked hard in the opposite direction. "Hello. You're a weird one, aren't you?"

Madeline's eyes bugged. "Pardon me. *I'm* strange?"

"You're pardoned."

The cat's mouth dropped open in outrage.

Tamara bristled. "She is not weird—"

Ravel dropped from the light fixture over the table. With a piercing screech, trailing sparks that looked more like flames, he flew into the squirrel's face.

"No!" Madeline yelled frantically. "Ravel, stop!"

At her command, the pixie fell back, still squeaking angrily. Most of the squirrel's whiskers went with him.

Myma raised a hand to her nearly bare cheek. "Oww. Well, you're not a very nice little thing."

From Madeline's shoulder, Ravel hissed. The tuft of his tail was puffed round as a dandelion in his ire.

Peg, who had stoically watched the entire debacle unfold in her kitchen, stepped forward and put a hand on the other witch's shoulder. "Myma, I think it may be time for you to head home, don't you agree? Wasn't there something you were working on there? Something involving new moon water, maybe…?"

The squirrel brightened visibly. "Oh, yes. Do you have any? I made mine into lemonade."

Peg placed the jug firmly in her arms. "Don't drop it. And dab some of this on your whisker roots tonight. They'll grow back by morning." She tucked a small glass bottle with a dropper lid into the squirrel's hand. "Have a lovely afternoon. Drive safely. Please do come by again. After Yule, maybe."

"Will do. Make more cookies." Without further ado, she left the kitchen. A moment later, the front door slammed.

The hedgehog calmly waddled to the refrigerator. Tamara and Madeline stared as she began to mix a potion they soon recognized as gin and tonic. The whole ordeal had taken less than ten minutes.

Tamara cleared her throat. "Sooo. Does she do that often?"

"Only about once a month." Peg finished mixing. She took a long drink, followed by a sigh of relief. "You two just got lucky enough to experience her with me today." She blinked at the empty cookie platter and the equally empty countertop around it. "Oh, that's nice. Seems she also made off with my pixie dust."

"I don't remember her being so..." Tamara searched for a charitable word.

"Stark, raving nuts?" the hedgehog supplied helpfully, adding more gin to her tonic.

"I was going to say 'out of touch with reality,' but that works too."

Ravel paraded victoriously up and down the table. He had a whisker in each hand.

"What on earth got into you?" Madeline frowned. She pinched one of the whiskers distastefully between her fore-finger and thumb and plucked it away from him. "We do not attack people. Even if they are being terribly rude."

"She made you pretty upset right then, didn't she?" Peg observed. "He's bound to you pretty tightly. Maybe he picked up on just how much."

The ginger looked stricken. "You mean *I* made him do that?"

"Not on purpose, of course. Try not to feel bad, honey. To tell you the truth, she probably won't even remember how she lost those whiskers tomorrow, poor thing. I think she might just be reaching that age."

Tamara snorted. "She looks pretty well preserved, if that's the case. You sure she doesn't need to be in a home or something?"

The hedgehog's quills rattled alarmingly. "I can't imagine how much trouble a senile witch in a nursing home full of unsuspecting non-witches would cause. Nor do I want to try to imagine it." She set her empty glass on the counter with a final-sounding thump. "Now. I believe I'm going to have a little nap."

Madeline stood immediately to collect her purse and pixie. "We'll be on our way. Thank you so much for your hospitality. The cookies were delicious."

Peg walked them to the door. "Come back any time, honey. You're always welcome here. Tammy, don't be a stranger. You don't always have to wait for me to send you a bird."

The coyote made a noncommittal noise, engrossed in coaxing a mason jar from her backpack. "Almost forgot. I brought you a present."

"Oh, what nice beets." The older witch accepted the jar with a pleased expression. Then the truth dawned. "You brought me these because someone gave them to you and you think beets taste like dirt, didn't you?" she accused.

Tamara sputtered. "What? No! Why would you think that?"

"Because I distinctly remember Tabitha forcing you to help us can them when you were a pup and you screaming 'beets taste like dirt!' as she dragged you inside. That's why."

Madeline quickly turned away, which did absolutely nothing to hide her giggle.

"If you don't want the beets—" Tamara began loudly.

Peg hugged the jar protectively. "You just run along now and catch some more pixies," she shooed. "Remember, you're up against time and their complete lack of self-preservation instincts."

They climbed into the truck. Tamara cranked her window down. "If you find any more sparkle-vermin, mind bringing them my way?"

"I promise." The hedgehog waved from the bottom of the cobblestone path. "If I see any of the others, I'll pass it on. Hopefully they won't have gotten as far as the other Holdings."

"Thanks. You might want to start asking around whether anybody knows if Auntie Gorse has a daughter or not, too. If she does, might be time to find her."

"Don't you worry about Myma Gorse, Tammy," Peg told her firmly. "She'll be just fine. Everything will turn out right in the end."

They pulled away down the lane. Morning slipped seamlessly into afternoon, bright sunshine bathing the fields and meadows. Redwing blackbirds called from the ditches, their songs rising over the incessant droning of grasshoppers.

In accordance with the wisdom of her elders, Tamara did her best to think only of the immediate, pixie-filled future, putting other creeping thoughts and cares aside.

Nature will take its course. Always has, always will.

CHAPTER SEVEN

Madeline was strangely subdued as they headed back toward town. Lost in thought, Tamara didn't notice the unusual silence from the passenger seat for several long miles.

"I'm sorry."

"Huh?" The coyote glanced over in surprise at the soft apology. "Why? You didn't do anything."

"I hardly think inciting my pixie to commit battery qualifies as nothing."

Tamara tried hard not to laugh as she drifted over the center line to avoid a fuzzy orange and black caterpillar inching across the road. "He didn't cause any permanent damage. Don't worry about it."

"I do worry, though. He only did it because I lost my temper. She's only an old woman, and I'm sure she didn't really mean to insult me—I shouldn't have let her bother me so much."

"If it makes you feel any better, she was getting under my fur too," Tamara admitted. "Gotta love it when the biddies start harping about why I haven't managed to get knocked up yet."

Arms crossed over her chest, Madeline huffed in second-hand offense. The tip of her tail wagged angrily near the floorboard. "How incredibly rude." Suddenly she turned, fixing the witch with a look of great determination. "Don't pay any attention to that nutty squirrel. You're beautiful exactly the way you are! I just know you won't have any trouble at all finding a husband when you're ready."

Tamara's chest clenched unpleasantly. Her hands tightened on the steering wheel. "Heh. Uh, thanks, Mads."

"You don't believe me, do you?" the ginger demanded. "You are beautiful! Trust me. I am a photographer. I am an authority on beauty."

"Right, right. I believe you. But, um…" She wouldn't get a better opportunity. Tamara took a deep breath and pressed on. "Look. My appearance has nothing to do with whether or not I reproduce. It's not going to happen."

"Oh." Madeline's ears flicked in confusion. "You don't want children? Well, that's fine. There are plenty of women nowadays who decide not to."

"It's not so much that I don't want kids, as much as I'm not interested in men."

Madeline stared.

"Romantically or sexually."

Bottle-green eyes blinked repeatedly.

"I am into women," Tamara said flatly.

"Oooooh." The cat began to nod slowly as if suddenly grasping a difficult mathematical concept. "Oh. I see."

It wasn't exactly a negative reaction. Tamara chanced a sidelong glance. "Come on. You really didn't suspect that already?"

"I try not to form conclusions about people based on circumstantial evidence," Madeline said primly.

"Good policy." Tamara huffed softly. "It's kind of refreshing to have somebody just accept it when I tell them and not try to change my mind for ten minutes."

The ginger's ears flicked backward in concern. "Who does that? The other witches? They don't treat you badly, do they?"

Tamara shrugged uncomfortably. The old seatbelt dug into her shoulder, fighting the movement. "No, not really. It's just… they're all old. They're old and they're stuck in this mindset that there's only one right way to do anything. Even Peg does it, and she's the most open-minded out of the whole coven now that Gran's gone." The tips of her claws dug into the worn, smooth leather of the wheel. "They don't treat me bad; they treat me like who I am as a person doesn't matter because it doesn't fit into this idea of what witches do."

"They think you should settle down and have children anyway?" Madeline guessed sympathetically. She softly stroked Ravel, who was snoozing across her knee.

"Like, it doesn't matter that I like boobs, because I'm a witch and a witch has to have herself a daughter, so I should just discard all my personal preferences and go get pregnant." The sun visor was very suddenly getting on her nerves. She swatted it up out of her line of sight. "It's idiotic. Last Beltane that friggin' beaver from Clearlake was all like, 'But you only have to grin and bear it once if you play your cards right! I have this great fertility spell you can use!' Can you believe that?"

"Um—"

"I don't even know why I'm telling you all this. I'm over it. It doesn't make me angry at all!" Static electricity crackled through her fur. The radio made an eerie scratching whine.

"Your hackles are up," the cat pointed out, not unkindly. "And we just ran a stop sign. It most definitely does make you angry. You have a right to be." A soft, graceful hand found her shoulder. "And you told me all of that because we're friends, and friends talk to one another about things that bother them."

Slowly, Tamara's muscles unlocked. She was able to stop throttling the steering wheel. Her palms hurt. "Sorry about the stop sign."

"No harm done. But we'll be back to town soon, so you

should probably not do that again. My mum and dad would be awfully put out if I wound up in hospital."

The coyote glanced over at her as they passed the small gas station that was the first sign of their return to civilization. "Has anyone ever told you that you're unnaturally nice?"

Madeline looked away almost bashfully. "I suppose I just know how you feel, is all."

For an instant, Tamara's heart stopped. Wild hope leaped up unbidden. "You—you do?"

"Well, perhaps I don't know exactly what you're feeling, since I don't have an imposing flock of elderly witches to contend with, but I certainly know how it feels to always be the odd one out. And to have people forever implying that you should just give it up and behave the way everyone thinks you ought to."

Okay. Right. It had been dumb to hope. She would never get so lucky that the first girl she'd had any interest in since college would swing the same way. But Madeline hadn't shown any discomfort at being trapped alone in a small space with her since finding out her preferences, either. Tamara would take what she could get. "I guess you do."

The cat beamed.

"So, you still want to be friends even though I'm a lesbian, huh?" She couldn't resist teasing.

"So, you still want to be friends even though I'm a non-magical pixie-sympathizing girly-girl?" Madeline asked innocently.

Tamara wanted to kiss her. "Smart ass."

"Better a smart one than a dumb one."

"Okay, point."

Madeline's giggles slowly tapered off. "May I ask you something?"

"Sure."

"Everyone keeps mentioning daughters. Why are daughters so important?"

"Well, traditionally, when a witch passes on, her daughter will come home to take over her Holding. That's basically just the land that we watch over and take care of. That way a witch's line can keep their Holdings for hundreds of years. It's kind of a point of pride. If you die and you don't have a daughter, then some other witch could show up to take your place. We're tied to our land pretty strongly, so a lot of them don't like that idea."

"What do the daughters do in the meantime?"

"Some of them never leave home. That's how it always used to be. A lot of them travel now, though. See the world. Learn new spells. Enjoy not having any responsibilities. Then they come back to their hometown when they're ready to have a daughter of their own and just live nearby, training up to take over the family's Holding someday."

"I see." Madeline frowned thoughtfully. "But what happens if a witch has a son instead of a daughter? Can they not take their mother's place?"

"Hmm. Good question." Tamara carefully stopped at the next intersection. "I guess they probably could. If they existed. Witches never have boys. Only girls."

"Never ever?" Madeline asked, clearly startled.

"Well, y'know. That's what they say, anyway." The coyote shrugged. "Magic is weird. That's just how it is."

The ginger slumped as much as her seatbelt would allow. "Now you've done it. My dreams that Harry Otter might have been based on a true story have been shattered." The back of her hand delicately met her brow. "Utterly destroyed. And he was such a charming lutrine in the films."

"Sorry, princess. Them's the breaks."

"No, no, don't try to make me feel better. I am completely inconsolable."

Tamara fought a smile with every ounce of her being and failed miserably. "What if I fed you tacos?"

Madeline sat up straight, ears and whiskers standing happily at attention. "Yes please!"

The bells above the door jangled cheerfully as Madeline led the way into the craft shop.

"Hi, welcome to Krafty Korner—oh, hey Maddie." Ellie smiled and waved from behind the counter. "What took you so long? I thought you'd be here an hour ago."

"Oh, you know. Things came up. I, um, met Tamara's aunt this morning!"

The gray tabby blinked in surprise as she noticed her friend's coyote tagalong.

Tamara raised a hand in greeting. "Yo."

"And then it was almost lunchtime, so we stopped for a bite." Madeline placed a paper bag on the counter. The aroma of grease and cinnamon wafted temptingly. "I brought you a snack."

Ellie brightened. "Hey, thanks, I don't get my break for another hour." She dug into the bag. "So, what did you come in for? Need more scrapbook stuff already? We got a new shipment of stickers in Tuesday."

"No, I still have plenty of supplies. We just need a few... bits and bobs."

"Odds and ends," Tamara supplied vaguely.

"Oh. Sure. Let me know if you need help finding anything." Churro crumbs clung to the tabby's whiskers as she munched.

"I'm sure we'll know it when we find it."

They made their way deeper into the store. At that time of the day, they were nearly the only customers. A serval pushing her kitten in a stroller browsed the yarn aisles. A graying badger considered the scale models with a critical eye.

Tamara drew a deep breath laden with the subtle scents of candle kits, potpourri, and paper. "Okay. Think like a pixie. What can we rig up to bring them to your porch?"

"Bells. Things that chime. Pleasant noises and colors."

Ravel peeked out from beneath the curtain of her hair, squeaking in agreement.

"You may look around," Madeline told him magnanimously, "if you are good. Do not break anything."

No sooner had she spoken than the pixie zipped away, trailing excited sparks.

"Was that a good idea?" Tamara wondered aloud.

"I want him to learn how to control himself when we're out and about, not only when I make him stay in my purse. He was fairly well behaved at Auntie Peg's house—minus the whole attacking someone bit—so I'll give him a chance." The cat smiled. "And besides, I know Ellie wouldn't kill me if something were to go wrong."

The coyote barked a laugh. "Okay, I take back what I said about you being too nice."

"Well, she wouldn't!"

They wandered into the seasonal crafts. The first aisle overflowed with warm colors, autumn leaves, and jack-o-lantern smiles. In the clearance section, however, summer-themed crafts and decorations were piled high.

Tamara pulled a giant garden pinwheel from a display stand. The head was roughly the size of a pizza pan and shaped like a flower, each angled petal a different rainbow hue. The witch gave it a spin, considering the whirling kaleidoscope that resulted. "I have no idea why someone would ruin a garden with something this obnoxious. But I think I have an idea."

Madeline had found a shopping basket. Over the next few minutes, it was judiciously piled with supplies.

"Okay, I think that should be good. We can come back if we need anything else." Tamara hoisted three of the pinwheels over her shoulder, the strangest harvest in history. "Let's roll."

At the checkout, Ellie looked anxious. One hand drummed nervously on the countertop. The other held a flyswatter.

"What's the matter?" Madeline asked, setting the basket down by the register.

The other cat's ears swiveled warily. "I don't want to be an alarmist or anything, but there is one hella big buzz-buzz loose in here."

"O-oh?" Now it was Madeline's turn to look nervous. "You don't say."

After a glance around the front of the store, Ellie slowly lowered the swatter and began to ring up their purchases. "You know, Mrs. Johansen was in here this morning for the quilting group meet-up. She was telling me how her neighbors at that big orchard down the highway had hornets as big as your hand invade their beehives." She scanned a ball of twine, a roll of duct tape, and a box of paper lanterns with quick, furtive beeps. "You don't think those things would make it all the way here, do you?"

Madeline fidgeted. "Oh, no, of course not. Why would they? I'm sure hornets are much happier there. In the country. And not in town."

Tamara nodded calmly. "You might've seen a cicada killer wasp. They're big, but they're not aggressive. Unless you're a cicada, anyway. Hardly ever sting people."

"You think?" Ellie hopefully scanned a package of glow sticks and a wind chime.

Madeline fluffed proudly. "Ellie, Tamara works for the forest service. You can absolutely take her word for it."

"Whoa, really? That's really cool."

"Mostly I just say 'yeah, that's an invasive species. Can we get rid of it or is all hope lost for this acreage?' Not very exciting." Tamara carefully leaned the pinwheels over the counter.

Ellie sighed, extending the handheld barcode scanner. "It is when you and all your friends are starving artists working part-time jobs and taking commissions. That's, like, a career." She scanned a large pack of bells and began to pull an assortment of long plastic tubes out of the basket. "What are you guys making, anyway?"

"It's a sort of... an interactive modern art sculpture," Madeline explained.

"With groan tubes? Your neighbors are gonna love you." The tabby flipped one of the neon-colored tubes upside down. A surreal, alien sound issued forth.

Ravel dove from nowhere with an excited screech.

Ellie screamed, disappearing behind the counter as the pixie buzzed over. The tube hit the floor with a pained noise as she crouched, arms tightly covering her head. "Oh my god, oh my god, oh my god—!"

"Yeah, that's definitely a cicada killer," Tamara said loudly. "Totally harmless, so don't worry. Just prop the door open and it'll fly out eventually."

"I'll get the door!" Madeline yelled. She chased her pixie toward the exit, yanking her purse open as she went.

Cautiously, Ellie peeked over the edge of the counter. Her ears were pinned back so far they couldn't be seen; her ponytail, in disarray; her striped tail, fat with frizz. The plastic googly eyes she had stuck to her name tag rolled wildly. "Is it gone?"

"Sure is." Tamara pulled out her wallet. "So, how about that discount?"

Madeline's apartment above the camera shop was accessible from the small parking lot behind the row of buildings by a narrow wooden stair. It was only a few blocks from the craft shop, so they had decided to drop off the pixie-baiting supplies before heading back to Tamara's.

"I bet these are fun in the winter," Tamara observed from a lower step as Madeline unlocked the door on the tiny landing at the top.

"I've had a couple near misses, but I always buy a bag of salt now to spread when it snows. That helps." The door swung open and the cat pranced inside, the bells in her shopping bag jingling merrily. "Come in, come in! Make yourself at home."

Tamara followed her into a very small foyer. On the wall to one side, a filigreed coat rack held a jacket and a sun hat. A shoe cubby against the opposite wall and several loose pairs at the edge of the mat indicated that she should remove her work boots. Propping the pinwheels in the corner next to a polka-dotted umbrella, she fought them off and ventured further into the ginger's domain.

A few steps down the hall, two doors faced each other that Tamara took to be a coat closet and the bathroom. Past the doors, the hall widened very slightly to allow a refrigerator, a sink, a small stovetop, and a miniscule slice of countertop. A rug shaped like a strawberry lay before the sink.

Beyond that, the witch stepped into a foreign land. *Does Rainbow Brite's pastel cousin live here?*

Suddenly feeling terribly out of her depth, Tamara crept into the studio apartment's main room. The hardwood creaked under her socked feet until she hit the edge of the white shag area rug on which a coffee table and two beanbag chairs sat. She dropped onto a beanbag made to look like a giant peach bun and gazed around in a state of subdued culture shock.

The sloping ceiling boasted a small skylight. The walls were painted baby blue. Strings of white lights had been tacked along the tops of them. Three full-length mirrors took over one corner, flanked by a large wooden wardrobe with roses carved into the doors. The bed against the opposite wall was a canopy affair of white metal, draped with lavender-colored hangings and piled with so many decorative pillows it looked like a pastry burdened with too much frosting.

There were fairies absolutely everywhere.

Framed drawings, posters, and prints of them took up a good portion of the wall space. Several shelves in the space that was left held rows of sparkling figurines of all kinds, while more fought for room in a crowded bookcase—every species, every color and style of flowing raiment, but all delicate, all ethereal, all winged and be-glittered.

"Wow."

"Home sweet home!" Madeline dropped the shopping bags on the table and pattered over to throw open the curtains over the sliding glass door that led to the small patio balcony. A fresh wash of sunlight brightened the room further.

There seemed to be enough room on the balcony for two lawn chairs, or maybe one modestly sized barbeque grill. A window box full of pansies and tiny model houses resembling mushrooms and tree stumps was fastened to the railing.

"What do you think? Can we convince the pixies to come here?"

Tamara fished the duct tape from the bag determinedly. "Heck yeah. Piece of cake."

A forlorn squeak drifted from inside the cat's purse.

She sighed, dropping into the other beanbag. It looked like a giant cheeseburger. "Well, I guess it doesn't matter now that we're home. You can come out."

"Your friend knew he was there," the coyote observed as Ravel made a grateful escape from his fabric prison.

"I didn't expect that," Madeline admitted, unpacking their purchases. "I thought no one would notice him as long as he didn't make any noise or knock anything over. We had to point him out to her at Java Flow that day. Even then, she didn't really see him."

"Right." Tamara thoughtfully rolled the tape from palm to palm. "I don't really have any experience with adults, other than you, who notice the fae without floating vehicles being involved, but I guess it's possible she could start to pick up on him if she's around you two enough. Is she an open-minded person?"

"She's an artist."

"So that's a yes. You told her I'm a witch, didn't you?"

The cat's ears turned down guiltily. "Well, yes. But I also told her about falling off a bridge and seeing a horde of pixies in the same breath. She didn't take it very seriously."

"Probably she's thinking 'witch' as in black hair dye, tarot cards, and tons of succulents." Tamara rolled her eyes. "No big deal. She can assume we're both crazy if she wants, as long as she doesn't get in the way or call the cops on me. I hate casting memory spells on the authorities."

"You don't have to worry about that." The ginger smiled fondly. "Ellie is one of the only people who have never treated me like I was crazy." She pointed to a piece of framed art on the wall by the bed. "She drew that for me when we were in high school. It's the sweetest gift I've ever gotten."

The piece was an incredibly accurate and detailed rendering of a high school-aged Madeline in colored pencil. She wore a flowing purple dress. Luminous moonflowers vined around her. Resplendent fairy wings unfurled from her back.

Tamara gazed at the drawing for a long moment. "When did you see the fae? The first time, I mean."

At first, she didn't think the cat was going to answer her. Then, after several long seconds, Madeline sighed. "I was six years old. We still lived in England, but we'd gone to Ireland on holiday. It was the week before Christmas."

Yule, Tamara's brain supplied instantly, *when the boundaries are weak. The Isles, where the worlds are close anyway.*

"We were staying in this charming little village in the hills. My uncle and grandparents and the whole family had come. It was lovely." Madeline plucked absently at the leader string poking from the ball of twine they had bought. "One evening after dinner it started to snow. I made such a fuss about it that my parents let me go out into the back garden to play."

"You left the garden, didn't you."

"The fields were so beautiful with the snow falling, and I only wanted to go out just a little way. I could still see the lights from the house. It was so quiet I could hear my breath, and the sound of the snowflakes landing on the dry grass." Green eyes went unfocused as she gazed down memory lane. "Then someone called out to me. It was the sweetest voice I'd ever heard—like icicles in the moonlight. I turned around and there was a lady standing there."

"What species?"

"Feline. She had long white fur and brown hair, like a sparrow's wings. Her eyes were like golden topaz. She was wearing a blue gown. She was the most beautiful person I'd ever seen."

Taking a similar form to lure its victim into a false sense of security, the witch thought darkly.

"She beckoned me over and I went to her. She smiled at me like she had known me forever. She put her hand on my cheek and said 'What a beautiful kitten you are. Would you like to see something lovely?' So I took her hand—"

Tamara's ears went back in alarm. "You did?"

"Yes, of course. And when I did, suddenly the fields behind her were covered in flowers instead of snow, and it was springtime, full of colors I'd never seen and birdsong I'd never heard. When I looked back up at the lady—I swear she didn't have them before—she had great, glittering wings down her back, like a moth dusted in starlight." Madeline's eyes were closed now as she lost herself to the memory, her expression so rapturous that she almost seemed to glow.

Tamara blinked hard.

The ginger *was* glowing. The glimmer was faint but unmistakable. Ravel floated around her, cooing adoringly.

Tamara had never actually met a fae-touched being in person before, but she had a feeling that she was seeing one now. "And then what happened?"

"I heard my father calling me. He sounded upset. So I let go of the lady's hand. She looked so, so sad." Madeline sighed quietly, glow fading as her ears drooped from their ecstatic perk. "Then I was standing in the field, all alone. No time had passed at all. But somehow it was morning. I walked back to the house and everyone made such a fuss. My mother hugged me and cried and cried. They'd been looking for me all night. Practically the whole town had been searching. But I know it couldn't have been more than a few minutes after I left the garden."

Despite the warmth of the sun-bathed room, Tamara felt her blood run cold. "Time was already warping."

Madeline looked up quizzically. "Hmm?"

"Time runs differently there. The fae realm. It's slower than ours. If a whole night passed in an instant then you were right on the border, about to cross over."

"Into fairyland?"

"Into fairyland." The coyote nodded grimly. "Thank your dad sometime. He probably saved your life."

"How do you mean?"

Tamara gaped, leaning forward in her bun-bag. "You were literally on the brink of being taken! Just a few more steps and you would've been gone from the mortal world forever."

Madeline's tail tip twitched in concern. "Forever?"

"People don't just stroll back from being kidnapped by a full-fledged faerie, Mads. Say you somehow managed to escape from the fae realm. Depending on how long you were there, you could have come back to a world where you were still six years old, but your parents were already eighty. Or dead. There could've been flying cars. Who knows."

"But... but she was a good fairy, I know she was!"

The witch rubbed at her forehead, struggling to get the point across. "Look. It's a fact. Faeries steal kids. I mean, not as much as they did in ye olden times, but it used to be so common that even non-witches picked up on what was happening. Why do you think all those creepy fairy tales exist?"

The cat's arms crossed stubbornly. "Why would a fairy want to steal a child from our world?"

"Enslave them. Eat them. Use them to test fae cosmetics."

"I absolutely refuse to believe that they could have such horrible intentions."

Tamara could have spent all day arguing the point with the writings of centuries of witches before her to back it up. Another glance around the room, however, a fresh look at all the fairy paraphernalia, convinced her that such a clearly lost cause wasn't worth the time or the budding headache.

"Anyways, let's just hope the worst we have to deal with is pixies." She shifted awkwardly. "But, uh. Thanks for telling me all that. I'm glad little you got back to your family."

"So am I. Even if it would have been wonderful to visit fairyland." Madeline held out her hand. Ravel stopped circling to settle on her palm. "And even if I did drive my family slightly mad after that. From then on I developed something of a fairy obsession."

Tamara snorted. "You don't say. I never would have guessed."

The ginger huffed and stuck out that little pink tongue at her.

Tamara laughed despite herself. "Kidding, I was kidding. Don't feel bad. Tons of kids go through a fairy stage, right?"

"Not quite like mine, I'm afraid," Madeline admitted ruefully.

"After we got home from holiday, fairies were all I would talk about. The only game I would play. Someone gave me a pair of costume wings and I refused to take them off, even when I went to school."

"Cute," the coyote uttered before she could stop herself.

"Cute when you're six years old, certainly. When you're ten or eleven... not so much." The cat's ears turned downward. "Eventually one gets tired of hearing the same thing over and over again." She looked down, stroking the purring pixie lolling across her hand. "You're only the second person I've told that story to since we came across the pond."

There had to be more to that chapter of said story—but Madeline looked like she'd rather not discuss it.

"Hey, look on the bright side." Directly against her nature, Tamara tried to point out the positives. "Near-death experience aside, if you hadn't run into that faerie back then, you wouldn't have grown up immune to memory charms and illusion spells. You've got an automatic one-up on every witch in the world. And you can see your sparkly pest pals. That's good, right?"

"Oh, absolutely. I wouldn't give that up for anything." She glanced up bashfully. "I know it's all been an inconvenience, but I'm so happy that I didn't forget about what happened on the bridge. Or about you."

"S'not an inconvenience," Tamara mumbled, staring hard at the floor by her feet. There was a hole developing in the toe of her left sock. "Just different. Not as bad as I thought it'd be."

The full force of Madeline's smile beamed across the little table at her, like the springtime sun determined to charm crocuses from the frozen ground. "Thanks for saying so. I'm glad I didn't ruin your plans."

Hopeless crushes had definitely not been part of the plan, but the witch thought she could pat herself on the back for rolling with punches that could no longer be denied. "Yeah, well. My gran used to say that any plan that can't be changed on the fly wasn't a very good plan anyway."

Madeline nodded seriously, whiskers twitching with mirth. "Your grandmother was undoubtedly very wise."

"She had a million-and-two wise old sayings for every possible situation. Used to drive me nuts when I was a pup. But now I remember most of them and drive myself nuts."

"I so know what you mean!" the ginger laughed delightedly. "My mum always folds her towels a certain way, and now that I'm on my own I find myself folding mine that same way, too."

Pixie-luring materials forgotten on the table, the afternoon slipped by quite unnoticed. When Tamara did notice, annoyance with herself flickered—and died away almost immediately.

Oh well. There's always tomorrow.

CHAPTER EIGHT

"Hold onto this tightly, all right? Mummy worked very, very hard for this piece of paper."

Tamara watched from the passenger seat of the Volkswagen as Ravel was given a check. He hugged it to himself importantly, the paper nearly as long as he was tall. "You sure it's a good idea to let him take care of that?"

"He likes it when I give him little jobs. It makes him feel useful. Besides, there's not much that can happen if we're not even getting out of the car."

The line of Saturday morning bank drive-through window traffic stretched through the parking lot and around the building. Rain came down hard and steady, the little car's wipers squeaking industriously as they crept along.

"So, the photo shoot went well?" the coyote asked, eyeing the pixie.

Parked in the cup holder, he had curled the check into a tube shape and was looking through it like a spyglass.

Madeline made a disgruntled sound and flopped forward in her seat, forehead hitting the wheel. The horn uttered an indignant little beep. "Oh my gooooosh. It was an absolute circus.

Give me a wedding any day. Engagement photos. Senior pictures. Anything but family portraits."

The client had seen the weekend forecast and asked to move the outdoor shoot up to the day before. Madeline had sent an apologetic text excusing herself from pixie hunting and that had been that. Tamara had headed out solo, scolding herself for being the slightest bit disappointed at the lack of company.

"Did the kids not behave?"

The cat shuddered. "There were five of them. The oldest was in third grade. As soon as I'd get one to stop picking his nose, another one would pull up her dress. Then someone would touch someone else and they would cry for five minutes. Then the baby spat up on the mum and we had to use his squirmy little body to hide the stain in the rest of the shots."

"I think I prefer checking ten truckloads of campfire wood for invasive insect species," Tamara decided.

"I just don't know how rabbits handle so many little ones. But anyway—I got a total of four shots in three hours where everyone was looking at the camera and no one's fingers were in their pants, nose, or other orifices. And they did give me a nice tip, and promised to leave a good review on my site, so I'm quite satisfied." The car inched forward. "How about you? Did you get any pixies yesterday?"

"One. Over by the high school."

"Was it causing trouble?"

"Kind of the opposite. I just happened to drive by there and felt like there was one nearby, so I stopped to look around. It was passed out in an empty two-liter pop bottle. Massive sugar crash."

"Oh dear." Madeline giggled as they finally pulled under the awning. "Okay, love, let's have the paper back."

Ravel handed her the check. He watched with great interest as she lowered the window and reached out, collecting the canister from the opening of the pneumatic tube.

"Now, we just tuck this in here with the deposit slip, and…" She reached back out to press the call button. "I'd like to deposit a check, please. Could I get fifty in cash and the rest in checking?"

The speaker crackled to life. "Sure thing. We'll have that right out to you."

The tiny door slid shut. Madeline pressed the second button. The canister rose majestically up the tube with a swoosh and disappeared into the upper bowels of the bank.

Ravel watched with huge, glimmering eyes. "Oooo."

In no time at all the tube descended. The ginger brought it into the car a second time, cracked it open, and pulled out her bounty. Her whiskers quivered happily. "Yay, groceries!"

"That paper turned into better paper," Tamara confided to the awestruck pixie as Madeline clicked the canister shut. "Then you can turn the better paper into other things. Like chips. And booze."

"Do not explain to him what booze is," the cat huffed. She reached out for the last time to return the canister.

Ravel darted over her shoulder. Before either girl could react, he zipped into the holding chamber. The door shut itself with a sparkle and a snap. The canister blasted up the tube with a pronounced thunk! and vanished, the pixie following hot behind.

Madeline screamed like a malfunctioning vacuum cleaner.

"Miss, are you okay?" the speaker crackled. The bank teller, a capable-looking opossum, peered at them over the top of the sports car currently parked at his window. By the squint, he was either fairly concerned or decently myopic.

The cat lunged out and jabbed the call button. "Yes! Yes, of course. Why wouldn't I be okay? There was just—ah—a spider! Yes, a spider, in my car. Thank you! Goodbye!"

Tamara's head thumped against the back of her seat from the violence with which the Beetle sped out from under the awning and whipped into the closest parking spot. She was laughing too hard to care. "Dude, he heard you screaming from behind the glass! That was amazing."

"Stop laughing," the ginger yelled, frantically unbuckling her seatbelt. "We have to get him out of there!"

"Hey, hey. Calm down." Tamara fought down a last snicker, laying a grounding hand on Madeline's arm. "Let's think this through. That tube goes straight to the teller, right? So he's not stuck in there. He'll get out as soon as they open—"

A ferret in a business suit dashed out the front door of the bank and down the sidewalk past the car, briefcase held protectively over his head. "Hornets! Giant hornets!"

At least a dozen bank patrons and employees followed in a shouting, flailing stampede worthy of a B-grade monster movie.

"There, see? He's out."

Madeline covered her eyes in despair. "Ideas, Miss Witch?"

"The little pest is bound to you. Summon him. Concentrate, focus on his energy, and order him to get his tail back out here."

"Okay, I'll try." The cat's hand moved to her temple. Her eyes drifted closed, lips moving soundlessly. Tamara was sure she could read the words 'right this instant' before forcing herself to look somewhere besides the other girl's mouth.

Silence descended. The patter of rain on the roof of the Volkswagen seemed abnormally loud.

A cascade of canisters shot down the pneumatic tube. Propelled by an unseen force, each one was bounced out by the one behind it and rolled wildly across the parking lot. Ravel zipped out behind the last canister. He passed the drive-through window in a sparkling blur and landed neatly on the Volkswagen's side mirror. His arms were full of twenty-dollar bills.

Tamara squinted. "Smart pixie."

Madeline's whiskers spasmed. "Oh no, you don't." She rolled down the window and seized the pint-sized robber by the scruff, whisking him back into the vehicle. "That does not belong to you. Drop it at once."

A couple of firm shakes and the pixie let go of his loot, squeaking in displeasure as the bills rained down in his mistress's lap.

"Are we going to jail?" Madeline asked with some concern as she tried to gather the cash up one-handed.

Tamara unbuckled. "You look good in everything, but I don't think orange is really your color. Give me the money and keep that—" she pointed at the pouting pixie, "—in here."

The witch stepped out into the rain. Countless drops of water falling from the sky, the rush of the wind, the subtle charge in the air at the head of the oncoming storm; Tamara reached out with her magic, energy tumbling over itself to heed her.

Several bank employees were valiantly struggling to chase down the canisters.

Tamara beckoned. The wind caught a nearby canister and rolled it swiftly to her feet. She scooped it up and quickly stuffed the money inside it. "Hey, excuse me," she called, jogging across the parking lot. Her waterlogged ponytail drooped. A buildup of energy followed closely at her heels. "This rolled over by our car."

A tall wolf in stilettos and a very stylish, very wet blazer accepted it without question. Her arms were already full of identical canisters. "Thank you very much! Oh, you're just drenched. Get back inside before it—"

Lightning flashed.

With a subtle sign, Tamara let the energy go. Freed, it flowed directly toward the nearest conduit. Thunder cracked deafeningly as the ATM went dark. So did the lights inside the bank. So did the security cameras trained on the drive-through and parking lot.

The wolf, dripping ears flat against her ruined hairdo, heaved a huge sigh. "I knew I should have called in today."

———

"Darn it, open! Open!" Madeline danced in place on her welcome mat, fighting to turn the key in a stubborn lock one-handed. Her other hand futilely tried to keep the rain pouring off the eaves from dripping onto her head.

Tamara stood passively on a lower step. Soggy to her skin, she watched with mild amusement. "Isn't it supposed to be witches who melt when they get wet?"

"I am made of sugar, so obviously it is me who will melt first."

The coyote barked a laugh as the door finally swung open and Madeline dove inside. Being much wetter, Tamara gave herself a hard courtesy shake before following suit. Her boots, sodden but much less muddy than usual, were carefully removed in the tiny foyer.

The bathroom door stood open, blocking the hallway. Tamara pushed it to just enough to squeeze by. The spell she wanted needed more space than the entryway.

She was peeling off her squishy shirt, flannel puddled at her feet, when the bathroom door closed. Madeline padded around the corner, wrapped in a towel. Tamara noted with some relief the yellow bra straps protruding from the top of it.

The cat was brandishing a fluffy blue bathrobe patterned with tiny green frogs and lily pads. She pushed it into Tamara's hands, relieving her of the dripping shirt as she did. "I'll just pop these wet things into the dryer."

"Oh, thanks. The drying spell doesn't really work on clothes without a clothesline."

Madeline's damp ears popped up. "Spell?"

"'ell?" Ravel peeped, peering out the top of the purse on the coffee table.

Tamara gathered her flannel off the floor, where it had made an obvious mark on the hardwood, and handed it over. "It just warms the air and circulates it around to dry hanging clothes. Or yourself. Whichever."

"Like a magical blow-dryer! Can I see?"

"You sure you didn't get enough of spells after the last one I cast on you?" the witch teased, stepping out of her wet pants.

"Incredibly sure. Let me just toss these in the dryer first—"

Tamara laid the bathrobe over a beanbag chair and glanced around the small room as Madeline scampered away, trying not to dwell on the fact that she was standing rather awkwardly in her underwear in a cute girl's living space. The horde of delicate, breakable fairy figurines stared back.

In the hall, the clothes dryer shut with a bang. What had first appeared to be a mere coat closet also held a small, stacked washer and dryer unit. Madeline was back in an instant amid the rumbling tumble, damp tail swishing excitedly from under her towel. "Ready!"

"Okay. I think it should be fine to do this here, but I don't want to break anything, so I'm going to add an element of containment to the original spell. Got any chalk?"

Madeline produced a fabric pencil, which worked just as well. She looked on attentively as Tamara drew a circle on the floor, roughly the size of a small wading pool, and marked off the containing runes. As if sensing that there was fun to be had, Ravel fluttered over and landed on the ginger's shoulder.

Tamara set the pencil aside. "That should do it."

Madeline was already in the circle, practically vibrating with excitement.

The witch stepped in beside her, barely more than a foot between them as they shifted to stay within the lines. Nearly toe to toe with the other girl, Tamara swallowed surreptitiously. "I'll bring it up easy. Brace yourself."

She pulled the energy thrumming around them into the circle in a slow, rolling build. The air began to move, warming as it swirled around them. The pixie's wings and the cat's hair began to flutter in the rising breeze. The ends of Madeline's towel began to flap.

In half a minute the dull, shop vac roar of the wind tunnel reached a crescendo. Tamara shivered happily as the hot air traced through her rapidly drying fur and stood her ponytail on end. One ear twitched rapidly as the pixie tumbled past it, caught in the tumult and shrieking with glee; not surprising given how he'd reacted to the leaf blower debacle.

Madeline laughed delightedly. She stood in a makeshift jumping jack, arms and legs spread wide as her fur stood on end and her hair swirled up like a ginger tornado. Her towel belled up like an opened umbrella.

Tamara stared dumbly at the white daisies on the other girl's cheerful yellow panties. *She coordinates her underwear.*

The sleek, creamy fur of the ginger's lower belly looked soft and silky as new butter. Her outer thighs, like her shoulders, were faintly striped. Her inner thighs—

The pixie hit Tamara in the face and clung. She loosed a highly embarrassing yelp. The wind abruptly died as her magical concentration shattered. Eyes screwed shut, she swatted ineffectively at the area around her face. "Get off! Get off, you make me itch!"

"Oh, dear." Tamara froze as a delicate but firm hand caught her chin. With a stifled giggle, Madeline peeled the pixie off the coyote's muzzle. Cradling its dizzy form to her chest, she ran a gentle finger over the bridge of Tamara's nose. "He didn't scratch you, did he?"

A black eye cracked cautiously open. "Uh…"

The cat glanced up.

Their gazes met.

The towel slithered to the floor.

"Oh my gosh," Madeline squeaked, whiskers going stiff and emerald eyes widening like forest pools as she seemed to realize how close they were. The hand she'd had on Tamara's face flew back to cover her own lips with a breathless whisper. "Are... are we having a lesbian experience?"

Tamara didn't know whether to laugh or scream. She settled on neither. "If we were, you'd know it. Trust me." She gave the cat's bare shoulder a conciliatory pat.

"Oh." Madeline frowned, ears angling in thought.

Ravel struggled upright in her cupped palm, snickering woozily. "'gain, 'gain!"

- / - / - / - / -

The rain had slowed to a steady patter as Tamara drove homeward. She drummed her claws lightly on the steering wheel, the old truck's tire raising an impressive splash from an overflowing pothole. Every few miles she glanced back at the little yellow Volkswagen following behind.

Pixie hunting having been a literal wash, they had decided to spend the afternoon finishing up the bells and whistles on the pixie-luring paraphernalia that would be installed on Madeline's balcony as soon as the weather broke. With the lack of space at the cat's tiny apartment, Tamara's place had been the logical next choice.

The witch was turning down the drive when a bedraggled crow swooped in front of the truck. She braked, rolling down the window. "What's up?"

Raven landed at her elbow. Raindrops beaded off his inky plumage. He uttered an ominous croak.

"Really. We'll see about that."

The crow launched off the windowsill and vanished into the foggy forest as Tamara killed the engine. A moment later, the Volkswagen rolled to a stop behind her. The coyote hopped out of the cab and jogged back to the smaller vehicle.

Madeline cracked her window. "What's the matter?"

"He says there's an intruder."

"Auntie Peg?" the cat wondered. "I hope it isn't that nutty old squirrel." Her ears flattened in distaste.

Tamara focused, shielding her eyes from the rain as she stared intently through the woods that hid the cabin from sight of the road. The muted energy of green, growing things and the scent of damp undergrowth rose around her. Her tail gave a wag of concentration. "No. I can't feel any magic. Whoever it is, they're not a witch." Despite the lack of palpable magic, though, she couldn't deny that the traces of sentient life she could feel were... odd. Very nearly normal, but ever so slightly off in a way she couldn't put her finger on. "I'm going to check it out."

Madeline turned off her car and stepped out onto wet gravel. "I'll come with you."

"Look, worst case scenario, someone's trying to rob me and I have to hex them. They could be armed or something. Stay here until I come back."

"But you might need backup!" The ginger hefted her folded umbrella like a baseball bat, whiskers stubbornly stiff. Ravel peeked determinedly from the hood of her raincoat.

Tamara rubbed at her eyebrow ring with a sigh. "Stay behind me. And be quiet."

They crept around the bend in the drive. The old oak tree loomed out of the drizzly gloom. Madeline's rubber galoshes squeaked faintly with each step.

"There's no car here," she whispered as they snuck toward the cabin. "Wouldn't robbers need a getaway vehicle?"

"You'd think." Tamara's ears went back. Her hexing hand twitched uneasily.

Going in by the front door was too risky. Crouching low beneath the windows, the two tiptoed along the outer walls. The soft patter of rain off the eaves and leaves covered what little sound of their footsteps the moss didn't swallow. The coyote nosed around the back of the house, sniffing and sensing for danger. Finding nothing immediate, she signaled Madeline on with a jerk of her head.

The pixiary stood, dripping but apparently undisturbed. The wards of protection gave off a faint sparkle as its inmates were sheltered against the cool and damp. The back door was, as always after the witch left home, shut tight and magically impassable. The kitchen window was wide open. A contrary curtain flapped over the sill.

Tamara's huff of annoyance was lost to the breeze. *Memo to me: cast a more comprehensive rebuttal spell.*

Finger to her lips, she beckoned. Madeline followed, close as a ginger shadow. The door swung smoothly, soundlessly open as they stepped into the mud room.

The inside of the cabin, usually dim thanks to the thick cover of the oak, was bathed in a gloomy false twilight—all but an ethereal glow from the far side of the kitchen. The pantry doors hung open. Inside, several dozen glass mason jars emitted a sickly green glow. Silhouetted against the eerie light stood an unfamiliar figure.

"Don't touch those!" Tamara roared.

With a scream of fright, the intruder whirled. Her bristling tail caught a row of jars, sending them crashing to the floor. A bloom of ghostly orbs escaped. Wide gray eyes shimmered green as the orbs rose quickly toward the rafters.

Taken aback, the coyote blinked. "You're the little shit from the park."

Behind her, Madeline sucked in a shocked gasp. "Young lady, where on *earth* are your clothes?"

The naked vixen bolted. Bare, nimble feet leaped the wreckage of the glass jars as she raced out of the kitchen and into the den with Tamara hard on her heels.

Barely through the connecting arch, Tamara tripped over something floor-level and moving. She went down with a loud curse, the fleeing girl's tail barely a hairsbreadth from her grasping claws.

The vixen reached the front door. There was a bang and a rattle as she assaulted the knob, trying desperately to make her escape.

"These doors don't open for trespassers," Tamara snarled. She struggled up, only to trip once more as a small, furry form darted from the shadows beneath the coffee table and sank tiny fangs into her ankle, just above the boot. "What the hell—?"

It was a feral red fox.

As the witch fought with her tiny assailant, Madeline hurried past, on course for the panicked girl. "Now, now, let's just calm down." She reached out soothingly. "I'm sure we can work all this ou—*ouch!*" A squall of feline discomfort erupted as Madeline was clocked squarely in the eye. The ginger crumpled to her knees, both hands held tightly over her face. Ravel shot out of her hood, high-pitched chatters of rage coming thick and fast as the vixen turned tail.

Tamara aimed a sharp kick at the animal clinging tenaciously to her pant leg. The fox disengaged with a squeal that caught the fleeing vixen's attention.

"Kory, run!"

Both foxes, bipedal and feral, burst past the floored witch and back into the kitchen. For just a moment Tamara worried that they might reach the open window, and her hand flew into the motions of a paralysis hex. Before it could be cast, a thing possessed exploded into the kitchen.

Raven swooped through the window, cawing to raise the dead. The vixen screamed and covered her head, ears flat with fear as his wings beat the air madly and sharp talons grabbed at her hair.

The ripple of energy caught Tamara completely by surprise. Her ears shot up, tail and hackles prickling as an alien, yet strangely familiar, feeling washed around her. If the life traces of a caterpillar's metamorphosis into a butterfly through long days and weeks had been condensed down into a single moment, it may have come close to what she was sensing.

There was a pop of displaced air, and quite suddenly the young vixen was gone. Two four-footed foxes scrambled on the hardwood, yipping wildly as they tried to avoid the angry crow. One leaped up and snapped at Raven, coming away with a mouthful of black feathers. The other ran pell-mell back into the den. Tamara, still on the floor, was so shocked that she didn't even try to grab for it as it dashed around her.

A wicker laundry basket descended from the heavens. The fox gave a shrill yip as it disappeared beneath the makeshift trap, the full weight of an angry photographer firmly pinning it to the floor.

"Punch me in the face will you, you little rotter?" Madeline seethed, claws digging into the strands of wicker. One green eye was half squinted and watering like mad. "I'll have Tamara turn you into a toad!"

The squealing from within redoubled.

Tamara finally forced herself to her feet. A series of short, broken yips turned her attention to the kitchen where her familiar had the second fox pinned against the front of the refrigerator. Claws buried in its neck ruff, the crow was delivering a volley of irate pecks between its flattened ears. Tiny black paws covered its eyes protectively.

"Okay, Raven, that's enough. Good job." As the bird launched back into the air with a triumphant caw, Tamara grabbed the fox by the scruff and hauled it off the floor. It curled in on itself as it was hoisted, resembling a fluffy red shrimp in her grasp. She tucked it firmly under one armpit. "I win. Now you do what I say. Bite me and I'll hex you so hard you won't move until Monday."

There was a somewhat squished whimper of acquiescence. Prisoner in tow, the witch marched back into the den.

Madeline was sitting on the laundry basket. She had produced a compact mirror from seemingly nowhere and was closely examining her reddened eye, oblivious to the soft whines emanating from the basket. Her pixie circled, cooing anxiously.

"Alright. I want some answers, and I want them now," Tamara ordered. The forthcoming silence was pronounced. She shook the vulpine dangling in her hold. "Come on, talk. Or change back to something that's able to talk."

Both the visible fox and the basket's inmate remained stubbornly quiet.

"Okay. Fine. We'll do it the hard way." Tamara's ears laid back in annoyance. "I got the other one," she announced loudly. "Mads, keep that one under control until I get this one skinned, then we'll switch out."

The basket uttered a terrified bark.

For the first time, the ginger's anger wavered noticeably. "Oh my, don't you think that's a bit harsh—?"

"Don't hurt him!" A very un-feral leg burst out of the basket as the wicker failed to contain an all-at-once full-sized teenage vixen. Madeline tumbled off of it with a shriek.

Tamara had a feeling she knew what would happen next and dropped the second fox a moment before another strange burst of energy produced the girl's very ruffled, equally naked brother in its place.

"Leave her alone!" He staggered up, one hand on his

undoubtedly bruised head as he planted himself between the witch and his sister. "It's me you want. It's my fault we're here."

"Damn it, Kory—don't lie for me," the girl yowled, struggling to extract her leg from the ruined basket. She kicked it off and launched herself at the boy, latching onto his arm protectively. "Breaking in was my idea!"

"If I'd been able to stop you, we wouldn't be in this mess!"

"Well, I should've listened to you when you tried to talk me out of it, so it's my fault!"

"Yeah, you should have listened. You never listen, even when I tell you something is a bad idea!"

"I knooow!" Fat tears rolled down the vixen's cheeks as she clung to her brother, clearly on the verge of hysteria. "I'm sorryyyy!"

Madeline cleared her throat rather awkwardly, darting completely flummoxed looks between the coyote and the intrepid teenage interlopers. Almost seeming to have forgotten both the seriousness of their predicament and their lack of clothing, the two had apparently patched things up and were hugging it out, the boy gently grooming his sister's ears with his claw tips as she sniffled.

She who thinks she's seen everything is just asking for a surprise from Mother Nature.

Tamara could feel a headache coming on. She rubbed tiredly at her forehead. "I have so many questions."

CHAPTER NINE

"First question. Where the hell are your clothes?"

Perched side by side on the witch's sofa, the twin foxes fluffed anxiously. Realizing that there was no other way out of the mess they had gotten themselves into, the two seemed resigned to their fates. It helped that Tamara had yet to make a move towards actually skinning anyone in the room.

"In our fort," the boy muttered. His knees pressed tightly together, tail tucked modestly over his lap. The white tip flicked nervously. "In the woods. By our house."

His sister apparently did not share his delicate sensibilities. "Clothes fall off us when we shrink," she said matter-of-factly, making no move to cover her bare chest or anything else. "It's so much easier to just hide them when we go on espionage missions."

Madeline frowned disapprovingly. She had claimed the armchair across the room and was somewhat preoccupied with holding half a bag of frozen peas to her swollen eye. "So you often sneak about in the nude and invade people's homes. Charming. Do your parents know about this little hobby of yours?"

"Uh, no. Duh." The vixen rolled her eyes so dramatically that most of her upper body got in on the action.

Tamara sighed, shaking her head in mild disbelief. "You need to cover your nips, kid."

She puffed defiantly. "Don't like, don't look."

"Modesty becomes one," Madeline sniffed around her peas as Tamara disappeared down the hallway.

"Jealous?" The girl grinned, cupping her own breasts. "You're totally jealous." Her brows waggled with wicked glee. "I'm only a sophomore. Who knows how bad you'll be losing by the time I'm done growing?"

The boy elbowed her, hard. By his pained expression, he wished to sink into the upholstery and vanish from the situation, possibly forever.

Madeline's pea-free hand clenched on the arm of the chair. Her tail began to wag sharply near her knees. "I would sooner be jealous of the cows at the dairy farm."

Tamara still wasn't entirely sure if the vixen was trying to cover up nervousness with her cocky attitude, or if she was really just that brash. Either way, the witch pointedly stepped back into the den in time to prevent further physical altercation. Over her arm draped two towels from the linen closet, which she tossed at her uninvited guests. "Just cover up so this can get marginally less awkward."

The towels were put to use with varying degrees of gratitude.

"Right. Second question." The coyote crossed her arms sternly, donning what she hoped was a no-nonsense expression. "What *are* you two?"

The boy looked up from tightening his towel kilt, ears flicking up in surprise. "You don't know?"

"In the interest of you guys being honest with me, I'm going to be completely honest with you." She took a deep breath and let it out in an annoyed puff. "No, I don't. I've never seen anything even close to this before."

"Oh." Wrapped in her absorbent makeshift toga, the vixen looked somehow crestfallen. "We... we were kind of hoping you would, actually. Because we're weird. And you're weird. But you're not weird like us, then, huh?"

Tamara's short whiskers twitched with wry amusement. The girl's moods seemed to change as fast and frequently as the springtime breeze. "I'm going to temporarily excuse the part where you broke into my house—which you shouldn't have even been able to find, by the way—instead of just *talking* to me." Well aware that she was, yet again, stepping into uncharted territory, she extended her hand. "Let's introduce ourselves. Tamara Ridgemount. Resident witch."

The girl made a noise reminiscent of an excited chick, wild chestnut hair bouncing as she shook her brother's shoulder madly. "I told you! I told you she was a witch! She has a crow and everything."

"Yeah, you weren't the one getting pecked by it." Rubbing ruefully at his cowlicks with one hand, he carefully shook Tamara's with the other. It was powdered with dried mud. "I'm Kory Anderson. This is my sister—"

"Kari." She flipped her tail winningly.

It was said among witches that once was happenstance, twice was coincidence, and thrice was the universe trying to tell you something. It had been a third meeting Tamara wasn't likely to forget. "I'd say nice to meet you, but I'm not sure how accurate that is yet. Good to know your names in case I need to curse you, though. Works a lot better when you specify your target."

In concert, the twins' ears flattened with concern.

During the course of the ruckus inside, the rain had picked back up. Deepening shadows seeped through the room. Steadfastly ignoring the conversation on the couch, Madeline kept to her chair, regally dabbing at her eye with the thawing peas. Ravel sat on her knee, warily watching the foxes.

Tamara glanced over her shoulder. She couldn't help but admire the brooding, almost gothic picture made by cat and fae and peas. "And the lady over there that you slugged is Maddie."

"You may call me Madeline," the cat informed them icily. "Not charmed, I'm sure."

The vixen's cheeks puffed out in frustration. "Look, I'm sorry I punched you. Adrenaline is a harsh mistress. It'll never happen again."

"I should certainly hope not."

"We really are sorry," Kory cut in, clapping a hand firmly over his sister's mouth before any more potential damage could be done. "We're very sorry. We never should have snuck into your house."

"Damn right," Tamara agreed amiably. "Good way to get shot. I hope you don't do that a lot. Big or small."

Kari pushed her brother's dusty hand off her pouting muzzle. "This was the first time, jeez. And we were careful. We waited until we knew you were gone." Her eyes narrowed. "This place is magic, isn't it? It took forever to find it, and we know every inch of the woods for miles around here."

"This is Oakridge. This house, the oak tree, the forest all around here. It's my ancestral Holding and it's supposed to be hard to find." The coyote fixed the teens with a serious stare. "Like I said, I'm writing today off. But I'm not the only witch in this area. Not all of them are as laid back as I am. If you don't want to disappear so hard your parents don't even remember you exist, you stay far away from any other place that feels like this place does. Get it?"

Kory leaned protectively toward his sister. "I knew something didn't feel right as soon as we crossed that creek. It just felt… wrong. Wrong like what you did in the road that stopped our jeep. Like what happened at the park."

"I felt absolutely nothing," Kari supplied helpfully.

"If you did, you would've turned back when I told you we should," he huffed.

"He's always felt stuff I can't," the vixen offered at Tamara's puzzled look. "Same as I can see stuff he can't. Like fussy-fluff's sparkly thing. And these green blobs." She pointed to a spot next to Tamara.

The witch glanced down in surprise. A glowing green orb circled slowly near her elbow. She grabbed for it reflexively, but it vanished in a blink.

"Oh." Madeline perked up a bit as another one appeared, bobbing in front of her chair. "What are they?"

Tamara blew at one irritably as it drifted past. "Will-o'-the-wisps. The ones that *used* to be in the pantry."

Kari shrugged sheepishly.

Green balls were popping up all over the room, drawn out by the murkier conditions. The one nearest to Madeline floated closer. Her pixie stalked it from the arm of the chair, tufted tail waving in concentration.

Head cocked, ears perking suspiciously, Kory studied the wisps. "Okay, I can definitely see them now. Are they dangerous?"

"Not really. They're just little clumps of energy." A wag of the coyote's tail sent one spinning. "People make them dangerous by following them when they shouldn't. You don't know how many hikers and campers get lost in the forest chasing these things."

"And you collect them because...?"

"Witchy reasons," she growled darkly.

Thunder rumbled. The foxes gulped.

A burst of cheerful music sounded, successfully ruining the drama of the moment. All visible will-o'-the-wisps popped out of existence. Madeline apologetically tugged her phone from her pocket. "Sorry. My 'remember to pick up milk' alarm."

"It's cool." Tamara straightened, cracking her back. "Alright, enough about me. I think it's time you two tell me the whole story."

The kitchen proved a better venue for the telling of tales.

She had been making an effort to clean up more since Madeline had begun making regular visits to her humble abode, but Tamara's hospitality skills still ranked near the level of a person who had, until recently, been classed somewhere close to 'mossy old hermit.' Despite that, she did what she could on short notice. An old kettle perked away on the stove as Tamara swept up the shards of glass by the pantry.

Raven had settled into his indoor nest on top of the refrigerator, neatly tucked amid the cereal boxes. Madeline and the fox twins sat around the table. A circle of slowly rotating witch lights glowed above it, as good as a chandelier on a gloomy afternoon.

Kari, elbows propped on the old wood, brushed snack cake crumbs from her whiskers. "I can't believe you carry tea bags in your purse."

The cat sipped primly from her mug. "God save the queen."

Tamara made a mental note to buy some tea. She tapped the head of the broom twice on the lip of the trash can. The attraction charm released, dropping the glass and dirt trapped in the bristles into the bin with a tinkle. Floor free of shards, she settled into the chair next to the cat. "Okay. Let's talk about these talents of yours. Start at the beginning."

"Well, it all started when a mommy fox and a daddy fox decided to make some baby foxes..."

Kory shot his sister a squinty-eyed glare. "I think you better let me do the talking for once, okay?"

She snickered but deigned to fall silent.

"So you've always been able to change like that?" Tamara prompted.

"Not always. We were in elementary school when it happened the first time. Around seven or eight years old, I guess. We were playing around in the woods near the house one day and it just... happened." He fiddled with his empty cake wrapper, folding it into smaller and smaller squares. "We've been able to do it ever since. We can't explain it."

"I don't suppose the moon was full?" Madeline asked, chin propped on her fist. She seemed fascinated despite herself. "Oh, but it's not even nighttime and you did it a bit ago. Never mind."

Both foxes perked eagerly.

"Are there really werewolves?" Kari looked delighted at the prospect.

"None that I've ever met or heard of." The witch tapped her claws thoughtfully on the scarred timber of the table. "What about your family? Can anyone else change like that?" She fixed the boy with a sharp black gaze. "Do they even know that you can?"

In the way of all teenagers avoiding a scolding, neither twin made eye contact.

"We only do it when we're alone," Kory mumbled at last. "When we were kits, it was just a fun secret, something for just the two of us to know about. Now we know what would happen if anyone found out."

Kari pulled the spoon from her empty mug, licking off the last traces of honey and tea. "We'd be kidnapped. Taken to a secret government lab. Experimented on. Never heard from again." She paused, considering. "I mean, if they even had to resort to kidnapping. Dad might just sell us."

Her brother threw up his hands in frustration. "Dad would *not* sell us to the government! We've been through this."

"He's an accountant. He'd sell anything if you gave him the chance. Remember those old whalebone knickknacks he hocked and Mom chewed him out because they were 'part of our cultural heritage' or something?"

Feeling like a referee, Tamara clapped a hand sharply on the table. "Can we stay on track, please? If I were a scientist, I'd want a refund."

Kari's mouth dropped open, tail bristling in offense. Kory bit his lip, obviously trying not to grin at his sister's ire. It wasn't hard to see which one was the alpha sibling and who usually hung back. Tamara decided it wouldn't hurt to put a few pinholes in the vixen's ego.

"So you discovered a hidden power at a young age that no one else in your family, apparently, has. Can you change whenever you want, or do certain conditions have to be met?"

"Whenever we want, really."

"Okay. Then do it now."

The boy fidgeted. "Now? Like, right now?"

Tamara nodded firmly. "Right now. Everything happened so fast earlier I didn't get a good look. If I'm going to help you figure out where you stand in the grand scheme of the universe, I need to see what I'm working with."

Kari stood with no hesitation. "Okay. With or without the catchphrase?"

A feline brow rose elegantly. "Catchphrase?"

"Uh, yeah. All heroes need a catchphrase when they do their transformation sequence, duh."

"Oh, of course," Madeline deadpanned. "How could I have been so foolish."

"I'm not really sure if—"

"Oh, come on." The vixen patted her brother's shoulder encouragingly. "What's the point of having a transformation sequence if no one besides us ever gets to see it?"

With some reluctance, Kory followed her to the middle of the kitchen. Tamara and Madeline watched with equal parts bemusement and curiosity. Ravel, tying the handles of two mugs together with the string of a used teabag, paid no attention.

The teens squared up, facing their audience. At some unspoken signal, they sprang into motion.

Kory flowed into a martial arts pose. "Kon-kon!"

Kari's curled hands met at her chest to form a heart as she twirled. "Love-love!"

They spun back to back, tails briefly entwining. "Kitsuneeee, *change!*" they chorused together, palms meeting for a fleeting moment.

It happened too quickly for the eye to follow. A double dose of the strange metamorphic energy washed from the twins. In the next instant, two feral foxes stood in a puddle of discarded towels on the kitchen floor.

Tamara blinked. "Somehow I'm even less sure what just happened than I was before."

"Ha! Er. Um. A-hem." Madeline did her best to cover a snort of amusement, instead clapping politely. "An anime transformation sequence. Of course. I should have guessed it. Well done."

The coyote's ears flickered in confusion. "What the hell is an anime sequence?" Sure she knew what anime *was*, but she'd never taken the time to watch any of it herself. If occurrences like this were the norm in that particular media, she was rather glad she hadn't.

"I'll explain it to you later," the ginger told her kindly, patting her arm.

Raven looked down with interest from the top of the fridge. His feathers rustled as he croaked thoughtfully. Back arched, tail bristled, one of the foxes growled warily up at the crow. The other scuttled under the cover of the table, hunkering beneath Tamara's chair with a whine.

"Okay, which one are you?" Tamara peered down at the bushy tail between her boots. "Without the boobs, you both look exactly the same."

An angry yowl preceded a bite to her boot.

"This is insane," the witch muttered. "Their bodies have changed but their brains are still fully sentient."

Madeline looked down into irritated vulpine eyes. "Is that usually not the case?"

"A really, really skilled witch could turn you into—oh, I don't know—a gecko, or something, but then you'd have a gecko brain. You wouldn't have the mental capacity to remember that you'd ever been anything but a gecko. But these two..." She glanced over at the fox that had to be Kory. He met her gaze and sat, tail curling neatly around his paws. "Changes in nature happen gradually, not all at once. This level of full-on transformation is fae stuff. *Faerie* stuff."

"But they're not fairies," the cat noted with complete certainty.

"Not in the slightest. I'd feel it." Tamara rested her chin on her hands pensively. "So what *are* you?"

Outside, rain pattered. The wind rustled the oak tree's wet leaves. Its soggy branches creaked ponderously in the breeze.

Tamara stood resolutely. "I need a book."

Kari scurried out from under the chair as it squeaked across the floor. Swapping a look with her brother, she trotted after Tamara as the coyote strode into the den. Kory and Madeline brought up the rear of the investigative procession.

Hands on her hips, the coyote surveyed the old bookcase. It was a solid oak affair, nearly floor to ceiling, overflowing with the combined collective efforts of generations of Ridgemounts. Books on every conceivable magical topic—spellcraft, astrology, mineralogy, indexes of plants and fungi—were stuffed into the overburdened shelves. Most of the old, leather-bound spines lacked titles.

"Do you remember which one it is?" Madeline asked, eyeing the less-than-orderly selection.

"Definitely don't."

Kari looked up from sniffing the bottom shelf with an incredulous yap.

"That doesn't mean I can't find it." Standing on tiptoe, Tamara plucked a small wooden box off an upper shelf. From among the bric-a-brac inside she fished a small, pale green crystal on a thin silver chain.

"Oooh, pretty," Madeline approved.

The witch stood very still, allowing the crystal to swing like a pendulum. Seated at her feet, both foxes watched it with interest, heads following its sway back and forth. When it finally stilled, hanging motionless before the bookcase, Tamara closed her eyes. Very slowly, concentrating hard on what she wanted, she began to move the crystal around the shelves.

On the third shelf from the floor, the crystal swung forward sharply, tapping the spine of a thick volume.

"There it is. 'Legends and Lore of the Witch's World: A Brief Record of Natural, Magical, and Ethereal Anomalies.' Haven't read this since I was a pup." Opening the book, she carried it back toward the light of the kitchen, already flipping through yellowed pages.

Kory hung back even as Madeline and his sister followed her into the other room. He stared up at the bookcase with wide-eyed wonder, tail wagging thoughtfully.

"Come back with your clothes on and I might let you read some of them sometime," Tamara called back casually. "The astrology ones are really interesting."

There was a moment's pause of surprise before the young fox bounded after them with a very pleased yip.

"Can I get a little space, please? It's hard to look with you all backseat reading."

Madeline and the twins stepped back sheepishly. Tamara

had been leafing through the hefty tome at the table for ten minutes, the other three leaning in from all directions. The foxes, at least, had reapplied their towels without prompting upon return to their bipedal shapes.

As if to prove her point, the next page she turned led to a promising lead: a hand-drawn sketch of a mighty bear warrior in full headdress descending in stages to all fours.

"Okay, here it is. This is what I was looking for." Sharp black eyes skimmed the pages rapidly. "Witches have their own take on the old transformation myths. Fewer wolves, more other species. It goes back to before there were witches—way back, when all of our ancestors were still druids and shamans."

"What's it say?" Kari demanded eagerly.

"Keep your towel on. It says: 'That the Shifters once existed, though likely never in great number, cannot be disputed. Innumerable accounts from our Sisters around the globe describe individuals of various species possessed of the singular ability to change their physical form, wholly reverting their bodies to the state of their feral ancestors.' Okay, this has to be it." Tamara read faster, more sure with every word. "'Incredibly, no magic to speak of is used in the transformation, the innate ability being acquired from birth in certain bloodlines.' Bingo." She thumped the book triumphantly with the back of her hand.

Kory's ears swiveled anxiously. "Is there more?"

"Plenty. Apparently, they can be traced back to the ancient inhabitants of certain places—'particularly, the puma and bear of North America; the jaguar of South America; the lion and leopard of Africa; the jackal of Egypt; the tanuki of Japan; and the fox tribes of multiple regions.' So the markers for it could theoretically be in your DNA."

Palms planted on the table, Kari bounced impatiently, tail waving like a car dealership banner in her excitement. "What else?"

Tamara skipped through several pages of references to the

other species. "Regarding foxes specifically, it says: 'Shifters have perhaps been reported most often in the vulpine lines. Of special note are those from the regions of Japan, the Celtic Isles, and Scandinavia. The Norse mythology of the non-magicals bears reference to the *fylgja*: a vulpine spirit that accompanies an individual in connection with their fate and fortune. *Fylgja* means "to go along with," similar to the mythical Irish canine spirit, the Fetch.'" She looked at the twins. "Where does your blood come from?"

"Norway and Denmark." Kory looked utterly mystified. "Mom has first cousins in Iceland."

Tamara smiled despite herself. "Well, there you go. Mystery solved. You're the proud products of Shifter blood."

Brother and sister shared a long, silent look. As one, they broke into huge grins.

"Wow."

"Uh, yeah, wow!"

Madeline allowed a smile of her own. She seemed to be slowly getting over the damage of the earlier scuffle. Both her pretty eyes could now open all the way again. "Isn't that nice? It's important to know where one comes from." She curled a lock of copper hair around her finger contemplatively. "But... if they aren't magic in the witchy sense, how can they do what they do?"

Tamara traced a claw tip through the paragraphs. "Hmm... Wait, here's something. 'While various origin myths hold that the first of the Shifters resulted from arcane relations of their tribes with the Fae Folk, the Shifters themselves claimed that their kind arose from ancient pacts forged with the Old Gods— the guardian spirits of nature itself.'"

Kari's ears perked.

Kory blinked guilelessly.

The witch's first instinct was to scoff at the idea. That powers as old and deep as the roots of the world could be at work in the bratty teenagers before her sounded, offhand, completely ludicrous. Then she thought again of the girl's uncanny Sight. The boy's supposed ability to Feel. The unnervingly alien, so oddly familiar energy of their shifting, as overwhelming as the change of a tiny acorn to a towering oak in the minuscule, infinite space of a breath. "…okay. I might buy that."

"This is the greatest day of my life," Kari breathed. "Oh my gosh. Is it hot in here? I think I need to sit down."

Kory's head cocked in concern. "What's wrong?"

"Did you not hear what she just said?" the vixen demanded. Before her brother could reply, she grabbed him by the fluffy cheeks. His whiskers poked through the spaces between her fingers, stiff with surprise. Stormy gray eyes nearly crossed as she leaned in close enough to whisper. "We. Are. *Gods!*"

"That is absolutely not what I said." Tamara closed the book with a loud thump. "That's the last thing I need—two underage prowlers with freaky transformative powers and delusions of grandeur."

Nose in the air, Kari flipped her tail with a huff. "See if you're getting blessed by *this* goddess."

"Cheeky thing," Madeline muttered.

"Speaking of blessings." Tamara folded her hands over the tome with businesslike aplomb. "We haven't discussed how you plan to pay."

Sudden silence descended over the kitchen.

Kari's tail lost some of its bluster. "I thought you said you weren't going to punish us for breaking in."

"I'm not. But you obviously came here seeking answers, which I have provided. Ergo, I did you a service. Witches always require payment for their services."

Kory reached automatically for a wallet and found nothing but the pocketless fabric of his towel kilt. "We'll pay, we promise. But can it be another time? All our money is back home."

"And I'll be honest: I've got about six bucks." Kari's arms

149

crossed petulantly over her ample chest. "Dad made us fill up the jeep yesterday."

"You'll find that we witches are very flexible when it comes to reimbursement. I'm an understanding person. You two don't have a lot of money, so how about something other than cash?"

The vixen's ears flicked curiously. "Like what?"

"Your brother's virginity should cover it."

Kari made a sound like a rusty screen door blowing open.

"You seem surprised," Tamara observed innocently.

Madeline's tail had poofed wide with shock. It switched back and forth in agitation as she stared, aghast. "You wouldn't."

"Why not? It's a very traditional form of payment. Pretty rare nowadays, those virginities—worth a lot more than they used to be when everyone had one they refused to get rid of. Probably enough to cover the answers you got today with a little more toward your next service."

"No!" Kari screeched, throwing her arms wide as she stepped between the coyote and her brother. "Not only no, *hell* no! You just keep your insidious paws away from him, witch."

Kory had been stock-still and silent for the duration of the conversation. The insides of his ears turned slowly pink. He swallowed hard, clearing his throat. "Actually, that might be doable..."

"Don't you dare go along with this, you perv," his sister yowled, swatting him hard with her bristled tail. "I'm trying to protect you from this other perv and you don't even appreciate it!"

"Hey, knock it off!" One fang anchored in his lower lip, he batted her fully-frizzed tail away from his face.

"Oooh, so this is why you still have that pesky virginity." Tamara shook her head sympathetically as the foxes scuffled. "Sorry, man. That's rough."

"You wanna go?" Kari demanded, rounding on her with fists

raised. "Magic or no magic, I'll kick your ass, right here, right now—"

Kory leaped forward and grabbed her around the waist, holding her firmly away. "Do I really have to remind you how hard we're *both* going to be screwed if you make her mad?"

The tea kettle descended onto the stovetop with a bang and splash of finality. Everyone froze.

"No one is having relations with anyone!" Madeline shouted. Her ears were pinned back, frazzled tail twitching like mad. "I'm going to have some more tea. Who else wants another cup of tea?" She stomped over to the countertop where her purse lay in repose and plunged in her hand, drawing forth a teabag. It was tied by the string to at least six other teabags. "Ravel, you *naughty—!*"

Unable to control herself any longer, Tamara began to laugh. "Oh my god, you all thought I was serious! That was amazing."

Kari's hackles slowly smoothed. Her fists uncurled as she casually flipped her hair back. "Pfff. I knew that."

"Oh, please. I so had you going." The coyote smirked toothily. "You should really work on not advertising so hard that you're each other's weaknesses, by the way. Someday, somebody's not going to be joking. Just a word of advice."

Madeline glanced up from picking moodily at the knot of teabag strings. "You ought to be ashamed, toying with their emotions like that. Teenagers are very delicate emotionally, you know."

"Oh, you're defending them now?" Tamara asked playfully. "I thought you were still mad about the panda eye."

The cat's mouth shut with a click of tiny fangs. She squinted suspiciously. "You're quite terrible."

Tamara really could not help herself. "I'm a very wicked witch," she cackled, tail wagging a mirthful rhythm.

The old kitchen had never seemed quite so lively.

It was late afternoon by the time the twins departed. The rain had finally blown out, leaving slanting sunbeams peppered through the trees. Lingering raindrops glittered, jewel-like, from every leaf.

Kory glanced out the window. "We should probably be heading home. We're supposed to go out to dinner tonight."

"Yeah, I guess." Kari sighed regretfully. She placed Ravel gently back on the table and turned to Tamara. "You were serious when you said we can come back, right? Your house isn't going to disappear the next time we try to find it?"

"Not to my knowledge." The witch's pierced brow rose. "Wait a minute. How did you know where to look for me, anyway?"

"We followed you home from the park last weekend. Well, we followed her following you." The vixen nodded at Madeline without a trace of guilt.

Tamara's ears flattened. "Little stalkers." Though, she had to admit that they'd done it well; they had stayed far enough behind that neither she nor the cat had noticed they were being tailed by the teens' jeep.

"Hey, it was a mystery that needed solving! All of a sudden your cars just disappeared into the woods. Vanished off the road without a trace. So then we really knew we were dealing with supernatural forces. Kory GPS'd where we were when that happened—"

"Because you made me."

"—and we figured out where it must be if we came in from the other direction, through the woods."

Tamara huffed. Witches took great pains to safeguard their private property. "You should have gotten lost."

"We did, like ten times. We kept getting turned around. That doesn't happen anywhere else in the forest, especially when we're changed, so we knew it had to be pushing us away from something. Every time Kory felt the weird feeling, we just turned around and went toward it."

"Fair enough." The coyote stood decisively. "Alright, scram. You've been here once; you'll be able to get back here again. But it better be when I'm home next time or I'll hex you until every hair on your tails falls off." Both foxes cast concerned glances at their tails. "And if you happen to find any pixies, bring 'em over and I'll give you something in exchange."

"Really?" Kari brightened. "I want a will-o'-the-wisp in a jar!"

Kory's tail danced eagerly. "I want to read your books."

"Catch some pixies first. Bargaining later."

Madeline looked on with some concern as the twins stood, obviously making ready to shift into their feral forms. "And you promise not to tell anyone about this, of course? Witches and pixies and magic?"

Tamara felt unreasonably touched that the other girl thought to ask.

The vixen fixed the cat with an unimpressed stare. "So she can claim we're insane and get us arrested for breaking and entering? No thanks."

Much more kindly, Kory smiled. "We have a lot of practice keeping secrets. We'll keep yours if you keep ours."

Madeline's whiskers quirked into an answering smile. "Odd ducks of a feather flock together, I suppose."

With a hop and a yip, the foxes changed. It seemed that the use of their transformation sequence was on an as-needed basis. Like living sunbeams, they skittered across the hardwood, fiery fur glowing in the warm light, and were gone with a swish of the curtains.

"I have doors for a reason, you know," Tamara yelled at the open window.

Very faintly, two yaps of merriment echoed from the forest

in stereo, quickly swallowed up by the trees and birdsong. Ravel squeaked what could only be a goodbye.

Hands on her hips, Madeline valiantly fought a fond expression. "They're not cute at all."

"Not in the least." The coyote leaned over the sill. Four sets of tracks crisscrossed the muddy ground below—two neat rows of tiny paw prints leading to and from the larger, clearly bipedal footprints directly beneath the window. "I hope they come back."

Madeline carefully collected the discarded towels. They were speckled all over with red fur. "Not to be mean, but are you sure? You've got rather a lot on your plate already, with the pixies and all."

And distracting cats, Tamara wanted to say, quite unable to ignore how lovely the other girl was washed in the glow of the oncoming evening, smelling of tea and honey and after-the-rain. "Well, like you said. Weirdos need to stick together. I may be alone, but at least I have connections. I could call on Auntie Peg, or even summon the whole coven if I ever really needed to. Those kits don't have anyone but each other."

"I can't imagine it would be easy hiding something that important from their family," Madeline mused thoughtfully, neatly folding the towels over her arm. The pixie swung happily from a string unwinding off one of the hems.

"Right. They're totally isolated. Nothing like them has been seen for Earth Mother knows how many generations, let alone in this neck of the woods. They might need somewhere to turn someday."

"That's awfully kind, for such a wicked witch," the ginger pointed out.

A flush raced up the insides of Tamara's ears. She cleared her throat loudly and pulled the screen down over the window with a bang. "A-and they're fascinating. I should study them. For magical science."

Madeline gave her a knowing look.

The coyote sighed. "Well. You should never get so busy with your own spells that you wouldn't help a neighbor with hers."

"Another wise witchy saying?"

"Seems like it fits the situation."

"Oh, indubitably."

The coyote offered a mock scoff. "Indubitably? What even is that word? Stop being so insufferably British."

Madeline stifled a giggle and sniffed haughtily instead. "Stop being so insufferably witchy."

"This witch will sic her terrible, murderous familiar on you."

"Well, I'll sic my pixie on you!"

Tamara shook her head sadly. "That's low. You know that flying glitter bomb makes me itch."

Teasing and laughing easily, the two managed to segue back into their original plan, finally pulling the truck and the Volkswagen up to the house and pulling out the pixie-catching crafting supplies.

Around them, the forest breathed. The earth turned. Change slipped slowly through the treetops.

CHAPTER TEN

There came a point at the end of each summer, September slipping away like a sparkling stream between the banks, when a sense of wanderlust overcame many witches. Tamara had never been exempt. On some days when the call became particularly bad, she would throw some food in her backpack, leave before dawn, and tramp the borders of her Holding until twilight, Raven tracking her progress from the yellowing foliage.

Such luxuries could not be afforded at the end of this particular season.

Sandwich in one hand, Tamara scribbled on a napkin with the other, a bright orange Java Flow pen jotting down figures. "So, that was seven on Monday, four yesterday, and five tonight."

Outside in the parking lot, carefully covered in the bed of her truck, a heavily warded birdcage held five very aggravated pixies.

"Plus thirty-two in the pixiary, plus Ravel, that's forty-eight. Minus the two that Peg can confirm got dusted, we're halfway there. Approximately." She took a large bite of deli roast beef and cheese, nose crinkling at the sharp bite of horseradish. "I wish there was a better way to know exactly how many actually got loose. Or how many others might have been... *poofed* since then."

Cradling her cup, Madeline sighed. "Yes, that would make things much simpler. But I suppose we just keep doing the best we can." She gently stroked Ravel, who was dozing across her knee. "I daresay we're doing well enough. If we're not doing well even with all this work, I just might cry."

It had been a hectic week.

Tamara had barely recovered mentally from the run-in with the mysterious fox twins before she had been called in bright and early the next morning by the DNR for a multi-day field survey. Madeline too had been kept busy, keeping the camera shop up and running while the owner went out of town. Through it all, the pixie traps on the cat's balcony had proven a success, pulling in several of the tiny fae a night. The two had managed to meet up only briefly each evening to covertly swap birdcages. One, filled with pixies, went home with Tamara to be emptied into the pixiary. The other, previously emptied, was left at Madeline's apartment for its next load.

"Your neighbors probably think you're dealing drugs. Or smuggling exotic birds. Or using exotic birds as a cover for dealing drugs."

"Which is exactly why we have met at the coffee shop this time," Madeline declared pointedly. "Well, that and lemon cake." A small dessert plate sat empty at her elbow, devoid even of crumbs.

The coyote was putting the last of her sandwich to rest when the door jangled open.

"Hey, Maddie! I thought you'd be here."

"Ellie!" Madeline looked up delightedly as the gray tabby cat approached their table. "What a surprise! How did you know I'd be here?"

The other girl waved a hand at the window. "I saw Daisy parked out front. You have the only yellow Bug in town."

"I suppose that's true. Sit down, sit down." While Ellie found a spare chair to pull over to the small table, Madeline covertly slipped the pixie's sleeping form off of her knee and into her purse. "Did you just leave work?"

"Yeah, I closed. Levi had a hot date, so I swapped him shifts. He owes me deets and a case of the good stuff." She sank into the chair with a grin, then turned to Tamara. "Hey, Tim-Tam, long time no see."

Mouth full of sandwich, unsure whether or not she should be offended by the sudden application of nickname, the witch waved awkwardly. "Sorry," she coughed, swallowing the last morsels. "Hi. Nice to see you again."

"Seems like you and Maddie have been hanging out a lot lately. Should I be jealous?" The tabby pouted exaggeratedly, whiskers drooping.

Madeline leaned over and threw her arms around her friend. "Good heavens, no. I'm sorry if you've been lonely. These past couple of weeks have been... very busy."

Ellie patted her on the head with a laugh. "I'm just teasing. I know you love me."

Tamara felt a little pang of envy at their easy affection. She hadn't consciously thought about it before—perhaps she hadn't allowed herself to think about it—but now she couldn't help but wonder how often she would actually be able to see Madeline when their pixie-catching work no longer meant they needed to interact on a regular basis and life could return to semi-normal.

"Oh, sweet." Ellie had glanced down at her phone. "There's still half an hour to closing. I'm gonna grab a pop. Be right back."

When she had left the table, Madeline looked to Tamara. "I'm sorry, but you don't mind if she stays, do you?" she whispered.

"No, of course not." If she couldn't carry on a normal conversation for thirty minutes, the coyote thought, she would admit that she might need more social interaction.

Madeline smiled gratefully as Ellie returned with a bottle in one hand and a giant chocolate chip muffin in the other.

"Score! Half-priced, end-of-the-day baked goods. So much tastier when they're on sale." The black stripes on her tail wiggled happily as she resumed her seat and began to peel the paper liner off the bottom of the muffin.

The ginger shuddered, watching with morbid fascination as the other girl took a large bite and washed it down with a mouthful of root beer. "I don't know how you can manage to take in so much sugar at one time. But half price, did you say?"

"Half price," Ellie sing-songed, waving the muffin enticingly. "But yeah, I don't know how you drink as much tea as you do at one time, so we're even." She peeked into Madeline's cup as if to prove her point, then blinked rapidly. "Oh my god. Are you drinking coffee?"

"I'm especially sleepy this evening," Madeline huffed, covering her cup defensively with one hand. "Well, I have been for a few days, really." She punctuated the statement with a dainty yawn.

"I don't believe it. Are you sure this witch doesn't have you under some kind of evil spell that's sucking all the England molecules out of you?"

Tamara took a sip of her chai and tried to look adequately evil. It was important to maintain appearances.

"Oh, you." Madeline swatted at the other cat crossly. "Don't jump to such conclusions. That's very stereotypical."

"Joking, joking." Ellie giggled, raising her hands in supplication. "But seriously, I've never met a practicing witch before. What's that like?"

"Well," Tamara answered slowly. "It involves lots of succulents."

Ellie nodded solemnly, wiping chocolate from her lip. "I knew it."

Madeline dropped her face into her hands despairingly.

"Succulents and other gardening. Long walks in the woods. Looking at stars. Collecting rocks and crystals. Occasionally attempting to foretell the future. I do not own a pointy hat. I do live with a crow, though."

"Nice!" Ellie munched at the last of her muffin. "I bet your house is cool."

"I like it. But I'm biased."

"It's a lovely house," Madeline assured. "Very interesting."

"Cool. We'll have to hang out sometime. Oh!" The gray cat disappeared briefly from view as she dove beneath the table to dig inside her messenger bag. "Maddie, I've been wanting to show you something." She popped back up with a sketchbook. "I finished my costume design for the Halloween match."

The ginger pulled her eyes and attention off the pastry case. "Wonderful! Let's see."

Tamara peeked over unobtrusively and saw that the artist had sketched herself in a superhero costume. Several angles showed the outfit in its entirety, from tights to cape to goggles made of what looked like giant bottle caps. Roller skates topped off the ensemble. "I like the eyewear."

Ellie beamed. "Thanks! My derby name is Choke-a-Cola, so I wanted to do something with a pop theme."

"Derby name?" Tamara looked again at the skates. "Oh, you play roller derby?"

"You know it. Proud member of the Indomitable Derby Dames. Almost undefeated."

"If you want to remain almost undefeated instead of dead on the track, we'll need to drastically cut the length of this cape. That's an open invitation for one of those mean girls to grab and throttle you." Madeline seized the pencil from the sketchbook's spiral binding and made rapid notes in the margins. "I'd say no more than two feet, at most."

"Aww. Okay."

"Can you alter the goggles yourself?"

"Oh, yeah. I've already got the polymer clay and paint for the bottle cap rims. And I was thinking maybe glue a bottle to the front of my helmet like a unicorn—"

"I will disown you."

Tamara watched the cats poke and tease, hashing out details on everything from the type of fabric to sequin use. Madeline was clearly deep in her creative zone, a state Tamara hadn't really seen before. She had a cute 'focus' face, nose scrunched and whiskers pudgy in concentration.

The moment was interrupted by a loud growl.

Wide-eyed, Madeline placed a hand on her stomach. Her ears flattened in embarrassment. "Pardon me."

"If you're that hungry, go get something else to eat," Tamara urged with a frown. She glanced at the purse hanging from the back of the ginger's chair and the napping pixie therein. "Remember, you're basically eating for two now."

Madeline's ears popped up in surprise at the reminder. "My gosh, you're right!" She jumped up from the table and trotted happily to the pastry case, long skirt a-sway and tail swishing happily. "Back in a tick."

Ellie sputtered wildly, mouth hanging open as she yowled after the other cat. "Madeline Annette Babcock! What have you been doing when I'm not around?! This is something you're supposed to tell your best friend!"

Tamara adjusted her bun awkwardly. "That didn't really come out right."

"I don't believe this." The tabby clutched the front of her hoodie in her despair. "We were supposed to live this revelation together. I was supposed to be the one you told first. I was going to have to be the one to buy the pregnancy test because you'd be too proper and scandalized to do it!"

"You had a plan for unplanned pregnancy?"

Ellie scowled at the coyote, claws sinking into the edge of the table. "Besties plan for all the emergencies. All of them."

"What on earth are you talking about?" Madeline returned rather bewilderedly to the table. She carried a pastry bag filled with no fewer than three butter croissants.

"The fact that you're pregnant!"

Madeline paused, bottom inches from her chair and the first croissant inches from her open mouth. "Whatever in the world gave you that idea?"

Ellie stared, as though the universe were playing some sort of cosmic joke on her.

"What I should have said," Tamara cut in loudly, "is that she's using as much energy as two people right now with how busy she's been, so she should eat more. There are no pregnancies occurring at this time. That I know of."

The tabby seemed to deflate in her relief. She slumped across the table, forehead cushioned by her sketchbook. "Oh, thank god. I seriously didn't want to have to go beat some random dude tonight."

Madeline sniffed. "Random dude, indeed." She took a massive bite of her pastry. "Oh, you're right; they're so much tastier when they're on sale."

"Excuse me," the rabbit barista behind the counter called. "We're closing in ten minutes. No rush, just a heads up."

Tamara waved by way of acknowledgment and turned to her companions. "I should get going anyway."

"Yeah, me too." Over her fright, Ellie stretched mightily. "Hoping to get a few panels done before bed."

"Ellie draws webcomics," Madeline confided between munches.

"About superheroes?" Tamara guessed.

"Sometimes. How'd you know?"

"Lucky guess."

They parted ways under the awning outside. The barista locked the door behind them. Crickets sang from the bushes around the café.

Ellie tugged her bike from the rack. "Take it easy, Maddie. Don't work too hard. And hey—if you're free on Saturday night, you should come out to the harvest fair."

"Gosh, is it that time already? Summer has just flown by."

Tamara's ears swiveled. She had known about the festival the town held at the fairgrounds every weekend closest to the autumn equinox, but she'd never felt the need to attend, even when dodging the invitations to Mabon activities that occasionally got thrown by members of the coven. Advertisement flyers hung at the farmers market and hardware store always sported smiling scarecrows and colorful gourds.

"You should totally come! It'll be fun. Krafty Korner's doing a face painting booth. And we're having a mini derby match in that big barn where they show the 4-H critters. Nothing official, just for fun."

"I suppose it would be big enough in there, wouldn't it?"

"Plenty of room for spectators in the bleachers," the tabby grinned suggestively, securing her bag's strap across her back. "Well, I'm off to draw the good fight. See ya later!" She swung herself onto the bike and pushed off, rolling away down the sidewalk with a passing blink of reflectors.

As soon as she was out of earshot, Tamara turned to the ginger. "Sorry I made your friend think you were pregnant."

Madeline laughed. "She's your friend now too, you know. And never mind, no harm done." She placed both hands on her belly teasingly. "At least you've taken responsibility for my magically bound pixie child."

"Pff. Don't remind me."

The cat giggled, hitching her purse gently higher on her shoulder. "So, anyway, about the harvest fair…"

"Have you been before?" Tamara asked.

"Oh yes, it's quite fun. There aren't any rides like at the county fair in the summer, but they do have crafts and games and treats and food trucks of all kinds. Bobbing for apples and cider pressing. A scarecrow dressing competition. Hay rides around the midway. And a bonfire."

"Do many people come?"

"As far as I know, it's very well attended. Everyone enjoys a reason to have a party. And then next month there'll be the big to-do at the Halloween Spooktacular before they close the fairgrounds down for the winter."

They had begun to drift across the parking lot as they talked. The old truck and the tiny yellow Volkswagen beside it were the only remaining cars. Cat and coyote stopped between them.

"So there will be a lot of people making lots of noise, lots of light, and lots of smells," Tamara summarized. "In one fairly centralized place in town. On the autumnal equinox."

"Well, yes." Madeline looked up at her, whiskers lifting rather hopefully. "Would you… perhaps like to go with me?"

Tamara nodded resolutely. "Let's do it."

Madeline stood a bit straighter. "Really? You will?"

"Absolutely. The boundaries between worlds blur on the equinoxes—not as much as Samhain and the solstices, but still enough that it'll stir the pixies up for sure. With that kind of commotion going on at the same time, you know the fair's going to get their attention." The witch drove a fist into her palm determinedly. "This is our chance to vacuum up another mess of them."

"Oh." For an instant, the ginger seemed to slump but righted herself at once. "Yes, of course, our mission! I'm sure we will find many pixies."

Her mind flipped through several tomes of witchy lore,

leaving just enough brainpower for a reply. "So we'll plan for Saturday evening."

"The shop is always closed by five. You could come 'round to my flat any time after and we could take one car to the fair. It's likely to be paid parking."

"I'll be there." A bang and an angry chatter erupted from the bed of the truck. The birdcage, draped with an old blanket, rocked dangerously. Tamara shot it a sharp glance. "Sorry. I better get those home."

"Of course." For a moment it looked like Madeline wanted to say more. As if thinking better of it, she climbed into the Bug. "I'll let you know in the morning whether I got any more pixies. Goodnight."

The witch waved her off as the little car puttered out of the empty lot. Two quick farewell beeps of the horn and the cat was off and away into the scant Wednesday night traffic. Unbidden, Tamara thought again of that time not too far into the future when seeing the Bug would become a much less common occurrence. She sighed. Chasing pixies was tiring, and frustrating, and highly annoying. But as long as there were pixies, there would, at least, be Madeline.

Sometimes the most beautiful flowers grow out of the most rotten compost.

A shriek of command rose from the covered birdcage, followed by a chorus of affirmation. There was a clatter of metal bars as the pixies mounted a coordinated attack on the walls of the cage. It rocked again, teetered, and fell over. The containment charms held, much to the displeasure of its captives.

Tamara rubbed tiredly at her eyebrow ring. "At least you little monsters are good for something."

CHAPTER ELEVEN

In direct defiance of her gloomy thoughts the night before, morning brought a crisp, sunny day upon the forest. It also brought Madeline, the second birdcage in one hand and a wicker basket in the other. The birdcage contained a small flock of grumpy fae; the basket's contents were a mystery.

"Good morning," the cat chirped as she trotted into the cabin. Her fatigue from the previous evening seemed to have vanished like the stars at sunrise. "What a gorgeous day! I'm so glad Mr. Jackson is back and I got the day off. It would be such a shame to be shut up indoors on a morning like this."

Tamara placidly stirred a spoonful of instant coffee into her steaming cup. "Mmm. Not bad for a Thursday."

"You know, it's funny, but when I was in school I never used to enjoy autumn very much. It just meant that I had to go back to school and do lots of homework and—and other unpleasant things." Madeline placed the birdcage on the floor and the basket on the table. "But now that I'm an adult, I find that I can simply enjoy the season as it is, and now I quite like it."

One side of the hinged basket lid popped up. Ravel poked his head out of it with a squeak.

Tamara took a sip of her coffee and waved at him with the tips of her fingers not taken up holding the mug. As much as she would never admit it to Madeline, the pixie was beginning to grow on her. "Life after structured education is a wondrous thing."

"Isn't it, though? We can just take a stroll and admire the leaves changing colors without having to worry about the next report or exam."

"Or football." The witch leaned against the counter, scratching absently at her upper arm. "I have never understood why everybody loves football so much."

Madeline grinned. "I'd much rather watch Ellie play roller derby." Her head cocked, tail swaying curiously as she slipped out of her jacket. "What do witches do in the fall? Are there certain things you do throughout the year?"

"We're really in tune with the seasons in general. It's part of being tied so closely with nature. Autumn is..." Tamara paused, considering. She had never found herself needing to put such a thing into words. "In the fall, there's this feeling of... fulfillment, I guess. All the plants have spent spring and summer growing. They've pollinated and made their fruit and seeds. Autumn is when they fulfill their purpose and send all those things out into the world to make more plants."

Madeline hung on her words, wide-eyed.

"But there's also kind of a frantic feeling, from the birds and the insects and animals. Like the monarchs and migratory birds. They know that the warm days won't last forever. They have to buckle down and get ready for that long flight. Some of them won't make it back to see next spring. And the ones that stay have to get fat and ready for winter. We do that, too—we, witches—gathering enough of what we use to make potions and medicine to get us through the winter. So everything's racing against time." The witch thoughtfully swirled the last of the coffee in her cup. "Nature needs winter so it can rest. But it's still a deep, dark, cold wait until spring. So autumn is also pretty melancholy. Mourning the seasons that have already passed, knowing what's waiting after the harvest ends. Dreaming about next spring. Hoping you're still here to see it."

The cat let out a wistful sigh. "That was the most beautiful explanation. You're so poetic."

Tamara's tail bristled in sudden embarrassment. "No, I'm not." She scratched awkwardly at the back of her neck. "Look, I'm just trying to tell you that I've got a lot of conflicting energies coming at me this time of year, so don't be offended if I get moody sometimes. The wind and the rain and the forest are always talking to me. I can muffle it, but it never really goes away."

"What do the other seasons feel like?"

"Winter feels sharp and soft at the same time. Like despair and peace. The starlight sings."

"And spring?"

"Spring is… euphoric. It's opening your eyes after being asleep for four months. Everything in nature is screaming 'gotta build, gotta grow.' It's really hard to block spring out." Tamara's claws were busily at work in the fur of her inner wrist. "Spring is… itchy." She blinked, only then realizing what she had been doing. "I'm going to take those things outside. Starting now, only one sparkle-vermin is allowed in the house at a time."

The pixies in the birdcage sulked, highly unimpressed. Madeline politely covered a giggle.

"Make some tea if you want," Tamara offered, hoisting the cage off the floor. "It's in the cabinet over the stove."

"You have tea?" The cat pulled open the cabinet door curiously. "You have lots of tea!" She pulled down box after box wonderingly—English breakfast, mint, lemon, Earl Gray, chai. "Did you buy all of this because of me?"

The coyote beat a hasty retreat out the back door. "Sorry, be right back."

It took her several minutes and one paralysis hex to get the new arrivals into the pixiary. Most of the flock seemed fairly content with their captivity, spending the days playing with the toys Madeline had provided and looking through the second-hand picture books that Tamara circulated for 'enrichment.' One of the most recent additions flew in the face of the norm. Tamara suspected the slightly smaller, much more assertive fae of orchestrating the birdcage tip the night before.

"I'm gonna call you 'Napoleon,'" she muttered, firmly locking the door of the converted coop. After a moment's deliberation, she added another containment charm for good measure.

The small but mighty pixie glowered, upside down, at her retreating back as its stiff but unharmed form was borne away to recovery by its henchmen.

"Giving the pixies that erector set might have been a bad idea," Tamara called from the mud room as she pulled off her boots.

"Oh, nonsense. It stimulates them intellectually."

"Promoting STEM skills in a bunch of sparkly trouble-makers is probably not what we want to do. I was just dive-bombed by a magically animated metal pterodactyl." The coyote stowed the empty birdcage in a corner and stepped back up into the kitchen. "Now I'm worried about how they even know what a pterodactyl *is*. As opposed to a dragon or something. Did we give them any dinosaur books—?"

She froze in the archway.

Madeline's wicker basket sat open and empty on a kitchen chair. The table had been cleared of its normal detritus of junk mail, partially folded laundry, stray crystals, and drying vegetation. Instead, it had been neatly laid with plates, glasses, napkins, and silverware for two. A small bud vase in the center contained a large yellow marigold.

"How do you like your eggs?" Madeline asked without turning away from the stove.

Tamara's eyes locked onto the bow of an apron tied above the base of the ginger's gently swaying tail. "Sunny side up."

"Me too!" The cat beamed, deftly cracking a succession of eggs into the little-used skillet. "They'll be ready in a moment. I've got bacon and English muffins, too. We could make little breakfast sandwiches. And there's orange juice in the fridge."

Tamara wandered to the fridge in a daze. "Why?"

"I like orange juice."

"Okay, yeah, but why the sudden breakfast?"

"Well, we've both been working hard this week. And I for one have been starving lately. Autumn nurtures the appetite, as they say. It's important to eat properly."

The witch opened her refrigerator and examined the contents with a critical eye. Part of a gallon of milk from the local dairy co-op; a handful of withered carrots; half a stick of butter; a few bottles of assorted condiments; more than a few bottles of beer. "I suddenly get the feeling Gran would be very disappointed in me."

Madeline busily transferred the eggs and bacon to the table. "Never mind. It's not easy to cook for one, especially when you're always on the go."

Tamara grabbed the bottle of orange juice and seated herself at her oddly clean table. "Well, anyway, thanks. You're just so nice. Unnaturally nice."

"Stop saying that. You're a witch—you're unnaturally everything!"

"Excuse you, witches are the most natural creatures in the world."

They were digging into the spread when a car turned down the drive. Tamara paused over her bacon as she sensed its approach, ears popping up and hackles rising of their own accord.

"What's wrong?" Madeline asked, layering her eggs with tomato slices. "Is it too crispy?"

"No. It's Auntie Peg." Tamara relaxed as the car drew nearer and she sensed the familiar magical aura more fully.

The ginger's ears swiveled, finally picking up the telltale crunch of tires on gravel. "Oh. I suppose I'd better put the kettle back on."

A few moments later, a polite but insistent rapping began at the front door.

"Come in," Tamara called, trying to banish the irritation of being interrupted from her voice. It wasn't every day—or any day—that she got to eat breakfast cooked for her by her crush. "Door's open, Auntie."

The matronly hedgehog waddled into the cabin and straight through to the kitchen. A loud rattling sound, like an activated call buzzer left unattended on a plastic restaurant table, accompanied her.

"Good morning, Tammy," Peg greeted loudly, voice rising over the buzzing. "I hate to drop in on you unannounced, but if you don't take this little glitter gremlin off my hands in the next ten seconds I'm going to personally guarantee that it buzzes its last." She held out a Tupperware container, quite old, avocado green. It vibrated alarmingly.

Madeline's whiskers stiffened in dismay. "Can it breathe?"

"Of course it can. It wouldn't be buzzing if it couldn't breathe."

The vibrations abruptly fell silent.

Tamara seized the container and sprinted out the back door without bothering to put on her boots.

The hedgehog snorted. "Dramatic thing."

Peg joined them for breakfast.

"All's well that ends well, isn't it?" Her spines rustled philosophically as she buttered an English muffin. "Good thing I didn't get stopped by that last train, though."

Madeline sighed, pouring the older witch a cup of Earl Gray. "Yes, quite."

"Now that I've resuscitated it, where did you catch it?" Tamara asked.

"Fitness Universe."

Both girls stared blankly.

"What?" the hedgehog grumped. "Because I'm an old biddy I'm not allowed to exercise? Don't judge."

"Please just tell me you don't do it in yoga pants."

"I have a perfectly respectable set of sweats, you impertinent pup." Peg's eyes narrowed warningly behind her spectacles. "Tight fabric won't hold up to my prickles. Anyway, as I was saying—I was coming out of my seniors' Zumba class and felt that itchy fae magic buzz, so I went poking around. Sure enough, there was a big to-do in the weight room. Some slim young weasel with no meat on his bones had one of those huge barbell weights lifted over his head with one hand."

"Pixie levitation?" Madeline ventured meekly.

"Exactly. I'm sure you've had firsthand experience. It waited until he got comfortable showing off for the crowd and then flittered off somewhere else. Put a hole right through the floor when it dropped."

Tamara winced. "Is the guy still alive?"

"He'll need that shoulder popped back into place, but other than that he got lucky. Everyone managed to convince themselves he just had a momentary surge of adrenaline or some such nonsense like that. Saved me a memory charm. Then a stair-stepper started running backward in top gear and launched a poor little fennec so high she almost touched a ceiling fan. Hopefully that gym has good insurance. I'd hate to lose my Zumba day."

"Well, you did stop the madness. And no one was seriously

injured. That's the important bit." Madeline nibbled at what was left of her breakfast, looking inordinately guilty.

"I still say juicing them would be easier. But what can you do?" Peg took a sip of her tea and looked around. "Speaking of, where's your little bundle of joy?"

"On top of the fridge." Madeline glanced up as Ravel peeked around the side of a cereal box. He squeaked crossly. "Oh, did I give away your hiding place? Mummy's sorry."

The pixie huffed, somewhat mollified. He disappeared once more. A moment later a rustling, crunching sound began.

Tamara looked up, a tiny smile hovering around her whiskers. "Raven's not going to be happy you're messing around in his nest. He might eat you. I might not be able to stop him."

"He would not." The cat pointed firmly with the butter knife. "No one is eating anyone. He and Ravel get along splendidly."

"Really? I think they're just keeping a respectful distance from each other."

Peg nodded contemplatively. "I suppose your crow might see him as a fellow familiar. One witch-bound creature will never hurt another. Not even an owl or a snake familiar would try to eat a bird bound to someone else."

"There are snake familiars?" Madeline asked.

"Some. Reptiles are rarer than birds, but they're certainly out there. Amphibians, too. Toads are very traditional. Opal Swiftwater down at Riverglenn Holding has a hellbender salamander for a familiar."

"Otter witch," Tamara clarified.

"Yes, her hellbender's name is Lucy, I believe. Myma Gorse—you had the pleasure of meeting Myma, I'm sure you remember her—has a rat snake."

Madeline took the mention of the strange old squirrel in stride. "Really? That's fascinating. I thought rodentia weren't overly fond of snakes."

"Most aren't. But then, Myma has always been rather… unique."

"That's a very charitable way to put it."

Bored with ransacking, Ravel flittered down from the fridge. He looped around the cat's head and landed at her elbow on the tabletop.

Peg rustled her quills in greeting. "Ah, there's the only well-behaved pixie in history."

"Ha! Well-behaved. Right."

Madeline pouted at the coyote, who used shuttling dirty dishes to the sink to move quickly out of poking range. "You have to admit he's much better behaved than all the other pixies, at least. He hasn't tied a single person's shoelaces together this week."

"Okay, you got me there."

The old witch chuckled. "So, what's it like to have a fae as a familiar, honey? Familiars are supposed to help you out, you know. Make themselves useful. Does he earn his keep?"

Madeline nodded eagerly. "He really does. If I drop something small, I never have to go hunting for it; he finds it for me right away. He's just as good at untangling things as he is at tying them up, so my wires and cords and chargers never get messy. He even braids my hair for me."

Tamara, rinsing egg yolk and crumbs off her plate, realized only then that she hadn't yet seen Madeline sport the same style of braid twice. She looked at the pixie with new respect.

"And he's taken to bringing me coins and things he finds on the ground. Tamara got him keen on money, accidentally. We had a bit of trouble learning not to take it from other people, but I think he's got the hang of it. I gave him a little jar and he brings coins in all the time. Sometimes buttons. One expensive-looking ring that I took to the police station."

"Doesn't that beat all?" Peg shook her head in good-natured disbelief. "I'd never have thought it could happen, but you've done a great job domesticating the little hooligan. Makes me happy that you can enjoy him for as long as you've got him."

"Forever and ever," Madeline purred lovingly, teasing his tail tuft with the tip of one finger.

"Mum," he agreed, grabbing the finger by its neatly polished nail and shaking it playfully.

An odd look flickered across the hedgehog's face. Tamara turned from the sink just in time to notice it. Her ears twitched uneasily as she fumbled for a hand towel. "What?"

Peg sat up straighter, gripping her cup almost guilty as she turned her attention to the junior witch. "What, what?"

"You had a funny look on your face. What were you going to say?"

"Nothing. I'm old and wrinkled. My face always looks funny."

Tamara's eyebrow ring performed an acrobatic feat. She crossed her arms over her chest, the wet fur of her hands spotting the deep blue checkers of her favorite flannel. The hand towel hung from the crook of her arm like an unspoken word. "Auntie."

"Has anyone ever told you that you look like your grandmother when you do that?" the hedgehog huffed. "It's disconcerting."

"Someone had to follow in her footsteps," Tamara grumbled.

Madeline glanced up. "Is something wrong?"

Peg sighed. "I'm probably going to kick myself for bringing this up, but Tammy explained to you what the spell of binding is before she cast it on you, didn't she?"

"Yes." The cat nodded attentively. "It ties the fae to you and they siphon off your life energy."

"Well, yes and no." The hedgehog swirled the dregs of her teacup, deep in thought. "That's the spell at its most basic. The way the magic works is, the fae and the witch are bound in a kind of feedback loop, with her natural, mortal energy and its fae energy just bouncing off each other like a static storm. The original intent of the spell is to enslave the fae and use it; use its magic, kind of like a living battery, to increase the witch's own power. And that goes on until the fae's magic is all used up and it dies."

Madeline's lips pressed into a thin line. "That's horrid."

"It certainly is, if you consider fae to be worthy of mercy or common decency. Some don't. But as I was saying, eventually, the bound fae has all of its power drained away by the witch who controls it. Cut off from the fae realm with no source of its own kind of energy to replenish itself with, it dies. Usually, by that time, the witch will have started to come down ill and strange with all that exposure to fae magic, so really it's a good thing that death does them part."

"Fairy magic can make you ill?"

"Not just sick; plain bonkers. Witches are meant to be in tune with the energy that comes from nature. *Our* natural world, in our plane of reality. The wind, the water, the sun, the stars, the animals, all the growing things—they all give off energy. Witches act like a prism, reflecting and magnifying that energy. We channel it with spells and charms and give it purpose. That's magic as we know it. We're not wired for any other kind of magic. Little bits of the fae stuff won't hurt, but use enough of it for long enough and it'll warp you like bad wood."

"But that won't happen in this case." Leaning back against the sink counter, arms crossed in thought, Tamara frowned pensively at Madeline. "She isn't a witch. She doesn't *have* any magic that could be corrupted by exposure to the fae stuff. I figured she'd get tired more easily, maybe need to eat more often. Nothing major. And she's not using any magic off the pixie, so he won't get drained and go poof. It's all good."

"Except that simply existing here in the mortal realm drains the little thing's magic, honey. A witch's familiar will live a long,

long time because it and its witch are on the same level, and it can thrive on her life energy. But with a fae, even a small one, once they're cut off from a source of their own kind of magic, a mortal's life energy won't keep them going indefinitely."

A drop of water disconnected from the faucet. Its descent into the metal sink seemed inordinately loud in the suddenly silent room. Ravel, nearly through with plucking the tiny petals off the centerpiece marigold, chirped curiously.

A heavy sense of dread descended over Tamara.

"I thought you girls knew that from the get-go." The elder witch heaved another deep sigh. She seemed to sag, looking far older than her usually cheerful countenance belied. "I'm sorry I had to be the bearer of bad news."

Madeline sat, back ramrod straight, in the wooden chair. Her hands clenched tightly in the napkin in her lap. "How long?" she whispered.

"What's that, honey?"

"How long do we have until being bound to me won't be enough to keep him—won't be enough?"

"Now that I couldn't tell you. But if being bound to you brought him back perfectly whole and healthy from the brink of dust, he has to be getting at least some sustenance from your energy. I'm willing to bet you've still got a good while. Maybe even a couple years. The ones in the cage look perky as ever, and the ones still on the loose have enough magic left to deadlift a hundred fifty pounds, so you're not in the danger zone yet."

"I see." The cat offered a short nod. Her ears angled backward. The tip of her tail twitched erratically, stirring what few specks of dirt and woodland flotsam on the floor that had managed to make it past the mudroom. "Thank you."

"No need to thank me for ruining your day," Peg assured dryly, rising stiffly to her feet.

"No, I really do mean it. Thank you for your insight. I'd rather know this now than be caught unawares by it later."

"That's a good attitude, honey. I don't care for being blind-sided myself." Peg waddled to the sink to deposit her empty cup.

Tamara drifted numbly aside to let her pass.

"Well, I think I've done about as much damage as I can." The hedgehog wiped her damp hands on the hem of her sweater. "Maddie, honey, thank you for breakfast. Keep your chin up. Things will turn out. Tammy, if you need my help, you give me a holler. I know you think you always have to go it alone for some reason, but I mean it."

The coyote swallowed the sudden lump in her throat. "Thanks, Auntie."

Peg showed herself to the door.

As the comforting feel of the older witch's magic faded away with her retreat, the practical station wagon rolling off down the forested drive, Tamara slunk back to the table. She dropped heavily into her seat. Her face dropped just as heavily into her hands.

"I'm sorry."

Madeline finally lost some of her rigidity, leaning forward to cross her arms on the tabletop. She stared at the pixie in his small mound of yellow petals, refusing to meet Tamara's eye. "You have no reason to apologize. You're not to blame for anything."

"I thought the binding spell was a permanent fix. I should have read it all the way through, first. Researched it more."

"If you'd have done that, he would have died in my hands. I hardly think that would have been the better of the two outcomes."

"He would've died, and you would've been sad, but only for a little while because then he was just a pixie. Now he's going to die anyway and you're going to hurt like you've never hurt before because now he's Ravel, and you love him."

"Nonsense. He is not going to die."

The coyote rubbed her face one last time and looked up. "Uh..."

"He is not going to die," Madeline told her matter-of-factly, "because you are going to send him back where he belongs. You told me yourself you can undo the binding spell. Do that, and then send him back to the fae realm with the other pixies."

Ravel shook off a flurry of petals and took wing, fluttering around the cat with a series of concerned squeaks.

"Are you sure?" Tamara asked softly. "Peg said you might even have a few years. That's better than nothing."

"Of course I'm sure. It's the only option, really." Madeline's whiskers finally trembled. Tears beaded at the corners of her eyes. "It would be terribly selfish to keep him. If he goes b-back, he'll have a good life. Even if it's not w-with m-m-me—!" Her face crumpled, voice breaking on a ragged whine. The tears spilled.

Tamara reached out helplessly as the ginger surged to her feet, nearly knocking the chair backward in her haste to leave the table. "Maddie, wait!"

Madeline dodged her hand and fled the kitchen, openly sobbing. The fluff of her tail disappeared into the den and around the corner, closely followed by a very worried pixie. A door slammed down the hallway.

Tamara sat alone in the kitchen.

She sat for a long time. There were no sunbeams to read for most of the day inside the cabin; a clock on the wall kept time with measured, accusing ticks. Every so often, her ears would twitch at a small, pitiful sound from across the house, but eventually even those fell quiet.

At last, finding no solace in inaction, the coyote slowly got up and began to wash what was left of the breakfast dishes.

Way to go, Ridgemount. She squirted an overlarge ribbon of soap into the egg-encrusted skillet. *This has to be the worst thing you've ever done. To the sweetest person you've ever met. Some way to help your damsel in distress.*

She attacked the skillet with vigor.

An hour after Auntie Peg's departure, Tamara had had enough. Armed with a glass of ice water and a box of tissues, she stared down the closed door of her own bedroom.

Part of her still wanted to avoid confrontation like a particularly nasty slime mold. A larger part, however, insisted that she try to offer the other girl some kind of comfort. Madeline hadn't tried to actually run away, after all. It was at least possible that she didn't really want to be alone.

She knocked softly. "Maddie, you okay? Can I come in?"

The silence stretched. Just when Tamara had begun to convince herself that the cat had run through the bedroom door accidentally while trying to flee the cabin and had fixed her mistake by escaping through the window instead, a small cough caught her attention.

"… yes." It was a very meek affirmation, but permission nonetheless.

Relieved, the coyote opened the door and poked her head in.

Madeline had taken refuge on Tamara's bed. She lay curled on her side atop the shabby, faded comforter, cheek pillowed on one arm. Ravel cuddled into her outstretched hand, peeping sadly at his mistress's distress. Tightly clutched in her free arm was Tamara's teddy bear.

"Hey. I brought you some water."

Madeline sat up slowly. Her perfect hair stuck up at odd angles and tangled over her shoulder. Her mascara had run. "Thank you."

"Feeling any better?" Tamara set the tissue box on the bedside table and sat awkwardly on the edge of the bed.

Ravel squeaked crossly at her closeness, clinging to the cat's wrist as she reached for the offered glass.

Green eyes, reddened from crying, wouldn't meet the witch's black stare as Madeline sipped at the cool water. "Not really, no. Now I just feel sad *and* ridiculous. I'm sorry I barged into your bedroom without permission. It was childish."

"You just got some really bad news." Tamara shrugged uncomfortably. She had very little practice in the consolation department. "Don't worry about it."

"I do worry about it. I am a blubbering disaster. I bungled up your ward and let all the pixies free—"

"We established that was an accident."

"—and made all this work for you, and then I forced my company on you, thinking I could help fix things somehow, but all I've done is make things more complicated." She tugged anxiously at the teddy bear's ear with her free hand, her own ears down, whiskers beginning their tell-tale quiver.

"Okay, whoa. I forbid you to cry again." Tamara crossed her hands in a firm time-out call. "We already tried crying and it didn't do any good." Grabbing the tissues, she waved the box. "Here."

Madeline took one and valiantly dabbed at her eyes. She blew her nose. "It did a good job of giving me a headache."

"Yeah, I bet it did." The coyote took the empty glass back and stood determinedly. "Hold on, I'll mix you some herbs for that."

"Yick! No."

Ravel launched himself airborne with a startled chirp as the cat flopped face down into the pillow. The resultant rush of air buoyed him upward, rustling several pieces of paper taped to the wall the bed abutted.

"Does it really taste that bad?"

"Loathsome," Madeline confirmed, slightly muffled in the pillow.

Tamara had to smile. She sat back down, the mattress squeaking slightly under her weight. She reached over and absently rubbed her finger over the loosened tape keeping a page of notebook paper stuck to the wall. A splotchy watercolor rendering of a small coyote, apparently riding on the back of a giant alligator, smiled back at her, but her attention was focused on something else.

It was a head trip, seeing someone other than herself lying across her bed. Under less serious circumstances, she might admire the sight. The copper cascade of the other girl's hair over her shoulders and the pillow. The graceful dip in the small of her back. The smooth, perky swell of her denim-covered rump—

Well, maybe she could admire, anyway. Certainly not act upon, but admire. In an entirely innocent and non-perverted way.

Tamara balled her hands into fists and placed them firmly in her lap. "Okay, no herbs. But only if you promise to cheer up." She took a deep breath. "We still have time. We can research. I'll ask around. If there's anything I can do to keep him with you without poofing, anything at all, I'll do it. I promise."

Madeline slowly left the safety of the pillow to sit upright once more. With all the suddenness of a Venus flytrap, she threw her arms around Tamara. The witch sucked in a sharp breath as the cat's warm, soft form slumped heavily against her. Her arms rose reflexively to wrap around the other girl's waist, supporting Madeline as she draped herself into the hug.

"I know you will," the ginger said into Tamara's shoulder. "I'll never be able to say thank you enough."

Tamara swallowed. "Just once is fine."

Having now been thrice embraced by the hug-prone feline, she was slightly more prepared this time. Rather than freezing up, she tried to relax into the contact. Hugs were comforting. Madeline needed comfort. Ergo, she would return the gesture without being an awkward frog about it.

The moment stretched.

Tamara breathed, the subtle scent of lavender and tea invading her senses with every inhale. Tiny prickles at her lower back raised the fur along her spine. "...are you kneading me?"

"Mm-hmm," Madeline purred, contentedly nuzzling her cheek against the coyote's shoulder. Her fingertips tightened and released, tightened and released in time with the gentle purrs.

Tamara had the sudden feeling that she might be sick. She shut her eyes, silently cursing every butterfly erupting in her stomach at the universally understood feline gesture of comfort and trust. "You're ridiculous." She hugged the cat a little tighter.

Miniscule hands landed on her chin and shoved. The witch's eyes snapped open. Ravel chattered angrily. Feet planted between Madeline's ears, he used the leverage to push Tamara's head away with all his tiny might.

Madeline reached up, snagging the pixie off her head. "Ravel, no! Tammy—*Tamara* is our friend. We do not push," she scolded, pulling out of Tamara's arms.

Ravel puffed as well as he was able. Arms hanging over her fingers, he made firm shooing motions. "Go! Go!"

Tamara stuck her tongue out at him. *Buzzy little meddler.*

He blew a raspberry at her.

"We should be going," Madeline declared loudly, covering her pixie firmly with her free hand as she slipped off the bed. "I'm sure I look a disgrace. I'll have to freshen up at home before my shoot."

"Another family portrait?" Tamara followed the cat out of her bedroom. The smell of her perfume lingered.

"Thank heavens, no. Senior pictures. I'm to meet the family when school lets out this afternoon." Madeline packed up her picnic basket with quick efficiency. "Meadow voles. Their son is on the swim team, so they wanted photos at the pool before it gets any cooler. Good thing; I always get busy with outdoor shoots as soon as the leaves start changing."

Tamara hummed in agreement, but her thoughts were now elsewhere.

Outside, the edges of the oak tree's leaves were beginning to brown. The ever-present energy it exuded, as constant to her as the beating of her own heart, had begun to dim almost imperceptibly in response to the slow waning of sunlit hours.

The equinox was two days off. A better chance to catch the remaining pixies and banish them back to the fae realm likely wouldn't present itself until Samhain—a dangerous time to be meddling with the boundaries of the worlds. Despite everything, they would have to press on.

Don't let the spells you can't cast stop you from casting the ones you can, she thought firmly, and mentally rolled up her sleeves.

CHAPTER TWELVE

"Cages."

"Check."

"Cage covers."

"Double check."

"Net, squirt guns, pillowcase."

"All check." Madeline gave a resolute thumbs up from the passenger seat.

Around the old truck, fairgoers swarmed. Across the dusty dirt and gravel parking lot, a banner proclaiming 'Fall into Autumn!' stretched grandly over the entrance to the county fairgrounds.

"Okay. I cast a concealment charm on the bug net, so no one should notice we're carrying one around for no reason. And if things get hairy, put these on." From the pocket of her jacket, Tamara pulled a pair of embroidered fabric wristbands. "I stitched a memory spell into them. If people look away from you while you're wearing them, they'll lose their short-term memory. Ellie can vouch."

"My very own magical items!" Madeline accepted the pastel bands reverently. "Weren't these all the rage in junior high?"

"Don't put them in the washer. The spell runes will come apart." Tamara watched unobtrusively from the corner of her eye, pretending to check the water level in her iron-laced squirt gun as the cat slipped the wristbands on and off, holding her hand against the fabric of her sweater to judge color and contrast.

She hadn't seen or heard from Madeline in two days. The witch had been careful to give her space after the bad news about the eventual fate of her pixie but was relieved to see that the other girl seemed to be back to her normal self. As normal as a fae-touched feline could ever be, anyway.

Tamara checked the breast pocket of her jacket for her own wristbands. "Ready to do this?"

The ginger's whiskers stiffened with determination. "Ready."

Ravel squeaked a war cry from a large exterior pocket of her current purse.

Leaving the truck with the carefully covered birdcages in the bed, they joined the crowd converging on the fairgrounds. The smells of fried food, kettle corn, and apples wafted temptingly. The sun, sinking slowly below the tree line, cast a pink and orange glow onto the undersides of clouds that had already lost the cotton ball billows of summertime.

"You seem a bit on edge," Madeline ventured timidly. "Is everything alright?"

Tamara plunged her hands deeper into the pockets of her jacket, choosing to blame the cool breeze rather than the antsy twitch in the tips of her fingers. "Yeah, I'm fine. Totally fine. It's just…"

"Just what?"

"Autumn makes me restless under normal circumstances. And this is sunset on the equinox. There's a lot of Power swirling around right now." The witch could feel it heavy in the air; energies strung wire-tight, ready and eager to act, to enable, to coalesce. A vague uneasiness crawled up and down her spine.

"I can't shake this feeling I should be back home." Someone shoulder-checked her, muttered an apology, and was gone into the throng before she could so much as give them the evil eye. Her ears angled back. "And I don't really like crowds all that much."

To her surprise, Madeline stepped closer and looped a firm arm through the coyote's own. "Well, of course you don't. You live by yourself in the woods. This must be quite overwhelming." A gentle hand patted her forearm reassuringly. "Don't worry. I'll stick right beside you. With any luck, we'll catch those pixies and be on our way in two shakes of a lamb's tail."

Tamara's flagging ears flushed hotly as the scent of junk food was overpowered by the far more enticing scent of floral soap and perfume—the same sweet smell that had lingered on her pillows after the cat's grief-fueled invasion of her bedroom two days ago. If the prim girl had any inkling as to the kind of dreams Tamara's subconscious had churned out that night, the witch highly doubted she would be walking so close. She swallowed. "Y-yeah. I hope so."

"Can you feel if any are nearby?"

Tamara concentrated, sending wary magical feelers out into the crowd. She winced. "I can feel them, but I can also feel hundreds of people and a pissed-off flock of starlings that can't forage on the midway because of all the people."

"So you can't pinpoint where the pixies are, exactly?"

"Right."

"Well, we'll just have to do things the old-fashioned way," Madeline decided pragmatically. "Let's look around and see if we notice anything strange. I know; we should drop by the face painting booth. Ellie can almost see them—maybe she's noticed something odd."

They rounded the corner of an exhibition hall, heading for the lines of game stalls. Tamara ran straight into a shark.

"Oof!" The shark staggered back with a compression of

plush stuffing. A white-tipped red tail flicked irritably from behind it. "Hey, watch where you're going!"

A young fox jogged around the corner. "Will you just let me carry that? You can't even see." His ears popped up in surprise as he caught sight of the coyote and cat. "Oh. Um, hello."

"Kory! So lovely to see you again." Madeline smiled warmly, no trace of her ire from the week before remaining. Ravel chirped a greeting from her purse pocket.

"Who is it?" the shark demanded.

Tamara reached out with a sigh and pulled the nose of the giant plushie out of the way. "Hi, Kari."

Finally able to see who she had walked into, the vixen behind it gasped happily. "*Majo onee-san!*"

The witch blinked. "Uh… what?"

"We had a test in Japanese class today," Kory volunteered helpfully.

Tamara shook her head with a sigh. Something told her she didn't want to know what Kari had said. "Never mind. Nice seeing you. Have fun, stay out of trouble, bye-bye now."

"Wait! Are you here to find the pixie?"

That got her attention. "You saw one? Here, tonight?"

Kory nodded attentively. "Yeah! Well, I felt it first, then Kari saw it. Back in the game booths."

"Aww, leave it alone," Kari whined with a frown. "It's not doing anything bad. It helped me win Sharkey."

Tamara's eyebrow ring quirked skeptically. "That I need to see to believe. Show us."

Kory helpfully led the way, bobbing in and out of the crowd. Without thinking, Tamara grabbed Madeline's hand and took off in pursuit, following the bright red beacon of the young fox's hoodie. Kari brought up the rear, waddling as speedily as she could while encumbered with her prize.

As they approached the booth, a maned wolf with a tall mohawk glanced up at the kits.

"Back for more, huh?" he asked, sounding highly irritated. "Well, sorry to ruin your fun, but I'm officially out of prizes." He stood on tiptoe, deftly looping a 'closed' sign over a peg under the colorful canvas awning where rows of stuffed animals should have hung.

Madeline looked up at the empty pegs. Her purse buzzed with interest. "So early in the evening?"

"It's the damnedest—sorry, darnedest thing I've ever seen. About ten minutes ago, all of a sudden, every single ball somebody threw went right in the grand prize cup!"

Tamara looked the game booth over. The wooden outer walls ringed a low, wide table in the center of the area, with just enough room between them for the barker to walk unhindered. The entire surface of the table was covered with what looked like glass dessert cups. The vast majority of the cups were clear, but scattered among them was the occasional red or blue cup, which she guessed must have determined a win for the smaller prizes. Directly in the center of the table, a lone green cup stood. Ping-pong balls were everywhere.

The wolf ran a harried hand through his mohawk. "I mean, it's not rigged or anything, but it's supposed to be really hard to get the grand prizes. When you aim straight, the balls bounce off the rims of the cups and land wherever. You gotta get a clear arc right down in the middle—or just get real lucky and have it randomly bounce in." His muzzle crinkled sourly, one fang poking out. "Boss is probably gonna fire me for this."

Madeline's ears fell. "Oh, dear."

Mind made up, Tamara stood a little straighter. "I don't see why your boss would fire you for a mistake that they made setting up your booth."

"Huh?" Sudden hope shone in the barker's eyes. "What mistake?"

"Well, clearly this game is set up directly in the middle of a wind tunnel created by these other booths over here," the coyote began in her best government official voice, gesturing vaguely with the hand not tracing signs behind her back. "Ping-pong balls are so light that even a weak breeze can move them once they're in the air. When the wind picked up a little while ago, it must have created the perfect conditions for a micro-vortex—pulled all the balls to the center of the booth. Right over the good cup."

The maned wolf clapped a hand to his forehead with a relieved laugh. "Well, duh! Oh man, I can't believe I didn't realize that. I should've just shut down until the wind died."

Behind them, the fox twins looked on in awe.

"It's not your fault," Madeline reassured kindly, gently blocking her purse pocket with one hand. Ravel released an antsy squeak. "You know those micro-vortices can be nearly unnoticeable."

"Yeah, guess so. I'll just have to tell the boss they gotta place the booths better next year." Mood much improved, the wolf swung himself over the wooden wall. "Well, anyway, sorry you ladies missed out on the windfall. Ha! Get it? Wind fall?"

Tamara subtly adjusted the bug net under her arm and forced a rather strained smile. "We get it. And no problem. We'll play some other games. Have a good evening."

The barker walked off with a backward wave, still chuckling at his own joke. The merriment of the fair swirled around the little group by the empty booth.

Kari peered out from behind her shark. Her large, doe-like eyes, shimmering silver in the twinkling lights, blinked innocently. "That guy's a real moron."

"No, this woman is a real witch," her brother corrected exasperatedly, waving a hand at Tamara. "How did you not feel that —that—thing that she just did while she was talking?"

"That 'thing' is magic," Tamara pointed out. She couldn't contain a small, rather proud wag. "But, anyway. Pixie. Being helpful and slam dunking balls into the prize cup for people out of the goodness of its glittery little heart. I don't buy it."

"Is it really so hard to imagine?" Madeline pouted.

"Yes. Was the barker getting upset?"

Kari grinned. "He was totally losing his mind."

"I rest my case."

Madeline stuck out her tongue at the coyote. With a snort of amusement, Tamara stuck her tongue out right back. Unable to keep up the grumpy charade, the ginger dissolved into giggles. Tamara's stomach flip-flopped like a half-stunned fish at the sound.

Kory's tail began to wag gently.

"Whether it was helping or not, it's gone now, I guess. But we'll find it!" Kari tucked her shark under her arm determinedly. "Just let me put this in the car first. And grab an elephant ear. Those things smell amazing."

"I don't know if you two 'helping' is a good idea," Tamara began warily.

Madeline put a cautionary hand on her arm. "Surely four hunters would be better than two? This is a fairly big place, if you'll pardon the pun."

Perfectly synchronized, the twins put on what was obviously their best begging faces—lower lips aquiver, eyelashes aflutter, velvety black ears back, hands clasped pleadingly.

Tamara sighed. "Like I'm going to win three against one. Okay. We'll meet up under the light pole by the 4-H barn in fifteen minutes. And I mean fifteen minutes! We don't have time to fool around." Her stomach growled loudly. "But we should get something to eat, so Maddie can keep her strength up."

"Oh my, how thoughtful," Madeline laughed, looping her arm back around the blushing coyote's elbow. "Lead away."

As luck would have it, a picnic table near the designated light was being vacated by a family of bobcats as the motley pack of pixie hunters approached. Kory ran ahead and flung himself across the empty tabletop, brushy tail waving triumphantly. "Claimed!"

"Well done." Madeline patted him fondly between the ears.

The twins had apparently eaten dinner before coming to the fair. Kory volunteered to stand guard over their seats and wait for Kari while the cat and coyote collected what they wanted from a flock of nearby food trucks.

Tamara was first back to the table. She unloaded a paper sack full of French fries, condiment packets, and two corndogs nestled into a cardboard boat. Squeezing mustard onto a napkin, she scanned the masses for a hint of ginger. Finally, she spied a splash of pink sweater at the tenderloin truck and relaxed, taking a large bite.

Elbows propped on the table, chin in his hands, Kory smiled guilelessly. "How long have you two been going out?"

Chunks of hot dog and cornmeal spewed across the table as Tamara hacked and coughed. "Wha—*what?*"

The fox leaned away from the mustard-scented detritus, ears back in concern. "Are you okay?"

"We're not dating," Tamara sputtered, thumping herself in the chest with a fist. "We just met two weeks ago!"

Kory's ears fell in confusion. "You're not? You're always together, though."

"We're on a time-sensitive mission. We have to be together a lot."

He looked almost hurt. "But… I can feel…"

The witch's eyes widened in panic. She had all but forgotten that while Kari could See magic and the fae, Kory could apparently Feel it instead. If that extended to the emotional energy of others… "What can you feel?" she demanded, more sharply than she'd intended.

Chastened, his ears flattened further. His tail wrapped defensively over his lap. His gray eyes wouldn't meet hers. "Nothing. Forget I said anything."

Clearly this kit was more sensitive than his sister. Tamara wondered how often being able to sense what others couldn't sense—or possibly what others wouldn't acknowledge—had gotten him into social trouble. Being a teenager was hard enough when you only had your own set of emotions to contend with.

"Hey. Look. I'm sorry, okay?" She looked furtively around the table for any sign that Madeline had returned from the land of the tenderloin. "I just—I like her, okay? But I haven't told her. So you're not wrong."

Kory seemed to uncurl slightly, his ears slowly lifting. "Why haven't you told her?"

"Because she has no interest in other women and I want her to continue to come around me for as long as she can stand my weirdness. So this silly crush is a secret. A secret that you don't utter to anyone, not even that crazy, boobular shadow of yours, got it?"

His whiskers jumped with a startled yap of laughter. "Okay, I get it. But you should really tell Maddie. She—"

Kari pounced him from behind. "I'm baaack! Look, the elephant ear guy gave us extra cinnamon sugar!"

"Ack," Kory managed around the arm lovingly wrapped around his neck.

Madeline returned a minute later. She bore a lemon shakeup, an apple fritter, and a breaded tenderloin so massive it dwarfed the bun it was served on. She also bore news. "There was a pixie at the apple fritter stall. It dropped the owner's keys into the deep fryer. She thought they just slipped out of her pocket."

"There was one messing with the dart game, too," Kari mumbled around a mouthful of sugary dough. "A little dude threw a dart at the wall and like thirty balloons exploded at the same time."

"How did they explain that one?" Kory asked.

A sticky paw wiped her muzzle. "Shockwaves."

Tamara rubbed her eyebrow ring despairingly. "Sometimes I wonder why I even bother casting perception charms on the people in this town."

Madeline munched worriedly at her tenderloin. She had a small spot of ketchup on her nose that Tamara dared not point out. "How are we ever going to catch them with so many people around? They're so quick."

High above their table, the light on the post flickered to life. Twilight was descending. The warm lights and music of the fair seemed more welcoming than ever.

"Could we lure them all to the same place somehow?" Kory wondered.

Tamara opened her mouth to answer just as a speaker under the light above them crackled loudly.

"Just a reminder, ladies and gentlemen: the Indomitable Derby Dames, our very own mistresses of the rink, will be putting on quite the show in thirty minutes in exhibition hall B. Glow sticks and necklaces will be for sale during tonight's Black Light Extravaganza, with all proceeds going directly toward team travel expenses for upcoming away meets. Be sure to come lend our lovely ladies your support!"

"Ooh, black light roller derby!" Kari wagged delightedly as the announcer repeated the message. "That's so cool. Man, I wish you didn't have to be eighteen to join the team. I'd be so good at that."

"You can barely skate," her brother teased with a grin.

She crossed her arms with an aggravated huff. "You don't have to be a good skater to fall into somebody and take them out!"

Madeline's mouth was frozen open around her apple fritter.

Bottle green eyes met inky black ones over the foxes' pestering. "Do you think…?"

"Oh, I think." Tamara's brows furrowed in resolve. "It'll be dark. It'll be loud. It'll be fast. Perfect cover." There was only one problem. "But there's no way we can guarantee the pixies will go into the barn in the first place with so much else going on to distract them."

"Leave that to me." Madeline hoisted her purse from the bench next to her onto the tabletop. "Rav!" Her pixie hovered into view immediately with a quizzical chirp. "Mummy has a plan and I need your help, alright?"

Tamara watched, mystified. The twins, finally noticing something afoot, paused their banter to pay attention.

Ravel rose out of the bag with an excited shriek and a faint sparkle in the gathering dusk. He hovered over the picnic table, casting the cat's features in soft golden light. "Mum!"

"Good boy. Now listen. Do you see that big building right there? The one with all the people going inside?" She pointed across the way to where spectators were already trickling into the exhibition hall. "I want you to fly around the fair and tell all the other pixies that you see to come to that building. Something very exciting is going to happen inside it. There's going to be a race, and things will glow, and everyone will shout and clap! Doesn't that sound like fun?" Beside himself with glee, the pixie shot several times around the table, chattering maniacally. "And when it's done, Tamara and I will bring all the other pixies home with us so they won't get hurt and go poof. Alright?"

"Ye." The tiny fae nodded enthusiastically.

"Good. Make sure they all get there by the time the big lights inside the building go out." Madeline took a deep breath and pointed firmly out at the fair. "Off you go!"

A stack of paper napkins scattered across the tabletop like blowing leaves as Ravel zoomed away. He skimmed the top of the corndog truck, banked around a giant cluster of pumpkin-shaped balloons tied to a helium cart, and was lost to sight.

For a long moment, the background hum of the fair was the only sound at the table.

"I want a pet pixie," Kari announced suddenly. "Hey, when you catch some more, can I—"

"Not on your life." Tamara crammed the last of the corndog into her mouth. The fries would have to be sacrificed. "Alright. We've got twenty-nine minutes to come up with the second half of this plan."

Madeline whipped out her phone and began to text madly. "I'll tell Ellie we're on our way over. She'll have left the face painting by now to get her gear on."

The remaining food was devoured. Madeline chugged her lemon shakeup like a champ. The party struck out with new purpose toward the exhibition hall, the coyote taking the lead.

Kory strode beside her, swinging the butterfly net thoughtfully. "It seems like you could only catch one at a time with this. How many pixies are there?"

"Three or four dozen. Approximately. If they're all here at the fairgrounds and Ravel manages to get them all in the barn at the same time." There were still too many conflicting energies banging around for her to get a bead on just how many were near, but the background buzz that gave away the faes' presence made her confident that most of the remaining uncaught pixies were, at least, close by.

"Oh." The fox's ears fell. "Then how are you going to catch them all?"

"First, I need to see what I'm dealing with inside. Then we plan."

They joined the crowd filing into the large building. Already, there had to have been at least two hundred people gathered inside, Tamara realized uneasily as they passed through the giant barn doors standing wide at one end of the structure.

Whatever magic she ultimately had to use would have to be cast under cover of darkness or she would also have to alter the memories of a good portion of the townsfolk.

"Look at all the glow sticks!" Kari looked eagerly at the table where they were being sold. She tugged at the end of her twin's tail. "Hey, how much money do you have left?"

"What happened to your money?" he demanded.

"I played some games and bought an elephant ear—an elephant ear that I shared with you, if you remember."

The boy rolled his eyes. "Okay. Let's get some glow sticks."

As the foxes scrambled off, Madeline led the way into the lee of a stand of bleachers. Several rows of them stood on either side of the makeshift oval track that had been marked off with white tape in the middle of the hall's concrete floor. In the rafters overhead, a rat technician climbed nimbly, adjusting black lights that had been temporarily installed for the event. A giant LED strobe light with multicolored lenses hung from a bracket above the center of the track.

"What do you think?" the cat asked loudly, tail swishing in concern. "It's awfully crowded, isn't it?" The din of excited chatter, shrieking young ones, and general merriment echoed.

Tamara's ears flattened. "Just a little."

"Are you going to be able to cast any spells without someone noticing?"

"Well, if something weird happens in the dark, surrounded by glowing stuff and spinning lights, and it's so loud you can't hear yourself think, everybody's perception of reality is going to be altered. So I might be able to get away with it."

Madeline's whiskers perked hopefully. "Maybe everyone will think it's special effects."

"Right. So if Ravel can lure them all in here—" Something bony collided with Tamara's back. She turned and came eyeball to eyeball with a snake. Shocked, she met its unblinking black gaze with her own. A forked tongue darted out to caress the tip of her nose.

Then a small, withered hand covered its smooth head. "Don't stare, Nathair. Gives folks the creepy crawlies."

Tamara shook herself, looking past the harmless rat snake. Its long, smooth form was half in and half out of the collar of an eye-searing fluorescent yellow rain jacket. Inside the jacket was a red squirrel. "Auntie Gorse!"

The old witch cocked her head. She blinked rapidly, like a slide projector searching for the right image. "Oh, hello there, Tabby. Good Mabon to you."

"Good Mabon, Auntie," Tamara replied automatically. So unexpected was the other witch's presence that correcting the case of mistaken identity didn't even occur to her.

Madeline nodded politely, if a bit stiffly. The snake followed the motion. "Good evening. So very nice to see you again."

Auntie Gorse held a candied apple. Watching the girls with one eye and the apple with the other, she took a large bite. Prominent front teeth sank into the red coating. Somehow, she managed to speak with moderate coherency through the resultant munching. "Nice night for a fair, isn't it? Should be a pretty autumn."

It was odd that an older witch wouldn't be home at their Holding whipping up a spell that needed the extra magical oomph that the equinox provided, or celebrating the night with other members of the coven. Tamara, however, who was doing neither of those things herself, withheld judgment.

The snake had come almost entirely out from the hood. It draped itself around its witch's neck, seeming totally at ease with the chaotic surroundings.

"Have you met Nathair?" Auntie Gorse asked, lifting a shoulder to shift her familiar. "I don't reckon he was with me last time we got together. He'd ate a bullfrog so big, this is the first he's moved around in ages."

Madeline leaned a bit closer. "He's lovely. His scales have such a shine." She looked up at the squirrel. "Nathair—is that Gaelic?"

"It is." Auntie Gorse looked pleased around the remnants of her apple. A sugary chunk clung to the end of one bent whisker. "You know that tongue?"

"I can't speak it, but I can recognize it when I hear it. My family emigrated from England when I was in primary school."

"Still have that pretty accent, don't you?" The squirrel tucked the stick and apple core into the pocket of her raincoat. "I was born in Ireland, you know."

Tamara's tail wagged with curiosity despite herself. "Really? I didn't know that."

"I sure was."

"You must have been very young when you came over," the cat observed. "You sound just like a local. Not that that's in any way a bad thing, of course!"

"It was a long time ago, child. A long time ago. Time just seems to melt into itself when you reach a certain age." Auntie Gorse's tail flicked, a wild twitch that didn't seem to be completely under her control. The snake bobbed on her shoulder. "You know, there aren't any snakes in Ireland. No snakes at all. Too cold." She chucked the reptile fondly under the chin. "Of course, legend says there used to be snakes before old Saint Patrick drove them all out. Snakes and witches aren't all that different, seems like."

"*Attention, ladies and gentlemen,*" the loudspeakers suddenly boomed. "*The show will start in ten minutes! Make sure to grab your glow sticks and find your seats before lights out!*"

The squirrel glanced up, tufted ears wiggling madly. "Well, that's my cue. See you later, youngsters."

"You're not here to watch the derby?" Madeline asked, surprised.

"No, I was only cutting through. Need to get home before

the moon gets into position. Got something big in the works."
Auntie Gorse gave Tamara a pronounced wink. Her open eye
scanned the rafters. "You never know what might happen on
Mabon."

Without waiting for a response, the old witch shuffled off
toward the exit. The snake familiar had disappeared back into
her coat.

Madeline gazed after her, green eyes wide with wonder.
"She seems remarkably less…"

"Nuts than she did last time?" Tamara suggested helpfully.

"I was going to say less confused. Less scattered, more
focused. More in touch with reality."

The coyote couldn't help but agree. It was almost like they'd
met a different person at Peg's house the week before. "It's
weird."

Madeline shrugged. "Well, you know how it is with the
elderly. Some days are better than others in the mental department. Perhaps she's having a good one."

Unfortunately, at the moment they had larger worries than
the eccentric squirrel.

Kory and Kari slipped out of the crowd. Kory's tail was
ringed with a series of pink, orange, and yellow glow necklaces.
Kari was covered in the things, around her tail and neck and
wrists in such a manner that she could probably be pointed out
from the International Space Station.

"We brought you one," the vixen chirped, snapping the centers
of a blue and a purple tube. Without asking, she fastened the ends
together and looped the finished blue necklace around Tamara's
left ear. "Sorry, 'black and brooding' wasn't a color choice."

Tamara pinched the bridge of her nose, hard. The blue necklace glowed in her upper peripherals as Madeline was likewise
lassoed with its purple twin. *They're only sixteen. They're only
sixteen. You were still learning priorities at sixteen.*

She'd also had more incentive to learn those priorities quickly.

Aloud, the witch cleared her throat. "Uh, thanks. That's thoughtful. But if you're really going to help us, try to focus. We have ten minutes to figure out how to trap a hypothetical swarm of pixies inside this building without getting the evening news involved."

Madeline, wearing her purple glow necklace like a coronet, suddenly stood on tiptoe and began to wave frantically. "Ellie! There's Ellie!"

Over the heads of the crowd, a gray-furred hand waved back.

"You made it!" the tabby cheered as Madeline, Tamara, and the twins squeezed their way to the edge of the track. "I was afraid you wouldn't come." She leaned over the portable aluminum gate segments separating the track from the bleachers and wrapped Madeline in a happy hug.

"Of course, I wouldn't miss it," Madeline assured with a breathless laugh, her cheek unintentionally rubbing Ellie's as she was squeezed. It came away smudged with the elaborate face paint the other girl wore. Each of the black stripes on her cheeks and the 'M' pattern half hidden by her bangs had been traced over with white paint, sure to glow impressively under the black lights.

"Hey, Choke-a-Cola!" A rabbit on roller skates, covered with more glowing accessories than even Kari, sped smoothly up to them. "Five minutes. Is your friend gonna take pics? The manager's okay with it."

Madeline looked back and forth bewilderedly. "Well, uh— that is—"

"Please, Maddie? Pretty please? I'm a jammer this time! Get one of me crossing the line." Ellie pointed to two lines tapped across the track. Between and above the lines stretched a huge cloth banner bearing the team logo, held up by jury-rigged flag-poles on either side.

The rabbit spun unconcernedly on her wheels, her neon green tutu flaring. "Could you take them from the middle over here? It would be cool to have the audience in the background with all their glowy stuff on."

Tamara looked up again at the banner, a few heads above the racers who would be speeding under it. An idea took root. "Can I come in with her?" the witch asked, stepping up close to Madeline. "I've never seen a roller derby before."

"Yeah, sure. Just get there quick!" The rabbit skated away toward where the rest of the team gathered near one of the starting lines.

Ellie followed, waving over her shoulder with a grin. "Get a good shot of me, Maddie. Not when I fall down, though—don't capture that for posterity. And thanks!"

As soon as they were out of earshot, Tamara turned to her posse. "Okay, I have a plan. We have zero minutes. Listen hard." She pointed to the flagpole on the bleacher side of the track. "You foxes: get to that pole and stay there. Maddie and me will be on the other side right across from you."

"Right," Kory nodded quickly. "Then what?"

The coyote pointed to Madeline. "She's going to make sure the pixies fly under that banner." She jerked a thumb at herself. "I'm going to make sure they get stuck in it. And you," she pointed firmly at the foxes, "are going to yank that rope holding this side of it up. We yank the rope on the other side, it all comes down, we wrap the little monsters up and make a run for it."

The ginger's whiskers stiffened in panic. "Wait, what?"

"Yeah! Good plan!" Kari bounced excitedly on the balls of her feet. "You can count on us."

Without further ado, the twins darted quickly away.

Plan in motion, Tamara acted. She grabbed Madeline's hand. "Let's go."

"But—but, wait!" Madeline mewled as the witch tugged her through a gap in the gates and across the track to the unoccupied middle of the tape ring. "I don't think this is going to work."

"Why not?"

"It's far too loud in here. Ravel would never hear me if I tried to tell him that everyone needs to fly that way."

"Remember how you summoned him out of the bank?"

The cat nodded slowly, making a show of pulling her camera out of her purse and testing the focus. The skaters who noticed immediately struck poses and began flashing peace signs.

"Do that, but instead of calling him to you, visualize the banner and tell him to go under it. I'm going to cast a Drawing spell—like a magic funnel web to pull all the pixies into it. When they're stuck, we pull the ropes and they're ours." Tamara's hand lingered on the aforementioned rope, held to the pole that supported that side of the banner with a series of simple loops around the cleat. It had most likely been rigged loosely to help the team set up and tear down quickly, but it would help her plan immensely.

Only a few yards across the track, the foxes reappeared. Better at weaseling than actual weasels, they squirmed through the crowd and were soon positioned against the barricades, within grabbing distance of the rope on their side. Kari caught sight of the coyote and gave an enthusiastic wave.

Then the lights went out.

CHAPTER THIRTEEN

There was a moment of deafening silence, then the crowd began to cheer. The black lights glowed to life as the LEDs started to flash and spin, spiraling colors across the floor. A dull, itchy thrum began to rise on the edge of Tamara's awareness.

The witch stilled. She closed her eyes, forcing her breathing to steady as she focused on the new stimulus. Slowly everything around her—the noise of the crowd, the echoing shouts of the announcer as the skaters began to roll, Madeline beside her peering anxiously around the barn through the cover of her camera—began to fade. A rush of fae magic rose up to take its place. Like an oncoming wave, it barreled toward her, swelling larger as it came.

Tamara opened her eyes with a gasp. The world popped back into focus, revealing a worried feline face.

"What's wrong?" Madeline shouted three inches from Tamara's nose, barely understandable through the ongoing din around them. Her whiskers blazed luminous white in the pallor of the black lights. The purple glow necklace diadem illuminated her eye shine, casting her fair countenance in an otherworldly light.

"Put your wristbands on!" Trusting that the other girl would do as she was bidden, Tamara ripped her own wristbands out of her pocket. Her fingers were weaving signs almost before the worn, familiar fabric settled against her fur. It would have been easier with a piece of chalk and a free space on the concrete to draw out the proper runes, but desperate times called for desperate measures. The patterns flew through the space between her hands, runes for drawing in and containing twining together and expanding like a Jacob's ladder only she could see.

From the edge of her vision, she caught the pack of skaters racing by, the breeze from their passing tickling the lock of hair that liked to flop across the side of her face when she forgot a bobby pin. They passed under the banner in a cluster to begin another circuit of the track.

A glowing, buzzing stream exploded into the barn. Pixies poured through the wide open doors, a cloud of them dozens strong. At the forefront zoomed a small, lone fae.

A loud chorus of oohs and aahs burst from the audience as the flock descended from the ceiling, the shower of sparks in their wake reflecting and refracting the ever-changing lights from above. The pixies dipped low over the track, following Ravel's lead as he honed in on a familiar figure—the curvy gray tabby stubbornly fighting her way through a crush of other skaters.

Tamara was seconds too late with the rune net. The last sign coalesced, completing the mat of magic just as the racers, closely followed by the pixies, passed under the banner.

Beside her Madeline wriggled with worry, camera clutched tight in both hands. "We missed them!"

"Tell him to bring them around again," the witch yelled, throwing her hands up as if she were tossing an overly large glob of pizza dough. Like a faintly glowing spider web, the net floated serenely upward and moored itself on the banner.

Across the track Kari gawked, pointing up at the banner and tugging her brother's arm. He nodded rapidly—being in on the magical conspiracy had no doubt opened his metaphorical eyes, even if he still couldn't See quite what his sister Saw—and grabbed for the rope, beginning to unwind it from the cleats.

Halfway around the track, the swarm was directly over the pack of skaters. Ellie seemed too focused on her mission to notice. With single-minded determination, she tried to squeeze past a sheep and the rabbit in the tutu.

Ravel dropped even with her ear.

The cat's head snapped to the side. The glowing pixie flew apace, inches from her whisker tips. Her eyes grew like waxing moons.

The flock of fae dropped in their leader's wake. Awareness seemed to strike the roller derby team all at once as the buzzing of dozens of tiny wings in their midst rose to a crescendo. General pandemonium erupted.

"*Hornets!*" the sheep shrieked, zigzagging in panic. "They're *huge!*"

A young pine marten covered her helmeted head frantically. "Oh my god, oh my god, I'm allergic to bees!"

The screams of the crowd swiftly morphed from cheers to exclamations of horror. Those standing began to run for the nearest exits. Those seated in the bleachers surged to their feet, some falling down the narrow aisles and stairs in their haste to descend to the ground. The skaters, trapped inside the rink by the temporary barriers, rolled pell-mell for the finish line and open ground beyond.

Ravel pulled away from Ellie. He swooped upward as they approached the banner once more, the other pixies hot on his tail.

Every fiber of her being tensed in determination, Tamara grabbed the rope—an instant before Tutu Rabbit careened into her broadside, arms and lop ears flailing as she was shoved off the side of the track. They fell to the concrete in a jumble of limbs and curses as the other skaters blitzed past, Tamara reeling from an elbow to the chest and a simultaneous knee to the gut.

"Please remain calm," the announcer beseeched shrilly, the sound system barely audible over the hysteria echoing to the rafters. *"Proceed to the exits in an orderly fashion! Please remain calm—!"*

On her back, the air knocked out of her, Tamara had a perfect view of the banner. Like comets strayed too close to a black hole's event horizon, the approaching pixies were pulled in, sticking to the rune net draped over it with little zaps like static cling. The flyers in the rear saw what was happening to those in front and tried to divert with a flurry of startled chirps, but momentum was not on their side. In a matter of seconds, the whole flock was affixed to the witch's trap.

Spewing panicked apologies, the rabbit clattered back up onto her wheels and rolled away. Tamara pushed herself painfully to her feet.

Squeezed tight against the gates, Kory and Kari withstood the flood of evacuating bodies. The far end of the banner fluttered as four foxy hands made quick work of untying it from the pole.

Madeline stood on tiptoe, camera bouncing wildly on the strap around her neck as she struggled with the rope Tamara had dropped. Before Tamara could move to help, the whole banner came down. It billowed out over the deserted finish line. The pixies, firmly stuck in their prison of witch magic and cheap fabric, squabbled in confused consternation as they parachuted down and landed safely on the floor.

"We got them!" Tamara wheezed happily, tail wagging even as she kept one hand over the general vicinity of her spleen.

Madeline bounced with glee beside her. "It really worked! I can't believe we really did it." Overcome by giddiness, she pounced into the witch's arms to deliver a crushing hug of triumph.

She'd already been tackled once that night, and much less pleasurably, so Tamara took it in stride. Without thinking, she hoisted the ginger off her feet and spun her around with a laugh, ignoring the twinge in her bruised side. "Who knew that little glitter bomb of yours could actually be helpful?"

Their celebration was short-lived.

"There's a police car outside," Kari yapped, squeezing through the barricade with Kory on her heels. "What should we do?"

Tamara's black eyes reflected the sudden flash of red and blue lights outside the open barn doors. Setting Madeline back on her feet, she assessed the situation with elegance and serenity. "Uh—well, shit. Okay. You kits get lost. Go out the back. If anyone stops you, you were hiding from the hornets in the bathroom."

Kory wavered, looking nervously between the girls and the angrily buzzing banner full of fae. "What about you?"

"Don't worry, we've got it covered. Go."

"You're welcome for the help," Kari sang. "See you tomorrow for our rewards!" Grabbing her brother by the hand, she tugged him toward the exit sign. In a moment their glow necklace-wreathed silhouettes had disappeared out the back door and bobbled quickly off into the gloom behind the big building.

Madeline dropped to her knees at one end of the crumpled banner. The rune net shimmered wildly in the still-spinning disco lights. "Sorry, sorry, loves," she soothed at the angry squeaks of the captives. "We'll have you out of there in no time at all. Tamara, help me fold this up—gently, we don't want to smother the poor things."

"You sure about that?" One eye on the police lights and the last of the building's occupants streaming out past them, Tamara collected the other end of the banner.

"Exceedingly sure. Oh, Rav!" The cat gently tugged the madly squeaking pixie from the net. "Don't worry, mummy's got you. It's all right." Her fae familiar free, she tucked him quickly into her bag and began to gather and fold expertly. "No, no, don't roll them up like a burrito; fold it like this, keep them all in the middle—"

In moments, the length of fabric had been gathered together and hung between them like a hammock. The pixies buzzed and chattered more amiably as they swung gently to and fro, muffled with a quick silencing charm. Charmed wristbands in place, the two hustled in tandem toward a small side door.

Outside, two security officers kept the crowd at bay. The police car seemed to be a golf cart with red and blue lights wired to the top.

A portly skunk with a metal trashcan lid held to his chest like a makeshift shield shouted through a megaphone. "All of the doors are being opened. When we confirm that the area has been cleared you will all be allowed back inside to gather your belongings. Anyone stung or injured during the evacuation, please proceed to the first aid tent."

His partner, a tall stag, scratched skeptically behind one antler. "Has anyone actually said they were stung?"

No one stepped up from the nervously milling crowd, though several did commence a limping journey toward the med tent.

"Excuse us," Madeline implored as they shuffled through the gawking onlookers.

"Excuse us, please. Everything is fine now. All of the, um, the *hornets* have gone."

The stag's eyes narrowed as they edged past the golf cart. He stared hard at Tamara. "Hey, don't I know you? You work for the DNR."

She kept her gaze studiously downward at the cloth she carried, willing the silencing charm to hold. "Yeah, that's right."

She raised her voice, a strange weight to her words. "Good thing it's going to be getting cold soon, isn't it? The first frost should kill all of these hornets off."

A murmur of relieved agreement rippled around the crowd.

The stag's walkie-talkie crackled to life. He grabbed it off his belt, breaking eye contact with Tamara. His posture relaxed instantly as he turned away to answer, facing the façade of the empty barn. "Ten-four. No serious injuries. No ongoing threat. Allowing civilians reentry at this time. Over."

"Walk faster," the witch hissed.

Madeline quickened her pace. "Do you know him?" she asked when they were safely out of earshot.

"No, but it seems like every time I have to take care of a situation that ends in somebody losing their memory, he's the guy on duty. The floating truck, the pygmy dragon forest fire, the hippocampus in the water tower—he makes everything more complicated."

"So he's your Inspector Zenigata?" Madeline giggled. "Foiling your perfectly executed jobs and being oblivious?"

"I... have no idea what that means."

"Ask the twins sometime. I'm sure they'll be happy to tell you all about it."

"Earth Mother forbid."

They were both giggling crazily by the time they jogged across the parking lot to the truck, the banner hammock swinging between them. The pixies inside seemed to have decided that they were on a ride rather than being taken captive and were cheering lustily with every particularly high bounce. For a brief, startling instant, Tamara felt genuinely glad that they had been caught before natural selection could doom them to glittery death. Madeline was obviously a terrible influence.

"Do you think they'll be alright back here?" the cat asked, peering into the truck bed.

Tamara lowered the tailgate one-handed. "They'll be fine.

The net should hold and they'll probably think it's fun. They think everything is fun."

Madeline beamed. "I know. Aren't they precious?"

"Let's just get them back to my place before anything has a chance to go wrong." The witch ruined her own warning by being unable to wipe the smile off her face.

———

They pulled out of the parking lot and joined the line of cars leaving the sights and sounds of the fair behind. Stars sparkled through the gaps in the clouds as Tamara steered them out of town and set a course for home. Success made her buoyant; happier than she had felt in months, and certainly the least stressed she had been since that night on the bridge when the whole misadventure had begun.

"Hey Ravel, is this all of them?"

On the floorboard between Madeline's feet, her purse rustled. The pixie popped out with a quizzical chirp.

"Are the pixies that flew with you into the building the only ones at the fair? Were there any that didn't follow you?"

He shook his head negatively, climbing out of the bag and buzzing up to alight on Madeline's knee. She stroked him adoringly.

"You did so well, love," she praised, petting between his ears with one fingertip. "I'm so proud of how well you listened. We couldn't have done it without you."

He preened contentedly at the praise.

In the darkness of the truck cab, Tamara took a deep breath. She was prickly as a chestnut by nature. Admitting what she was feeling, even to herself, was sometimes like pulling teeth. Still, she would be remiss if she didn't bully herself into it now. She let out the breath in a long exhale. "We couldn't have done it without you, either."

The cat's ears pricked, shifting the purple glow necklace she still wore around them. "Huh?"

"If you hadn't been there commanding him, there's no way I would have been able to pull that off by myself. Actually, I probably wouldn't have been able to catch a single one of them tonight." Tamara kept her eyes on the road, the broken dashes of the centerline catching the headlights and vanishing behind them one after another. "The other day you said… you told me that you were just making things worse by trying to help me. That's not true."

Madeline stared silently, mouth open in surprise, green eyes shining in the faint dashboard lights.

"What I'm trying to say is, thank you. You've been a huge help. So thanks for not letting me chase you off when I said I could do it all myself. I'm really glad you wouldn't take no for an answer."

A suspicious sniffle came from the passenger seat. Madeline dabbed at her watery eyes with a wristband. "I'm so glad I could help in some little way." She looked over, tiny fangs nipping at her lower lip. "W-would… would it be all right if I called you 'Tammy' from now on?"

"You know there's only one person on this green earth who calls me 'Tammy' now and gets away with it, right?"

Madeline's ears fell.

Tamara sighed. "Yeah, you can call me 'Tammy'."

The cat let out a little mew of happiness, wiggling in the embrace of her seatbelt as if trying to hold herself back from embracing Tamara on the spot and running them all off the road. "Thank you. I promise not to do it in front of people if you'd rather."

Tamara snorted. "In front of the coven, you call me 'Miss Witch.' Might make them take me more seriously by example."

"Oh my, do you think I'll have reason to meet your whole coven someday?"

"Well, you already know three of its members and haven't forgotten any of us yet. Hang around long enough and you're bound to meet everybody. There aren't all that many witches in these parts."

"So you'll still want me hanging about once we've caught all the pixies?" the ginger asked shyly.

"Well, yeah." Tamara did her level best to sound nonchalant. "Kind of seems like a waste if you didn't, you know? Someone like you who can see the fae, who's got natural immunity to some of our spells; I could teach you a lot. Not actual magic, but you'd probably be pretty good at divination."

"That sounds lovely." Madeline breathed a happy sigh.

They had reached the edge of the forest. A waxing moon, nearly full, glimmered through the trees. Stray leaves blew across the empty road, early heralds of the season now upon them.

"So, do you think we've caught all of the pixies now?" the cat asked. "How will we know for sure?"

"We can't, really," Tamara admitted as they approached the drive leading to Oakridge. "I'll just have to wait and see if anything else happens in town. But we definitely got most of them." She flipped on the turn signal. "It might actually be a good idea for me to send the ones we already have back to the fae realm tonight."

"Tonight?" Madeline squeaked in alarm.

"It's Mabon—the equinox—until sunrise. It would be a lot easier for me to open a pathway for them tonight, while there's excess Power flowing." She glanced over at Madeline, who had curled up small in the passenger seat and was holding her pixie tightly to her chest. "Just the wild ones tonight. If there are any left out there, we might need Ravel's help again."

"Yes, of course." The cat heaved a sigh of relief.

"I promised to try to find a way for you to keep him, remember? I have until he starts getting weaker to do it. Don't get ready to say goodbye yet."

The old truck pulled up to the cabin, headlights illuminating the tips of the longest, lowest hanging branches. The edges of the leaves had begun to tint. By the end of October, the tree would be a pillar of deep red visible to half the forest. Tamara reached up to touch the tip of one fondly as they climbed out of the truck.

"Let's get these little monsters in with the others for now. There's a lot of prep work in making a Pathway to the fae realm. I need to collect some things."

"I can stay and watch?" Madeline asked hopefully, managing to drop the tailgate on her own.

"Yes. As long as you promise not to touch anything. Or get too close. Or try to make a break for 'fairyland' or something."

"I will be on my very best behavior. Pinky promise."

They hauled the banner full of their sparkly spoils back to the pixiary. The little beasts definitely liked Madeline better, whether by virtue of her sweet demeanor or the lack of conflicting magical energy surrounding her. Whatever the reason, Tamara left her to add the arrivals to the group in the cage for what would be, hopefully, a very short stay.

The small fae were in high spirits, jittery and on edge.

"Some of you haven't gotten to stretch your wings in so long," Madeline fussed, locking the door of the coop behind her. "Not to worry; you'll all be flying free back where you belong before sun up." She shook her hands, the last traces of the dissolving rune net trailing from her fingertips like spider silk.

"They're just up in arms because of the equinox. They can feel the pull from the other side. Which is good—hopefully they'll make a beeline for it when I open the doorway." Tamara crossed the yard behind the cabin, a bucket of supplies in hand. Her crow familiar swooped after her, a spot of darker shadow among shadows. "How many do we have in total?"

"With the ones we just added, one hundred and seven, counting Ravel."

"More than we thought." The witch set the bucket down on the old garden bench at the base of the oak and moved to help Madeline, who was wrestling with the roller derby banner. Together, they folded the massive cloth into a parcel the size of a rolled sleeping bag.

"I'd better let Ellie know that we have this. If the team went back inside for it and found it missing, I'm sure they're quite upset." The cat fished her phone from her purse. Her whiskers stiffened in the sudden light from the screen. "Oh my goodness."

"What's wrong?"

"She's tried to call me four times and sent seventeen texts in the last forty-five minutes!" Madeline winced. "Some best friend I am, only thinking of her now. I'm sure she's terribly worried after all that. I'd better call her back."

"Good luck." Leaving the cat to her business, Tamara set about making a small fire in the rocky ring not far from the oak. It would be a far cry from the bonfires of Samhain, but it always felt off to light spell casting with anything but firelight. It would suit her purpose.

Madeline paced nearby. "There's certainly not a very good signal out here, is there? Oh, Ellie, there you are—"

Tamara clearly heard the yowling on the other end.

"Yes, yes, everyone is perfectly fine," the ginger assured, holding the phone away from her ear with a wince. "No injuries at all. I'm so sorry I didn't think to call or check my phone before now, but things escalated rather quickly—what? Yes, I have several very good photos... of the hornets, you mean? Erm, possibly. Why? Something strange about the hornets?"

Tamara looked up from her smoking kindling with interest.

"Right now? Um, I'm afraid I'm a bit tied up with—yes, I am with Tamara, how did you know? Well... no... that's not... of course she has nothing to do with anything, what makes you say that?" Even in the paltry lighting, Madeline looked inordinately guilty. Lying, it seemed, did not come naturally. "Anyway dear, I wanted to let you know that we have the team's banner—yes, the derby banner, it came down in the hubbub—and I will absolutely get it back to you as soon as possible—tomorrow. Now I must run; bad signal, you know. Goodbye!"

"That sounded productive."

Madeline slumped onto the bench with a deflated sigh. "I'm fairly sure Ellie did not see any 'hornets' this evening. She was all up in a clamor to look at the photos I took."

A small, cheerful crackle had engulfed the dry leaves and twigs. The coyote warmed her chilly palms over the infant fire. "It must really suck, doubting reality as you know it."

Madeline huffed. "Yes, I'm sure it must be very nice for witches, who never have to cope with such trivial things."

"Hey, don't worry about it. If she comes to the conclusion that fairies are real and it breaks her brain, I'll just erase her memory. Do a hard reset back to the end of August. Everything will be fine."

"Let's not, if we don't absolutely have to. Losing track of a whole month will make her question her mental state just as much." Madeline watched the little fire thoughtfully. "Would you get into trouble somehow if she figured out that pixies exist on her own and you didn't make her forget? You've already gotten three non-magical tagalongs in as many weeks."

Tamara stood, brushing the loam off the knees of her jeans. "Well, I don't think you count, since I did try to make you forget and it didn't work. I gave it my best shot and Fate said no. And I'm pretty sure the fox brats don't count either. Shifters should be a gray area, at the very least. So having one normie who knows about pixies and what I do for a living wouldn't be the end of the world. May have to swear her to secrecy in a sacred circle, though."

"And you really wouldn't be punished for it?"

"Some of the real sticks in the mud in the coven wouldn't like it, but unless I was on national TV telling everyone about our existence, they wouldn't interfere. Witches only butt in on each other's business if one of them is being a danger to everyone else. Or if one of them specifically asks the others for help. Even then, the rest of the coven doesn't *have* to do anything; it's just rude to ignore your Sister when she asks you for help. That and it's nice when your skill is acknowledged as valuable and desired. It's flattering."

Madeline giggled. "O great and powerful witch, please impart upon me your limitless wisdom!"

"Did I mention it's also understood that the one doing the asking then owes the one doing the helping a favor?" the coyote asked pointedly, retrieving her bucket. "Anyway, if Ellie decides she can handle the truth, we swear her in and move on with life. If she loses her shit, I gently alter her truth. No worries."

"That's a load off my mind," Madeline confessed. "I suppose I'll find out which it'll be tomorrow." She stood decisively. "But for now, what can I do to help? What does opening an interdimensional doorway entail, exactly?"

"First, you need to make some tea."

The ginger blinked. "Tea?"

"And coffee for me. We need to stay alert for another few hours. At midnight the moon will be almost exactly at its highest, and it's almost full. That will help me a lot to work magic this big."

"This is so exciting," Madeline bubbled. "One coffee, coming right up! Oh, but don't start getting ready without me. I want to see everything!" She dashed for the back door.

At the fireside, Ravel watched her go. Seeming reassured that she wasn't going far, he returned to the task at hand—dropping dry leaves and small twigs into the flames from above.

Tamara snapped her fingers at him with a frown. "Hey, be careful. Watch the updrafts, they pull up embers."

Raven cawed sulkily at her from the roof of the pixiary.

"No, I do not like him. You're obviously getting senile." The witch looked fondly up at her familiar. "I know it's late. Take a nap. I'll call you down when it's time."

With a skeptical croak and a hard stare, the crow pushed off and disappeared into the lower branches of the oak in a few quick flaps.

Tamara watched him blend into the darkness beyond the firelight. Then she looked up through the tree branches. Though the leaves still blocked her vision, the ebb and flow of unseen energy told her all she needed to know. Far above, the moon was on the rise.

Three cups of coffee, a pot of tea, and half a package of cookies later, the time was drawing nigh.

Tamara moved the last crystal into place. "There, that should do it. It's as ready as it'll ever be."

Madeline watched, owl-eyed, from the bench they had moved over to the fireside. The last mug of tea steamed tranquilly between her hands. "It's lovely."

Two parallel rows of clear crystal quartz gleamed in the light of the small candles spaced evenly between them, forming a short path that stopped at the base of the oak tree. On its rough bark, the coyote had spent a painstaking hour chalking out complicated runes in an intricate arch that formed the outline of a doorway. Standing out against the dark wood, framed at the bottom by the juts of the ancient tree's thick roots, it looked unearthly and vaguely ominous.

"Where will it open? I mean, do you know the exact location in the fairy realm?"

"No. There's a lot about the fae realm I don't know—no one does. Not that they talk about, anyway. I saw just a glimpse through the pathway last time. It looked just like my forest, but… not. Kind of twisted and wrong."

"And all the pixies went back without a fight then?"

"Yeah. As soon as they felt the worlds brush, they went absolutely nuts, and when I opened the bird cage they couldn't fly through fast enough. Seems like they're done with the mortal world when you refresh their memory of where they came from."

"Well, that's… that's good. It will make things much easier for us if we can just pop open the door of the coop without worrying they'll disappear into the night again."

Tamara didn't miss the worried glance the cat cast at her own pixie, who was dropping acorns into the empty bucket nearby. "Do you want to put him in the house for this?" she asked gently. "I'll get one of the cages out of the truck."

"No, no. He can stay with us." Madeline rolled the mug absently between her fingers, ears at half-mast. "He's not a prisoner. If he wants to go with the others, I won't keep him here."

"Are you sure? If he gets across the border, the binding spell will definitely break. He won't come back to you."

"That's alright. The fairy realm is his home, after all. It's where he really belongs. Any time I have with him is borrowed time in the first place." It seemed the other girl had done some soul-searching and come out relatively at peace.

The witch nodded solemnly at her decision. "I understand." She glanced up through the branches, judging the moon's position. "Okay. Let's get this show on the road."

"What should I do?" the cat asked, ears popping back up.

"Go stand by the cage. When I say, open it up and then get out of their way. Either they'll fly right through or we get to catch them all over again."

Madeline moved into position. Standing to one side of the pixiary, she laid a hand on the latch. When it opened, the door would be between her and the evacuating fae. "Ready."

Raven, who had begun stirring in the tree as soon as his witch's intentions reached him, hopped to the end of his branch with a flit and flutter. Shaking the last vestiges of sleep from his wings, the crow coasted down and banked in for a landing on her shoulder. Tamara reached up to scratch his soft, downy breast feathers. With a deep, centering breath, she started up the path of crystal and candlelight.

A loud pop echoed through the darkness behind them.

Ravel shrieked.

Madeline screamed.

Tamara jumped like she'd been shot, tail bristling in defense. She spun to face the sound with a hex crackling at the tips of her fingers. Raven's claws dug into her shoulder, a flailing wing bashing her in the ear as he tried to keep balance.

The singed, smoking remains of a green acorn lay in the dirt near the fire. Ravel stood like a tiny statue, eyes huge, a second large acorn held over his head in both hands.

Tamara pointed at him with all the threat she could transfer into one finger. "No. More. Acorns. In. The. Fire."

"Ravel, this is a serious occasion!" Madeline shouted, fright-puffed tail thrashing in exasperation. "Come over here this instant and behave yourself."

He dropped the nut sheepishly and zipped over to her side, a shower of sparkles brighter than embers in his wake.

Tamara heaved a deep sigh and willed her hackles to go down. "Let's try this again."

Raven mirrored her last dirty look at the pixie with an irate caw. Witch and crow continued up the little path.

At the foot of the tree, Tamara stopped. *Okay, Ridgemount. Just like last time. Nothing to be afraid of.* She took a last, deep breath and closed her eyes. *Magic and life are meant to be risky.*

Her feet shifted in the dirt and sparse grass, finding a strong stance. She imagined the rough pads of her soles growing down into the earth through the bottoms of her boots and felt the energy of the earth rising up into her body. Arms at her sides, all her fingers spread, she felt the lifeblood of her forest pulsing through them, felt Raven's bird-quick heartbeat as his life energy bled into her own. Head tipped back, face to the sky, she spread her awareness as far as she could and opened herself fully.

The Moon around our Earth. Our Earth around the Sun. The Sun, one star of countless. The stars, seeds of the galaxies. The galaxies, adrift in space. The universe—all things existing as they should. So mote it be.

Tamara felt a moment of euphoric weightlessness. For a fleeting eternity, she was one with the All, the power of the cosmos flowing through every part of her being, eclipsing and enfolding her into part of the infinite Whole.

Raven brought her back to earth. A sharp beak to the ear and a croak of warning reminded her of her terrestrial tethers.

With more than a bit of longing, the witch refocused herself, reaching out for her earthly anchor. The ancient oak before them was the bastion of her ancestral grounds. Roots locked deep within the soil and rock, branches stretching high into the air, it bridged the spaces between elements. With Power streaming through her from below, from above, and from all around her, she placed her hands against its bark.

The arch of white chalk blazed bright. The runes swam like quicksilver. The space inside the magical doorway began to warp. The dark, rough bark of the tree melted away like sugar as the realm of mortals and the realm of the fae grew closer, replaced with a swirling silver mist.

Behind her, Madeline let out a gasp of awe.

Feeling a surge of triumph, Tamara pushed with her hands and her will. *Open.*

Somewhere, on the other side, something pushed back.

CHAPTER FOURTEEN

A bolt of pure fear coursed through Tamara. Instinctively she tried to pull back, to draw herself and her magic away from the yawning gate already opening at her feet. *Close! Close!*

The opposing power followed. Stronger by far than anything she had ever felt, it sent shocks like icy fire through her fur and across her skin. The door had become a long, dim tunnel between gnarled, twisted tree trunks. Darkness pooled at the edges, swirling like smoke into the nebulous silver mist.

Far down the tunnel, a ray of white light gleamed.

The pixies in the coop began to chatter and buzz wildly. Some of them clung to the chicken wire in the spaces where no iron was woven, shaking the thin walls in their frenzy.

"Tammy, can I let them go now?" Madeline's anxious voice cut through the white noise of blood pounding in her ears. "Tamara? Is everything alright?"

The realization that the situation was no longer under her control hit the witch like falling through ice she had thought was solid into a bottomless winter lake. The Pathway was no longer hers to close. She tried to back away without taking her eyes off the tunnel and tripped over her work boots. Cawing in alarm, Raven launched himself off of her shoulder as she sprawled backward on her tail.

Madeline broke from the pixiary and dashed toward them.

"Maddie, no," Tamara yelled hoarsely. "Run away, run!" Scrambling backward across the ground like the world's most awkward crab, she struggled through the cloud of her fear for something, anything, to defend them—a hex, a curse, anything at all. She came up empty-handed.

The cat reached her as her back hit the side of the garden shed. Madeline dropped to her knees beside the coyote, gripping her upper arm and trying to hoist her to her feet. "What's happening?"

The pixies in the coop suddenly fell silent.

A figure stepped through the doorway.

Tendrils of mist curled around heavily embellished leather riding boots as they picked a nimble way down through the tangle of the oak's roots and landed confidently on solid ground. In them stood a tall snow leopard. Fur of alabaster and storm-cloud gray ringed with deep violet spots gave off a faint glow, eclipsing the light of the dying fire. A long, luxurious tail curled in question as the feline straightened his ornate purple and gold doublet, taking stock with luminous amethyst eyes. A circlet of golden leaves and purple berries rested on his brow.

"Well, that's not bad at all. In fact, I'd say it's rather quite good. Eddie, what do you think?" He turned to address the door in the tree. Huge, moth-like wings of black and purple velvet draped his back like the finest of capes.

Madeline's mouth dropped open soundlessly. Her claws sank into Tamara's arm. Neither girl moved.

A moment later, a second figure emerged from the mist. Just as tall and significantly more stocky, a chocolate Labrador made a slightly less graceful descent. He sighed with the patience of the long-afflicted. "You look brilliant, as always, Your Highness.

Very regal and mysterious. But I wish you would have let me go first."

"You worry too much." The snow leopard waved a hand dismissively. A swirl of sparkling light followed it, coalescing in midair into a perfectly formed mirror. He observed himself, stroking his whiskers approvingly. "Oh, very nice! Even better than I thought. Definitely keeping this one."

Power seeped from him in waves. Tamara's skin crawled beneath her fur at the creeping itch of fae magic, stronger than a million pixies combined.

"But I was right. This is certainly witches' work," the feline mused, absently waving the mirror away into nothingness as he took in the chalk door, the oak tree, and the candle-crystal path. "It just oozes mortal magic. Note the judicious use of sparkly rocks. Witches can't resist sparkly rocks. There should also be a cauldron around here somewhere."

The dog beside him glanced warily around the yard as if said cauldron might attack from the shadows, floppy ears perked alertly atop a shaggy haystack of brown hair. Plain beside his resplendent companion, he wore a simple green tunic crossed in the front with a leather belt. Slung across his broad, wingless back were a bow and quiver.

Searching brown eyes traced curiously over the pixiary, across the tool shed, and made contact with Tamara's. His slowly wagging tail went stiff in surprise. "Your Highness?"

"I wonder where they've gone? One doesn't usually roll out the welcome mat and then disappear—"

"Your Highness."

"Eddie, please, I know we're on business, but I wish you'd stop calling me that."

With a low growl of impatience, the dog grabbed the leopard by the face and turned his head toward the shed. "There they are."

The other's tail poofed in shock when he noticed the coyote

and cat crouched in the ferns. He recovered gracefully. Shooing off the hands bending his whiskers, he hurried toward them. The ghostly echo of silver bells rang faintly with every sprightly step.

Tamara forced herself to her feet without taking her eyes off the faerie. Her hand groped, blindly searching, along the wooden wall at her back.

"Hello, my good ladies! Absolutely charmed and delighted to make your acquaintance. Dreadfully sorry if I startled you; my presence has been known to overcome the occasional delicate constitution with awe and admiration—"

Tamara's hand closed around something solid. Without thinking, she swung it as hard as she could. The leopard let out a startled squawk as the brush of an old straw broom caught him upside the head, knocking the circlet lopsided.

"Tamara, what are you doing?!" Madeline shrieked. She threw her arms around the witch in horrified disbelief. "This is not how any of the fairytales go!"

Tamara kept whacking mechanically, swinging low to catch the intruder in the gut. "This isn't a fairytale! This is real life, and he's going to enslave us or murder us or eat us, so *run!*"

"Madam, please, I know our kinds have had their differences in the past, but—ow!—I assure you that I have only the purest of intentions—will you stop that, this is my best jacket!"

The broom was suddenly wrenched out of Tamara's hands. The Labrador held the handle out of her reach with a frown. "I thought you said witches ride on brooms, not bludgeon people with them."

"Perhaps my sources were slightly outdated." The leopard replaced his circlet with a pout. "Ahem. Now then, I believe we somehow got off on the wrong foot. Allow me to introduce myself." He flourished an elaborate bow. "I am Prince Alexander of the Fair Folk, acting sovereign of the Summer Courts, Land of the Deep Forests and Clear Waters. And this is my retainer, confidante, former ward, and dearest friend, Edmund. Say hello, Eddie."

The dog cocked his head skeptically, propping the broom back against the shed. "Are you sure they invited us?"

"Of course they did. They opened the door."

"Hell no, I did not 'invite' you," Tamara snarled, hands balling into fists. "There was no invitation of any kind. You hijacked my Pathway!"

"An open door is an open door, my dear. They work both ways. Now, with whom do we have the pleasure of speaking?"

The coyote crossed her arms stubbornly. "No one."

Madeline groaned, covering her face in mortification. "Do please forgive her, Your Majesty. She's not used to conversing with royalty." Dropping her hands, she grabbed the hem of her jacket and did a little curtsey. "My name is Madeline, Madeline Babcock, and this is my very good friend Tam—"

"Wait, don't tell him that! Names have power!"

"Oh, fear not, my good witch." The faerie prince waved off her concern with an airy hand. "I already know you by your magical signature. I've no need to resort to such base tactics as that."

Tamara felt ill.

"But I must inquire: if you didn't open a way between worlds to invite contact, why did you open it? Not up to any mischief, I trust." His amethyst eyes became a little sharper.

Tamara suppressed an involuntary shiver.

"Oh no, not at all," Madeline rushed to explain. "We've been working for weeks to find all the pixies that escaped from your realm and capture them before they could get hurt, and tonight we were about to send them back when you arrived. See?" The ginger gestured beyond the shed to the pixiary. "All whole and unharmed."

Alexander drifted curiously over, Edmund close at his heels. The pixies, which had been remarkably quiet and well-behaved since his appearance, sent up a chorus of eager peeping very much unlike the unholy screeching Tamara was used to when she approached the coop.

"Look, Eddie, I was right! This is where the little sprites came from." Without hesitation, seeming unbothered by the wards and iron reinforcements on the coop, he pulled open the door.

Tamara gasped. "Wait, don't—!"

The pixies streamed from the coop. They did not make a break for the forest, however, or even the open path to the fae realm. They flocked around the prince, chattering and cooing happily. Their golden glow surrounded his silver-white. Some perched on his outstretched hands. Others draped over his arms. The smallest, most assertive of the lot touched down in the middle of his circlet with an air of great satisfaction.

He laughed, ears flattening as they were tickled, wings flaring in delight. "What charming little creatures! Who would have thought the mortal realm could produce such gems?"

Tamara and Madeline shared a bewildered look.

"I think they like you, Your High—Alexander." Edmund gently shooed away a pixie trying to tug an arrow out of his quiver.

While part—a large part—of the witch wanted to invite her unexpected "guests" to take the flock and leave immediately, some other small part of herself that valued the answers to riddles over self-preservation made her hesitate. She cleared her throat uncomfortably. "So, uh. What's so special about these pixies? There are tons of them in the fae realm. Right?"

Prince Alexander, covered in pixies, wings at full mast, turned to her with a puzzled frown. "No, certainly not. I'd never seen one before a few days ago. A door opened up from the mortal realm and all of a sudden they were flying about a garden party at Court, turning mead into vinegar and levitating puddings. The nobles were enamored."

It was impossible to calculate the difference in the flow of time between the mortal plane and that of the Summer Courts, but it wasn't a giant leap to assume that a few days for the prince could have been a few months for Tamara. "That may have been the first bunch that I opened a Pathway for," she said slowly. "It was right after Ostara—the spring equinox."

"Are pixies maybe not as common in the fae realm as witches have always assumed?" Madeline asked her worriedly. "Have we been dealing with an endangered species?"

"No one else in the palace had ever seen one, either." Edmund had taken his quiver off his back and had one hand over the opening protectively. Several pixies circled, waiting for the dog to let his guard down. "We host dignitaries and visiting nobles from all of the Four Kingdoms. Some of the nobility are many centuries old. If the little sprites were native to our world, someone would have known about them before now."

"Yes, they caused quite the hullabaloo. There was almost a fight over who got to keep one for their own." The prince had at least ten pixies cuddled to his chest with the joy of a child holding a litter of small pets. "Hopefully these will make enough to go around."

Madeline clasped her hands happily. "The other fairies like the pixies? I'm so glad. The people in our town aren't so fond of them."

"Who wouldn't like them? They're so playful and clever! You never know what mischief they'll get up to next. Just delightful."

Tamara could feel a stress headache coming on. "Pixies have to be from your side of reality," she protested. "They *are* fae. When tears open between the worlds they come pouring out in swarms. When they die they turn into pure magic dust. Nothing in the mortal plane does that. They don't belong here. Which is why I was trying to send them back over there."

"Oh. Well, that's a puzzle, isn't it?" Looking significantly less bothered, Prince Alexander slowly wandered across the yard.

The pixies followed like planets orbiting their sun. Careful of his tiny entourage, he settled on the garden bench. The fire had burned down to embers. With a snap of his well-manicured fingers, it blazed bright in a rainbow of dancing flames. "Tell me, what do witches think causes these tears?"

"Fae magic is unstable and blows up like a geyser sometimes," Tamara answered warily, trying not to dwell on the fact that she was discussing magical science with a being that could, if it chose, incinerate her as easily as breathing. "That rips reality and we can feel it over here. And pixies escape and cause chaos almost every time."

"That's actually very close to the truth. I'm sure it must be quite vexing to you mortals—your world is very plain and boring, after all."

The coyote gave the faerie a dirty look that he politely ignored.

"At any rate, there have been two swells of excess power from my world to yours unusually close together; the one three days ago, a few hours before the pixies came, and another this morning. We have a rather loose definition of abnormal, but that qualifies. I was preparing to investigate myself when you so kindly opened the door for me. I assumed you were trying to make contact."

"I wasn't. I was trying to return some fae pests before they used up all their magic in a plain, boring world and died."

"And we will gladly take them, my good witch. But I must repeat, they are from the mortal realm. I can feel it in their bones."

"Do you think," Edmund said suddenly, "maybe these pixies aren't so much from one realm or the other, as they are a byproduct of both?"

Everyone stared.

The Labrador's tail gave a sheepish wag. "Well, you say they always appear when rifts open between the worlds. You never see them at any other time. Maybe all the fae magic pouring into the mortal plane coalesces and makes something brand new—these pixies. We haven't seen them on our side because mortal magic fluxes rationally and never breaks the barrier the opposite way, so pixies aren't created there."

No one spoke. The rainbow fire popped a green spark.

His ears flattened. "It was just a thought."

"Edmund," the prince said slowly, "have I told you lately what a clever, good soul you are? You think such wonderful thoughts."

The wagging of a chocolate tail kicked into overdrive.

"That's… a pretty good theory," Tamara admitted grudgingly. "It's not like witches are known for their use of the scientific method. Lots of pixies come through the holes, so everyone just figured that they flocked over there like sparrows or insects."

"Not an unreasonable assumption to make," Madeline assured her kindly. "Is this the first witch and fairy magical research collaboration? How exciting!"

It might have been the first civil conversation between a witch and a high-level faerie on record that hadn't ended in a fight to the death and destruction of half the countryside, but Tamara felt it wise not to say so.

Prince Alexander nodded enthusiastically. "I do so agree. I know magical mortals and the Fair Folk have had some rather nasty interactions over the centuries, but I've never quite lost hope that things can change. Just look how productive this meeting became after everyone stopped getting hit with cleaning implements."

Tamara flushed darkly and laid her ears flat to cover it. "You startled me," she growled petulantly.

The prince laughed. "All's well that ends well. You accomplished your mission of mercy, in a way, and my kingdom has gained a wonderful new treasure. I wonder if they'll be able to sustain their own population."

The witch fought not to roll her eyes. "I just hope these random breaches aren't going to become a regular thing. I'm not going to dedicate my life to re-homing displaced fae that the universe decided to create on the wrong side of reality."

Prince Alexander's good mood seemed to falter, despite the multitude of pixies he still wore. "Yes, I have to agree with that assessment. There are usually long intervals between the times our realm touches yours without someone meaning for it to happen. That it happened twice in so short a time naturally makes one question why."

Madeline fidgeted urgently nearby. "Um, if I may ask—why do fairies come to our world? Do they come often?"

"Not nearly as much as we used to, I'm afraid. Your world has changed in rather staggering ways in a very short time. It's much more dangerous. Just one or two of your centuries ago, all we had to worry about was running afoul of a powerful witch, but now there are guns and bombs and all manner of horrible things. We still do pop by from time to time, though. I'm sure this world will always fascinate us."

"I'll never understand why," Edmund muttered.

Tamara looked the dog up and down. He was saturated in fae magic, but under it all, she could feel without a doubt that he was mortal. A mortal who would age very, very slowly as long as he remained in the fae realm, but mortal nonetheless. Where he had come from, or when he had come from, she couldn't begin to guess, but the witch had her own private theories.

"I met a fairy once," Madeline told the prince shyly. "When I was a little girl. I've never forgotten it."

He brightened approvingly. "Ah, so that's where you get your lovely glow from. I didn't think you were a witch. You don't have the eyes for it, anyway."

Edmund frowned. "You met one of the Folk and didn't go with them? Why?"

"I'm afraid my family would have missed me terribly. But I treasure the memory."

"That's... that's nice." The Labrador's tail gave a somewhat feeble wag.

Madeline carried on blithely. "Now I can see the pixies when others can't, and witches' memory and illusion spells don't seem to affect me. Tamara says it's because of the fairy I met."

"It certainly is. Once you've seen the glamour of the Fair Folk, no other illusions will stand a chance against your eyes," the prince boasted. "And one of these little rascals chose you, if I'm not mistaken?" He looked down pointedly.

Ravel was industriously trying to pry a gold button off the front of the royal doublet.

Tamara couldn't hold back a snort. It was somehow comforting that the sparkle-vermin respected a ruler of the fae realm exactly as much as it respected her: not at all.

Madeline snatched her pixie away, tail curling around her knees in embarrassment. "I'm not so sure that 'chose' is the right word, Your Majesty. He was injured and about to die. Tamara bound him to me magically. It saved his life."

The coyote crossed and uncrossed her arms uncomfortably. "In my defense, she asked me to do it."

The prince studied Ravel intently. Forgetting about the button for the time being, the pixie had latched onto the cuff of his mistress's sleeve. He tugged insistently, pointing at the prince and chattering excitedly as if to show her an amazing discovery.

"Now that you say it, I can faintly feel the binding tying him to you," Alexander mused slowly. "It's not something I've ever seen myself. Though too many of the Fair Folk have been lost that way, enslaved and swallowed up by the witches and druids."

A chill rolled down Tamara's spine at the words, and the way one royal purple eye rolled to fix on her almost lazily, seeming to pierce through flesh and bone to the innermost workings of her soul. For a moment she was sure that this was how she would die—murdered beneath the very tree that had sheltered her fore-mothers by an ancient being of terrible power that she herself, in her foolishness, had allowed into the middle of her Holding.

"But that doesn't seem to be the case here!" The faerie laughed suddenly, all smiles and silver bells once more. "He seems quite happy with you, dear lady. As happy as any that are taken in by my noble acquaintances will be, I'd wager."

"I hope so." Madeline nuzzled her pixie obliviously.

Edmund allowed a small smile. "You're very kind, for a mortal."

The ginger's ears dipped bashfully. "That's very nice of you to say, but he wouldn't be here for me to dote on if Tamara hadn't been kind first and helped me save him. Do you know, all of the other witches just exterminate the pixies because they cause trouble or use their dust for spells and such? But Tamara caught as many of them as she could to send them where we thought they belonged, even though it was so much more work than just letting them run free until they all died. She's incred-ibly kind and good."

Once again Tamara found herself pinned under the faerie's thoughtful gaze like a beetle to a specimen board. It was not a pleasant feeling.

"Is that so? Well then, it seems I've been twice lucky this evening." Alexander stood decisively. A dozen pixies took flight with petulant squeaks. "It would put my mind at ease to have an ally on this side of the coin, so to speak. Someone powerful who can keep a weather eye out in case these pesky rifts between our homes continue."

The coyote managed a strained laugh. "Powerful? Yeah, right. I'm the youngest, least experienced witch within a day's drive of here."

"That may be, but not just any of your kinswomen could open a flawless Pathway like this and still have the energy to be upright and swinging afterward. Clearly you have got raw Power in spades—which means piffle if that's all you've got, but you had the tenacity to capture a hundred pixies and the decency not to harm any of them. I would be going out on a limb making a pact with a witch, but the evidence seems to say it may just turn out to be a good idea."

Madeline beamed. "I promise you won't regret it!"

"I do not make deals with faeries," Tamara declared firmly.

The cat deflated. "Why not?"

"Making deals with the fae never turns out well in any story."

"Oh, come now," Alexander huffed, spotted tail twitching in un-princely impatience. "You have nothing to lose from the arrangement. I would even be in your debt. Doesn't the idea of a favor owed appeal?"

"I especially don't want you to owe me any favors."

Madeline threw up her hands. "Now you're just being difficult."

"When faeries return favors, it's always in a way that back-fires on you," the witch argued. "Like, you ask them for a million dollars and they give it to you, but when you take it to the bank you immediately get arrested because a million dollars was mysteriously stolen from their vault an hour ago. Or you ask them to magically make you the best singer in the world and they do, but now you can't talk anymore, only sing your words for the rest of your life. Stuff like that."

Madeline looked at the prince askance.

He offered a charming, though somewhat guilty, smile. "In the defense of any favors I may one day make good on, some of our lower-born countrymen may have occasionally been known to take shortcuts when one isn't incredibly explicit with the details of one's requests."

"They get lazy," Edmund supplied helpfully.

"Yes, thank you, Eddie, that is one way to put it. Rest assured, as acting sovereign of one of the Four Kingdoms, I would of course cut no such corners."

Tamara heaved a flustered sigh. "Look, I appreciate the offer, but I don't need any favors. And you wouldn't even be indebted to me in the first place. I'm a forest witch." She threw her arms wide, encompassing the dark, quiet woods surrounding them. "I watch over the forest here within my Holding and wherever else I can. If reality tears, I patch it. Pixies run rampant, I catch them. Chaos unfolds in my town, I stop it. It's what I do every day. No one owes me anything for it."

The dog and the faerie blinked at her in surprise.

"Isn't she heroic?" Madeline whispered loudly over the crackling of the chartreuse and tangerine fire.

Tamara's building headache was now in full swing. "Mads. Please stop trying to help me."

"She's certainly not a miserly old crone crouched beside a cauldron," Edmund mused with a wag. "Not what I thought a witch would be."

Her ears angled back without her permission. "Give me a few years."

"All the years you desire, my good witch," Alexander laughed. "Well then, if that's your final decision, I suppose we had better be on our way. It wouldn't do to wear out our welcome."

Tamara bit back a sarcastic reply and settled for a quiet hum of relief. She wasn't strong enough to banish the otherworldly duo without their consent. If the faerie decided to stay and take over her territory, she would be powerless to stop him.

"You're really going so soon?" Madeline asked, ears and whiskers drooping sadly.

"For the moment, I leave knowing these lands are in capable hands. But fear not, sweet lady." The glowing leopard drew himself up with a grand flourish, the eddy from his spreading wings tumbling several unwary pixies through the air like cottonwood fluff. The noble and dramatic effect was somewhat dampened by the small pixie still clinging stubbornly to his circlet. "For I shall return!"

"Wait, what?" Tamara's tail bristled in alarm.

"Really, you will?" Madeline asked delightedly.

Extending one needle-sharp claw, the faerie neatly sliced the top button from the front of his coat. Ravel watched with utmost interest as the button was pressed into Madeline's palm. "If ever you should need our assistance, just call. You won't even owe us any favors." He winked charmingly.

Tamara shuddered as Madeline held the token to her chest in protective disbelief, heedless of the fae magic it exuded—strong enough to burn a witch like a brand if she were stupid enough to touch it.

With a squeak of enthusiasm, Ravel suddenly flew upward into the darkness. A moment later he came back to earth with a shower of shimmer, clutching a round object that he presented proudly to the prince. It was an acorn.

"A gift, for me? How very kind."

"Wait, no, you can't have that," Tamara yapped in startled panic.

Alexander tucked the seed quickly inside his doublet. "Sorry, a gift is a gift," he declared with excessive cheer. "I will treasure it always."

Ravel chirped happily at his success, twirling an airborne pirouette.

The prince pet him indulgently on the head with one finger. "Such a nice little creature. You must take after your caretaker." He swept into an exaggerated bow, gathering Madeline's hand and pressing a kiss to her knuckles.

The cat, free hand and gold button over her heart, nearly swooned.

Tamara's hackles performed a military salute. A growl bubbled up behind her teeth, white-hot anger pooling behind her eyes and sparking in her fingertips.

"Are you through, *Your Highness?*" Edmund called, narrowly averting disaster. The eye roll in his voice was almost palpable. "The night grows old. The sprites grow restless." A pixie dove into his unguarded quiver. "Hey!"

"Yes, yes, let's get these little devils home to their eagerly awaiting public." Seeming unaware of how close he had come to assault with the most painful hex Tamara knew—the one with the boils and the hair loss and the horrible rash—the prince strode toward his retainer. The proud plume of his tail curled behind him, beckoning. The pixies followed it like a flight of tiny sky lanterns.

Ravel zipped after them.

Startled from her dreamlike daze, Madeline gasped. She reached for her retreating pixie, hand outstretched. Then she paused. Happiness replaced by trepidation, she fidgeted with the gold button, waiting. Ire instantly cooled, Tamara put a supportive hand on her shoulder.

Halfway across the yard, Ravel looked back. Seeing that he wasn't being followed, he beckoned Madeline with an excited chirp.

She breathed a hitched little laugh. "No, love. Mummy has to stay here."

The tiny fae frowned. He flittered back to her side to take hold of her sleeve, tugging insistently toward the tree. "Go. Go."

"Rav, mummy doesn't belong in Fairyland. I belong here." She gently pulled her sleeve from his clinging hands. "But... if you want to go with them, you may." She smiled bravely through watery eyes and quivering whiskers. "It's alright."

Edmund and Alexander had taken notice of the small drama unfolding. They paused to watch with twin expressions of intrigue.

The prince, surrounded by a cloud of his minuscule followers, had one foot in the tunnel of the Pathway and one braced firmly on the tree roots. Tamara realized with a blink that he was holding the door, as it were, waiting for a single pixie to make a choice.

The choice did not take long. Ravel's long ears fell as the realization that Madeline really wouldn't come with him sank in. He wavered in midair like a pendulum, looking from the ginger to the prince and back again with confused, fretful chirps. Then, turning a philosophical loop-the-loop, he buzzed up to land on Madeline's shoulder.

"Oh, you little darling!" she cried, turning her head to nuzzle him. Tears of happiness glittered in her cheek fluff.

Tamara rode a silent surge of relief.

Alexander beamed. "Well done! What a good little fellow. Loyalty is a very desirable quality, you know."

From his perch, the pixie waved an amiable goodbye.

"Farewell, then, new friends, until our paths cross once more." Alexander waved grandly back, three more pixies clinging to his hand. "Remember, I am merely a summons away."

That was exactly what the witch was afraid of. She sidled closer to Madeline with a sour look.

"Goodbye!" Madeline waved rather wistfully. "It was such a delight to meet you, Your Majesty. Thank you for looking after the pixies."

"A pleasure, my dear. They'll be in the best of hands. If you'd ever like to visit them—"

Tamara grabbed Madeline close and snarled.

Edmund shoved the prince firmly through the door. Alexander disappeared with a startled, somewhat less than dignified meep. The cloud of pixies poured into the hole in pursuit of his silvery glow.

"Goodbye." The dog offered a congenial nod over his shoulder, then he too stepped through. The last of the pixies followed.

For a moment, the yard was still. The fire, once more the orange-gold a fire should be, crackled softly. The last of the silvery mist eddied around the door in the oak. Inside the tunnel, the glow began to fade.

It flared back to life as Prince Alexander's head and shoulders popped back into view. "Also, do please at least consider letting me know if you notice any more of those pesky reality rips. We're only a short eternity apart, you know—"

"Will you come along?" A brown furred arm reached out, grabbed the prince by the collar of his doublet, and yanked him back into the depths.

"Yes, yes. You're such an impatient pup."

"Well, you'd go on all night if I let you—"

Their voices faded into nothingness.

This time, Tamara felt the faerie's retreat from the mortal plane. The slow burn of otherworldly magic bled slowly away, save for Ravel's tiny spark and the dull pulse of the button now in Madeline's possession. The runes on the tree glowed faintly as the misty archway beneath them closed, wisps coalescing and taking form until finally there was nothing left but hard, solid tree bark.

The energy emanating from the venerable old tree was distinctly grumpy.

Tamara let her grip on Madeline finally loosen. Moving on autopilot, she left the ginger's side. By the time she caught up with herself, she had dumped Ravel's acorns out of the bucket and knelt by the goldfish pond. Bucket sloshing, she crossed to the oak. The chalk runes vanished with a hard splash. It did nothing to quiet the deep sense of unease that lingered in her chest. Her head throbbed.

Madeline sank down on the garden bench. Holding her pixie to her chest with one hand, she wiped her eyes with the back of the other. "Well, goodness. That was certainly an experience, wasn't it?"

"Yeah," Tamara agreed hollowly. "An experience."

With a flap and a shaking of leaves, Raven descended from the oak. He landed on her shoulder with a worried caw.

"I'm okay," she promised quietly. "Don't worry. It's gone." The witch wasn't sure if she was trying to reassure her familiar, or herself.

"Do you really think he'll come back?" Madeline asked. "Surely fairy royalty has better things to do than drop in on mere mortals."

Tamara tried to ignore the thinly disguised hope in the other girl's voice. "Probably. As much as I really wish that wasn't the case. He has an anchor."

"A what?"

"An anchor. Something from this world that gives a fae being a grip on this time and place." Tamara glanced at Ravel, ears back. "That acorn he took came off the Oakridge tree. It's full of my family's magic and this land's signature. If he opened a Pathway of his own on the other side, it would lead him back here whether I welcome him or not."

"Oh, I see…"

The wind blew, rustling the trees in the dark forest around them. The last intact log in the dying fire shifted and fell in half with a soft crack and a spurt of embers.

Tamara shivered. "Let's go in."

"Let's."

She doused the fire with another bucket of water. Madeline helped her gather up the crystals and burned-out candles, still neatly aligned along the ground. Raven clung to her shoulder as they went in the back door, clearly deciding to err on the side of caution for the night's roost.

Kneeling in the mud room, one boot off and unlacing the

other, Tamara came to a sudden realization. "Damn it. I still need to take you home."

It was past one in the morning. The thought hadn't seemed daunting hours before—all-nighters were just par for a witch's course sometimes—but now, head aching, pride wounded, magical energy depleted, the thought of driving into town and back was enough to make her massage the spot between her eyes and hold back a whine.

Madeline, shoes already off, stopped in the threshold. Ravel flew ahead into the kitchen as she twiddled her thumbs nervously. "I certainly don't want to impose, but perhaps would it be alright if I stayed the night? You look awfully tired."

Tamara nearly groaned in relief. Her crow took flight as her shoulders slumped, winging after the pixie with a croak of warning that likely had something to do with the nest behind the cereal boxes. "Yeah. Thanks. I promise I'll take you back first thing in the morning."

The cat brightened both figuratively and literally. Behind her, a witch light floated down from the rafters to illuminate their way into the cabin. "Oh, no need to worry about that. The shop is always closed on Sundays. I can get back at any time. Maybe we could stop for breakfast?"

At that moment the coyote would have agreed to stop for a full spa mani-pedi if it would allow her to go to sleep in the next ten minutes. "Sure. Whatever you want. Come on, I'll change the sheets for you."

"Oh, there's no guest room?" Madeline followed, surprise evident in her pricked ears.

The back bedroom had been devoted to the craft for longer than Tamara had been alive. She tried not to dwell on the loft upstairs, closed off for close to a decade. "I'll sleep on the couch."

"Nonsense. You look haggard. I'll sleep on the sofa and you'll get a good night's rest in your own bed."

"Don't start with me, Powderpuff. I could bench you, easy."

"Well, I could... stun you with a camera flash, I suppose? And then trip you into the bed?" The ginger's tutting and fussing followed her down the hall.

Bedtime was a slapdash affair.

Tamara pulled the spare sheets out of the linen closet. She did not own a single pair of real pajamas, a fact that had never bothered her before but now made her tail try to hide between her legs as she offered Madeline an old t-shirt to wear to bed. (It said 'Sarcasm: Just one more service I offer' on the front.)

"Thanks! Do you have a pair of gym shorts?"

She had exactly one pair of shorts. They were khaki, knee length, and covered with large pockets and zippers. "No, sorry."

"That's alright," the cat assured. "This shirt is almost a night-gown, anyway. I'll just sleep in this and my knickers."

Tamara let her headache and the nagging feeling that she had begun to live like a hobo distract her from the thought of Madeline sleeping in her bed in her 'knickers.' She slunk off, hoping against hope to find a spare toothbrush.

By some small miracle, she found one at the bottom of a bathroom drawer. She also found and threw together some headache herbs from the jars overflowing the medicine cabinet. Madeline was right—they tasted terrible. After brushing her teeth, half to kill the taste of the potion and half to keep from being a complete cretin, she returned to her bedroom with the spare toothbrush.

"Hey, I found you a—"

Madeline was bent over the bed. Her perfect tail curled in the air as she industriously smoothed the fresh fitted sheet over the small mattress. The hem of the shirt Tamara had loaned her rode up her hips. Her panties were the blue of a summer sky with a thin strip of white, lacy elastic at the waist and leg holes where fabric met the peaches and cream fur of the ginger's upper thighs.

That night Madeline had quite literally met Prince Charming—tall, light, and handsome in shining raiment. A fairytale made flesh and fur. The fulfillment of a lifelong yearning. And her underwear was a sight that, now more than ever before, Tamara was sure she would never, ever be allowed to see beyond the casual accidents that happened when gals were being jolly good pals.

The witch flipped off her ceiling and the general universe beyond.

"What did you say, dear?" Madeline didn't look up from smoothing.

"I said I found you a toothbrush." Tamara looked away as the cat put one knee up on the mattress, leaning farther over to straighten a corner. "A new one. Still in the box."

"Thanks!" With the ease of one with a flair for the domestic, Madeline applied the top sheet and the faded blue comforter. "There we are, all nice and cozy." She straightened, turning to Tamara, hands landing on her hips in a businesslike manner. "Now then, Miss Witch, in you get."

"I'm so not in the mood to fight about who gets the bed."

"Likewise. Therefore…" She grabbed the second pillow off the floor, the one the coyote usually wound up tossing off the bed in her sleep every night, and plopped it ceremoniously at the foot of the bed. "We will share."

Tamara stared at her blankly. "It's not big enough."

"It's a bit snug, but we'll fit. Ellie and I used to squeeze into her twin bed all the time when we were in school. It'll be like a slumber party! Won't that be fun?"

"I have never in my life been to a slumber party."

"All the more reason to have one now, then." The cat's white whiskers stood out stubbornly. "I'm going to go brush my teeth. When I get back, I trust that *someone* will
be ready for bed."

The nerve of this girl. As if she could stand there in her

underwear and one of Tamara's shirts and tell a witch what to do like the duchess of... of... of somewhere. Those glittering green eyes and pudgy, determined whiskers were awfully distracting.

Tamara huffed, slapping the toothbrush into an expectantly outstretched hand. "Bossy."

"Thank you." Head primly inclined, Madeline left the room. The fluff of her tail disappeared into the dimness of the hallway.

A burst of pure affection warred with the supernova of anxiety lingering in the coyote's chest. Conceding the battle, Tamara oozed into the motions of undressing. Her ponytail fell loose in waves of surrender. Blue jeans and flannel were tossed at the laundry basket in the corner. The dresser was combed through. Madeline's clothes lay in a neatly folded pile on top of it. The presence of the button, tucked into one of the pockets, had thankfully faded to the barest background hum.

With every movement, her energy and motivation flagged. When Madeline returned Tamara was sitting on the edge of the bed in a clean, carefully inoffensive tee and boy shorts, staring blankly at the hairbrush in her hand.

The cat blinked. "You've got your hair down."

Tamara ran a hand through the plain, sandy brown strands self-consciously. "Happens occasionally. Alternate Saturdays every third month."

"Would you like me to brush it for you? Or braid it? That's a very traditional slumber party staple."

The witch's tail began and aborted a wag in the same breath. "It's pretty late."

"Yes, yes, of course. Some other time, then." Looking inordinately guilty, the cat slid under the blankets at the foot of the bed. Her feet carefully did not touch Tamara. "Rav," she called, "we're going to bed. Are you sleeping—? Oh. Will it be alright if he sleeps down here with me?"

Finally kicking into motion, Tamara ran the brush briskly through her hair. "Yeah, fine."

"Are you sure? I thought pixies make you itch."

"As long as he doesn't touch me, it's okay." She dropped the brush on the bedside table with a wry smile. "Don't tell anybody, but I think I'm getting immune. Compared to that token the faerie gave you, I can barely feel him."

The pixie in question zipped into the room, momentarily lighting up the hall outside the door with his golden glow.

"Land somewhere, Tinkerbell," Tamara growled halfheartedly. She snapped her fingers. The witch lights circulating in the rafters descended, dimming as they came, and bobbled out the door. Refusing to acknowledge that there was anything weird or awkward about the second party in her bed, she slipped under the covers by the pixie's buzzing light. Her legs carefully stretched out on the side where Madeline's weren't.

Ravel settled on Madeline's pillow. She placed a hand over him lovingly. A little sigh of tired contentment broke the quiet. "I still can't believe he chose to stay with me. Or that I met another fairy, after all this time."

"I can't believe we lived through it," Tamara grumbled into her pillow.

"He seemed like such a nice fellow. He was trying so hard to be friendly. Do you really think he would have hurt us?"

"Maybe. Probably. I don't know." The witch fought the urge to curl around her scruffy teddy bear while in the presence of company. "The rulers of the fae courts are rulers for a reason. They're the strongest, the most magically powerful. Half the time, even a weak faerie can kill a witch before she can subdue it enough to cast the binding spell. One of their royalty..." She shivered, burrowing deeper into the covers.

"You really must tell the other witches to stop with this binding business," Madeline said, quietly but clearly unhappily. "Just about anyone would kill in self-defense."

Tamara lay quietly for a long, long moment.

From her books and the teachings of her elders, she had understood that non-magical persons could always be made to Forget. Then came Madeline.

She had also understood that pixies were devoid of brains and personalities, existing only to make life as difficult as possible. Then came Ravel.

She understood that faeries were evil, murderous, child-thieving tricksters.

She thought of a time long ago and the thick, scaled, sun-warmed body of a massive timber rattler draped docile in her small arms. A strong, steady, work-worn hand ruffled the hair between her ears. *Once you know what makes it tick, Tammy, nothing in this whole big cosmos can scare you.*

"I'll submit it for discussion the next time the coven gathers. I don't think it's something many witches do anymore—at least not the ones I know, anyway—and they might not even listen to me, but I can bring it up."

"Just making the attempt puts you a cut above the rest." Madeline's tail shifted under the blankets. The end of it settled over the coyote's own in companionable solidarity.

Tamara offered a feeble wag in return. "Goodnight."

Despite herself, toes and tail warm, she drifted into a blessedly dreamless sleep.

CHAPTER FIFTEEN

"Pass the syrup, please."

The coyote's hand hovered over a small rack of glass bottles. "Which one?"

"Blueberry."

Morning sunbeams spilled through sparkling windows and lit up the cozy diner. The aroma of coffee, bacon, and sausage gravy permeated the warm air. The industrious clink of cutlery on dishes accompanied the background buzz of relaxed Sunday morning conversation.

Madeline wiggled happily as rich, purple syrup puddled atop her stack of fluffy pancakes. The sugary pool mingled with pats of melted butter and flowed down the sides in sticky rivulets. "Mmm, this looks delish."

Tamara picked at the plain waffle in front of her. The chicken strips on top steamed gently, golden and crunchy, speckled with flecks of pepper.

Ravel, sitting on an overturned coffee mug next to the cat's orange juice, reached over to dip a shred of nibbled hash browns into her syrup.

"Does he eat a lot?" Tamara asked.

"No, not really. He'll eat something if I offer it to him, but only little bits. I don't think he really needs to."

"Probably not. Being bound to you should be enough to keep him going." Tamara made a mental note to watch the pixie more closely. There was always a chance he might start trying to eat more corporeal food to compensate if the cat's life energy stopped sustaining his metaphysical strength.

"You're not eating very much either," Madeline noticed, frowning at the witch's plate. "Is something wrong?"

In truth, Tamara felt like she had the equivalent of a magical hangover—the nagging headache that even her potions couldn't completely erase, the lingering exhaustion, the fresh regret of poor life choices made in the not-so-distant past.

"Nothing," she lied, chasing a bite of waffle with a gulp of strong black coffee. "It's good."

"Oh, I'm glad." Madeline beamed, tucking away a forkful of pancake. Her whiskers quivered with pleasure, catching the gleam of a slanting sunbeam. "We're supposed to be celebrating, after all."

The pixies had been returned to—or, more accurately, foisted onto—the fae realm. They had run up against a powerful faerie prince and lived to tell the tale. Their mission had been neatly accomplished with relatively few casualties and she was, somewhat unbelievably, sitting across the table in a snug little diner from Madeline, who seemed quite happy to be there.

It should have been a celebration, but Tamara couldn't shake the quiet sense that something, somewhere, still wasn't quite right.

"So, what are you going to do now that we don't have to catch pixies every day?" the ginger asked.

"Just... things," Tamara mumbled lamely around a chicken tender. "Research the prolonged existence of fae creatures in the mortal world. Prep for winter. Other stuff I've been putting off when I probably shouldn't have."

"You did have a big project that needed your attention. It isn't like you were just slacking off," Madeline pointed out.

"Yeah, I guess. What about you?"

"Lots of things. I'm booking up for photo shoots as the leaves turn. I've got sewing projects I haven't touched in weeks. Goodness, I really should post something to my blog. My followers must think I've fallen into a pit."

Tamara, who admittedly knew a lot more about stars and succulents than social media, felt a ping of self-satisfaction that she could still follow the conversation. "Do you have a lot of followers?"

"Oh yes, lots." The ginger puffed with pride.

"What do you blog about?"

"Photography, mostly, but also a bit of fashion. I have a side account for the clothes and costumes I make. And of course I reblog whatever pretty things catch my eye—aesthetic posts, nature shots, cute creatures, other people's art. But getting likes and comments on my own projects is the most rewarding. It makes you feel not so alone, you know?"

Tamara allowed herself to imagine what an all-witch social media network would be like. Magicspace, maybe. Witchstagram. Showing off how well the fungi garden was growing to someone other than her familiar. Sharing tips on how to coax fussy crystals to grow big and strong. A bustling barter thread for excess potions and slightly-used magical items. "I can sort of see the appeal."

Madeline smiled somewhat wistfully. "Still, having followers isn't the same as having friends you see in real life."

"I bet you're looking forward to being around people again." The coyote tried not to sound bitter. Madeline was classic popular girl material. She probably had dozens of friends that she'd had to put on the back burner to chase a witch chasing pixies on a multi-week field capture.

Bemused, the cat dipped a corner of her napkin in her water

glass and wiped Ravel's sticky muzzle. "Well, I've been able to spend a lot of time with one friend recently, but I should make some time for Ellie before she gets lonely and goes off to find a boyfriend."

Tamara huffed a laugh into her coffee. "The worst."

"Not that I don't wish her happiness," Madeline hurried to assure, making guilty little hand motions. "But whenever Ellie gets a boyfriend, she tries to pair me up with one of his friends, and it never really works out."

A pierced brow quirked. "Oh?"

"Um. How should I put it? I'm beautiful." The cat announced it matter-of-factly, her beauty as obvious as the blue of the sky.

It was a truth the witch couldn't dispute. Not that she wanted to dispute it. "Uh-huh."

"It's not hard to get a fellow to take me out. But I'm also fairly eccentric, so it doesn't take long for people to realize that there's something not quite right about me. Now I wonder if they somehow subconsciously sense that I'm—what did you call it? Fae-touched? Anyway, none of the fellows I've dated have stuck it out for long. Especially when they find out that I... well..." The insides of her ears turned pink in the sunlight, then angled down in embarrassment. "I don't really like to be *intimate* before I know someone quite well. That frustrates a lot of men."

"Screw them." Tamara dropped the words with the force of a Command.

Madeline reared back with a shocked gasp. "What, literally?"

"No, not literally! Figuratively. With a broomstick. No, a rake. If they can't see what a good person you are, they're not even worth the effort it'd take to flip them off." Ears back, the witch glowered. "If you ever need me to cast a curse at some jackass—"

"I'm sure it won't come down to that," Madeline soothed through a fit of embarrassed giggles.

"I can give them permanent whiskey dick. Intermittent hemorrhoids. Crotch crabs the size of walnuts."

Overcome with laughter, the ginger snorted adorably into her hands. "That's absolutely terrible!"

"I'm a witch. Terrible is my forte."

"That is such a lie and you know it." The sunbeams pouring over their booth had nothing on Madeline's unsteady smile. "Um, Tamara? Tammy. Listen." She fiddled with her napkin, the damp patch tearing easily. "I've had this thought—silly, really, I'm sure—but I've had it several times now, so. Maybe sometime you and I might possibly—"

A young gray squirrel suddenly materialized at their table. He had a loaded serving tray on each arm and a stack of menus precariously balanced on the considerable brush of his tail. "Hey, no hurry or anything, but is this gonna be on one check or two?"

"One," Tamara answered instantly. "I got it."

"Awesome, I'll be back with that." Without so much as a glance at the pixie shredding open sugar packets on the table-top, he zipped away into the crowd, the stack of menus wobbling alarmingly but somehow refusing to topple.

"You don't have to do that," Madeline protested. "I have money."

"Don't worry about it. Call it a thank you for that time you made me breakfast." The coyote waved the notion away. "Anyway, what were you saying?"

"Oh. Um, I'm afraid I've lost my train of thought. Shall we finish up? I'm sure there's someone else waiting for this table. The after-church crowd will be out and about soon."

Tamara's hackles rippled up at the reminder of the impending Midwestern Sunday brunch flood. "Eat faster."

They tucked back into their food with more purpose.

In her purse on the seat beside her, Madeline's phone

buzzed. She fished it out one-handed and glanced at the screen over her orange juice. "Oh, dear. I was afraid of that."

"What?"

"It's Ellie. She says she'll be at my place in half an hour." The cat cast a mildly concerned look at Ravel, who chirped back curiously.

Tamara crunched into her last chicken strip. "Do you want me to be there for this?"

Madeline's ears flattened beseechingly. "Please? I may need moral support."

Or a memory cleanse on the fly, the witch thought. Good thing she was flexible.

Madeline flitted nervously around her apartment.

From the beanbag chair shaped like a cheeseburger, Tamara watched passively as the ginger fussed with an electric tea kettle in the small kitchenette.

The pixie helpfully ripped the wrappers off a small pile of teabags that smelled faintly of peppermint. He bumped a teacup, sending it tumbling off the edge of the narrow counter.

The cat caught it deftly, almost absentmindedly. "Do you think I should tell him to hide when she gets here, or just act natural?" She placed the cup daintily back on its saucer. "I don't want him to scare her. Or vice versa. That is to say, if it turns out that she can see him and hasn't convinced herself that we're all mentally compromised."

"Maybe have him settle down somewhere, at least. It'd be less of a shock if she does see him if he's not buzzing around like an undead cicada."

Madeline turned slowly away from the tea to fix her with a very strange look. "A *what* cicada?"

The witch sank lower into her cheeseburger chair. "Forget it."

"You know you can't just say something that specific and not elaborate."

Tamara groaned. "Fiiine. But let me just preface this by saying that necromancy always causes more problems than it solves and is classified as a black art for a reason."

"And knowing that, you wanted to see if you could do it, so you tried it anyway?" the ginger asked shrewdly, hands on her hips in fond consternation.

"Hey, I picked something completely safe to resurrect," Tamara defended, palms up. "Necromancy is basically the drug use of the witch world. Almost everybody tries it once, regrets the heck out of it, and never does it again—or they get addicted, try to build an army of brainless undead minions, and the coven has to spend a Saturday cleaning up the mess."

"I'm guessing the former happened in your case. So, what happened with your cicada?"

"It rose up just like it was supposed to. Started buzzing like it just molted that morning."

"And?"

"And it got away. I forgot to give it orders and it flew off while I went to the bathroom. It hid from me and buzzed its little undead head off. I'd be about to find and smash it and it would shut up just long enough to move somewhere else. I tried to cast a Finding charm, which didn't work because it clashed with the magic I used to resurrect the stupid thing in the first place. Same thing with the Silencing charm. I tried to hex it to death but it was already dead, so it just kept buzzing."

"O-oh, my." Madeline tried valiantly to keep a straight face, lower lip caught under one tiny white fang. "What did you do?"

"I spent a lot of time outside. After a couple of weeks, the spell wore off and its shell started to fall apart—stop laughing, it was actively terrible!"

The cat wiped away a tear of merriment. "Maybe all young witches should have to resurrect a cicada to teach them a valuable lesson about the pitfalls of necromancy."

"Like we had to drag that dumb crying baby doll around in high school to show you how much having babies sucks and prevent teen pregnancy?"

"I think it was meant to teach us responsibility, actually—" A loud barrage of knocking brought a sudden end to the conversation. "Oh bugger, it's her." The ginger's tail poofed with instant nerves. "Ravel, go sit down somewhere and be a good, quiet boy until I say so."

The knocking grew more insistent. "Maddie, you home? You better be home!"

The pixie took flight obediently as Madeline hurried toward the door. "Just a moment, I'm coming!"

Tamara watched the tiny fae land on a low shelf of the small bookcase near the bed. It was strewn with shiny rocks, a purple candle in a glittering holder, and a glass jar nearly full of loose change that she wondered if the pixie had collected. A tiny dollhouse bed that looked like it had never been used sat in a corner, covered by a satin handkerchief counterpane. Ravel settled just as the door banged open. Suddenly motionless, he blended into the myriad figurines scattered around the room.

Madeline stepped back into the kitchenette, tail swishing nervously as her friend crowded into the small entryway. "Good morning, Ellie. Come on in, I've just put the kettle on."

The gray tabby didn't pause. "Have you seen the paper?" She waved a roll of newspaper frantically, hopping on one foot as she tried to pull off a sneaker. "It's on the morning news, too!"

"Let me see that." Madeline intervened, taking the paper before the other girl could topple over. Flipping it open, she read the headline aloud. "'Giant hornets fire up fall festival: spectators flee roller rampage!' Oh dear. Last night was a bit of a fiasco, wasn't it?"

"Uh, only a bit? That was like being part of a natural disaster." A green sneaker hit the tile, shortly followed by its twin. "I tried to find you, but they wouldn't let anybody go back in and the crowd outside was crazy."

"I know, everything was topsy-turvy. We left as soon as we'd grabbed the banner."

"Why didn't you just bring it over to my place last night?" Ellie demanded, squeezing past Madeline to step into the living space. "I was really worried. Oh." Her eyes narrowed at the coyote in the beanbag chair. "I guess I should've figured you'd be here, too."

"What is that supposed to mean?" Madeline demanded, whiskers quivering defensively.

"Every time I've seen you for basically the past month, you've been with her." The gray cat stuffed her hands into her hoodie pocket uncomfortably. "Look, since you're both right here, I'm just gonna say this. Something freaky happened last night and I don't know what's going on, except that it *wasn't* hornets and I know that she—" she jerked her chin at Tamara, "—is involved somehow."

Prepared for some level of confrontation, Tamara stayed where she was, relaxed and non-threatening. "What makes you say that?"

Foregoing the open, peach bun-shaped beanbag chair next to her, Ellie began to pace the small apartment. "I just find it very weird that you show up out of nowhere, my best friend starts spending all her free time around you, and all of a sudden all this strange stuff starts happening around town."

"That's reasonable."

Madeline took a seat on the empty peach bun. Her hands clasped and unclasped in her lap, eyes darting covertly from her friend to the bookcase where her pixie sat and back again. "I'm sorry, Ellie. Really, I am. I haven't been a very good friend these past few weeks. But there's a very good reason for it, I promise."

The pixie on the shelf sat still as a stone, even when Ellie came so close that the restlessly flicking tip of her tail almost touched him as she turned away.

"Okay, but you're not denying that something happened last night."

"Of course something happened last night." Flustered and guilty, Madeline began to knead the material of her skirt over her knees. "We were all there. It was in the Sunday paper."

"What the paper said happened isn't what really happened and you know it." The tabby's ears pinned back accusingly. "I saw—"

Tamara's pierced brow rose. "What did you see?"

Ellie wavered, ears back, but pressed onward. "Not hornets, that's for damn sure. Bees don't swarm at night, or trail sparkles, or glow in the dark."

"Are you sure it wasn't the weird lights messing with your head?"

"Yes, I'm sure! I know what bees and wasps and hornets look like. Those things were not bugs. Or birds. Or bats."

The witch took a steadying breath. Even with a plausible explanation offered, an out for the cat to latch onto, she refused to let go of what she'd seen. This was the point where Tamara would normally deploy memory-altering measures. She glanced at Madeline, who looked back helplessly.

"So, what exactly do you think you saw, then?" Tamara asked carefully.

"It looked like... I..." Suddenly faltering, Ellie turned away. She prowled over to the bed and sat down on the edge of it with undue force, bouncing a bit as the springs adjusted. Pulling one of the many small, fluffy pillows into her lap like a shield, she frowned challengingly at the coyote. "You tell me."

Madeline swallowed audibly. "It was—"

Tamara cut her off with a firm hand on her arm. "No. Don't say anything."

The ginger's mouth snapped shut.

"Maddie!" Ellie's claws dug into the pillow entreatingly. "Why are you listening to her? I'm your best friend!"

"And you know you're about to cross a line," Tamara told her firmly. "You want to know what's really going on? Then Name it." She let the smallest strain of Power into her tone. "We can't confirm or deny anything if you can't even say what you believe."

The other girl broke under her intense gaze. Her eyes darted around the room as she hesitated, caught in an almost audible internal struggle between what her eyes and her common sense told her she had seen and what a lifetime of conditioning told her was impossible.

Ravel sneezed.

Ellie's head jerked up. Her striped tail frizzed atop the bedspread. "What was that?"

Madeline fidgeted like she was tied to a termite mound. "Um —ah—that was—you see—"

Eyes huge, ears pricked on high alert, the tabby zeroed in on the source of the noise. On the bookshelf, the pixie remained as frozen as any of the dozens of resin and ceramic fairy figurines on display. Ellie slipped off the bed. "So, uh, Maddie?" Her voice had gone higher, almost squeaky. "This is that ball joint doll you were sending me pictures of a couple weeks ago, right?"

"Oh. Er, yes. I did send you some shots of him. Of it."

"It's pretty different than your other fairy stuff, huh?" Ellie crouched slowly, only an arm's length from the bookcase. "Are the eyes glass? They, uh, look pretty well made."

Ravel didn't blink. He barely seemed to breathe.

"This flocking on the body is amazing. It's almost like real fur..." She slowly lifted a hand, reaching forward.

Tamara braced herself and began to trace signs.

Madeline gnawed at her lower lip in trepidation. "Yes, yes, but it's quite delicate, so perhaps you shouldn't—?"

The tip of the tabby's finger collided solidly with a tiny stomach. The pixie screamed.

Ellie shrieked like she'd stuck a claw in a wall socket. Ravel zipped away in a shower of alarmed sparks as she threw herself backward away from the bookcase, scooting madly across the carpet until she hit the side of the bed. "It's real! It's real!"

Madeline leaped up from her beanbag. "Ellie, it's alright! He's perfectly harmless." She held out her hands, which the pixie immediately flew into. "There, there, Rav. Don't worry, Ellie won't hurt you. She's just surprised."

The other girl continued to scream.

"Okay, that's about enough of that." Tamara waved her hand decisively. Blessed quiet instantly prevailed as the Silencing charm took effect. "Okay. Better."

The sudden lack of sound from her own throat seemed to startle Ellie out of her hysterics. Her mouth closed in a little 'o' of surprise before opening again, tentatively, obviously attempting to create noise. A very quiet puff of air was the result. Her eyes narrowed as she tried to look down at her own lips.

"How long will that last?" Madeline asked the witch, stroking her riled pixie soothingly.

"Sundown."

The gray tabby's eyes bugged in disbelief. Soundless protests tumbled from her rapidly moving lips as she patted her face in alarm.

"Or until I nullify the charm. Which I totally will, if you promise to calm your heaving bosoms."

"I rather think that's the better course of action." The ginger sank gracefully down onto the rug by the side of the bed. Shifting Ravel onto her shoulder, she set her free hand supportively on her friend's arm. "Ellie, I know this is all quite a shock, but screaming is only going to get the police unnecessarily involved."

"And your memory altered like a dry-erase board in a room full of second graders," Tamara added helpfully.

"Yes, also that," Madeline agreed. "Only, I'd very much prefer it—I think you would too—if you didn't get made to forget. So won't you stay calm and let's talk about this?"

One hand on her throat, hazel eyes fixed on the pixie, Ellie offered a slow nod.

"Good. Glad we have an understanding." With a small sign and a simple wave, Tamara deactivated the charm. "You can talk."

The tabby tentatively opened her mouth. "Ah? Ah! Aaaaaaahh—" The vowels stretched into an alien trill as vocal cords were reconfirmed.

Tamara shot her a look.

"Sorry!" Powder-gray hands hastily covered her mouth. "Holy crap, that was so weird!" Her awed gaze peeled away from the coyote, over to the strange creature on her friend's shoulder, and back again. "That's... That's a fairy. Like, a *real fairy.* And you're a real witch. Like. For *real.*"

"It's a pixie, not a fairy." Tamara dropped back into her bean bag. "But yeah. For real."

Ellie's ears flattened, dazed. "Wow."

"There now, isn't this better than screaming?" Madeline looked pleased as punch. She gently coaxed her fae compatriot off her shoulder and into her palm. "Now then, let me introduce you to Ravel! He's sort of like my familiar. Remember that day at the Java Flow when the milk steamer sprayed butter? That was him playing jokes before he learned better. Right after that..."

Tamara listened without comment as Madeline regaled the other cat with the tale of their adventures, from the pixie's high-impact encounter with a minivan to what had really happened at the harvest fair the night before.

Ellie too listened quietly, ears perked, the inky black tip of her tail twitching intently. Ravel lost interest halfway through and took off, buzzing aimlessly around the room and drawing her eyes away from the story every few seconds.

"… and that's what happened. Thank you for lending us the banner, even if your team didn't realize it. We never could have done it without a net that big."

The gray tabby sat silently on the rug. She stared down at her hands, lying limply in her lap.

Madeline frowned, concern and sympathy written all over her fair features. "I know this is a lot to take in. It's alright if you need some time to adjust."

"So everything you told me was true." Ellie looked up, meeting the ginger's open, emerald gaze. "About how you fell off a bridge, and Tamara—a real-life witch—saved you, and a hundred pixies flew out of fairyland."

Madeline fluffed rather sheepishly. "Yes, all of that was true."

Tamara couldn't help but smile at the memory. It had become a very good memory, against all odds. "Honest truth. I can vouch."

Ravel buzzed back into the cats' space. The faint trail of glitter he perpetually exuded caught the glint of the first afternoon sunbeam through the small apartment's skylight and sparkled brilliantly as he hovered, considering, then landed on Ellie's knee. As she had not long before, she reached out very slowly. The tip of her finger, claw blunted by habitual chewing, hesitated inches away from the fae.

"He survived getting hit by a car," the witch pointed out. "Barely, but still. You won't hurt him if you touch him."

"Go ahead," Madeline coaxed with a smile. "He won't mind."

Ravel squeaked as the finger closed the distance and gently ruffled his short, dusty blue-gray tummy fur. He grabbed her nail with a grumble and gave it a perfunctory wiggle.

Madeline gasped with delight. "Where did you learn how to shake hands? What a clever boy! Such good manners."

The reality of physical contact with a creature from another plane of reality seemed to seep into Ellie like groundwater through layers of bedrock. "He's... really alive. A little magic pixie. And everything you said was..." She looked back up at her friend. "Everything you told me when we were kids was true too, wasn't it? You really did meet a fairy when you were little. You did almost go to fairyland."

"Oh yes, that's all true, too. Actually, it turns out that's why Tamara's witchy memory magic never worked on me, and why I can see the pixies! It's called being 'fae-touched.' It's all worked out terribly well, actually."

"Maddie." The gray cat took a deep, unsteady breath. "I'm so sorry."

The ginger's ears popped up in surprise. "What?"

Tamara sat up a little straighter on her beanbag.

"I'm so, so sorry." Ellie hung her head, ponytail slithering forlornly over her shoulder. "You were telling the truth this whole time and I never... it's not like I thought you were *lying* about it, but I didn't... I just couldn't..."

Realization dawned. Madeline offered a rueful smile. "You couldn't completely believe it. I understand."

"I'm sorry." Pulling her hand back from the pixie, Ellie scrubbed beneath her eye with the heel of her palm. "I'm a terrible friend."

"No, of course you're not."

"I am! After everything that happened to you because of the fairy thing, you still trusted me enough to tell me about it, and I didn't believe you." Rocking onto her knees, she leaned forward and threw her arms around Madeline. "I'm sorry."

Ravel took to the air with an annoyed chatter as his mistress returned the surprise embrace. Abruptly, Tamara felt she was about to be swept out of her depth.

"Ellie, it's alright, really. I'm not upset."

"Well, you should be! You're the sweetest, nicest person I've ever met, and you were *telling the truth* the whole time, and all anybody ever gave you was shit for it when they should have been falling over themselves to be your friend. I'm sorry."

Madeline wrapped her arms around the other girl, pulling her into a tight hug. "Now listen here, you. No more apologies. You've never been anything but a brilliant friend to me. Sure you might not have been able to believe that I can see creatures everyone thinks are imaginary, but you've never called me stupid, or mental, or told me to grow up and stop obsessing over fairytales. And I'm sorry that you had to be in the dark for the past few weeks, thinking I was abandoning you to spend time with Tamara."

The coyote in question looked away uncomfortably. Such open affection between the cats was disconcerting.

"You're allowed to have other friends besides me," Ellie muttered, somewhat muffled. Her face had been lost to the ginger's perfect *décolletage*. "I'm glad you have other friends besides me. Just...don't forget I'm your bestie?"

"I will absolutely never forget you are my bestie." Madeline rested her chin lovingly between soft, gray ears. "And now that you've got over your denial about magic, I can tell you all about the amazing things I've learned, and you can experience them with me! It'll be wonderful."

They had discussed what would happen if Ellie decided to accept the knowledge of magic and fae as part of her reality. They had discussed it, but now that it had happened, Tamara found a small, selfish part of herself annoyed about it. Almost bitter.

I'm jealous, she realized, watching the felines happily hug it out.

She had come to take Madeline's undivided attention for granted. Was Madeline going to start wanting Ellie around every time Tamara got to see her? Sometimes was fine, but every time seemed unreasonable. Would she even willingly spend time with a grumpy loner with someone as bubbly and fun as Ellie around? Was she ever going to stop squeezing the tabby's face into her boobs?

So what if she has a best friend? No big deal. But will I ever be a good enough friend to get a boob-hug? No, wait, thinking that probably automatically makes me the worst friend. Ugh.

Madeline uttered a sudden gasp of realization. "Oh my gosh! I completely forgot."

"Forgot what?" Ellie blinked in confusion as the ginger pulled away, holding her at arm's length.

"I haven't told you what happened last night after we ran away from the fairgrounds with the pixies. Tamara opened a pathway to the fae realm so we could send the pixies back where they came from. Well, we thought at the time that was where they'd come from—"

"Whoa, okay. Hang on. She did what?" The tabby looked over at Tamara with wide eyes.

The witch gazed back, trying with all her being to look the correct blend of cool, mysterious, and aloof. "I bridged the gap between realities."

"She used magic to open a door to fairyland," Madeline bubbled. "It was brilliant! There were crystals, and candles, and mist came out of the doorway she drew. And then." She took a deep, dramatic breath. "You will never guess what happened."

Ellie leaned forward eagerly, hanging on every word. "What? What happened?"

"A fairy came through the doorway. A real, honest fairy like the one I met when I was a girl. And he was a prince!"

The gray cat's eyes were round as saucers. "No. Freakin'. Way."

"Yes. One hundred percent way. He had a crown and everything."

The tip of Ellie's tail twitched with frenetic interest. "Was he hot?"

Madeline tittered, the insides of her swiveling ears pinking prettily. "You have absolutely no idea."

Tamara stood abruptly with a crinkle of Styrofoam beanbag filling. "Okay, well. I think I'm gonna hit the road."

"What? Now?" Nonplussed, Madeline too got to her feet. "But it's only—" She glanced at the flower-shaped wall clock with a little start. The position of the sunbeam on the floor confirmed that morning was becoming early afternoon. "Oh. I suppose we have been at it for a bit. But are you sure you won't stay for a while longer? I completely forgot to make tea."

The cups and husked teabags sat pristinely on the small counter. The electric kettle, having long since switched itself off, had cooled. Tamara strode purposefully past them.

"Yeah. Thanks, but last night really took it out of me. I just need to go decompress for a while. Get another good night's sleep. 'Can't magic your best if you don't get good rest,' right?" She stole a glance back at Ellie, who was riffling intently through her messenger bag. "You guys can keep getting caught up."

"Maddie, you have to tell me the whole story about the door to the fairy world," Ellie called. "I have *got* to draw a comic of this!"

Caught in the middle of the room, the ginger cat wavered. "Well, alright then. If you're sure. I'll see you sometime soon, then?"

"Sure." Careful not to suggest a time frame, the witch laced up her boots. "See you around."

Tamara stepped out onto the small landing. As she turned to close the door, Madeline disappeared from the short hall back into the main room. Ravel swooped into view for an instant, chasing the flicker of her tail around the corner.

"Okay," Ellie implored, "tell me everything. I'm ready."

Sketchbook pages rustled. "Give me all the details. What did your hot fairy prince look like? What was he wearing? Hunk body or boy-band body?"

A bashful giggle. "Oh, gosh. Well, he was—"

Tamara pulled the door shut with a firm bang.

CHAPTER SIXTEEN

Autumn hung in the still, dry air. The sun beat down hot, but the breeze whipping Tamara's ponytail through the open window was tellingly cool as the old truck rumbled down the backroads as fast as the pothole-ridden pavement would safely allow. Every flight of birds from the ditch rows, every snatch of waning insect song, every wave of browning cornstalk pulsed with the knowledge that summer was past. The season of gathering and scattering had begun.

The coyote felt both strangely detached from the world and as if a noose were tightening around her neck.

All of the restless yearning so typical at that time of year had up until then been held at bay by the pressure of her mission, of finding the pixies as fast as she could and removing them from the mortal plane. She also suspected that Madeline's near-daily company had gone a long way toward fending off the creeping malaise of the seasonal shift. With both distractions suddenly gone, her internal clock seemed to have gotten with the program. The backlog just happened to be hitting her all at once.

Part of her was glad that life could now return to normal,

while another part of her already missed the urgent sense of purpose. Part of her was honestly glad that Madeline could confide in her closest friend again, while another part raged at the knowledge that she now had to share the ginger's time. Part of her wanted nothing more than to go home and sleep for a week, while another part insisted, almost manically, that she be anywhere else—preferably as far into the wilderness as she could get. Such was the dichotomy of autumn.

Tamara forced herself to keep the truck pointed toward Oakridge. For one, she only had a quarter tank of gas. For another, disappearing from civilization without so much as a sleeping bag was entirely possible for a forest witch, but definitely much less comfortable. She needed supplies.

A plan brewing like October rain, she felt marginally better as the hidden drive into her Holding appeared from the forest to meet her. The relief lasted until she turned up the gravel path and her home came into sight.

A jeep was parked near the cabin. Two foxes were waiting on the porch.

"Where have you been?" Kari demanded, shooting up off the worn wood like a firecracker had gone off under her tail. The thick brush of it quivered with irritation. "We've been sitting here for two hours!"

Tamara almost threw the truck into reverse. Instead, she killed the engine and stuck an elbow impudently out the window. "And that's my problem, how?"

Kory trailed his sister down the steps. "What she means is, we weren't sure when you were coming back, so we've been waiting very patiently." He shot the vixen a pointed glance. "Right?"

"We didn't try to break in," she confirmed. "Didn't even check to see if the window was open. Can we have our rewards now?"

The boy's tail gave a cautious wag. Tentative hope lurked in his frosty gray eyes. "Please?"

With a mighty sigh, Tamara cranked up the truck window. "Yeah, okay. I do owe you. But just a short visit. I have places to be."

The foxes followed her inside, delighted as the front door swung open to admit them all. The witch reminded herself again to ward the windows as she wiggled her boots off by the door. Even if the twins seemed to have learned their lesson about trespassing, it wouldn't hurt for the old place to be more secure. Especially if she was going to be gone a while.

"Pick whatever book you want," she told Kory, waving vaguely in the direction of the tall bookcase in the den. "You can bring it back whenever you finish it—unless I need it before then. Then I'll just summon it back."

He needed no second bidding.

Kari wriggled eagerly. "And me?"

"Still got your heart set on a will-o'-the-wisp?"

"Yes!"

"Come on, then." Tamara led the way into the kitchen.

The vixen's eyes immediately zeroed in on the pantry. "I remember where they are, you know."

"I hope so. If you already forgot about all the carnage you caused last time you were messing around in here, you might need a doctor." Ignoring the stink eye sent her way, Tamara pulled open the old, wooden doors. "Lucky for you I had enough empty jars to collect them all again." Auntie Peg probably wouldn't be pleased about losing all the mason jars she had loaned her, but hopefully not mad enough to cut off her canned green bean privileges. "Here."

Kari accepted the lidded jar giddily. She held it in her cupped palms, peering at the very faint, translucent sphere inside. "How do I take care of it?"

"You don't. Just don't take the lid off unless you want to lose it. It should glow in the dark for at least a couple months before it burns out."

"It feels tingly." Her claws, for once clean, chimed gently on the glass. "Thanks."

"Thanks for your help last night, I guess."

The vixen's hand darted past her to point into the depths. "Why is there a jar of nails in your pantry?"

Tamara shrugged. "I keep a lot of stuff in there. Will-o'-the-wisps, nails, potion ingredients, seeds, moon water. Stuff."

Kari withdrew another jar. "Whoa, cool! What kind of potion do you make with pasta sauce?"

"Uh... spaghetti?"

Wide-eyed, Kari placed the sauce back on the shelf. The jar next to it was clearly labeled 'nightshade' with masking tape and permanent marker. "You keep energy balls, poison, and potential tetanus in the same place as your food. How are you still alive?"

"Oh, didn't I tell you? Witches are immortal. I'm three hundred and twenty-four years old."

The vixen's short whiskers stiffened in disbelief. "You're lying!" Her ears flickered, betraying her uncertainty. "Aren't you?"

Tamara grinned toothily as she swung the pantry doors closed. "Yeah, I'm lying."

Kari scowled. "Why do you keep trying to trick us?"

"Because it's fun." A one-fingered salute met her honesty. "Hey, it's not my fault you're prime targets. I don't exactly have a lot of people I can tease with false witch facts. The rest of them *are* witches."

"One of these days you're gonna be trying to tell us something real important and we're gonna think it's a lie," Kari decreed pointedly. "Your credibility will be zilch. It could mean the difference between life and death. Is that really what you want?"

"From now on, I'll preface all the true things I tell you with a kick in the butt, so you'll know I'm being serious." The coyote shooed her from the kitchen.

She went reluctantly, hugging her jar. "So, wait, why don't witches really just use magic to make themselves immortal? Because in *Harry Otter*—"

"Discard any supposed knowledge of magic you learned from *Harry Otter*," Tamara instructed firmly. "I've read those books. They're fun, but not very accurate on a lot of points." She steered them toward the den. "To answer your question, witches are too in tune with nature to want to live forever. Whether it's a mayfly or a bristlecone pine, everything has a lifespan and then it dies. Even the mightiest oak falls eventually. Even stars burn out and collapse. It's the most basic law of nature. Eternal life is in direct opposition to our core beliefs."

"Oh." Kari considered. "I'd still be tempted. Think about what you could do in the stock market if you lived hundreds of years. You'd make a killing."

Tamara had the vague recollection that one of their parents was in accounting. It showed.

In the den, Kory was consumed with considerations of his own. He sat cross-legged by the bookcase, a tome in each hand. His tail wagged across the floorboards in gentle thought as he sized each of them up.

His sister draped across his back, leaning down to rest her chin between his ears. "Whatcha readin'?"

"Nothing, yet. I can't decide."

Tamara looked at the books he had chosen. One was an old folio on astrology; the other was the book on magical myths and lore she had consulted the week before to help decipher the mystery of the twins' shape-shifting abilities. "Take them both."

He looked up in surprise, Kari's head lifting by default. "Really?"

"Go ahead. You look like a kit who knows how to take care

of library books. Don't let anybody else see them, though. Might be hard to explain to your parents why you have an ancient text on magic."

"Don't worry," Kari assured. She separated from her brother, puffing with confidence. "I'll tell them we took up tabletop gaming and it's a prop rulebook."

"That 'prop' is at least two hundred years old."

Her chin jutted defiantly. "I'm very good at convincing."

"Just don't let my books get hurt or confiscated. Circle of trust, kid. Don't break it."

Kory hugged the volumes protectively. "I won't. I promise."

Of the two, Tamara was currently more inclined to take him at his word. She dropped an impulsive hand, ruffling his already messy cowlicks. "Good. Try not to hide them with your Play-boys. Parents have a sixth sense for those."

"I do not have Playboys!" he yipped indignantly, the insides of his ears burning instantly red.

"Yeah, nobody keeps magazines anymore." Kari's eyes rolled as she stated the blatantly obvious. "All our porn is on our phones. Maybe you really are three hundred years old."

Tamara casually flipped her off.

A faint caw from outside made it past the sturdy walls and dusty windows. Sensing his witch's approaching presence, Raven had winged his way homeward. It was entirely possible the crow had sensed her restlessness and could feel what was coming. He'd had many years of practice.

The coyote stood straighter. "Okay. Time to move out, you two. I have things to do this afternoon."

Kari rocked on the balls of her feet, hair and tail swaying gently as she peered into the canning jar. "Is your girlfriend coming over?"

Tamara flinched as the unintentional barb landed. She had almost managed to distract herself from any untoward feline-related thoughts. Her hackles fluffed. "I don't have a girlfriend. I'm happily single."

Clearly picking up on something she didn't mean to be broadcasting, Kory's eyes widened in alarm. He scrambled to his feet, tucking the books under one arm. "Okay, well, thanks again. We'll see you later."

Kari acknowledged the hint and blatantly refused to sign for it. Her ears flattened in disapproval. "Oh, please. It's totally obvious you and Maddie are a thing. Or if you're not a thing, you should be a thing. Kory, shouldn't they be a thing?" She glanced at her brother for validation. "He would know. He can always tell when people are about to hook up at school."

Tamara gave him a hard, squinty stare.

Kory wilted like a moonflower under a spotlight. "I didn't say anything, I swear! It's just really kind of obvious that you like her, okay?"

Watching the boy clutch the books to his chest like a shield, every line of his posture wary, Tamara felt like she'd kicked something small and defenseless. Sweet Earth Mother, she had no practice being any kind of wise, sensitive mentor figure.

Kari bristled, ready for battle at her sibling's side. "Hey, whatever your deal is, it's not his fault."

Tamara huffed a short sigh of defeat. "Sorry. I'm not mad at you."

He didn't look convinced.

"No, Maddie isn't coming over. She's hanging out with a friend. She's been spending too much time around here anyway —she's got a life outside pixies and bitchy witches. And I've got seasonal maintenance to do on my borders. I'm getting a late start this year. So I'm a little tense. It's pretty common for witches to get wound up in the fall."

Kory uncurled slightly at the explanation. Kari looked somewhat mollified.

"Take your time with the books. Don't lose your wisp. I

won't be home for a while, so give it a week or two before you come back around."

With a soft creak, the front door swung open to beckon them out. The vixen gave it a calculating look.

"Don't even think about it," Tamara advised. "It wouldn't let you out when you weren't supposed to be in here, so it sure won't let you in if I'm not around. You got what you wanted in here, anyway."

"Yeah, but I haven't had a chance to snoop around at all yet."

The witch tried and failed not to think about little foxy hands prying into her spaces. Pillaging her belongings. Disorganizing her tools and potions. Opening her underwear drawer. It was a disturbingly realistic scenario. "Get out."

"Kidding! I was kidding. Why do you get to joke about stuff and I can't?" the young vixen complained as she was shepherded toward the door.

"Because she's an adult," Kory pointed out reasonably, following his sister. "And she could probably turn us into toads."

"All of the toads," Tamara promised ominously. "All of them."

The twins shuffled out. Soft, sly ribbiting sounds and muffled snickers followed them down the porch steps. Tamara had a feeling that her threats of magical revenge weren't having quite the intimidating effect they once had, and it hadn't even been two full weeks. She watched the teenagers climb into the jeep with a sigh so deep it made the lock of hair escaping her hair tie flutter.

With a burst of flapping, her familiar landed on the porch railing a few feet away. Sidestepping down the plank, Raven settled at her elbow and demanded preening with a few well-placed pecks.

Tamara scratched his breast feathers absently as the jeep rumbled off down the drive and out of sight amidst the fading green of the forest. "If that's what it's like to have siblings, I'm so glad I'm not going to have children."

The crow cocked his head with an assortment of clicky croaks.

"Yeah, well." The witch let her gaze wander from the panorama of the forest up to the tips of the oak branches hanging across the drive, dipping even further than usual under a bounty of ripening acorns that would soon begin to shower the roof of the cabin with a barrage of incredible noise. "It'll work out. It always does."

Maybe if the next Witch of Oakridge Holding wasn't any daughter of hers, that lucky soul might stand a better chance of being competent at life.

Tamara turned on her heel. "I'll be ready in ten."

Fluffing his feathers back into order, Raven settled in to wait.

True to her word, it took no time at all to pack. The hall closet surrendered her camping backpack, larger and sturdier than her day-to-day standby. Her sleeping bag was already bundled into the straps on the bottom. Moving mechanically, she stuffed in a few clean clothes and a smaller bag full of a hairbrush, toothbrush, floss, and bar of soap.

On her way to the shed for a tarp and some rope, she dialed the DNR office extension. Within minutes, a block of pre-scheduled time off appeared in the computer system's payroll file.

Back in the cabin, a few utensils and an enamel mug joined an assortment of jerky, granola bars, trail mix, instant oatmeal packets, and a tiny jar of coffee to fill the last of the space in her backpack. She clipped her water bottle and a small cooking pot to a hefty ring on the side. An outside pocket held a coil of fishing line and a palm-sized mint tin full of hooks and sinkers; she would catch and forage for the rest. Sustenance accounted for, the coyote hurried from the kitchen.

Her phone remained, face down on the counter.

A final check of the locks. A quick ward on the cabin's

windows. Tamara adjusted the straps of her backpack and clipped the lower support around her waist. Without a backward glance, she left through the back door.

Crow wings tousled her hair as Raven swooped around the side of the house to land on her weighty backpack. Assured of his company, she struck out for the rear of her immediate property. They passed the oak tree, which seemed to rustle in wordless understanding. Empty but for abandoned toys and puzzles, the sight of the deserted pixiary offered no comfort. With a breath of wind and a whisper of trees, the witch and her familiar disappeared into the forest.

The relentless march of civilization against wilderness had made it considerably more difficult in recent decades for witches to feed their wanderlust in traditional ways that didn't involve motor vehicles and highways.

Luckily for the local coven, pockets of woodland skirted and divided the farmland fields for nearly endless acres. A knowledgeable witch could move unseen back and forth across the patchwork of the countryside, never quite intruding on any other witch's borders or calling down the ire of the farmers. Little streams and a few true rivers crisscrossed the land, offering water and fish. Depending on the season there were mushrooms, wild carrots and onions, mulberry trees, and the occasional thicket of blackberry brambles.

Using the resources available to the fullest, Tamara was gone for five and a half days.

On the morning of day six, she awoke at dawn to the routine riot of birdsong. Their calls had lost the flirtatious notes and territorial squabbling of spring and summer, replaced with the urgency of flocks banding together for imminent migration.

Fog hung heavy in the forest that morning. Drops of

condensation clung to leaves that had taken on a definite hint of orange and brown. Snuggled in her sleeping bag, Tamara was glad for the tarp lean-to she had roped up between two saplings.

She wasn't very good at lying in bed, even in the dead of winter. Crawling out of her makeshift shelter, the coyote stretched hard and began her day.

The embers of her fire from the night before, neatly banked with ash before she slept, fanned easily back to life with a few dry pine needles from the shelter of the tarp. Water from a nearby creek soon boiled and became coffee. Her backpack, warded against midnight tampering by feral mice and raccoons, yielded a crunchy but acceptable breakfast.

Tamara sat on a log by the small fire pit, soaking up the warmth of the flames as she sipped her coffee and munched handfuls of granola. With the forest canopy shrouded and barely visible, she reached out her senses to find where Raven was roosting.

Instead, she ran up against a very different signature of life energy. She nearly choked on a chunk of granola. "What in the actual hell—?"

Several minutes later, a twig snapped at the edge of her small campsite. A four-footed red fox trotted out of the gloom. Laying eyes on the witch, it threw its head back and uttered a vulpine shriek of triumph.

"Hello, Kari," Tamara greeted flatly.

An answering bark echoed from the surrounding woods as the vixen reared on her hind legs and swiftly made the shift to bipedal.

"Ha! I knew we could find you. Piece of cake." The girl's smug grin melted into an uncomfortable grimace. She crossed her arms over her bare chest. "Jeez, it's cold out here. You got an extra jacket I could borrow?"

"What's wrong with being small and fluffy?"

"If I go back to small and fluffy, I can't talk."

Tamara fished a piece of jerky out of her jacket pocket and nibbled delicately. "Oh, what a shame."

Gray eyes narrowed. "We got up at four in the morning on a Saturday to find you and make sure you weren't dead in a ditch somewhere. You're really going to make me stand here in the buff?"

"I have nothing to do with the choices you made at four o'clock." Regardless, the witch pawed through her backpack. Sniffing a wrinkled hoodie, she deemed it passable and tossed it over. "Here, you can wear that."

Kari gave it a suspicious whiff. "It smells like fish and smoke," she complained, holding the shirt away with a grimace. "When's the last time you had a bath?"

"Yesterday, for your information. In the river. Right after I caught the fish you smell. It was delicious, by the way. Wear that or be naked, your choice."

Kari shrugged into it with a series of grumbles. The black DNR logo hoodie was big on Tamara. On the smaller girl, it hung far enough down her rusty flanks to offer some degree of modesty if she didn't bend over too ambitiously. She took a careful seat on a rock close to the fire, gingerly pulling the hem of the hoodie between the thin fur of her rear and the cold stone. "Gotta say, I have to give you props for getting in the river when it's basically October."

"Warming and drying spells are a witch's best friend."

"Wha? Hey, that's not fair! You cheated."

Before the issue could escalate into a squabble, Kory bounded from the slowly dissipating mist. Dew soaked all four dainty black paws. A smattering of milkweed seeds decorated the thick brush of his tail. He yipped a greeting, several of the milkweed fluffs taking flight as he wagged enthusiastically at Tamara.

The coyote looked him over bemusedly. "Damn. Why are

you so stinkin' cute when you're shifted?" She pulled out another stick of jerky. "Here. Want a bite? It's teriyaki."

His ears pinged upward with a whine of interest.

Kari uttered an indignant gasp. "Hey, we're twins—we're equally cute! You can't feed him and not me." She made grabby hands from her rock as her brother, rather smugly, took the offering gently between his teeth. "Give me some, too. Please? Teriyaki is our favorite."

"Nice manners. Good girl." Tamara passed her the last stick of jerky. The vixen ripped off a rebellious mouthful. "Okay. Now that you've conned me out of half my breakfast, mind telling me what you two are doing out here? We're miles away from town."

"That's why we had to get up at four in the morning," Kari grumbled, still chewing. "I already told you: we were trying to find you and make sure you were okay."

"Why would you think I wasn't okay?" Tamara asked suspiciously, adding a handful of small sticks to the fire. "I told you I was leaving for a while."

"Yeah, but apparently you didn't tell Maddie."

Tamara stared over the rim of her mug. "What?"

Kory made a squeaky sound of affirmation at her side, ears flat in clear disapproval. One half of the witch's brain figured the boy was hesitant to shift forms because he didn't want to be seen in the nude again. The other half fumbled over what Kari had said.

"Okay, story time." The vixen scooted forward to the edge of the rock, propping her toes closer to the fire. "So yesterday after school we went by Java Flow to get a pumpkin spice latte— because it was Friday and also it was allowance day—and we saw Maddie, so we went over to say hi."

"Right." The witch nodded attentively. "And?"

"She looked like she got dumped, failed a class, and her gold-fish died. She was super sad. She tried to be all 'pip pip luvs, sunshine and rainbows!' but Kory can always tell how people really feel. Even *I* knew she was lying."

"Why was she sad?" Tamara demanded even as she dreaded the answer.

"Well, *somebody* didn't answer her phone for three days. You never texted her back or answered when she called, so she thought you were mad at her. She went to your house to say sorry for whatever it was she did to make you mad and found your dead phone laying somewhere."

"Wait, wait, how did—how'd she even get in?"

Kari shrugged impatiently. "How should I know? Bottom line is your truck was there, your phone was there, but you weren't there. She was totally freaking out thinking something terrible happened to you."

"But you told her I'm okay?" the coyote nearly begged. "You told her I just went wandering, right?"

Kory nodded rapidly, snowy muzzle remarkably expressive.

"Yeah, duh. That made her feel better for a minute, and then she got all worried again and started blabbing about poachers, and traps, and it's getting colder at night, and what if you fell in a hole and broke your leg out in the middle of the woods without your phone and couldn't call for help. Stuff like that."

Face in her hands, Tamara laughed a laugh that toed the line between helpless amusement and hysteric guilt. "Oh my god, Maddie... What does she think people did when they went backpacking before cell phones?"

"I guess she thinks there were no survivors. But *anyway*—I, because I still feel kind of bad for punching her in the face, and my brother, because my brother is just a really good person, volunteered to come find you and make sure you're not actually dying in a hole with a broken leg."

The forest carried on around them. Birds discussed migration routes. Wild squirrels berated one another in the treetops.

The creek burbled in the background. Tamara sat silently on her log. A green twig snapped in the fire.

"So, I guess that's it," Kari said finally. "We found you. You're still alive. We'll tell Maddie."

Kory whined sadly, ears falling.

"No." The witch took a deep breath, throwing a glance at her tiny shelter. "It won't take long to break camp. If I push it, I can make it home by this evening. I'll call her myself."

A happy, chirrupy fox screech echoed as Kory's tail began to stir the leaf litter.

"Yeah, no kidding," his sister huffed, wrapping her arms around her knees. "The adult made a good adulting decision. It's a miracle."

"Stuff it, kid. Adulthood is complicated."

"Are you really that surprised that she was worried about you?"

"It's a novel experience, yeah."

The vixen's nose wrinkled in confusion. "Why? You disappeared into the woods for a week without saying anything or taking your phone with you. Most people would get worried." Her whiskers twitched wryly. "I mean, we run off into the woods all the time, but if we went camping for even one night without telling Mom and Dad, we'd be grounded until we finish high school."

Tamara swigged the last dregs of her coffee, now cold. "That's a little different. Most witches operate solo. And we're safer in the wilderness than just about anyone else."

"Yeah, but still. Parents are weird like that. Doesn't your family ever worry?"

"Nobody's worried about me for a long time."

A small black paw landed on top of her boot. Kory's chin rested gently on her knee. Soulful silver eyes stared up at her.

"What? I don't have any more jerky."

Kari groaned dramatically, throwing up her arms in teenage

despair. "Forget it. We're leaving. Tell Maddie she can treat us to a coffee if she really, really wants to. We won't say no."

Tamara snorted. "I'll be sure to pass that on."

The vixen stood resolutely. She peeled off the borrowed hoodie in one smooth motion and tossed it back to its owner. Before the bundled fabric had landed in Tamara's hands, Kari was small and four-footed once more. She pounced on her brother with a high-pitched war cry before darting off into the underbrush.

Kory shot off in hot pursuit. A well-aimed body slam tumbled Kari nose first into a carpet of umbrella plants with a startled yip. Then both twins were lost to sight among the trees.

"See you around, brats," Tamara yelled into the mist.

There was no reply.

Even if a witch lost track of exactly where she was in the forest, she could always home in on the direction of her Holding. It was pure luck that the foxes had found her when they had. Two days ago she had been much further afield, more than a day's travel on foot from Oakridge. As far as the coyote could tell, at a quick march with minimal stops, she could make it back before sundown.

Mind made up, she grabbed her cooking pot and set out for the creek. Again she reached out for her familiar. *Raven. I'm heading home.* She wasn't entirely sure if the faint caw of acknowledgment that came back was actually carried on the breeze, or just a ghost echoing through their bond.

With a small smile, Tamara doused the fire and began to break camp.

CHAPTER SEVENTEEN

Gut instinct serving her well, the witch crossed the borders of her land around dinnertime. Twilight was beginning to fall, the air growing chill as she passed beneath the ancient oak and the back of the cabin came in sight.

A light glowed in the window.

When Tamara had been a pup and her grandmother was the Witch of Oakridge, her home's doors had opened themselves for Auntie Peg. Perhaps they still would; the old hedgehog was practically family, even if necessity hadn't brought her to the property while no one was at home to receive her in many years. But as far as Tamara knew, the cabin had never willingly admitted anyone else if its witch wasn't there to explicitly invite them in.

Sparing a passing thought that she should probably be more worried than she was, Tamara crept to the kitchen window and peeked in. The room was empty. The light seemed to be shining through from the front of the cabin. Feeling like a burglar at her own home, she stole around to the front of the house.

A yellow Volkswagen was parked next to her truck. Even

knowing what she would see, the witch found a likelier window and peered into the den.

Madeline was curled in the armchair. Her pixie draped languidly across the back of it, apparently asleep. The warm glow of a nearby lamp, several witch lights corralled beneath the shade, kissed the copper in her hair as she fiddled with something in her lap. One hand held it steady while the other moved rhythmically to and fro.

Tamara realized that she was sewing. A lump caught in her throat.

She watched the cat for several minutes as dusk deepened, soaking up the domesticity of the scene as the evening chill settled against her fur. Only the sudden beating of wings as her crow came in for a landing on the porch rail behind her broke the spell.

The front door creaked open with her first step toward it. A rush of warmth greeted her as she stepped inside. A whiff of something hearty and delicious in the air revealed that Madeline had been doing more than sewing. Made impatient by several cold nights in the woods, Raven flew over her head and headed for his kitchen nest.

The ginger's head jerked up as the bird flapped noisily past. "Tammy!"

Ravel raised his chin from his crossed arms, yawned a truly unimpressed yawn, and went back to sleep.

As if such a situation happened every night, Tamara gently shut the door. She slid off her backpack, breathing a sigh of relief as the weight finally left her shoulders, and knelt to unlace her boots. "Hey, Mads."

Madeline set her sewing aside and hurried from the chair. For a moment it seemed sure she was about to throw her arms around the witch, but several feet from her target decorum seemed to prevail. "Welcome home! I'm so glad you're back safe.

And I'm very sorry to have intruded—twice now—while you were gone, but..."

"How did you get inside?" Tamara set her boots beside the door with uncharacteristic neatness. "I warded everything before I left."

The cat fidgeted sheepishly. "I came over on Wednesday to talk to you. Your truck was here, so I thought you must be home and came up to knock on the door. It just swung open, so I took it as an invitation. The same thing happened this afternoon."

Tamara had had two girlfriends in college and one in high school. None of them had known she practiced magic in the truest, most literal sense. She hadn't felt comfortable inviting any of them into her home even under close supervision.

"It was an invitation. Apparently, Oakridge thinks you belong here. *Mi casa es su casa.*"

"Oh, I'm so glad you're not upset. When the twins told me this afternoon they had found you and you were headed home, I thought I'd pop by to give you a proper welcome. Are you hungry? I made some soup. It's chicken and noodle."

Several witch lights followed them into the kitchen where Madeline ladled up some soup that had been gently simmering on the stovetop.

Tamara accepted a steaming bowl full. "Thanks. Smells delicious."

The witch couldn't help but notice that the tiny bowtie pasta had definitely not been an ingredient from her own kitchen. Or that the entire kitchen seemed to have been given a thorough cleaning. Or that her grandmother's favorite everyday cauldron had been used to make the soup.

"I hope you enjoy it. It's my father's recipe—plenty of chicken and cream. Just the thing for someone who's been hiking the woods all day."

Tamara swallowed a spoonful. It was decadent, clearly full of butter and cream. It warmed her all the way to her toes. She savored the wonderful taste and the pleased expression on the girl in front of her. Then she stuck her tongue out at the cook.

Madeline frizzed with shock. "Gah! Your tongue is purple!"

"You used Gran's pot." She giggled helplessly, nodding at the dented, well-loved copper cauldron on the stove. "She enchanted it when I was just a pup and never wanted to eat. Anything you cook in it turns your tongue weird colors."

Green eyes widened in fascination. The cat dove for the silverware drawer, produced a spoon of her own, and quickly sipped some soup. Her little pink tongue emerged bright blue with yellow spots. "Oh mah goth, ith blue!"

Stay here, Tamara wanted to say. *Make me soup. Be adorable. Be silly. Be here every night to meet me.*

"Would you mind if I made a pudding in that pot at some point?" Madeline asked.

"Make all the pudding you want. I bet Ellie would get a kick out of it."

Tamara decided to eat dinner on the couch. After almost a week sitting on rocks and logs and sleeping on the ground, such a thing seemed like the epitome of luxury. She settled into its soft, lumpy embrace with a contented sigh, cradling the warm soup bowl in her hands.

Madeline tucked back into the armchair and took her sewing back up.

"So," Tamara began between spoonfuls. "The kits said you were worried about me."

Madeline concentrated very hard on threading a needle. "Erm. Yes, I was rather. Did you mean to leave your phone when you went off?"

"Yeah. I needed to be alone for a while. I never take it when I go out into the woods like that."

The cat made an unhappy sound. "You didn't mean to come home yet, did you?"

"Well… not really. But I also can't stay gone forever. I'd have been back in a few more days, anyway. I was almost out of coffee."

"Oh, goodness." Madeline reached for a pair of tiny scissors in the basket by her feet and neatly snipped a string. "A catastrophe in the making."

Tamara offered a lopsided smile. "Next time I'm going to disappear, I'll give you a heads up."

"You don't have to do that. It's really none of my business where you go or when. Not to mention, you're a forest witch in your natural habitat. Surely nothing bad could happen that you couldn't handle with your magic and your smarts. I was just being silly."

"And yet you sent your vulpine minions to hunt me down."

"They offered to check up on you!"

On the back of the chair, the dozing pixie cracked a baleful eye at Tamara's loud laughter.

"They're tenacious little cusses. They can barely drive and I already wouldn't want to get on their bad side. Imagine what they'll be like when they're legal." She chewed a bite of chicken thoughtfully. "They're fast, too. Four-paw drive covers a lot of ground. They could be pretty useful for tracking and running errands. Too bad they lose their pockets when they shift." She eyed Madeline's sewing. "Maybe you could make them little foxy fanny packs."

"I'm sure they'd charge you an arm and a leg for the service."

The witch watched curiously as her needle moved through deep blue and purple fabric with quick, efficient motions. "What are you making?"

"My Halloween costume. I only have a month to finish it, and I've got so many photo shoots coming up. I don't want to get behind and run out of time."

"Let me guess. It's a fairy costume, right?"

Madeline inclined her nose with a dainty huff. "Perhaps it is, perhaps it isn't. And perhaps you'll just have to come to the Halloween party to find out."

"I bet you've gone as a fairy for Halloween every year since you moved to a country that celebrates that holiday," Tamara teased. She was somehow sure that Madeline had been the cutest tiny feline fairy. And that she was currently the most beautiful.

"I plead the fifth."

Done with her soup, the coyote dropped her spoon into the empty bowl with a satisfied sigh. She found herself unwilling to leave the soft embrace of the sofa to put it in the sink. Conceding as little movement as possible, she leaned forward to put the bowl on the coffee table instead. A neat pile of papers caught her eye among the crystals and shells scattered across the scuffed surface.

"I brought in your mail while you were gone," Madeline told her, noticing her reach for the stack. "I promise I didn't snoop."

"You're not a crazy teenage fox with more boobs than common courtesy, so I believe you." Tamara leafed through the small pile, pulling out the single magazine. "Oh, nice, my Nat Geo. Love these." She set it aside to start on before bed.

"I don't suppose witches get utility bills, do they?" Madeline asked, eyes on her needle and thread. "The little light baubles are wonderful, but what powers the appliances?"

"Raw energy. The cabin pulls it from everywhere—the wind and the growing plants, mostly, but in the winter when the growth stops and the trees are bare, it gets a little solar exposure. Gran's mother worked that magic back in the thirties when appliances started getting mainstream. Cooling spells to keep ice frozen and food cold are easy, but apparently she really wanted a washing machine."

The last envelope, hidden behind the junk mail she never could figure out how to stop from arriving, had been addressed by a slightly messy hand. It immediately snared Tamara's attention.

"If only everyone were as eco-conscious as witches."

"Mmm-hmm." Distracted, she slit the envelope open with one claw. Inside, as she had come to expect, were two folded pieces of ruled notebook paper. A few tiny pieces of jagged edge still adorned the side where they had been torn free of the spiral binding. Unfolding the first paper, she scanned a letter in large, wobbly handwriting.

"Tammy, are you okay?"

"Huh?" Her head jerked up guiltily.

Madeline straightened her fabric with some concern. "You have a strange look on your face. Is everything alright?"

"Yeah, fine. I just got a letter."

"Oh, really? It's so nice to get a real letter in this day and age." The ginger refocused her eyes on her sewing. "Is it from a fellow witch? Do they live too far to send a bird with a message? Or maybe they don't have a familiar that flies?"

Tamara's mouth opened one step ahead of her conscious decision-making processes. "It's from my little brother."

"What—?" The cat looked up, mouth agape, and jammed her needle into the pad of her finger. "Oww, bugger!"

Ravel shot a foot into the air with a shower of glitter at her surprised shout. He landed on the arm of the chair, chattering anxiously as Madeline stuck her finger in her mouth with a vexed pout.

Tamara fought the immediate urge to reach over and take the cat's injured hand into her own. "Do you need a band-aid?"

"No, I'm fine. Just a little poke." Madeline frowned down at her fingertip. "I'm sorry to pry, but I distinctly remember you explaining that witches never give birth to male children. So would this be a half-brother on your father's side?"

Tamara considered the paper in her hand. "If I do a little more explaining, can you promise me something?"

"Yes, of course. What am I promising?"

"If we wind up seeing Auntie Peg again soon, don't mention this to her. I'm still working out what to tell her. If I should tell her anything."

"I won't utter a word." Madeline's ears swiveled in anticipation as she gathered her agitated pixie into her lap, stroking him soothingly.

Tamara in turn gathered thoughts she had never spoken aloud to any living being but the crow in the other room. "Half-brother, yes. But on the other side. It shouldn't be possible, but he's definitely a witch. He's got the magic, the black eyes, the works."

The cat's tail, poking from the bottom of her skirt to dangle off the chair, twitched in confusion. "Auntie Peg doesn't recall your grandmother having two grandchildren? That's a bit difficult to forget."

"He was born after Gran died. He'll be nine next summer. He lives down south with his—" She cleared her throat, forcing the unsavory word out despite herself. "With *our* mom. He's never been up here for Peg to see. I've not even met him in person yet."

"You haven't?" Madeline looked even more lost. "But I thought—goodness, this is a bit awkward. I've been operating under the presumption that your mother was also deceased."

The witch snorted humorlessly. "Might as well be, for all the difference it's ever made."

"But if your mum is still alive, and witches pass their Holdings on from mother to daughter, why are you the witch here instead of her?"

"It's… complicated." Tamara set the letter aside and unfolded the second piece of paper. As she'd come to expect, a colorful drawing had accompanied the letter.

Wisely, Madeline let that line of conversation die. She leaned forward in the armchair, peeking at the picture.

"He always draws a picture when he writes." Tamara held it up for the cat to see. "Usually it's of him doing something he did that week, or he'll draw me doing something I told him about doing myself." She had a crayon drawing of herself and Raven, the first one he had ever sent, tucked away in her special things drawer. "Playing on the playground, going fishing, riding alligators. Y'know. Cute kid stuff."

"Are those giant flames coming out of a cauldron?" Madeline asked worriedly. If the house in the illustration was to scale, the purple scribbles erupting from the pot were higher than the roof.

"Might be fire, might be a pup trying to show an abstract concept like magic with a box of markers. Apparently he's got a knack for potions."

"What's his name?"

"Tomlin. He goes by Tommy."

"Tomlin." The cat tried it out, whiskers pudgy in contemplation. "Tommy and Tammy. You're a pair!" She smiled warmly. "He sounds adorable."

"Yeah, he does." Tamara carefully tucked the letter and drawing back into their envelope. "Honestly, it's been super weird. Trying to wrap my mind around him, I mean. Not just that he's a male witch and he's not supposed to exist. You go twenty-three years thinking you're an only child and all of a sudden you find out you're not. And they're not even a baby; they're this small *person* that's been out there all the time, and you never knew. It's kind of surreal."

Emerald eyes widened. "You've only known you have a sibling for a year? Your mother never bothered to tell you before then?"

"Like I said, it's complicated." The coyote slid the envelope between two pages of the National Geographic. "Weird witch family issues."

"Well, I can't say that I understand, because I don't. You

witchy types are quite mysterious, after all." Madeline's fingers, gentle as her teasing, trailed down Ravel's wings. The pixie had dozed off once more in her hands. "But thank you for telling me about your brother. It makes me happy when I learn new things about you. About your life."

Tamara's ears ignited with a sudden flush. She looked quickly away to cover it. "I'll tell you more. Some other time."

"Some other time," the cat agreed. She glanced out the window into the darkness. "I'd better be on my way. I have a shoot tomorrow morning I should be rested for."

"On a Sunday?"

"Engagement photos. The young couple wants them taken on the grounds of their church, before the morning service. It's very sweet. All the roses around the building are still beautiful, and they have a gazebo. I hope the weather cooperates."

"I bet you'll be in luck." Tamara forced herself off the sofa before she could become one with the cushions. She ferried her bowl to the kitchen and put the lid on the soup cauldron, moving the cooling pot to the refrigerator.

When she came back to the den, Madeline was packing up her sewing basket. Ravel circled lazily overhead as he waited for her to finish. When she tucked in the last of the fabric he dove, settling into the pile with a pleased chirp. "Be careful, love; there are still pins in that."

Tamara fidgeted awkwardly, hands in her pockets. "Well. Uh. Thanks for dinner. And being here to welcome me home."

"I was happy to do it. I'm sorry again for being such a worry wart and making you cut your alone time short."

"You can come next time," the coyote blurted. It wasn't what she had planned to say at all, but something prodded her to roll with it. "If you want to, I mean. Camping may not be your thing."

"Really?" Madeline lit up with excitement. "You'd really let me come with you? I've never been on a camp out before. I wouldn't be a bother?"

"You weren't a bother catching pixies. You won't be a bother wandering around out in the woods." She would, however, probably need to invest in a proper tent. The thought of the soft feline sleeping on a tarp under a lean-to was farfetched, at best.

The ginger beamed. "I can't wait. When should we go?"

"Soon, before the nights get too much colder. I have an extra sleeping bag you can borrow, but nobody's first experience sleeping outside should involve frost advisories. Check your schedule and let me know if you have a couple days free next week."

"Will do. My first camping trip—this is so exciting!" Madeline wiggled happily, gazing at the witch with shining eyes.

"Yeah, okay. Hugs." On a hunch, Tamara opened her arms. In a moment, they were full of fluffy sweater and happy cat.

"I promise to listen carefully and wear sensible shoes."

Tamara allowed herself a moment to savor the hug. While it wasn't quite a boob hug—she was too tall for that at this angle—it was still very nice. A soft purr vibrated against her chest. From the sewing basket on the coffee table, she swore she saw the pixie roll its eyes. "You really like hugs, don't you?"

"Everyone needs hugs," Madeline said firmly. Her arms tightened a fraction around Tamara's ribs, as if afraid she would escape. "Physical affection is very important. Especially when one lives alone."

"Witches are allergic to affection."

"Such lies you tell."

If she looked down just a tad and moved forward just a hair, their noses would touch. Before she could become too tempted by the thought, she patted the other girl between the ears and stepped back. "Alright. Get going. I swear I'll charge my phone and reply as soon as you text me."

"I'll hold you to that." Madeline collected her purse and sewing basket. "Goodnight, Tammy. I'll be in touch."

Tamara walked her to the door. With a quick wave of her hand, a witch light wove its way down from the ceiling and out onto the porch, illuminating the cat's way down the steps and to her car. She watched from the doorway until the Bug disappeared down the drive with the parting beep that always signaled its departure.

She hadn't planned on a grudging return to civilization yet, but that had certainly been worth coming back for.

The witch light followed her back inside. Alone again but for the soft rustle of a nesting crow from the kitchen, Tamara took a moment to regroup. All of her gear needed to be unpacked. Her smoky, fishy, dirt- and moss-covered rambling clothes needed to be washed. A shower with hot water suddenly sounded heavenly. And she needed to pen a reply to her brother's letter sooner than later.

Deciding that unpacking and laundry could wait until morning, the witch wandered to her bedroom. She was whistling tunelessly to herself and pulling clean clothes out of her dresser when something caught her attention out of the corner of her eye.

Her teddy bear sat on her pillow. That in itself wasn't odd—the stuffed bear was always somewhere in the vicinity of the pillow if she hadn't knocked it down behind the headboard in her sleep—but Tamara's teddy bear had not done anything but slump or flop in the better part of two decades. She dropped the shirt she was holding and went over.

The old toy had been transformed.

Hesitantly, Tamara lifted it off the pillow. The shabby fabric of the body held up under her hands, holding its shape instead of its usual rag doll limpness. She turned it over, inspecting the seams. One stood out a hair more than the rest. The body had been expertly opened, emptied of its ancient, flattened stuffing, and washed. It smelled faintly of floral soap. Stuffed with new fluff, it had been sewn up almost undetectably. Two shiny button eyes had been stitched to its formerly blind face, as black as the witch's own. A blue satin ribbon had been tied around its neck in a neat bow.

Halloween costumes hadn't been the only use for Madeline's sewing kit.

Tamara sat on the edge of her bed. She looked down at the stuffed toy in her lap for several minutes. Her heart performed a sweet, painful samba around her ribcage. *This girl,* she thought hazily, *is obviously trying to kill me.*

An indeterminate amount of time later, she forced herself up. Her cell phone was still on the kitchen counter, dead as December chrysanthemums. She plugged it into the socket nearest her bed. The collected energy pulsing through the cabin's walls had the screen blinking to life in minutes.

It took more than one try to turn the camera around, but Tamara managed. She flopped backward onto her pillow, tucked the bear under her chin, and snapped the first selfie she had taken in years.

//Tammy Bear says thank you// she typed, and sent the image off.

Less than a minute later, a reply pinged in. //Tammy Bear is most welcome <3//

The witch nearly dropped the phone on her own face. She stared up at it, at the tiny heart that capped Madeline's message. Rolling onto her stomach, she smashed her muzzle into the pillow and unleashed a muffled howl of agonized delight. The phone slid off the bed with a thump as her tail wagged helplessly.

The shrill cry of an irate crow yanked from the brink of sleep sliced through the air.

"Cute girls put hearts in their texts all the time!" she yelled. "It doesn't mean anything."

It didn't mean anything. It *couldn't* mean anything. Not when Madeline was pining for her prince charming.

Who was she kidding—it wouldn't have meant anything even if Prince Alexander had never come into the picture. Tamara was not the kind of fairy tale hero who got to neatly wrap up her quest, get the girl, and live happily ever after. That wasn't the way her story went. She had learned years ago to be content with mediocrely ever after.

Her tail finally came to its senses enough to stop wagging, flopping limply to the comforter at the pointed reminder to herself.

On the other hand, she reasoned, it was pretty obvious that Madeline was fond of her, if only in a purely platonic capacity. Friendly affection that went so far as cooking for her and fixing her teddy bear was nothing to sniff at. Tamara had no doubt that if she asked Madeline to help with another magical crisis, the cat would be on her doorstep in a heartbeat without worrying about danger or consequences or whether or not her fashionable clothes might get ruined.

A real friend is the one who comes closer while the rest are running away from your new charm's test run.

It might not have been exactly what she wanted, but Tamara was more than grateful for what she had.

CHAPTER EIGHTEEN

The countryside slipped into October like a velvet gown. Yellow and orange leaves began to overtake the green of the forests across the fields. Brittle cornstalks rustled in the cooling breeze, waiting patiently for harvest. Combines trundled up acres of dry, golden soybeans, blanketing the county in a fine layer of dust.

Pulling into a parking space at the sporting goods store, Tamara cranked up her truck window and swiped the sleeve of her flannel over the dusty dashboard in irritation.

It was a sunny Tuesday afternoon. A rack of kayaks in all colors of the rainbow glowed invitingly from the storefront. Displays of decorative hay bales, pumpkins, and potted chrysanthemums decked the sidewalk in front of the grocery store next door. Skirting a stand of fly fishing rods, the witch entered Doggy Paddle Canoe & Sport Co. and wished quickly that she hadn't. On the wall inside the doorway, a rubber bigmouth bass attached to a plastic plaque began to flop and sing in panicked, jerky jolts.

The Jack Russel behind the counter looked over with shining

eyes, ears perking over his ball cap. "Howdy! How can I help you today, miss?"

She squirmed under the barrage of barely-restrained enthusiasm. "Uh, yeah, hi. Camping section?"

"Straight back past the fishing gear, take a right, past the running shoes and hiking boots. Give a holler if you need a hand." His short tail quivered in subtle hope as he leaned over the counter to point the way.

"Thanks." Tamara resigned herself to asking for 'help' at least once. Even her charcoal briquette of a heart couldn't justify denying such obvious need in a fellow wanderer of the cosmos. The bass's tinny electronic singing followed her further into the store.

The aisle full of tents and portable shade canopies was easy enough to find. Tamara stood with her hands on her hips, critically assessing her options. She was determined to offer Madeline the best first camping experience possible, and that required a certain standard of lodging.

A picture on the packaging of a large canvas yurt showed the warm, homey tent strewn with throw pillows, draped with knitted afghans, and strung with fairy lights. That made it her immediate first choice, but the three-hundred-dollar price tag and difficulty of portability made the reality of it a no-go.

Maybe something more simple. This A-frame looks pretty easy to put together. Should be light enough to backpack with, too. Lost in thought, she didn't notice she was no longer alone until it was too late.

"Hi!"

Tamara yelped and spun on her heel, the packaged tent raised over her head like a bludgeon.

Ellie laughed, striped tail wiggling playfully around her knees. "Nice to see you, too."

Breathing harder than was strictly natural, Tamara lowered the tent and took stock of the gray tabby before her. She hadn't even noticed the singing bass announcing someone else coming into the store. "Hi. What are you doing here?"

"I was grabbing some groceries next door and saw you come in." The cat was laden with several cloth shopping bags. Bright hazel eyes roamed the aisle. "You don't already have a tent? Maddie said you go camping a lot."

Tamara tried to look suitably dignified. "I usually go pretty primitive. Take a tarp and use it to make a lean-to between some trees. I didn't think Maddie would enjoy that very much."

"Yeah, maybe not." Ellie absently rubbed at her nose with the back of her hand, shopping bags weighing down her arm. "She told me you invited her. It's really nice of you to buy extra stuff just for her."

The coyote's awkward noises were thankfully cut short as the canine from the front counter popped around the corner, a spring in his step. Tamara suspected the spring was perpetual.

"Still finding everything okay back here?" he asked hopefully. "Need any help?"

"Yeah, I do have a question." Tamara held out the tent package she still held. "This says it's for two people, but it seems kind of small. Should I size up?"

"Good question. Two-person tents can hold two people just fine, if you don't mind being a little squished and don't have much gear you can't leave outside. If you want some elbow room or you want to keep your gear in with you, go with the three-person."

"Right. Thanks." Trying hard not to think about being squashed into such a small space with Madeline—maybe zipping their sleeping bags together for warmth, feeling the soft feline curling into her side as they slept, waking up with the other girl wrapped snugly in her arms—Tamara put the tent firmly back on the shelf and chose the larger size.

As the dog continued on his rounds, Ellie looked curiously at the tent Tamara had chosen. "You know, Maddie's pretty cuddly. She'll probably end up sprawled all over you like a starfish, anyway. Might as well get the two-person one, it's cheaper."

The witch coughed, subtly angling her ears to hide a blush. "I guess if she can't help it, she can't help it. But I'll get this one anyway. Then we'll have space for a third person. Y'know, if you ever wanted to come with us or something."

"Hey, thanks!" Ellie followed her back to the main aisle. "I might take you up on that. Just, like, next summer."

Tamara decided not to mention the possibility of warming spells cast on sleeping bags. She was coming around to the idea of Ellie tagging along during her Madeline time, but she wanted at least one chance to have the object of her affections alone in the forest she loved, attention undivided.

They made a loop of the rest of the camping section.

"Do we need a lantern?" Tamara paused to eye a display of Colemans. "I see well enough in the dark that I don't bring one. Cats can too, right?"

"Totally. Don't sweat it, Maddie will be fine. Worst thing you might have to worry about is her refusing to sit down anywhere and get the butt of her designer pants dirty. Actually, you should force her to sit down on a rotten stump, right on some toadstools. It'll build character."

Tamara surreptitiously picked up a small, collapsible tripod camping chair.

Ellie grinned. "Or spoil her. That works too."

Tamara paid for her purchases. They bid the Jack Russel goodbye, promising to come again, and set off the singing fish one last time as they left the store. A city bus pulled away from the stop in front of the grocery and chugged past them as they stepped out onto the sidewalk.

"Hey, wait!" Ellie yowled. She ran a few yards after its retreating bulk before reason prevailed, slowing her sneakers to a stop on the concrete. Slumping under the weight of her grocery bags, she pouted as it turned onto the road and rumbled out of sight. "Well, crap. I guess that's what I get for stalking people instead of waiting for the bus."

"You don't have a car?" Tamara asked, balancing the tent bag across her shoulders. Come to think of it, she had only ever seen the tabby on a bicycle.

"I don't really need one. I can ride my bike to work and stuff, and I can take the bus when the weather's bad or I need to go shopping. My teammates give me lifts to matches and practice. It's environmentally responsible!" Her whiskers suddenly drooped. "Also, cars are kind of expensive."

Tamara, still driving the truck her grandmother had bought almost twenty years ago, could relate. "Stupid expensive. Want a ride?"

Ellie blinked. "You don't have to do that."

"No, I don't have to. Want a ride?"

Tail frizzing with happiness, Ellie followed her toward the truck. "Maddie was right—you *are* a sweetheart."

Tamara grumbled halfheartedly as she swung her new tent into the bed of the truck and reached for the tabby's grocery bags. That fluffy photographer was determined to destroy her reputation. "I am a dark, brooding, curse-casting witch, and don't you forget it."

"Yeah, okay. Whatever you say." The cat climbed energetically into the truck cab. "Hey, do you like pizza?"

Half an hour later, in a booth at the pizzeria down the block from Ellie's apartment complex, Tamara wondered if she was losing her touch or if all cats had some sort of buffer against witchy intimidation.

"What toppings do you like?" Ellie asked. The tips of her ears twitched over the top of the menu she held.

"Eye of newt, wing of bat, slime of frog."

"Here I thought you looked like a pepperoni person. Split some breadsticks?"

Tamara frowned. "Like I said, you don't have to buy me lunch just because I drove you home."

"Drove me home, and helped me carry my groceries up three flights of stairs, and didn't turn out to be a vampire bent on draining my best friend of her lifeblood." Ellie closed the menu with a flap of laminated pages. "So two cokes, a large pepperoni, and an order of sticks. Sound good?"

"You thought I was a *vampire?*"

"It was one of my top five best guesses."

The coyote decided not to ask about the other four. "It was broad daylight the first time we met."

"Some vampires walk the day as well as the night." Ellie wiggled her fingers mysteriously and made an exaggerated face that exposed her tiny feline fangs. "Haven't you ever seen Duskbright?"

The teenage vampire fantasy-romance had been a cult classic among the girls in high school. Tamara had even been on the library's waiting list for the first book once. "I was actually going to start reading the series, but… life happened, I guess."

"You should read it! The books are better than the movies. Then you can help me tell Maddie how great they are."

"She never read them? I'm kind of surprised."

"Yeah, no, I tried years ago and she wanted no part of it. Because fairies are 'absolutely real' but sparkling vampire lynxes are 'absolute twaddle,' y'know." Ellie rolled her eyes affectionately. Then she froze. "Uh, I suddenly feel like I should clarify this since I'm talking to a real live witch right now, but vampires *aren't* real, right? They're still fake?"

"To my knowledge, vampires are not real and are still fake."

An otter waitress noodled up to the table. The cat placed their order with marked relief.

While they waited for their drinks, Tamara twirled a napkin on the smooth tabletop with the tip of one claw. "So. Besides not being impressed with vampires, what was Maddie like in high school?"

"Hmm." Ellie stroked her whiskers in thought. "She was sweet. Bubbly. Dressed like a pastel Lolita most of the time. Had pictures of fairies and unicorns taped up inside her locker. Sewed the straightest stitches and baked the best cupcakes in Home Ec."

The witch snorted. "So, basically she was the same person she is now."

"Maddie's always known who she is. I know she looks like a fluffy pushover, but she won't change for anybody. That's part of why I liked her so much when we met. She was just as nice to the cheerleaders as she was to the nerds, but she never tried to get attention or make people like her."

Tamara's heart and assorted other organs swelled with pride for their sweet, deceptively strong friend.

The waitress wiggling by to drop off their sodas proved a welcome distraction.

Ellie attacked her drink like she had survived a week in the Mojave. She took several long swallows, then daintily licked her whiskers. "Aaahh. Good stuff."

"Little bit of an addict, then?" Tamara asked, raising a brow at the half-empty glass.

The tabby gulped another unapologetic mouthful. "I am a caffeine-powered artist. Coffee is gross. This is my blessing and my curse."

"Maddie showed me the portrait you did of her with fairy wings. You're really good."

Ellie pushed what was left of her soda aside, a wide and somewhat sly smile overtaking her striped cheeks. "If you think that piece from like nine years ago was good, wait until you see what I can do now. Which brings us to the perfect point for me to show you a thing."

Sipping warily at her soda, Tamara tried to brace herself as a familiar sketchbook was pulled from the cat's messenger bag. She really didn't want to see a bunch of drawings of the fairy prince's handsome, snooty face, but felt it would probably be rude to say so this early into tentative companionship with Madeline's best friend.

With the ease of familiarity, Ellie flipped through the book until she found the page she wanted and eagerly handed it across the table. "What do you think?"

The coyote accepted it and glanced down in resignation. Her mouth dropped open as her eyes widened. It wasn't Prince Alexander's face staring back at her, but her own.

"Here are your breadsticks," a peppy voice chirped. The otter waitress, appearing suddenly at their side, glanced down at the sketchbook. "Oh, hey, that's really great! It looks just like you. Killer Halloween costume."

She set the breadbasket on the table with a shimmy of lutrine approval, collected Ellie's empty glass, and noodled away again. Tamara didn't look up.

The sketch took up most of the page. Tamara's uniform of ratty jeans and baggy flannel had been replaced with tight pants and a medieval-ish top tied over the chest with laces. Belts and chains looped her waist where a dagger sheath and potion bottles hung. Clunky work boots had been replaced with calf-clinging leather. A long black witch's cape with a ragged hem billowed from her shoulders. Raven perched on her outstretched arm, wings mantled dramatically. Crystals and crow feathers fluttered from her ponytail.

"Do you like it?" Ellie asked eagerly. A quick gray hand corralled a breadstick onto her plate. "There was a pointy hat, but Maddie made me take it out."

Black eyes, huge and watery, finally lifted from the sketch-book. "You made me look so cool. Thank you."

"Yay!" Ellie squeaked a happy victory. Her breadstick performed a slam dunk of celebration into the cup of hot cheese sauce. "I'm so glad you like it. I just got this, like, tidal wave of inspiration when Maddie told me about all the awesome things you do."

"It's not that awesome," the witch mumbled. Suddenly bashful, she quickly turned to the next page.

"Uh, yeah, it totally is," Ellie argued around a bite of bread and cheese. "Resurrecting a mythical creature from the brink of death, weaving a net out of pure magic, opening a gate to the fairy world—you're pretty much the coolest thing ever. I so wish I could've seen all that."

Ears laid back in embarrassment, Tamara slouched lower in her booth seat. The next page was full of sketches of Ravel: the pixie in flight, in repose, with tiny hands full of half-braided ribbons. The page after that caught her breath. It was Madeline in profile from the shoulders up, smiling lovingly at the pixie hovering a few inches from her nose. Ellie had added some colored pencil to the sketch, and the pixie's golden glow lighting the peaches and cream fur of Madeline's cheeks was reminiscent enough of that first night on the bridge that Tamara felt herself go loose and warm all over with affection.

"Is Maddie mothering that pixie not the cutest thing you've ever seen?" Ellie demanded.

"Er. Yeah. Pretty cute." Better the other cat think that the pixie was a key factor than figure out just how adorable Tamara thought her friend was. "Not a pet I'd pick personally, but he really seems to make her happy."

Ellie wiped her mouth and folded the napkin thoughtfully. "You have no idea."

Something in her tone made the coyote look up with a quizzical cock of her head. "Oh?"

"Fairies kind of mean a lot to Maddie."

Tamara snorted, but not unkindly. "I gathered."

The tabby continued to toy with her napkin, claws perforating it with pinprick holes, as if considering how much she should say. "Did she tell you about what happened to her when she was a kitten?"

"She told me about almost getting kidnapped by a faerie and never seen on this plane of reality again, yeah."

"Did she tell you she got bullied at school because she wouldn't shut up about fairies after that? So bad it was part of the reason her mom accepted a job overseas and they moved here? Or that her parents put her in therapy?"

"What?" Tamara's ears flew upright in alarm as she fumbled the sketchbook. "No. Why'd they do that? Because she was bullied?"

"Because she was a little kid who went missing for a whole night and came back with a story no one could believe, then kept obsessing over that story. She showed up dry and warm after hours supposedly lost in the snow. She must have been with *somebody*. Her dad got this idea that someone did something terrible to her and her little kitten brain made up the fairy story because she couldn't cope with what really happened."

"Oh." The witch suddenly felt squeamish. It was one thing for her own spells and charms to make someone forget something between one blink and the next, or subtly begin to believe that maybe they really hadn't seen what they thought they'd seen. She couldn't imagine being trapped in some well-meaning doctor's office session after session, kindly being told that her memories were just a pleasant cover-up for horrible abuses. "No. She didn't tell me that."

"So, yeah." Ellie shrugged uncomfortably. "After going through all that, getting concrete proof that fairies and magic really do exist was probably the best thing that could have ever happened to Maddie. That's why she loves Ravel so much." Her whiskers suddenly pulled up in a grin. "Other than him just being an adorable little bean, because that's definitely part of it, too."

That Madeline had the strength of will to keep believing her own version of what had happened, no matter how fantastic and improbable it may have been, was almost miraculous. Tamara mentally added 'validation of sanity and entire world-view' to the pixie's importance and decided that finding a way to keep him alive in the mortal realm was more important than keeping herself above the daisies.

"Here you go! Sorry about the wait." Their waitress returned, pizza pan balanced on one hand and a full glass of soda in the other, pulling the witch back to the present. "Let me know if I can get you anything else."

Tamara handed the sketchbook back across the table before Ellie had a chance to get grease on her fingers. "Thanks for showing me. You're really good."

"Why, thank you. I'm glad my humble artwork gets the witchy seal of approval." Her ears flickered impishly. "And this means you won't be mad that you're a main character in my new comic, right?"

Strings of cheese bridging the gap between the pizza pan and her plate, Tamara glanced up. "Wait, what?"

"I'm drawing a comic!" Ellie's grin was wide and infectious. "Check it out." She flipped open the sketchbook to an as-yet-unseen page, pointing out draft sketches and notes. "Maddie is the perfect plucky heroine. Ravel's the perfect animal mascot. And you're the perfect cool, bad-ass, magic-wielding co-heroine."

At a loss, the coyote settled for a garbled noise around her slice of pepperoni.

"I'm still working on plot details, but I think Maddie's

camera is some sort of enchanted device that helps her track down magical creatures and items and stuff." All the sketches of a plucky, determined Madeline looked fairly true to the cat's real-life fashion sense. "Pretty sure the story starts out how you two actually met, on the bridge, but she said she'd disown me if I drew her tripping on her heels and falling, so I'm thinking in the storyline her character is there to investigate a magical disturbance, not take selfies."

"Probably for the best," Tamara managed. "Do I get my name changed to protect the innocent, or something?"

"Sure, if you want. What do you want it to be instead?"

"I'll have to think about it." 'Nightshade' was probably much too corny.

Ellie wiggled happily, finally reaching for a slice of her own. "I'm so glad you're cool with this. It's going to be my best comic yet."

The witch shrugged. "I guess there's no harm in it. Even if people found out you modeled the characters on your actual friends, they'd never believe the story wasn't complete fantasy."

"Exactly! It's the perfect setup." Dropping the slice on her plate, Ellie brushed the crumbs off her hands and picked up her sketchbook again. "A mysterious occurrence draws the main characters together. Worlds unexpectedly collide. An unlikely partnership leads to friendship." She flipped the book around for Tamara to see. "Allies appear from the other side to help combat the darkness!"

Tamara was less enthused at the rendering of the faerie prince and his Labrador retainer, but she would admit that without having ever laid eyes on them herself, the tabby had used Madeline's descriptions to get her drawings very close to life. She declined to comment on their action poses—Prince Alexander, apparently wielding a swirl of purple fae magic as a weapon, hadn't struck her as the type who dirtied his hands with combat. "I'm not sure I'd call those allies. And I'm not sure a plague of pixies really qualifies as darkness. Annoyance, yeah, but maybe not darkness."

"Like I said, I'm still working out the plot. There has to be some kind of evil for the heroines to fight, right? Maybe an ancient curse. Or a super powerful magical villain!"

"Well, let your imagination run like the wind, I guess. There are good witches and not-so-good witches, but believe it or not, there aren't many super powerful magical villains in our history." Which was probably something to be thankful for, she thought lightly, washing down her last bite of crust.

"Oh, and there has to be some kind of romantic subplot. That's a given."

The coyote choked on an ice cube. "Huh wha—?"

"Mm-hmm." Little fangs dug deep into the pepperoni, Ellie smirked like the proverbial cat getting the canary. The 'M' on her forehead danced beneath her bangs as she wiggled her brows.

"Between who? Whom? Which characters?" Tamara demanded between coughs into her napkin.

"Hmm. Dunno. Haven't decided yet. Any ideas?"

The witch glowered, ears back to their extreme. "Pair me up with that faerie and I'll hit your drawing hand with a paralysis hex. You might be able to sketch again by next midsummer."

"Okay, okay!" Ellie raised her hands in surrender, one still gripping half the slice of pizza. "Peace out, girl scout. No fairy prince for you. There are lots of options."

"Like what?" Tamara asked warily.

"Well," the cat pondered, nibbling thoughtfully, "could be anything. Ravel could meet a cute girl pixie and that would add plot tension about whether he decides to go back to the fairy realm with her or stay with Maddie. Or maybe the prince is betrothed to a powerful fairy princess for political reasons, but he's secretly in love with someone else."

The coyote snorted. "Yeah, himself. Guarantee you that guy

is super vain. It's a common flaw of the fae folk." She took another slice with a carefully neutral expression. "But for plot purposes, it should be the cute, plucky heroine, right? That's the traditional way to go."

"Mmm, maybe." Ellie swirled the dregs of her second glass of soda. "Traditional isn't always best, though. Plucky heroine and handsome prince is totally predictable. Maybe the prince is actually in love with his bodyguard, but the difference in their stations would never allow it, or something."

"There are gay faeries?" Tamara had never had reason to wonder whether or not the fae operated under the same romantic principles as mortals. "Guess there could be."

Ellie crossed her arms, whiskers pudging up stubbornly. "It's my comic and if I say there are cute gay fairies, there are cute gay fairies."

"Totally fair."

"As far as anybody reading this goes, they're not gonna know any different, so I might as well make made-up fairy culture inclusive. I mean, for that matter, maybe the heroines should just get together. Strangers to allies to friends to lovers is a great trope."

Throat suddenly rebelling, the witch fought to swallow a large mouthful of cheese and crust that clearly wasn't going down without a fight. She thumped herself hard between the collarbones, tail flopping like an eel on the pleather of the booth seat.

The tabby carried on obliviously. "You'd be okay with it, right?" she asked, wiping a hand on the knee of her jeans and pulling a pencil out of her bag. "You just said no to shipping your character with the prince, not no to shipping her with anybody."

"I don't think Maddie would be a big fan of that," Tamara coughed finally. Her eyes watered.

"Why not?"

"She could have the fictional version of herself paired up with a handsome faerie prince, or have the fictional version of herself paired up with a surly witch. The better option is kind of obvious."

Plate and napkins swept aside to make room for the sketchbook on the tabletop, Ellie was already focused on drawing. She offered only a noncommittal noise.

"Hey, are you listening?" the witch demanded, panic and hackles rising steadily as the artist's pencil skated smoothly across the paper.

"Sorry, can't hear you over the singing of my muse. I actually really like this new plot angle. Is there anything special witches do to show romantic interest in somebody?"

"No. No, there isn't."

Ellie glanced up for a moment at that, ears back at an unimpressed slant. "Well, that's boring. I'm making something up. How about giving them a charm with a feather from your familiar—?"

"Oh, wow, look at the time. Is it that late already? I really need to get going." Tamara twisted around in the booth and waved a frantic hand at the startled waitress who had been wrapping bundles of silverware inside napkins. "Excuse me, check please!"

Leaving the restaurant a minute later with a warm take-out box and her metaphorical tail between her legs, the coyote could almost feel the cosmos laughing at her. *Sometimes one well-timed retreat can save you ten spells worth of embarrassment.*

After all, she hadn't been lying about needing to be on her way. She had a camping trip to plan for.

CHAPTER NINETEEN

"We should probably stop and make camp soon. It gets dark pretty fast this time of year."

Evening sunbeams slanted through the orange and golden canopy, illuminating a ballet of falling leaves as they spiraled gracefully to the forest floor. Acorns and buckeyes fell with more purpose, hitting the loam and the packed dirt of the trail with quick and certain pops.

"Alrighty-roo!" Madeline ran the last few steps down the length of the fallen tree she had been walking like a balance beam and jumped off the end, purple sneakers coming back to earth with an explosion of accumulated leaves. The pompom on her crocheted beanie wobbled wildly between her ears as she raised her arms in happy triumph. Ravel squeaked encouragingly, doing a loop-the-loop in the air above her head.

Tamara was contractually obligated to smile at the ridiculously adorable picture. "Just so you know, you look like you're about ten years old right now."

"Playfulness should not be relegated only to childhood," the cat said primly. She did a little wiggle, straightening the pink and purple stripes of her matching crocheted scarf against the front of her white puffy jacket. "How far have we gone?"

"About eight miles, give or take. Pretty nice little hike."

"Oh, that's a lot! No wonder my feet are starting to get sore." Madeline followed readily as the witch struck out again up the trail, winding at a slant up a small woodland gully. A creek, choked with leaves, trickled sluggishly at the bottom. "Where are we going to stop?"

"There's an old wildfire clearing not too far from here. Should work for the night." Tamara's tail wagged gently in time with her steps. Not even the added bulk of the tent and extra supplies she'd packed to support a second body could weigh her down on such a beautiful evening.

Their camping adventure had started off on exactly the right foot. Madeline had matched the witch's pace all day, at times almost dancing around Tamara in her enthusiasm, her pixie flitting among the trees around them like quicksilver. From time to time, the ginger's camera would make an appearance as she snapped a photo of the pretty stream, or an especially graceful tree, or a wild chipmunk scaling an old stump, cheeks bulging with foraged treasure. It was exactly as Tamara had hoped the day would be.

They left the main trail, following a small deer path through the undergrowth. Tamara led the way, doing her best to convince the brambles and saplings not to grab too rudely at the feline photographer following close behind her. A short time later, the denser vegetation gave way suddenly to a wide ring in the trees. The sky appeared, turning orange with sunset light, as they left the cover of the forest and walked out into the clearing. The grass and weeds underfoot were slowly being covered with a blanket of fresh-fallen leaves. The occasional fallen log or craggy stump poked up from the ground.

"Ooh, how lovely!" Madeline cooed, raising her camera.

"It is pretty nice. In the spring this whole place is covered in crocuses and bluebells."

"Then I'll have to come back here for a shoot," the cat decided, snapping away determinedly. "Maybe in costume. It looks like somewhere the fairies would come to dance in the morning dew."

"No faeries," the witch declared loudly. In direct opposition to her order, the pixie buzzed by close enough for the breeze of his passing to stir her ponytail. She unbuckled and slipped off her pack with a huff that was mostly for show. "I'm going to get the tent set up and a fire ring built before we lose the light. See if you can find some kindling."

Madeline took off her own, much less hefty, backpack and placed her camera gently atop it. "Right. Just little branches, then?"

"Dry branches are good. Check the pines over there—pinecones make great fires. There should be plenty."

Keen to help, Madeline bounded off with Ravel in glittery pursuit. The pixie's sparkle faded into the stand of pine trees separating the clearing from what Tamara remembered was the start of another set of farm fields.

A gust of wind whispered through the pines, floofing the coyote's fur against the growing chill. It had been a brisk day, October thick in the clean air. Hiking had kept them comfortably warm since they'd left Oakridge after lunch, but as the sun neared the end of its downward journey and the breeze picked up through the increasingly-thinner foliage of the wood around them, Tamara was glad that the lighter-furred cat had upgraded from a variety of fashionable jackets to a real coat. Resolve redoubled, she unfolded the tarp across a level spot in the grass and set to pitching their tent.

By the time Madeline made it back, a huge bundle of sticks in her arms and coat pockets stuffed with pinecones, the small

A-frame was upright and staked firmly into the ground. Two unrolled sleeping bags lay neatly side by side inside it.

"Will this be enough?" Madeline asked, setting her armful down next to the fire ring the witch had dug in the moist earth. Wobbling through the air with a pinecone almost as big as he was, Ravel tossed it down with a triumphant chatter.

"Oh yeah, that's—" The pinecone hit Tamara on the snout and bounced off into the weeds. "—that's great. Thanks." She rubbed her nose, shot the pixie a scowl at the tug of pine sap, and knelt to arrange the kindling.

The tip of one claw traced a rune as old as time. With a simple snap of her fingers, the invisible mark flared hot and red. Glowing like an ember, it curled itself around the nearest twig. A tiny fire sprang to life.

Madeline blinked at her. "So that's how you started a fire instantly on the equinox. I was too busy placating Ellie to notice."

The coyote offered an innocent wag. Using magic wasn't lazy; it was *efficient.* "What? Expecting flint and tinder?"

"Heaven forbid. You never do anything the way I expect you to."

Tamara yapped a surprised laugh and began gently adding a few pinecones to the small flames. "Yeah, well. Same to you."

As evening fell, they settled in. Tamara unpacked a tiny foldable grill and the cheese sandwiches they had pre-made back in her kitchen. While the sandwiches toasted over the fire, she urged a tiny kettle to boil.

"This is delightful," Madeline decreed. She perched on her new tripod chair near the fire like a princess sitting for a portrait, tail curled neatly over her lap. "What else does one do on a campout?"

Tamara shrugged and handed her a chipped enamel camping mug trailing steam and a teabag string. "This is pretty much it once the sun goes down. Enjoy the fire and listen to the night. Maybe read a little bit. Watch the stars come out."

"Ooh, can we do that?" the cat asked. "I'd love an astronomy lesson from a witch." Her eyelashes fluttered winningly.

"Sure. We'll let the fire die down and go out to the edge of the field. Should be a pretty good view." Something round and white flew by in the periphery of Tamara's vision, followed by a squeaky pixie laugh. Her hackles went up in annoyance. "Get out of those marshmallows, you little cretin!"

Grilled cheeses eaten, untainted marshmallows toasted, they sat by the dying fire until it turned to embers. Twilight lay heavy over the forest. The last crickets sang from the weeds and leaf beds. Tamara knew, innately, that the first frost wasn't far away.

"It's so quiet," Madeline marveled, ears swiveling as the breeze stirred crunchy leaves. "Don't you ever get lonely out here on your own?"

"It's hard to really be lonely when you're a part of nature, and nature's all around you," the witch answered evasively. "But," she added quickly at her companion's rather crestfallen look, "it's kind of nice to have somebody to talk to for a change. Raven's good company, but he's usually a crow of few words."

"Oh, I'm glad." The cat fluffed happily, then glanced to the sky. "Do you think it's dark enough to go stargazing?"

Tamara looked away, into the almost complete darkness of the forest. Her night vision had reasserted itself after being weakened by the glow of the firelight. She stood with a nod. "I think so. You might want to bring your chair."

Eagerly, Madeline unzipped her backpack. "I brought a little picnic blanket, actually. So we'll both have somewhere dry to sit." She pulled out the folded lump with a pleased noise. "Ravel, Tammy and I are going to go look at the stars for a while. Can you be a love and watch the camp for us? Make sure no naughty creatures disturb the tent?"

Drawing himself up to his full few inches of height, the pixie saluted his mistress importantly. Tamara silently pitied any feral raccoon or opossum that had the bad luck of wandering into the meadow.

They set out across the clearing. Leaves crunched beneath every heavy, booted step Tamara took. Beside her, the cat's lighter footfalls produced a cheerful crinkle. As they reached the pine trees, Tamara felt a hand catch her sleeve.

"It's a bit spookier in the dark, isn't it?" Madeline commented, squeezing a little closer against her side.

The witch had to laugh. "You've been eyeball to eyeball with one of the most powerful magical beings there are. Trust me, that's the scariest thing you'll ever run into. Everything else is cake." Still, she obligingly bent her arm and let Madeline take hold of it. As they followed a deer trail through the softly whispering pines, it was almost too easy to imagine the other girl clinging close to her in affection rather than nerves. Tamara did her best to squash that wayward imagining.

On the other side of the trees, they emerged near the top of a small rise. Down the hill, newly-harvested fields stretched for miles. The sky to the west was smudged a deep, deep blue as the last, lingering light of sunset slowly disappeared. Higher above and to the east, the darkness was smattered with stars.

"Oh, what a perfect spot! You can see the whole of the sky." Madeline unrolled the blanket and shook it out onto a level-looking patch of grass. She sank gracefully onto it and patted the place next to her invitingly.

"Yeah. I'm glad it's clear." Tamara plopped down beside her with considerably less grace, but did remember to keep her hiking boots off the edge of the blanket. No sooner had she settled in than the cat pressed close to her once more.

"A bit chilly, isn't it?" Madeline said blithely, snuggling against her side.

Tamara did her best to ignore it. "Well, yeah. It is October. Are you too cold? Want to go back and build the fire up?"

"No, no, I'm sure I'll be just fine. Please tell me what we're looking at."

The southern sky stretched out before them. More and more distant points of light winked into view. Tamara pointed westward. "That bright one about to set behind the tree line is Venus. When it's up, it's the brightest object in the night sky. Besides the moon, I guess."

"Well, it stands to reason that a planet named for the goddess of love would have a commanding presence." The cat's voice took on a playful tone. Her soft cheek suddenly pillowed against Tamara's shoulder.

The witch froze. Seeking warmth was totally natural; instinctual, even. She couldn't fault the silly cat for that. Cheek nuzzles seemed a bit excessive. Were casual cuddles just something Madeline did with all her friends? Tamara tried with limited success to launch her attention skyward. She cleared her throat. "The bigger bright one up to the southeast is Jupiter. The smaller one over there is Saturn."

"I saw the rings once. My parents took me to a program at an observatory. The astronomers let all the children look through one of the telescopes."

Tamara's mind drifted at once to the small telescope in the back bedroom, scolding her past self for not thinking to bring it along. "I have a telescope. We can take it out sometime and get a closer look. The middle of an ice storm when the power goes out in town is a great time to see everything without all the light pollution."

"Oh, really? I would love that ever so much." Madeline leaned in even closer still. A purr vibrated between them. Behind them, a fluffy feline tail shifted until the length of it curled around, draped over Tamara's, and molded snugly to the curve of the coyote's bottom and hip.

Tamara's own tail went bottlebrush-stiff. She bit her tongue against a stunned sputter. "Uh—Orion will be rising soon, right over there," she stammered, pointing almost desperately to the eastern horizon. "That little 'V' shape is the face of the constellation Taurus the bull. Oh, that little cluster of stars right above him—those are the Pleiades, the Seven Sisters. A long time ago, farmers used the position of the Pleiades to help them know when to harvest. They used to peak in the sky on Samhain. It was the start of the new year for the ancient Celts. The beginning of their winter."

"It will be winter for us soon, as well." Madeline sighed softly. "Time for snuggling up with someone special, drinking hot cocoa, and watching the snow fall... How awfully romantic." The tip of her tail flicked back and forth, tickling the top of Tamara's thigh.

Enough was enough. Tamara turned her head, broad brown nose nearly bumping a smaller pink one. "Look. I don't know if you know this, and maybe it's completely by accident, but you're totally putting the moves on me."

"Oh, you've noticed? Is it working?" Madeline asked hopefully.

The gears in Tamara's mind locked up in unison. "Uh... what?"

"I said, is it working? Are you at all tempted to engage in romantic activities with me? I'm afraid I'm not very good at this flirting business."

"That's what I thought you said." It barely made any more sense the second time. The coyote was sorely tempted to pinch her own arm to make sure she hadn't dozed off by the fire. "But why are you saying it?"

"Because I am trying to have a lesbian experience with you, you daft thing!" Madeline nearly shouted, pulling away to throw her hands in the air despairingly. "I've only been trying to drop hints that I was interested for weeks! I wasn't sure who was meant to make the overture in this case, since we're both women, but I did hope you'd at least guess at my feelings. Did you really not cotton on?"

Tamara slowly, slowly leaned backward until she flopped flat on the blanket. The stars took up her whole bewildered field of vision. "I'm asleep, right? I'm dreaming. This is a dream and I'm going to wake up face down in my own drool, sad and alone."

"Oh, you," Madeline huffed crossly. "Honestly, I thought I was being very forward. I was beginning to think you were being thick on purpose so as not to hurt my feelings with an outright rejection." Her dainty hands, covered with mittens, folded and unfolded in her lap. Her ears angled down under her pompom beanie. "You can still do that, though. Reject my advances, I mean. I'm not foolish enough to think that just because I'm a woman you would automatically be attracted to me. I'm all too aware that someone like me might not be at all your type—"

Tamara pushed herself half upright again, sweaty palm pads catching on the blanket fabric. "Wait, what?"

The cat fiddled with the tassels of her scarf, not quite meeting her eye. "Well, you know. I can be a bit silly and soft and whimsical, and you're quite practical and tough. A bit too cool for someone like me, really, but one never knows if one doesn't try. If you aren't interested, I promise not to make a fuss. We can forget I ever said anything and we can simply be good friends." She chanced a fretful glance upward. "At least, I do hope we still can."

Tamara sucked in and let out one long, calming breath. Against astronomical odds, this was actually happening. It was vital she not screw it up. "Mads, in case it wasn't glaringly obviously, I am absolutely interested. You are for sure the silliest, softest, sweetest, *nicest* person I've ever met. And I thought you were the prettiest the first time I laid eyes on you swooning around on a bridge in the moonlight."

"Oh! Oh, my." Madeline giggled bashfully, mittens coming up to cover her cheeks. Her tail waved happily. The stars seemed to shine a little brighter. "Then, does that mean that you would consider going on a date with me?"

"This is a date," Tamara declared, utterly serious. "Starting right now. If you want it to be."

"Yes!" The ginger dove in with a happy mew, throwing her arms around Tamara in a tight hug. "Absolutely yes. I'm so glad I listened to Ellie and made the first move."

"Oh, no. That crazy artist had a hand in this?" Preoccupied with hugging Madeline back, the witch could only grumble a little bit. Her soft warmth and pervasive lavender fragrance made being grumpy very difficult. "I'm almost afraid to ask."

"It seems I wasn't as good at hiding my feelings from her as I'd thought. I should have known; she does know me better than anyone besides my parents. Once she pried a confession out of me, she said she supported me completely and insisted that this campout would be the perfect opportunity to tell you how I feel. For some reason, she seemed to think that you might feel the same way."

Tamara huffed, equal parts amused and exasperated. "Guess I should be flattered that she moved from thinking I was a vampire out for your blood to thinking I'm good enough to date her best friend so fast."

"You bought her pizza, even though she was meant to be treating you. That's an instant path into her heart." Madeline laughed merrily, the bright sound trailing off into a purr. "If tonight didn't pan out, her next plan was to arrange a slumber party for the three of us at my flat and then back out at the last moment, leaving you and I alone with only one bed."

"We've already shared a bed," Tamara pointed out, because her inner snarkiness could not be contained. "Everyone's virtue came out intact."

"Yes, but not whilst I was wearing lingerie."

If the sight of the cat's everyday undergarments had been impressive the whole two times she had caught a glimpse, Tamara could only imagine the sight if Madeline was putting effort into it. The insides of her ears went hot. "Maddie, we've only been dating for two minutes. Try to wait at least a week before pulling out the big guns. Give me a fighting chance."

"And relinquish my advantage? Never." She giggled impishly, nuzzling into the collar of the coyote's jacket.

Kiss her kiss her kiss her kiss her— Tamara's brain screeched very unhelpfully. She rested her chin carefully between Madeline's ears. "So, uh. I'm not a guy."

"The fact had flittered across the periphery of my awareness, yes," Madeline deadpanned.

"Smartass. What made you decide you wanted to go out with me, anyway?"

Madeline had the decency to look a bit bashful, but did not remove her arms from Tamara's shoulders. "Well, I will admit that there was probably a bit of hero worship happening at first, what with how you saved me on the bridge, and then saved me from being run over, and then saved Ravel's life. I was simply ecstatic to know that magic was real, and you were magical, so I suppose I was rather in awe of you. But as we spent more time together and I got to know you as a person rather than just a personification of magic, I realized how very kind and funny you are. I was delighted that you seemed willing to become my friend." Her long, white whiskers tickled the coyote's muzzle as she smiled. "And then when you told me about your romantic leanings, well. Forgive me if my mind began to wander."

"You've never gone out with another girl, though, right?" Tamara had to ask.

"I can't say that I have, or that I've ever really considered it before now. But none of the young men I've been out with have been anything to write home about, let alone saved my life. Or taken me on a grand adventure. Or looked half so cute with such a messy hair bun and leaf bits in their fur. I'm willing to give it a go."

Joy swelled through the witch like bubbles in a rushing snowmelt brook, like a warm spring wind through unfurling buds. "Does that mean I can kiss you?"

In lieu of an answer, soft mittens wrapped around her cheeks and reeled her in. Determined green eyes took up Tamara's field of vision before she was soundly kissed by petal-soft feline lips. Every strand of fur stood up. Against her will, her tail began to thump the picnic blanket.

"Wow," she whispered as Madeline pulled back, looking

entirely pleased with herself. "Do you still buy those little fruity tubes of lip gloss everybody used in middle school?"

"What?" Madeline squawked, ears and whiskers quivering in disbelief. "That's all you have to say? You are impossible."

Tamara yapped delightedly as she was pounced, toppling over onto the blanket as the cat poked and tickled her sides determinedly. Her tail wagged in a very un-witchy fashion under the tangle of their legs. "I'm sorry, I'm sorry!"

"No mercy! You are *utterly* impossible. And I am utterly impossible because I'm besotted with you anyway." Seeming convinced that she had taught Tamara a sound lesson, Madeline flopped down beside her. Her head landed on Tamara's shoulder. Both her legs and tail wrapped around one of the witch's own like a fluffy ginger squid. "Now, may we please resume the astronomy lesson? I promise I am actually interested. It wasn't entirely a ploy to finagle you into a romantic situation."

"It's nice to know I'm valued for my smarts *and* my charm." Tamara curled an arm around the cat, warm and snuggly against her side in the chill of the autumn night. Dear Earth Mother, if she woke up the next morning and it turned out this was all some sort of wild dream, she silently vowed that she would ask Madeline out herself. Anything for a chance to keep feeling this almost weightless happiness. "Okay. You can still kind of see the summer triangle, over there in the west. The bright star up there at the top is Deneb. It's part of Cygnus the swan…"

In the velvet dark above them, the stars and planets slowly turned. *Nature never hurries, but it always gets things done on time.*

Fortune telling had never been one of Tamara's fortes. It was reassuring to know that whatever the cosmos had in store for her immediate future, she would make her next journey into the unknown with a hand in her own and a fellow traveler by her side.

Back in the meadow, a pixie buzzed diligent laps around the silent tent.

A swift vulpine shadow at the edge of the grass perked his ears and earned an eager squeak, but a closer look proved that the feral fox was not one of the pair he knew. It regarded the small fae with curious but wild eyes before slipping away again into the darkness.

Ravel came in for a landing on top of the tent where two poles joined together. He perched there, glowing like the star atop a fir tree, soaking up the ambient signals of the forest. Not far away, a bit to the south on the other side of the tall pine trees, he could very clearly feel the bright little pulses of *happy happy happy!* emanating from his mistress. Shimmering eyes rolled at the outburst of affection that was most decidedly not aimed at him. Still, the grumpy, serious witch pleased his mum so much. He would not pull her whiskers out.

Bored with guard duty, the pixie had begun to contemplate loosening up the tent stakes when a ribbon of power rippled over the treetops from the north. Instantly reminded of the night he had come into being, and of the moment when the wonderful, glowing Great One had stepped out of the oak tree, Ravel shot into the air with a flurry of interest.

By the time he rose above the trees the power was already fading. Slightly disappointed, he looked thoughtfully out over the shallow valley on the edge of the northern horizon. A cold wind combed through his short fur. Gossamer wings vibrating harder to fight the chill, Ravel dismissed the incident with a flick of his tufted tail and dove for the shelter of the tent far below.

Whatever it had been, clearly it could wait until tomorrow.

ABOUT THE AUTHOR

Robin lives in east-central Indiana with two cats and a guinea pig, none of whom would make good familiars. In addition to writing, she enjoys camping, hiking, travel, reading, and chasing chipmunks out of her garden. She encourages you to go outside daily, touch grass regularly, and disappear into the woods periodically.

Say hi on Fur Affinity: sillyneko345

ABOUT THE PUBLISHER

FurPlanet productions is a small press publisher serving the niche market that is furry fiction. They sell furry-themed books and comics published by themselves and most major publishers in the community. If you can't get to a furry convention where they are selling in the dealers room, visit their online stores: FurPlanet.com for print books and BadDogBooks.com for eBooks.

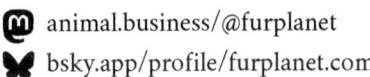

animal.business/@furplanet
bsky.app/profile/furplanet.com

www.ingramcontent.com/pod-product-compliance
Lightning Source LLC
Chambersburg PA
CBHW071203020726
47502CB00002B/519